Praise for the Allison Campbell Mystery Series

DEADLY ASSETS (#2)

"The mystery is firm and well-explained, and great fun to follow, but it's the rich relationships Tyson has created that this reader will carry away from the book...I will be following Allison Campbell and her cohorts with a great deal of interest in all the books to come. There had better be a lot more."

– Stephanie Jaye Evans,
Author of the Sugar Land Mystery Series

"A mystery is only as good as its characters, and *Deadly Assets* is filled with vivid people who will keep readers turning the pages to find out what happens to them...Allison herself is savvy and likable, with an unusual job that promises many satisfying installments in this well-written series. Highly recommended!"

– Sandra Parshall,
Agatha Award-Winning Author of the Rachel Goddard Mysteries

"Tyson creates a tense, engrossing tale by weaving vivid descriptions with thrilling threads of family secrets, greed and the shadow of an unknown threat. The Allison Campbell mystery series is not to be missed!"

– Laura Morrigan,
Author of the Call of the Wilde Mysteries

"Dark and edgy with multiple layers of intrigue, the Allison Campbell series keep me up late trying to piece together Tyson's intricate puzzles. I love the complexity of this mystery."

– Larissa Reinhart,
Author of the Cherry Tucker Mystery Series

"Tyson crafts characters who are real and we can believe in which makes us willing to follow them anywhere. Excellent page turner. Can't wait for the next installment."

– Shannyn Schroeder,
Author of the O'Leary Series Contemporary Romances

KILLER IMAGE (#1)

"An edgy page-turner that pulls the reader into a world where image is everything and murder is all about image. Great start to a new series!"

– Erika Chase,
Author of The Ashton Corners Book Club Mysteries

"Wit, charm, and deliciously clever plot twists abound...the author has a knack for creating characters with heart, while keeping us guessing as to their secrets until the end."

– Mary Hart Perry,
Author of *Seducing the Princess*

"This cleverly revealing psychological thriller will keep you guessing...as the smart and savvy Allison Campbell (love her!) delves into the deadly motives, twisted emotions and secret intrigues of Philadelphia's Main Line."

– Hank Phillippi Ryan,
Mary Higgins Clark, Agatha, Anthony and Macavity Award-Winning
Author of *The Wrong Girl*

"Nancy Drew gets a fierce makeover in Wendy Tyson's daringly dark, yet ever fashion-conscious mystery series, beginning with *Killer Image*. Tyson imbues her characters with emotional depth amidst wit, ever maintaining the pulse rate."

– Deborah Cloyed,
Author of *What Tears Us Apart* and *The Summer We Came to Life*

"An intriguing psychological thriller. The book reminded me of Jonathan Kellerman's Alex Delaware series...I loved the book, it's dark and hopeful at the same time. Five stars out of five."

– Lynn Farris,
Mystery Books Examiner for Examiner.com

DEADLY ASSETS

DEADLY ASSETS

An Allison Campbell Mystery

WENDY TYSON

HENERY PRESS

DEADLY ASSETS
An Allison Campbell Mystery
Part of the Henery Press Mystery Collection

First Edition
Trade paperback edition | July 2014

Henery Press
www.henerypress.com

This is a work of fiction. Any references to historical events, real people, or real locales are used fictitiously. Other names, characters, places, and incidents are the product of the author's imagination, and any resemblance to actual events or locales or persons, living or dead, is entirely coincidental.

ISBN-13: 978-1-940976-21-1

Printed in the United States of America

For Ben—technical advisor, best friend, life partner, soul mate.
Thanks for always waiting while I finish "one more page"
and for believing I could write a book.

ACKNOWLEDGMENTS

The pool of people to whom I owe gratitude only grows with each novel. First, I have endless appreciation and admiration for my agent, Fran Black of Literary Counsel. Business advisor, beta reader, cheerleader, friend, chocolate connoisseur...you must need a separate closet for all of these hats, Fran, yet you seem to wear them so effortlessly. Your advice and friendship have been invaluable. Thank you for believing in me.

Many thanks to Rowe Copeland at The Book Concierge for her editing, friendship, tireless work and creative ideas. A true gem.

To Kendel Flaum (editor extraordinaire), Art Molinares and everyone at Henery Press—thank you for giving Allison such a wonderful home.

Thanks to all of my early readers and tireless supporters, especially Marnie Mai, Mark Anderson, Sue Norbury, Angela Tyson, Edie and Sam Newman, Jennifer Brown and, of course, Carol Lizell (once a teacher, always a teacher—you still have the sharpest pencil around!).

To my family...thanks for putting up with "Purple Mommy Minion" before every deadline and for being my most vocal PR team!

And finally, many thanks to mystery readers, who make all of this possible, and to the wonderful community of mystery and thriller writers. We may all write about murder and mayhem, but I have never met such a warm and welcoming group of people.

~ Wendy

ONE

The hawk fell from the sky like a bomb, its body graceless in death. It plummeted through a canopy of oaks, their foliage laced with the vestiges of afternoon sun, and landed just feet from Allison's bumper in a limp, twisted heap. Heart racing, Allison slammed on the brakes. She bolted out of the car in time to see a young woman emerge from the forest. The woman wore a rifle slung over one shoulder, a rucksack across the other. A wild mane of black hair flew behind her like a cape.

"That one's mine," the woman shouted. "Don't touch it!"

Allison glanced down at the dead hawk with equal parts sympathy and disgust. She certainly had no intention of touching it.

"Bastard's murdered a dozen chickens in two weeks. Damn thing had it coming." The woman leaned down, grabbed the bird by the throat and shoved it into the canvas satchel. Finished, she looked up at Allison as though registering for the first time the presence of a stranger on her property. "Who are you?"

"Allison Campbell. The image consultant." Allison started to hold out her hand, but with a second look at the rifle, opted instead for a friendly nod.

The woman harrumphed a hello, wiped her hands on her jeans, and gestured toward the house behind them. "I suppose you're here for Francesca."

"Is she ready for me?"

The woman shrugged.

She was in her late twenties, lean and muscular, and now that she was closer, Allison could see the face beneath the hair. Beautiful features—dark almond-shaped eyes, a regal nose, full lips, and high, defined cheekbones—clashed with an almost savage indifference.

Allison tore her gaze from the woman with the gun and looked around at her surroundings, too startled by the bird to have taken in the Benini estate—the home of her potential client, Francesca Benini—before now. The house lay sprawled across a hilltop, fronted by woodland that sloped down to the angry edge of Cayuga Lake. A winding driveway meandered its way up the hill, ending in a semi-circle in front of the house. The town of Ithaca was visible in the distance, an urban island in a sea of forest and farmland.

The house itself stood as testament to Benini Enterprises' dwindling finances. A dilapidated three-winged monstrosity with a triple gabled front, a look-out tower and multiple entries, its wood trim was in desperate need of paint. Small patches of stucco had disappeared off the fascia, leaving scars like pockmarks across the broad façade. The building's height blocked out the sun and shadows slashed across a yard that was unkempt around the edges.

It was a warm August day. Storm clouds bruised the distant skies, and a sticky breeze offered no relief from the heat. Allison wiped the sweat beading along her brow. Her attention now back on the young woman, she asked, "And you are?"

But before the woman could respond, the front door flung open and a tall, athletic-looking man in his early forties came down the steps toward them. He was slim, with broad shoulders and narrow hips, and his movements were quick and elegant, especially for a man of his height. A day or two's worth of stubble gave a rakish air to a strong nose, sharp cheekbones and smooth olive skin. And, most noticeable of all, were his cerulean-colored eyes, which pierced Allison's own with a knife-like gaze.

He flashed Allison an apologetic smile. "Please ignore my sister, Maria. I'm Alessandro Benini. Most people call me Alex." He held out his hand. "You must be here for my aunt. Let's get you inside where it's cool." To Maria, he said, "Don't just stand there gawking. Do something with that bird."

By now, blood had soaked through the canvas bag and a small circle of crimson was pooling near Maria's sneakered feet.

Undeterred, she hoisted the bird over her free shoulder and threw Allison one last glacial glance before disappearing back in the direction of the hill and the barn beyond.

Allison said, "I hope I'm not disrupting things. Your sister seemed a bit surprised to see me."

"Not at all." Alex started toward the house. "It's me who should apologize. Maria can be insufferable. Don't take it personally. She hates everyone. Horses constitute her social circle. And people," he smiled, "including her family, are just an annoying fact of life."

Allison followed him through the double entry and into a large reception area. The inside of the home was as well-seasoned as the outside. Although the rooms were grand, the ceilings high, and the floors marble, the gold-toned wallpaper had faded to dull yellow and the Oriental rugs scattered in each room were muted and matted with use. Heavy brocade drapes covered the windows, blocking out any remnants of afternoon sun, and lending a dark and musty gloom to the already bleak interior.

They walked through a hallway, past a dining room and a formal parlor and into a screen-enclosed sun porch that ran the entire length of the back of the house. Two white wicker chairs, a wicker rocker, and a small white-painted table constituted the only furniture. Six large potted ferns stood sentinel along the back wall.

Alex said, "Sit, please."

Allison chose a wicker chair and sank into a floral seat cushion that had probably once been a bright and cheerful scarlet but had since weathered to the color of dried blood. The view from her seat made up for any lack in the decor.

Below the porch, laid out in a sweeping vista, were the family's vineyards. Row upon row of grapes, their vines trained and twisted over wire trellises, lined the side of the mountain like troops on the march. To the right and left of the vineyards, two swaths of dense forest stretched their way down a steep hill toward the town of Ithaca. A battered barn was next to the woods. Four horses grazed in a pasture corralled by a split rail fence.

Allison watched a young colt prance along the barrier, surprised it chose not to jump over something it could have so easily cleared. Sitting back in her seat, she said, "The view is beautiful. Do you ride?"

Alex had been standing by the window. At the sound of Allison's voice, he turned and took the seat across from her, folding his lanky body into the chair with exceptional grace for a man.

"We all ride, except Aunt Francesca. She's not terribly adventurous. In fact, she hasn't left this house for as long as I can remember." He smiled warmly, as though to minimize the seriousness of his remarks about his aunt. "She'll be down in a few moments. Until then, I'm afraid you're stuck with me."

Allison nodded. There was something about this arresting stranger that she found unsettling.

His eyes shone with an amused intelligence, at once world-weary and good-natured, as though he had seen it all, but life still entertained him. Only, she couldn't tell if they were sharing a joke—or if the laugh was on her.

"You're Paolo's son, then? Francesca's nephew."

Alex nodded.

"I'm so sorry about your father. Francesca told us what happened when she called. How is he?"

"Doing poorly, unfortunately. The stroke was severe. Maria and Francesca were the only ones here when it happened. They didn't find him until...until it was too late to do much about it. He was awake for a few days. Now...now, he's in a coma."

"Again, I'm so sorry."

"Thank you, Allison." Alex glanced at his watch and sighed. "I imagine Francesca is under the assumption that if she works with you, she'll be fit to run Benini Enterprises?"

Startled by the sudden shift in topic, Allison said, "She must believe it's possible, or she wouldn't have invited me here."

"The notion is ridiculous."

Allison sat up straighter, feeling protective of a woman she hadn't even met yet. "Tell me, why do you say it's ridiculous? That's a strong word."

"Because she's a sixty-three year old woman with no business background. Benini Enterprises, while considerably smaller than it once was, is a four hundred million dollar company with locations in Italy, the Balkans, and the United States. How can she go from housebound to corporate leader practically overnight?"

"Are you sure that's what she has in mind?"

He frowned. "As you said yourself, why else would she have contacted you?"

"If not Francesca, then who will take over if your father has to step down?"

"My brother Dominic is the natural successor, I suppose. Although Maria will disagree. But then, that's nothing new." He sat back in the chair. Allison saw a man at ease with people, a man who was comfortable being the center of attention. A man with his own agenda?

"And you, Alex? Are you in the family business as well?"

This time, Alex's smile had a wistful quality to it. "Me? It depends whether you consider-"

But before he could finish, a woman entered the room. She was short—very short—with a thick-set body and deep-set brown eyes that shone with energy of purpose. Her gaze darted between Allison and Alex. "Thank you, Alessandro. You can leave us now."

"Allison, my aunt, Francesca Benini." Alex stood, and shifting his gaze to his aunt, said, "I was entertaining your guest in your absence."

"I can see that." Francesca's tone was flat. She walked to where Allison was now standing and offered her hand. The older woman's fingers were tiny, but her grip was startlingly firm.

Francesca surveyed the room, settled her eyes back on Alex. "Tell me, where is Simone?"

"Not feeling well."

"Again? She should be at the hospital. With Paolo."

Aunt and nephew stared at each other for a full minute, some unspoken communication going on between them. Silent tension blanketed the room. Eventually, Alex was the one to break it. "I'll leave you with my aunt," he said. "It was a pleasure talking with you, Allison. I trust we'll see each other again."

The last statement was said with a charmed smile and laughing eyes that made Allison wonder whether Alessandro Benini always got his own way. "Perhaps," she said, lifting her chin. She kept her tone neutral, aware of Francesca's judging stare. "It was nice to meet you, too."

After Alex left the room, Francesca sat on the seat he'd vacated. The older woman took a moment to appraise Allison, making no attempt to hide her approval of Allison's pale pink linen suit, her cream sling backs and matching Gucci purse. She glanced at Allison's hands."Do we make you nervous, Ms. Campbell?"

Allison looked down at her fingers and was relieved to see that they gripped the sides of her chair with steady strength. "Not at all. Alex was a pleasant companion."

Francesca smiled wryly. "Of that, I have no doubt." She turned her head to look out the window. Allison followed suit, and together they watched Maria down by the barn, leaning over an over-sized, silver pail. Maria appeared to be scrubbing something, her long, slender arms submerged in murky water. She looked up toward the house, as though she'd felt the weight of their stare, but after a moment she gave her attention to the thing in the pail again and resumed her chore.

Allison glanced back at Francesca, evaluating her with an image consultant's eye. Not only was Francesca small, but she had a stocky, muscular build that would be tricky to clothe. Right now she wore black polyester pants and a loose short-sleeve sage sweater. Allison pictured her in a tailored pants suit, something that would lend credibility and an air of power. Francesca's head was covered in short, thick, wiry curls, peppered with gray—nothing a shapely cut couldn't handle. She had pug-like features and pale skin, with moles dotting her cheeks and neck. Like her niece and nephew, her best features were almond-shaped eyes fringed by long, lush lashes. Her irises were deep brown like Maria's, although they lacked both Alex's perpetual amusement and Maria's disdain. Instead, Francesca Benini projected the resolve of a woman on a mission.

Allison said, "How can I help you, Ms. Benini?"

"Let's do away with the formalities, shall we? Call me Francesca. "

Beneath the crisp words lurked the faint, melodic remnants of an Italian accent. Allison knew that Francesca was from a village in Calabria, in Italy. Her older brother, Paolo Benini, the CEO and President of the family business, Benini Enterprises, had a stroke less than two weeks prior. That's all Francesca shared with Vaughn when she'd called the week before, upset and demanding to be seen right away.

"Do you like wine, Allison?"

"I do."

"Do you have a favorite?"

"I'm no connoisseur, but I suppose it would be Pinot Noir."

"A fine choice. We grow Riesling here in the States, both dry and sweet. But that's primarily for house use. These grapes can't compare to those grown in Europe. Other than California, the U.S. climate's just not right." She turned toward the window again and rubbed her palms up and down along the length of her thighs. "In Italy, we grow six different types of grapes. That's just on our property. We own half the land in our town, but we also own acreage in other parts of Italy and Europe, and we pay growers in Greece, Macedonia and other Balkan countries to raise grapes. In addition to wine, we're importers—specialty foods from Italy, olive oil from Greece, home goods. But it all began with a small vineyard, sixty-five years ago."

"Your father started the business?"

"Yes. With help from my grandmother. She was a shrew, but she had a keen sense of business and knew how to turn nothing into something."

"And now your brother runs the business?"

"He *ran* the business. Make no mistake, Allison. Paolo won't recover from this. Despite the fact that they"—she gestured back toward the main part of the house, and Allison could only assume she meant Simone and Paolo's kids—"don't seem the least bit concerned, he is not going to make it. Even if his body survives, he'll be a vegetable. This company is mine, too. It was my father's intent for me to run it if something happened to Paolo. I have to do my part."

"And that's where First Impressions comes in?"

Francesca nodded, but her eyes held a resigned, wary expression. Allison wondered about the sudden shift. What wasn't she sharing?

"So what's your main goal, Francesca? We should start there."

"I need to take command. Although we are a privately-held company, we still have shareholders, some of whom are very powerful in their own right. I have to instill confidence in these people, especially those in Italy. Our families go way back. Seeing a woman at the helm will be tough enough. But if it's me? I'm afraid it will take a miracle." She stared at Allison. "*You* must be that miracle."

Allison considered this. Alex had made it sound as though Francesca's world had been very small—limited to the walls of this massive, intimidating home.

Perhaps she was agoraphobic or suffered from social anxiety. Perhaps she simply disliked people. Whatever the reason, she'd have to leave this house if she wanted to change. And change could be painful and laborious.

"Can I ask you a candid question, Francesca?"

"If we're to work together, I would expect nothing less."

Allison paused. She appreciated Francesca's pointedness—was it sincere? "How much time do you feel you have to...well, to make these changes? A month? A year?"

Francesca's eyebrows shot up. "Oh, heavens, not that long. The business is failing and the vultures are already circling. A lot is at stake. Weeks, maybe."

"You'll need to come to Philadelphia."

Francesca's hands danced wildly in her lap.

Allison continued. "My office is outside the city. We'll arrange for a suite nearby. You'll be comfortable and well-attended. We can meet regularly over the course of several weeks, until you feel you're ready."

"And what, specifically, will we do?"

"That depends on you, Francesca. You'll decide, with guidance from me and my team."

"Team?"

"I oversee everything, of course. And I can help you with public speaking, dressing for success, navigating corporate culture, things of that ilk. But we also have a whole cadre of specialists who can help. We can even get you a business tutor, if that's what you decide you need, someone from a local MBA program."

Francesca frowned. "Oh."

"Not what you expected?"

"To the contrary. Simone, my sister-in-law, bought me your book for Christmas. *From the Outside In.* Simone's very thoughtful that way." Francesca's sour expression said that Simone was anything but thoughtful. "I know exactly what to expect."

"But?"

"No 'but.' It's just a lot to take in, that's all."

Allison chose her next words carefully. "Are you afraid to leave this house? Because if so, that's okay. Sometimes people have anxiety issues that require treatment and even medication. We can help you, but it will take time. Treatment doesn't happen overnight."

Francesca laughed sharply. "Oh, that's priceless. I'm not agora-phobic, if that's what you mean. Alex may have filled your head with such hokum, but it's far from the truth."

"He did mention that you haven't left this house in years."

"And I have my reasons for that. But things have changed and now, it seems, I have no choice." She offered an empty smile, the venom gone as quickly as it had arrived. "Tell me, can we start today?"

Surprised, Allison said, "Today was just an initial consult."

"The gentleman I spoke to said you would be prepared to get started right away."

Allison shook her head. She'd already been making arrangements in her mind, sorting through her new-client to-do list. But she hadn't planned to start immediately. "If you really want to do this, we can pick you up and take you to Villanova. Next week?"

"Sooner. Today. I don't have a minute to waste."

Curious, Allison pulled out the next day's schedule. Open until the afternoon. Vaughn had blocked almost two days for the trip, anticipating travel time, and so Allison had packed an overnight bag just in case. It made a certain sense to start the intake process right away. And although the woman's request was unorthodox, given her situation and sense of urgency, Allison could accommodate it.

"I'll need to make hotel arrangements."

Francesca dismissed the notion with a wave of her hand. "I won't hear of it. We have beautiful guest quarters. You'll stay here."

Allison hesitated. "If you're sure."

"I couldn't be more." Francesca stood. "I'll see you to your room. I'm afraid we no longer have full-time help. Connie left the last time Paolo tightened the belt. But we have a cook. That's something, yes?"

Allison smiled. "Shall I make arrangements for next week as well? At my offices?"

Again, that look of wary resignation. "Will I need to book a car? I don't fly."

"That won't be necessary. We can come and get you. It'll require a little time to line everything up. Next Friday? Then we can get started over the weekend so that we don't lose any time."

"I guess that will have to do," Francesca said. She led Allison back toward the main portion of the house. "But no longer than that. Once the vultures smell rotting meat, it doesn't take long before the carcass is picked clean."

TWO

Clouds pressed in, painting the sky with a heavy coat of gray that matched Allison's mood. It was nearly six o'clock on Thursday evening. Allison was unpacking her small overnight bag and placing her few belongings on padded hangers in the guest walk-in closet. She had nothing formal for dinner, so her pink suit would have to do.

She hung up black pants and a cream blouse for tomorrow and carefully tucked her platform sling backs under a foot stool. After a quick call to Jason, her ex-husband and current boyfriend, asking him to take care of her dog Brutus, she sat on the lounge chair in her suite and looked around.

True to Francesca's word, the guest quarters were generous. Two rooms—a bedroom and a study—flanked a full bath. The bedroom was furnished with heavy antiques. A four poster canopied bed, with down mattress, comforter and richly upholstered shams, stood against one wall. On the opposite wall sat an ornate, carved dresser topped by a thick slab of champagne-colored marble. A chaise lounge completed the bedroom.

All of the suite's linens, bedding and fabrics wore a designer touch, with coordinating patterns of cream, butterscotch and brown. The overall effect lent a comfortable charm to the decidedly masculine rooms. But the bathroom was Allison's favorite. Nearly as large as the bedroom, it had two sinks, a bidet and a Roman-style sunken bath that hinted at the wealth the Beninis must have once had. Allison eyed the bath longingly. No time for that now.

Leaning back in the lounge, Allison tapped her colleague Vaughn's phone number. Vaughn answered on the third ring. "Guess where I am?" Allison asked.

"Hawaii?"

"Funny. At the Benini estate."

"Still?"

"Still. I'll be here until tomorrow." She gave Vaughn a quick run-down of her meeting with Francesca. "She's in a hurry to get started."

"You're staying at her house? Isn't that a little...weird?"

Allison laughed. "Under normal circumstances, yes. The Beninis have the room, though, and I could use the crash course in Benini culture if I'm going to work magic in such a short time. I need you to do some things."

"Name 'em."

"We need to come back up and get her next Friday. Do you think you can clear my schedule for next Saturday? Maybe a portion of Sunday, too? After that, find a few hours a day for the next two weeks. And start to line up the gang. Errol for hair, Natalie for make-up, Kenneth for voice and diction. Call Neiman Marcus...try Annette for personal shopping."

"So you want the works?"

"No nutrition, at least not for now. But include Dr. Keith for a psych consultation. Francesca may balk, but truthfully, she'll need all the calm she can get. Dr. Keith's good at helping people deal with anxiety."

"Got it."

"Thanks." Allison thought through her intake checklist. "What am I missing?"

"It's not what, it's who. You received another urgent call today. From a woman named Denise Carr."

"Don't recognize the name."

"She manages musicians. She'd like you to meet with her client, Tammy Edwards, next week. She asked for today or tomorrow, but I explained that you were in Ithaca."

"Why the urgency?"

"Tammy Edwards—she's known as Swallow, how do you like that for a nickname?—will be on the next season of America's Next Pop Star. Heard of it?"

"Of course. It's one of those reality shows. People sing in the hopes of becoming famous."

"Yep. According to Denise, Tammy was discovered by a music executive while singing a solo in her church's choir during a wedding he attended. He signed her on the spot and had her audition for this show. She made it."

"So why the image consulting now? Isn't it a little after the fact?"

"It's all a little odd because Tammy already has a music contract. But the show doesn't prohibit it, and her manager thinks the show will be good exposure. Denise—that's the manager—says the kid has no stage presence. That she was basically raised by wolves."

Allison rose. She walked to the window, parted the heavy drapes and looked outside.

The sky had darkened to a surly charcoal and although dusk was more than an hour away, it looked like night had fallen prematurely.

"Where's she from?"

"Scranton."

"What's wrong with Scranton?"

"Nothing."

Allison let the drapes fall. "I've known you for a long time, Vaughn. I can hear the hesitation in your voice. What's up?"

"Ignore me," he said. "Denise Carr just rubbed me the wrong way. It's nothing."

Allison doubted it was nothing, but she knew Vaughn wouldn't tell her until he was ready. "So when did you get Tammy in?"

"Monday."

"So soon?"

A weary sigh from Vaughn. "Afraid so. You'll get back tomorrow, you're giving a speech at that business luncheon on Saturday and beginning on Monday, you start long sessions with Tammy Edwards."

"Well, at least I have next Sunday night free."

"Actually-"

"Uh-oh."

"I had to reschedule your Recently Divorced group. I made it for Sunday night."

"Were the ladies okay with that?"

"I offered to refund their money, but they requested that timeslot instead."

Allison laughed. "Who likes to relax?"

"Relaxation is overrated. Besides, you're up there in the beautiful Finger Lakes. Have some wine. Enjoy the view."

Lightning flashed outside. Seconds later, Allison heard the distant rumble of thunder. The lights in the suite flashed off and on.

"Sightseeing's not in the cards." Allison glanced at her watch. "Dinner in fifteen, then a session with Francesca afterwards." She closed the drapes as the lights flickered again. "I'll call you tomorrow when I'm on my way back?"

"Please. And don't let the ghosts get you. I read something about the old Benini estate being haunted. Someone died in that house."

"Lovely," Allison said. She slipped her shoes on and looked around the room. Shadows danced in the falling gloom. "Ghosts I can handle. It's Francesca's vultures I'm concerned about."

Dinner was a tense affair.

Allison arrived at the dining room to find Francesca and Maria sitting side-by-side on one end of an enormous walnut table. At its center was a bouquet of white roses surrounded by tiny white candles. Twenty matching carved armchairs sheathed in worn velvet surrounded the table, and an eight-armed chandelier hung low over the table's center, its spray of crystals reflecting the centerpiece's candlelight like so many scattered diamonds. Allison imagined this room had been beautiful during the height of the Benini's wealth, but right now, with the storm raging outside and the shadows cast by the candles, Allison felt a chill that she was certain had nothing to do with the air conditioning.

Allison sat across from Francesca. Next to Maria, another woman perched on the edge of her seat as though ready to fly.

With a note of rancor, Francesca introduced her as her sister-in-law, Simone Benini. Simone was an older, less wild version of Maria. Just as beautiful, despite the age difference, she had thick ebony hair tamed into a chignon, accenting sharp cheekbones and a softly-bowed mouth. A fitted black dress with lace overlay left little to the imagination.

Simone regarded Allison in an almost feline manner—mildly interested, mildly contemptuous. "Thrilled to meet you," she said.

Outside, the sharp crack of thunder followed a flash of lightning. Francesca rubbed the back of her neck before glancing at the pocket doors that led back into the hallway. She's nervous, Allison thought, and wondered whether her client was anxious about their upcoming sessions—or something else. Something that was feeding the strain in this room.

"Allison, I trust you found your room comfortable?"

Allison smiled at her host. "It's lovely, Francesca. Thank you."

Francesca fluttered her fingers, waving away the compliment. "It's nice to have company. Isn't it, Simone?"

Before Simone could answer, Alex Benini walked into the room. He nodded his hello to Allison and kissed his aunt on the cheek, ignoring Simone and Maria. Allison watched him hesitate by the head of the table, but only for a second. He slid the chair back and sat to Allison's left. As he was positioning his chair, he leaned toward her and whispered, "Now begins the fun."

"Where's Dom?" Francesca asked her nephew. "With Paolo?"

Simone and Maria exchanged a glance.

"I don't know where my brother is, but I doubt he's with Father. Jackie, do you know?"

A plain-faced woman with short, gray hair had entered the room carrying a massive tray. She put the tray on the buffet and began placing salads on each charger. "I'm afraid I don't."

Allison looked down at the beautiful arrangement on her plate. Field greens, roasted beets, candied walnuts and goat cheese, topped off with a single nasturtium. She wished she felt hungry.

Maria grunted. She shoveled a forkful of salad greens into her mouth, keeping her linen napkin balled in her fist on the table. Simone glanced over at her daughter, grimaced in disgust, and picked up her own salad fork. She traced the tines across a slice of beet and looked over at Alex.

"Are you staying here tonight?" she asked. With a knowing smile in Allison's direction, she said, "He only stays when it's convenient. The rest of the time he goes catting at those clubs with his brother. Isn't that right, Alex?"

Alex stabbed a piece of lettuce and held it to the candlelight. He moved his wrist back and forth, examining the leaf, in no rush to respond. "Sometimes I need a break from this house, Simone. I can't imagine why." He turned to Allison and said, "But that has nothing to do with my relationships, as my stepmother would have you think. Dom has his own house. Getting away lends...perspective."

With the last word, he took a hard look at Francesca. Her face tightened, and then slowly readjusted, taking on the visage of a painted mask. Allison regarded her, curious about the relationship between Francesca and her family. Was this a show meant for Allison's benefit, or was every gathering this fraught with tension?

The wind pummeled against original lead windows, shattering the sudden silence with a slow, steady rumble. The lights flickered once, twice, then went out. Simone gasped. Allison's eyes took a moment to adjust to the dim light of the centerpiece candles. She saw Jackie, the cook, rushing in with a flashlight and two candelabras. The cook placed the candles on the table, on either side of the centerpiece.

"Shit," Maria said. "The horses."

"Always with the horses, Maria." Simone took a sip of wine, hands trembling. "Your father's dying and that's all you can think about." She let out an ugly laugh. "What do you think, Allison? How would you like to add my daughter to your clientele?"

Allison refused to take the bait. She said instead, "Do you have a generator?"

It was Alex who answered. "We do. It only handles the most urgent needs—the refrigerators, emergency lighting, air conditioning and the cooling system for the wine cellars."

Allison tried to detect irony in his voice—wine cellars over lights?—but if it was there, she couldn't read it.

"Allison, are you looking forward to working with my aunt?" Maria asked.

Before Allison could respond, the stealth-like Jackie was back with another tray. Efficiently, she removed the salad plates and the chargers and replaced them with steaming dinner plates.

When all of the plates had been served, Jackie said, "Grilled halibut with cilantro garlic butter, sautéed spinach and roasted fingerling potatoes. Finished just in time. Does anyone require anything else?"

"More wine, please," Alex replied. "One of our Italian reds." Turning to Allison, he said, "Back in Calabria, we make a nice Magliocco

Canino blend that you might enjoy. I realize that we're having fish, but your palate will adjust, yes?"

"Of course."

Jackie left to fetch the wine and Allison had a short reprieve while the others ate. She looked around, watching the candles flicker, throwing shadows across the cavernous room. Francesca was quiet. She'd barely touched her food. When Jackie was back with the wine, she poured the jeweled red liquid into each person's glass.

When she got to Francesca, Francesca covered her glass with her hand and shook her head. "Not tonight, Jackie. But thank you."

"Francesca here has noble roots, you know," Simone said. "Her great-great-grandfather was the Duke of Calabria. Isn't that right, Frannie?"

"You know better than anyone, Simone—it's not blood that matters. We no longer live in a world that cares about heritage. Today, *anyone* can get ahead. Through marriage, luck or otherwise." Francesca aimed her words at the empty wine glass, but her tone made it clear whom she was talking about.

"Well...at least I haven't hidden away from the world, so scared of the past that I have no future."

"Although that's all about to change, isn't it Aunt Francesca?" Alex asked. He spoke quietly and without any bitterness. But Francesca reacted. She looked at Alex with a peculiar mix of loathing and concern. Allison blinked, and when she looked back at Francesca, her client was silently examining her hands, face once again dispassionate, as though the exchange never occurred.

Between bites, Allison watched her hosts. They were quiet for a spell, but the storm outside continued to rage, and each flash of lightning illuminated faces marred by anger. The stale air smelled of fish and Simone's cloying floral perfume. Allison felt the beginnings of a headache wrap its talons around her temples.

Breaking the silence, Simone said, "Paolo never wanted you to run the business. He didn't think you could do it. Because"—She spoke rapidly, in a shrill voice that rippled with the undercurrents of a Brooklyn accent, her words hurdling over one another in an effort to escape and wound—"because you're a shut-in, Francesca. How can you possibly lead a corporation?"

Francesca slammed her hands down on the table, rattling her dishes and causing everyone to stare. "Is that what you think?"

"Yes, it is. And so does everyone else. But they're just too goddamned afraid to say anything." She stared at Francesca, daring her to argue. "Why would you stay all these years? Tell me. And now you want Benini Enterprises?"

"The ghost," Maria said. "The martyred Gina."

Francesca looked sharply at her niece. "Nonsense. This is all nonsense."

"There *is* a ghost," Maria insisted. She fixed her stare on Allison, and her eyes held the insatiable gleam of a madwoman. "Gina. My father's first wife. She haunts this house. My mother doesn't like to think of her, do you Mother? Because Father still loves her. He loves a ghost."

"Stop it, Maria," Simone hissed, her face now deathly pale.

Undaunted, Maria continued. "If you listen at night, you'll hear her. She makes a long, slow, heinous moan. At first you'll think it's the wind in the woods, but then you'll realize it's coming from inside the house."

"Stop it!" Francesca stood and threw her napkin on her plate. "I need some air." Everyone watched as she disappeared through the pocket doors.

"Brilliant, Maria," Alex said. "You can't get through dinner without behaving like a lunatic?"

"Gina was *your* mother, Alex. Maybe if you focused on your family instead of your libido, you could hear her. She's been driving me crazy for years."

"Crazy is right. *You* need help."

Allison stood up from the table. She wanted to find Francesca, although she didn't even know where to start. She turned to Alex, who seemed the most solid of the group, and said, "Where do you think Francesca went?"

Alex untangled himself from the chair and walked to the window, clearly in no hurry to retrieve his aunt. He pulled aside the heavy drapes and glanced out into the night. "Typically she would retreat to the grotto. But it's still raining." He turned around. "The library, perhaps. I'll take you there."

"It's true you know," Maria called out as they were leaving the room. "Don't let my brother lie to you. Gina is still here."

Allison started to turn back toward Maria, but she felt Alex's gentle restraining hand on her arm. Even as they walked through the threshold back into the hall, Maria's screams were deafening. "She was murdered, you know. By Francesca. Poisoned!"

THREE

"What was that about?" Allison touched her face with the back of one clammy hand in an effort to calm herself. She and Alex were walking briskly through the home's inner corridors, following the path of emergency lighting past the kitchen and walk-in pantry. Allison's heart beat wildly. She felt caught, trapped in these walls. It wasn't just the talk of murder and ghosts. It was also the sheer tension, the blanket of gloom that weighed down on this family like a load of cement.

Alex stopped at a narrow white door at the end of a hallway. Unlike the other doors, which were framed in thick, ornate white trim, this door was a lonely slab of timber, faded white and unadorned, a glass doorknob its only nod to beauty.

Alex turned, smiled wryly. "I warned you—my sister is difficult."

"Does she *enjoy* upsetting everyone?"

"I've never been able to figure out whether Maria is a devil or an angel. Since she was a little girl, she's been different. She claims to hear things, know things. She can be unbelievably cruel, yet I have seen her tend to baby birds and injured deer, devoted to their care. She's amazing with the horses." He shrugged. "We're isolated here, Allison. She, Simone, and Francesca, especially. It can have an effect."

Allison could understand that. She hadn't been in the Benini home for a full day, and she was already gauging how long she could last. She craved sunshine, people. Fresh air. Outside, the wind continued to wail. The emergency lighting didn't waver, though. For that, Allison was grateful.

Alex moved closer. In the shadowy light, his striking features drew her eyes. The slope of his nose, the curve of his lips. The bad-boy charm of his laughing, blue-eyed gaze. Even now, in the midst of the abysmal night, he looked amused. Goosebumps prickled Allison's skin, and she rubbed her bare arms.

"Are you cold?" Alex asked softly.

Allison shook her head. She tore her eyes away from the searching concern reflected in his. "Can we please find your aunt?"

After a long moment, a moment in which time seemed to stand at attention, Alex grabbed the glass doorknob and pulled open the tiny Alice in Wonderland door. A dark and narrow set of steps greeted them.

Allison looked up, amazed. "I would have never known this was here."

"You'd be surprised. There are many nooks and crannies in and around an old house like this. These steps lead to the library. When I was a child, Francesca brought me up here often. We would read for hours." He motioned with his chin brusquely. "Wait here. Let me grab a flashlight."

Alex disappeared into another room, and Allison stood still in the threshold of the library stairs. She thought of Francesca, a prisoner in this house for decades. Or a willing inhabitant, a ghost-like presence herself, walking these gloomy halls without the benefit of nurturing company or laughter? And what about Maria's allegations. Had her client killed someone?

Oh Allison, this place is getting to you, she thought. How could you believe Maria? You're letting your own imagination take a fantasy vacation.

But was she? Ghosts, shut-ins, a charming, mysterious man...this place had the makings of a Gothic novel.

"Sorry."

Alex's baritone interrupted her thought. He returned with the flashlight and shone the beam up the wooden steps. "You'll have to trust me a little." He held out a hand. With reluctance, Allison accepted it. His skin was warm and smooth.

He started up the stairs. Allison followed closely. The walls were close—*too* close—and she had trouble breathing. She closed her eyes for a second to regain her composure, not stopping for fear Alex would stop. She didn't trust herself to be stuck for long in such a tight space. Not with her anxiety level as high as a Russian satellite.

When they were finally at the top of the two-floor flight, they entered an octagon-shaped room lined with bookshelves on seven sides. Allison let out a sigh of relief, both because they had made it, and because Francesca was sitting at the far side of the room, huddled in an old arm chair, a book in her lap.

Francesca had placed a battery-powered lantern on a shelf behind her, a lantern powerful enough to light all but the farthest recesses of the room. Allison looked up in awe. The bookshelves reached at least ten feet high along the walls. In them, every size and shade of book binding imaginable faced her, a collage of color. Above the shelves was a bank of divided light windows, each about a foot tall. Two armchairs had been placed in the center, atop the worn wooden floor. A small, round, and weathered Oriental rug, its colors long since faded, warmed the floor between them. The effect was a cozy reading nook, oddly-shaped, reeking of age, and filled with a rainbow of literature.

If Allison had grown up here, she had no doubt she would have escaped to this retreat, too. Even with the rain pounding on the roof and the other-worldly flashes of lightening, it beckoned.

"Aunt Francesca?" Alex said.

Francesca looked up from her book and smiled. "Ah, Allison. Welcome to the library." She closed the book—a large leather-bound volume—and regarded Allison with guarded warmth. "I'm so sorry you had to witness that little tirade downstairs. Alessandro will tell you, I'm not usually so sensitive. But, well, the prospect of leaving, I suppose, has me a little off balance."

"Aunt Francesca, you don't have to do this, you know."

Francesca held up a hand. "Oh, I'm not afraid to go, Alessandro. I just have a lot on my mind." She stood up from the chair—a wide, slip-covered armchair that had certainly seen better days—and walked over to where Allison and Alex were standing. "Leave us, Alessandro. Check on Simone. She's the one you should be worried about." With a glance at Allison, Francesca said, "Simone is...easily shaken."

When Alex didn't move, Francesca said with a tsk, tsk, "Go on now. We'll be fine. I'll see Allison to her room."

Alex looked reluctant to leave. He said, "Do you need anything else from me, Allison?"

Allison shook her head. "Thank you for helping me. I'll be fine."

With a nod to Allison and a fleeting kiss on his aunt's cheek, Alex disappeared down the stairs, his flashlight bobbing in the darkness. When she heard the door at the bottom of the steps close, Allison said, "Are you sure you're alright, Francesca?"

"I'm as well as I can be right now." Francesca made her way back to the armchair and sank down into its softness. "Sit. You may as well get comfortable."

"What happened down there?"

"Just Maria spouting off. She has a way of getting under everyone's skin. It's not always a bad trait." She picked the heavy book up and placed it back on her lap. "In a house like this, where dust collects in every crevice, you need someone who will scare the spiders out from their hiding spots."

"And Maria is that person?"

"She not only scares the spiders out from their hiding spots, she crushes them with her candor."

"Does your family have a lot of spiders, Francesca?"

"What family doesn't?" Francesca picked at the hem of her blouse, rolling the fabric between stubby fingers. "I've just been here too long. I recognize them all. I know their favorite niches."

"Why *have* you stayed?"

Francesca contemplated her hands, the cover of her heavy book, the seam that ran along the arm of her chair. "I'll give you some materials to read when you leave. They may or may not shed light on this family."

"That's a very enigmatic response."

Francesca burst out with a hearty and unexpected laugh. "You can scare a few spiders yourself, I bet. Although with more finesse than our Maria." She sighed, all traces of humor again gone. "Some might say I'm being dramatic. Perhaps. But once we get started, I'll share more of my story. And then you'll understand." She shrugged. "Or you won't. But I read your book, and while you portray yourself as a lady who helps cultivate image, I sense the reason you do so well is because you understand what's beneath."

"I try."

Francesca regarded Allison with a look, weighing how much she wanted to say. Finally, she tilted the cover of the book she'd been reading so that Allison could see it was a Bible, its red leather cover well worn.

"I wonder, do all people find religion when they age?" Francesca's face tightened. "Don't answer that. The ramblings of a woman who's had no wine but who's drunk on the romance of thunderstorms."

"A lovely sentiment, Francesca. And I imagine many people feel closer to God as they age. Wisdom, mortality, openness to the possibilities...who knows. Does it really matter why?"

"Perhaps not."

Warming to the intimate setting, Allison asked, "Who's Gina?"—although she knew the answer.

"My sister-in-law. Paolo's first wife."

"Is what Maria said true? Did Gina die here?"

Francesca nodded. Allison watched Francesca's hands claw against the Bible. "She took her own life when the boys were young."

"Oh, I'm so sorry."

"It's in the past," Francesca said stoically, but the quiver in her voice betrayed her. "Let's talk about the reason you're here. Benini Enterprises. We can start with my brother." When Allison nodded for her to continue, she said, "Paolo is a good man, but no genius. I've had his ear over the years and have helped him where I could, when Simone or Dom or someone else was not interfering." Francesca gave a crooked smile. "No business school for me, I'm self-taught. I have read every treatise on business management and finance imaginable. If allowed, I could run this business. If *allowed*."

"By Dom?"

Francesca sighed. "By all of them."

"But surely you have some allies?"

Francesca appeared thoughtful. After a few seconds, she said, "No. As a matter of fact, I don't have a single one." She looked up, brightening. "But you will be my ally, Allison. That is, if you'll have me."

Allison looked at the walls of books, at Francesca's earnest expression and the Bible gripped in her hands. She mustered a smile. "I'll have you."

Francesca nodded. The Bible now clutched to her chest, she rose and grabbed the lantern. "Let's go. I'll fill you in on some practical details about Benini Enterprises when we head back downstairs. And then I'll lead you to your suite. You have a long drive tomorrow."

Indeed, she did, although Allison was too caught up in Francesca's family to worry about the next morning's drive. "Tell me, Francesca," she said as they headed back down the narrow steps, "do you still come up here often?"

Without even a backwards glance, Francesca said, "No, actually. I haven't been to the library in years."

It was well after midnight when Allison fell into bed, exhausted. The night air had stilled to a ghost of its former self, and Allison closed her eyes to the gentle patter of drizzle. Francesca had filled her head with details about the Benini business. Gone were the older woman's sentimental ramblings, replaced instead by a determined zeal to get started. Together, they'd created an initial plan. And business acumen and leadership skills were to be the main foci.

Allison took a deep breath, inhaling the scent of clean cotton. Francesca's family—the whole odd lot of them—still made her uneasy, but she forced her mind to think about work. In work, she found comfort. Before she drifted off to sleep, her last thoughts were of Francesca Benini's hands clutched around that Bible and the name Gina Benini. She listened for Gina's other-worldly moan, but if the dead woman was calling, her voice was drowned out by the sounds of Allison's own rhythmic breathing and the rain showers outside.

FOUR

Other than making the necessary arrangements for her client's future visit, Allison didn't have time to consider Francesca Benini or the woman's unusual family. She had another client visiting on Monday—Tammy "Swallow" Edwards, the eighteen-year-old ingénue from Scranton, Pennsylvania. After talking to Vaughn days before, Tammy's manager, Denise Carr, contacted Allison directly to discuss the budding star. She wanted to impress upon Allison that the girl had a voice like an angel but the social skills of a monkey on Xanax.

Tammy's parents had been unable to bring Tammy to First Impressions, so Denise brought Tammy down herself, leading the girl with a hip-swaying nonchalance that said she owned the place. Long, straightened, blond hair clashed with eyebrows left to their natural state. Skin-tight red skirt, red and hot pink floral blouse painted on to breasts that were no stranger to Victoria's Secret's line of push-up bras. Black heels so high that she practically shuffled into the Client Room. A heavy dose of red lipstick that made pillow-thick lips compete with a strong Slavic nose. Denise Carr was a cross between Wall Street arm candy and the star of an eighties metal band video.

Denise sat next to Tammy and patted her hand. "Tammy's not comfortable with people, Ms. Campbell. We need to help her slither out of her shell. She has a glorious music career ahead, if we can convince her that people don't bite."

Choosing to ignore Denise's unfortunate descriptors, Allison regarded Tammy. The kid was the polar opposite of her manager. Denise's initial description had been a bit unfair, but not completely off the mark. Tammy was skinny and tall—nearly six feet—with lank, mid-length brown hair and a strong, almost masculine, facial bone structure. She had a long face, prominent nose and chestnut-brown, soulful eyes. Doe eyes. But it was hard to see those eyes because Tammy hid them behind her hair.

In an attempt to engage the teen, Allison said, "The thing to remember, Tammy, is that a performance—any performance—is not about you, really. It's about the audience. It's hard to feel self-conscious when you're focused on other people's needs."

Tammy remained intent on her left thumb nail.

Denise said sharply, "Ms. Campbell is talking to you."

"It's okay," Allison said. "Why don't you leave us now? We'll be fine. Right Tammy?"

"Uh-huh."

Denise said, "Do you think you can help her?"

Allison's first impression was that Tammy's was a problem of communication. The girl might have a voice that won her a spot on America's Next Pop Star, but she wouldn't open her mouth to speak. And Allison loathed to admit it, but here, Denise was spot on. It was hard to garner an audience's affection if they couldn't connect with you.

"I can help her with presentation. But what about voice? Does she need a voice coach?"

"She has a voice coach. Anyway, singing is not her problem. If you've watched the show, you know half the time will be spent answering questions, engaging the audience. That's what we need you for."

Allison said, "Does that make sense, Tammy? Do you want to tackle things this way?"

Tammy mumbled, "Sure."

"Oh, my." Denise smiled apologetically. "She packed clothes for the week. I know you're putting her up at a hotel. That's fine. My agency will pick up the tab. Her parents aren't in a position to pay right now. But no one's worried about that." She patted Tammy's hand again, a gesture meant, no doubt, to be reassuring. Allison couldn't help focusing on Denise's coral-coated talons, which she didn't find remotely comforting. "Because we believe Tammy will be well worth the investment."

Allison smiled. "Shall we get started, Tammy?"

Tammy shrugged.

"You'll be okay," Denise said. "I'll pick her up on Friday?"

Allison stood. "My colleague Vaughn will drop her off. Say noon? At her house?"

"All the way up there? That seems very out of your way."

"Vaughn's headed to Ithaca for another client. Tammy's house is directly on the way. It's no trouble at all."

Denise looked at Tammy. "Does that work?"

Tammy shrugged again.

Denise shook her head. "See what I mean? How is she going to win over an audience if she can't even answer a question?"

Allison tried fifty ways to get Tammy to talk, but the most she got was a curt nod and a mumbled yes or no. The kid wasn't rude, simply agonizingly shy.

Allison would have chalked it up to meeting a new person, but Denise said this was status quo for the young musician. How the girl could stand in front of thousands of people and sing, she had no idea.

It was a hot, soupy, Philadelphia day in August. Allison had chosen a sleeveless charcoal sheath dress, but with the air conditioner on, she needed a sweater.

She rose from her seat across from Tammy and excused herself. She kept a cardigan in her office. Retrieving it would buy her a few minutes to think strategy.

When Allison returned, sweater in hand, Tammy was gone.

"Tammy?" Allison called. "Tammy!"

No answer.

She hurried through the client room into the kitchenette. No Tammy. The bathroom door was open, the space empty. The offices to First Impressions were not that big. Where could she have gone? Allison decided to go room by room. But each one—and every closet and nook—came up empty.

Great, Allison thought, two hours in and the kid's already quit.

A bird flying by a window caught Allison's eye and she happened to glance outside at the small parking lot below. There was Tammy, sitting on the curb next to Allison's Volvo, hunched over her tall, thin form, arms around her legs, head on her knees, rocking rhythmically back and forth.

Allison let out her breath slowly, unaware that she'd even been holding it. Quickly, she tossed the sweater over the back of a chair and headed outside. She sat next to Tammy on the curb, doing her best to keep her dress from riding completely up to her backside, and echoed Tammy's posture.

They sat in silence for almost fifteen minutes, the flimsy shade offered by the Volvo doing little to mitigate the stifling heat. But Allison knew better than to talk. After the work she'd done with another teen, Violet, years ago while still a graduate student in psychology, and then based on her relationship with the difficult Maggie McBride, Allison understood that kids would speak when they were ready. She just hoped it happened soon in this case, before they both melted.

Finally, Tammy said, "I want to go to the Ellen and James S. Marcus Institute for Vocal Arts. At Juilliard."

Surprised, Allison said, "That sounds like a great goal."

Tammy shook her head. "Not happening."

"What do you mean, it's not happening?"

"I'm going to record an album."

"Recording an album and going to school are not mutually exclusive."

Tammy sighed, gaze still locked on the black pavement under her Converse high-tops. "You don't get it."

"Then help me get it."

"I sing pop music."

"And I hear you're pretty amazing."

Rocking again, Tammy turned to Allison, her sad eyes brimming with tears. "I want to be an opera singer."

Allison thought about that in the context of what she knew. Denise, Tammy's manager, had said that Tammy was discovered by a music exec while singing in a church choir. She was encouraged to try out for the pop star competition and won a spot on next season's show. Denise *never* mentioned opera.

But Denise had also said that the family was a challenge. Tammy's mother was allegedly meek and docile, and her father a burly, brusque man who worked two jobs—a toll booth operator and a maintenance man at a local landfill—to pay for his brood. He called the shots, and according to Denise, right now he had dollar signs in his eyes.

Understanding all of that, Allison thought she also understood Tammy's despair. An education at Juilliard meant tuition money. And even if she got a scholarship, school meant lost income—income that would be invaluable to a family with seven children under the age of eighteen.

Tammy wouldn't want to disappoint.

Classically-trained opera singer was a far cry from pop music reality television star. One just may pay the bills in the short term. But, it seemed to Allison, that the other could be a fulfilling, long-term career. Especially if it was your true passion. And what a gift to know your true passion at such a young age.

Allison took another look at Tammy, trying to envision her on stage, dressed in the elaborate costumes of an opera star.

With that bone structure and that frame, she could pull it off physically. And perhaps with a little coaxing, Tammy could pull it off mentally as well.

"I see," Allison said finally.

Tammy wiped her eyes with the back of a grubby hand. "Can you help me?"

Allison tapped manicured fingernails on hot cement. *Could* she help? She took a deep breath. "In a way, perhaps. Have you told your parents how you feel?"

Tammy shrugged.

"Let's start with all this shrugging. I want to help you, Tammy, but you need to meet me half way. That means you need to communicate, hard as it may be. And shrugging does not count as effective communication."

Tammy looked up. "Fine. I mentioned it once. My father said there was no money for college and that was the end of it. I don't argue with my dad."

"When was that?"

Tammy started to shrug, thought better of it, and said, "A few months ago, maybe."

"And how do your folks feel about the television show?"

"My mom hates the idea. She's pretty religious. My dad seems fine, though. He hooked up with Denise after the executive for the record label called him."

At least Tony Edwards wasn't trying to manage his daughter's career himself. That was something. Allison wanted to meet the Edwards family in person. Perhaps that would be next. Was Tony the domineering father Denise had painted him as, or was there more nuance here, more to the story than Denise's simple depiction? She was betting on the latter. But one thing was certain—although Allison wasn't a counselor and had no intention of putting herself in the middle of the family's struggles, she *could* help her new client help herself just by doing her job.

"Here's what we're going to do." Allison stood, tugging down her now-wrinkled dress. "We're going to put you in the best position possible to advocate for your own future. That means you need to trust me. Do you think you can do that?"

Tammy, now standing, was the same height as Allison, despite Allison's three-inch heels. Tammy nodded, her eyes downcast.

"First lesson, Tammy. Look at me when you respond. Eye contact is important. It tells people you're interested in what they have to say. It provides a connection with your audience. And it's easier to speak articulately when you have that connection. You want that, don't you?"

Tammy raised her head so that they were just about eye-to-eye. "Yes," she mumbled.

"Now say it like you mean it."

"I understand. And I'll trust you," she said in a stronger voice, a voice that hinted at the talented singer she was alleged to be.

"Good. Very good," Allison said. "Now let's get back inside where it's cool."

It was after eleven when Allison finally crawled into bed between her two favorite guys—her ex-husband-turned-boyfriend Jason and her Boxer dog, Brutus. She wasn't sure who was the noisier sleeper. But only Jason woke up after she entered the room. He flipped on the bedside light, blinked a few times and smiled when he saw her.

"You're late," he said without a trace of accusation.

Allison sat next to him and leaned down to kiss his mouth. "Yeah, got caught up with the kid. She's pretty damn amazing, actually."

"This is the rising pop star?"

Allison nodded. "I finally convinced her to sing opera for me. Her voice made me weep."

Jason sat up in the bed, gently pushing Brutus over to the other side of the mattress. "You sound like you like her."

"She's extremely shy. Just getting her to address people directly will be a challenge. And she doesn't speak up, even when it's in her own best interest. But those things can be dealt with." Allison thought back to the scene in the parking lot. "It's the bigger picture I'm worried about. Lots of people are suddenly making decisions on her behalf. I'm not sure who has her best interests at heart."

Jason smiled. "Leave it to you to find the wayward kid in need of protection."

Allison took the good-natured ribbing as it was intended. She grabbed a pillow from underneath Jason's shoulders and hit him squarely in the chest. "Oh yeah?"

Jason grabbed her wrists lightly. "It's what I love about you." He pulled her on top of him and hugged her close, his hands already trailing their way toward the hem of her chemise.

"Not so fast," Allison said, but she stayed in his arms. "I have to be up early tomorrow. Breakfast with the kid, then a business luncheon."

"Who's with Tammy after that?"

"Vaughn's carting her around to various appointments, but she and I will have sessions throughout the week."

Jason brushed Allison's ear with his lips, sending a tingle that reached her toes. "When does she leave?" he whispered.

Allison kissed Jason deeply before answering. She let her hand wander across his chest, down his tight stomach, before trailing one fingertip across a thigh. He moaned.

"I'm saying good-bye to Tammy on Friday morning and hello to Francesca Benini that evening. Vaughn's driving one back and picking up the other."

Jason put a warm hand under Allison's silk nightgown. He kissed her, hard, while tracing a finger from the sensitive peak of one breast to the other. Allison shivered.

"Then Vaughn's the one who needs a good night's sleep." Another kiss, deeper, harder. "Not you."

FIVE

The kid said exactly two words during the entire drive to Scranton: whatever and no. She sat slouched on the passenger seat of Vaughn's BMW with the hood of her black sleeveless hoodie hiding her face. For most of the drive, she slept. When she wasn't sleeping, she had her head pressed against the window of the car, iPod on, headphones in. After they passed Allentown, Vaughn offered to plug the iPod into the car's sound system just to have something to listen to. That's when she said "whatever."

Vaughn was surprised to hear classical music come out of the speakers.

But his attempts to engage Tammy in any type of conversation were met with blank stares or watery smiles. At one point, about thirty miles from Scranton, on the Pennsylvania Turnpike, Vaughn asked if she'd like to stop at a rest stop to use the bathroom or grab something to eat. That's when she said "no."

Vaughn shrugged. "Suit yourself."

Traffic was light, cruising was easy. It was an uneventful drive.

And so Vaughn made it all the way to her house in Scranton in a little over two hours, arriving almost an hour sooner than they'd anticipated. He pulled up in front of Tammy's home on Linden Street and parked next to the curb.

The house was a half a double on a street of twin homes. It was blocky, with a fading front porch that spanned the width of the house and a pair of vinyl-clad windows above that. Chain link fencing ran alongside a shared driveway. Whatever yard they had in the back would have been the extent of green space because the porch started within two feet of where the sidewalk ended. It was not a big house and

Vaughn, who had been raised in the slums of Philly, wondered how the Edwards family reared seven children there.

Vaughn noticed a Chevy Cavalier in the driveway. He followed Tammy up the steps to the porch and waited while she opened the front door. She threw her bag onto the floor and stood, blocking the entranceway. The house behind her was dark.

"Dad!" she yelled. There was no answer. She shrugged. "No one's here."

"We're early—Denise wasn't expecting you for another hour. Isn't your mom home?"

Tammy shook her head. "That's my dad's car outside. When he works at the landfill, sometimes he carpools."

"Are you okay by yourself?"

Tammy's eyebrows shot up. "Seriously? I'm eighteen."

Vaughn smiled. Kid was right—and I'm getting old, he thought. He glanced at his watch. If he got on the road now, maybe he and Francesca could be back to Villanova at a reasonable hour. It'd be nice to hang out with Jamie tonight. Catch a movie, talk about Jamie's new job. He felt more distant from his twin now that Jamie had a life outside of their apartment. He was happy for his brother...happy, but change could be tough to swallow. Even good change.

"Okay, then," he said to his charge. "Allison will be in touch. You'll be down for a few weeks later this month. In the meantime, I'm sure she gave you homework? Make sure you do it."

Tammy started to shrug again. She seemed to think better of it, raised her head and looked Vaughn in the eye. Echoes of Allison. Vaughn smiled. His boss was in Tammy's head already. Didn't take long. Never did.

"Thanks," Tammy said finally. She gave a wan smile. "Bye."

Tammy turned and disappeared into the darkness.

On the second leg of his trip, Vaughn wasn't so lucky. An over-turned tractor trailer on Route 81 shut down the highway in both directions and Vaughn idled his car on what had become a parking lot. As a consequence, he didn't arrive at the Benini estate until after five in the evening. It took him two passes to find the turn-off that led to the

Benini property. The small wooden sign marking the family vineyard had faded over time and was partially hidden by a dense patch of trees, across from the lake. Vaughn was a city boy. While he might have appreciated the countryside in photos, he'd have preferred to pick up his client somewhere less isolated. Somewhere with fast food joints, gas stations and even the occasional mugger.

Not built for off-roading, the BMW staggered its way up the steep driveway toward the mansion. Portions of the path were paved, although the blacktop had seen better days and Vaughn, concerned for his car's undercarriage, took the drive very slowly. If it hadn't been for that fact, he might have missed the woman on horseback. She was behind him, in the woods that lined the drive, and he caught just a flash of her face and the movement of the horse's tail behind a tree.

Another flash of movement, and then the woman repositioned the horse so that the pair was parked behind a large pine tree. Vaughn couldn't make out the woman's face, but he sensed her watching him.

He kept going. The drive was S-shaped and at least a mile long. Must be a bitch in the winter, he thought. At the top, the driveway passed through an iron gate, which was closed. Vaughn pulled up to the small gate house, climbed out of his car and looked around. The sentry house was dark. He opened the door and glanced inside. One shattered window, covered in plastic, advertised that it hadn't been used in quite a while. Vaughn glanced behind him. Maybe that chick on the horse could tell him how to get in.

Frustrated—they were expecting him, after all, so the gate should be open—he took a closer look. The lock was not completely fastened, giving only the appearance of being secured. He pulled the padlock apart, hooked it over the iron loop and pulled the heavy gates to each side. They opened with a screech. Then he climbed back into the car and pulled through, not bothering to re-close it once on the other side. He drove the rest of the way in second gear, his eyes on the house up ahead of him. Allison was right. It was right out of a Victorian novel.

Francesca Benini was ready and waiting for him by the front door, three large suitcases—hard, red relics from the sixties—and one small black one piled in the family's huge foyer. Vaughn took one look and wondered how he was going to fit them in the tight trunk of his car. And what the hell was this woman doing—moving in with Allison?

Vaughn picked up two of the suitcases and put them in the car. Only one would fit in the trunk, so he placed the other on the backseat. Francesca followed him outside with her small black bag and her purse, clearly anxious to get going. Vaughn opened the passenger door for her before heading back to get the last bag. That's when he saw his stalker. She was walking up from the barn at a fast clip, her curvy form doing justice to tight jeans and a black, fitted tank top.

As he tucked the last of the bags in the backseat, he stole another glance at the woman. Why had she been watching him in the woods? Shy? Or secretive? She was over the hill now and only about one hundred feet from where they stood.

Francesca made no move to acknowledge her, just stared straight ahead, fingers tapping against her thigh, ready to get on the road. Vaughn pushed his curiosity aside. But as he pulled away, he snuck a final glance in his rearview mirror. Before the distance distorted his view, he noticed two things about the stalker from the woods. One, she was about the most beautiful woman he had ever seen. And two, she was carrying a shotgun.

"That would be Maria," Francesca said as they made their way toward the highway. "My niece."

"What's with the gun?"

"She kills animals that attack her chickens."

Francesca's eyes were closed. She'd leaned her head back against the leather and had her hands spread out in her lap. She seemed focused on her own breathing.

"Would you like some music?"

"What kind?" Francesca asked without opening her eyes.

He ran through a list of options. She settled on Mozart.

They sat quietly for a long leg of the trip. Traffic had returned to normal, and while Vaughn drove, he thought about his date the next night with Mia, Allison's former mentor. Things had been easier now that their relationship was out in the open, but Mia wanted to have "a talk," which, in his experience, was never a good thing.

Francesca sat inert beside him. After some time, she said, "So tell me, did you talk to my niece?"

"No. She was coming over the hill, from the stable. Before she got close enough to say anything, you were ready to leave." He chose not to mention that she'd been following him in the woods.

"It's better that way. I wouldn't want your image of our family clouded by your impression of Maria."

He smiled. "Not your favorite relative?"

"To the contrary. Of Paolo's kids, I suppose she's my favorite. She's at least candid about her intentions."

"And what are those intentions, if I can ask?"

"You can and you may. Maria wants to run Benini Enterprises."

"Is she capable?"

"If being feisty and having street smarts makes you capable." Francesca sighed. Her tone softened. "Maybe with training. Now, she is too impulsive and impatient, like Simone."

"Simone's her mother?"

"Yes. Although mother is a term that suggests maternal feelings and nurturing behavior. I don't think Simone has ever exhibited either. She's more like an older sister competing for attention."

Vaughn looked at her with a half-smile. "No love lost between the two of you?"

This time, Francesca opened her eyes, although she kept her head back against the seat rest. "Is it that obvious?" She smiled, but it was a sad smile and Vaughn felt a tug of empathy. "I was raised by nuns in a convent boarding school. I started when I was five years old. *Five*, Mr. Vaughn. My own mother was weak-willed. She let her mother-in-law, my grandmother, make the decisions. And my father's mother was, well, let's just call her opinionated. She had strong views about the role of girls."

"Seen but not heard?"

"Neither seen nor heard." Francesca pursed her lips. "My family is from Calabria. Paolo, my brother, was raised to believe he could do no wrong. Not by my father—he was a smart man who took a small plot of land and turned it into an empire. No, it was not my father. It was my grandmother and, by way of submission, my mother."

"Paolo runs Benini Enterprises?"

"He *ran* the company. For the last thirty-one years, since the death of my father. Now, I'm afraid, Paolo's tenure is over. The stroke may not have robbed him of his life yet, but the doctors are quite certain it has robbed him of his faculties."

"And the company?"

Francesca smiled, with a pained twist of the lips. "After all these years, that burden is mine."

"If you don't want the burden, why take this on? Why not just let one of Paolo's kids run Benini Enterprises?"

"Why indeed."

Vaughn slowed as the traffic before him rounded a bend on Route 81. He thought about the distraught woman who'd called him for Allison's help. Somehow he couldn't reconcile that Francesca with the one who sat next to him, quietly confident and oddly unemotional.

"You and your brother are close?"

"Very. Paolo is older than I am. He's long been my protector and advocate within the family, first when it came to my grandmother and, later, his wives. It was Paolo who invited me to live at the family's American estate when it became clear to everyone that I was not meant for marriage or a so-called normal life. And it was he who insisted I stay connected to the business when our father died."

"But he didn't let you help run the business?"

Francesca didn't answer. Vaughn was thinking he had pushed the line of inquiry too far when she said, "Learned helplessness."

He searched for the connection. "Seligman's work?"

"Yes, those awful experiments where animals were taught that they couldn't help themselves no matter what, so they simply learned to endure. That's me, Mr. Vaughn. I have learned over the years—through many different lessons—that life is not fair. I stopped thinking I could change things."

"Until now?"

Another silence. Francesca's eyes were closed again. "Perhaps."

"Can we stop?" Francesca said. They were still on Route 81, somewhere between Scranton and Wilkes Barre. "I'd like to use the ladies room."

"Of course," Vaughn said. "I'll get off at the next exit."

The next exit took them toward Pittston and a truck stop off Route 315. By now it was dark outside and the vast parking lot surrounding a Perkins restaurant and connected service area looked like a truck graveyard.

Vaughn pulled up outside of the restaurant area. "Are you hungry, Francesca? Would you like to stop for dinner?"

She had unbuckled her seat belt and was slowly stretching her legs out in front of her. "If you don't mind, I'd prefer to get where we are going. Although if you want something—"

He didn't and he said so. They agreed to meet back at the car in fifteen minutes. Vaughn watched the older woman enter the truck stop. Then he took out his mobile and called home. Once he was certain Jamie was fine, he dialed Allison's mobile.

"Things going well?" she asked.

"As well as can be expected. Although it will be close to midnight by the time we arrive." He filled her in on the traffic and on their discussions so far.

Allison was quiet for a moment. "At least she opened up to you. It's a start."

"I think you're going to have a long haul with this one. Her goal seems so unattainable. She's definitely motivated, though." He flashed back to the look on her face when she mentioned that the business was her burden now. "Motivated in the way of a martyr going to the grave for her god. Or something."

"*Something* is right. That house...her family. But we enjoy a challenge, right Vaughn?" Allison laughed. "So I'll see you in about two hours?"

"Give or take."

Vaughn took another look at his watch. They were supposed to meet back at the BMW at 9:25, but it was 9:35 and Francesca still wasn't there. He was reluctant to leave the car in case she returned. He hadn't asked for her cell number. Stupid on his part. He'd wait a few more minutes and then go look for her.

At 9:45, tired of waiting, he scribbled a note to Francesca, tucked it under the windshield and walked inside. To the left of the entrance was the restaurant. He scanned the crowd, looking for his client, but didn't see her. Same luck in the convenience store and coffee shop. Finally, refusing to acknowledge the tennis ball lump in his belly, he asked a truck stop employee to search the women's restroom for someone who matched Francesca's description.

"Is that the only bathroom?" he asked when the employee came out alone.

"There's a shower area in the rear and a bathroom in the restaurant."

After a moment's hesitation, the woman agreed to check each of these. Ten minutes later she returned. "I'm sorry, sir, but I looked twice in each location and checked every stall. I didn't find anyone who looks like your friend."

Vaughn asked to see the manager. He explained the situation to a skeptical-looking older man with a thick mustache and bald head that glistened under the fluorescent lighting, providing a detailed description of Francesca, down to her clothes and the leather-banded watch she was wearing. The manager chewed his lip. Finally, he nodded. "I'll make an announcement."

Vaughn heard the cackle of the intercom, listened to Francesca's name being called, and waited. After ten endless minutes, he knew he couldn't put off the inevitable any longer. He dialed Allison's number. After a quick explanation of what had happened, he asked for Francesca's cell phone number.

"She doesn't have one."

"Shit. I was afraid of that."

Allison asked, "You've searched the entire place?"

"We're still looking."

"We'll have to contact the family. She may have called them or they may know something." She paused. "But I'll wait until I hear back from you."

"I'll call as soon as I can."

Vaughn asked the manager to contact security. Together they scoured the outside parking areas and outbuildings, questioned sleepy truckers, but no one admitted to seeing her.

Vaughn couldn't overcome the rising dread boiling in his gut. From tennis ball to bowling ball, and growing.

Where the hell was Francesca?

Vaughn finally called Allison back at 11:48 p.m.

"Yes?" Her voice was not quite so even now.

"No sign of her." Vaughn took a deep breath. He could hear the weariness in his own voice. "It looks like Francesca is missing."

Allison didn't respond. Vaughn heard her mumble something to someone in the room with her. A second later she was back on the line.

"Vaughn, I'm afraid there's more." She hesitated. "Denise Carr called about twenty minutes ago. Tammy wasn't at the house when her parents returned tonight. They haven't heard a word from her. They think she ran away from home." Another pause, and Vaughn swore he could hear the beating of her heart through the phone. "Or she was kidnapped."

SIX

Allison opened her eyes, hoping for a brief second that it had all been a nightmare. But Jason's worried face said otherwise. He was sitting on the edge of the bed dressed in cargo shorts and a Patagonia t-shirt. The day-old stubble on his face gave him the haggard appearance of a new father. He smiled weakly when Allison sat up, and he handed her a cup of strong coffee.

"The police called me back about Tammy Edwards. Nothing so far. They've filed a report with the NCIC."

"And nothing from Francesca's family?"

He shook his head. "They're not being particularly cooperative."

"What does that mean?"

"The sister-in-law insists that Francesca has been clinically depressed for years. A danger to herself. That this was the first time she was really left unattended and...well, now this happened."

"She thinks she ran away?"

"Not exactly."

Horrified, Allison said, "Not suicide?"

"She hasn't actually used the word. But yes, that's what she's suggesting."

"That's quite a leap. And what about a body? She couldn't have gotten far. It would have turned up by now."

Jason smoothed the covers out around Allison's legs, picked at a microscopic piece of lint. "Maybe. Although it was a truck stop. She could have gotten a ride before Vaughn even started looking for her." He gently pushed the hair away from Allison's face with the back of his hand. "How well do you really know this woman, Al?"

"Francesca? Not well at all."

"So, it's possible that she took advantage of the situation and did something drastic. Ran away, hurt herself?"

"Why go to all the trouble of arranging to meet me? Why not just do something from the house in the Finger Lakes?"

"Opportunity. Impulse. We both know people's reasons for things don't always make sense."

Allison took a sip of coffee. It was searing and rich and, despite how appreciative Allison felt that Jason made it for her, it flowed into her stomach like an acid bath. Allison closed her eyes. She flashed back to others whose actions didn't make sense...murdering two people, framing a young girl. No, it was certainly a bizarre and often cruel world.

The beginning of a migraine wormed its way into her brain. It wouldn't be long before the throb was all encompassing. Add to that a pleasant side of nausea.

She forced another swallow of coffee and said, "Anything from Tammy's family?"

"I figured you would reach out to them when you woke up." He looked at his watch. "It's eight-thirty. You didn't get to bed until well after four. If you want to sleep a little longer, I'll cover for you."

"No, I'm fine. Maybe a migraine med, if you don't mind. Then give me a half hour and I'll be ready to roar."

At half past nine that morning, Allison was tired of waiting for a call back from the Edwards family, so she dialed Denise Carr's mobile number.

Tammy's manager answered on the third ring.

"No one is blaming you," Denise said immediately, insinuating, of course, that everyone was blaming Allison.

"Well, that's good, I guess." Allison sank into the oversized chair in her living room, a relatively new purchase. Actually all of the living room furniture was new. Her own nod to moving on, she wondered? Brutus curled on the floor next to her, his giant head on her foot. "I assume then that she hasn't shown up?"

"Nothing. Nada. Zilch." Denise gave an overly-dramatic sigh of frustration. "The Scranton police say they are investigating, but I'm sure they hear teenager and immediately think runaway. Plus, she's eighteen. Technically an adult, free to come and go as she pleases."

"Do her parents think she ran away?"

"Her parents don't know what to think. She's incommunicado, sure, but a runaway?" Denise made a clucking sound. "Doesn't seem like it. And why now, before her dream competition?"

Yes, indeed, why now? "I've tried to call the parents, but they haven't returned my calls."

"Like I said, Allison, no one blames you."

"Blames me for what?"

"Look, it may seem incriminating. She goes to you, spends a few nights, you do your head stuff with her and the next thing we know, *whoosh*. She vanishes. But let me be clear. No one blames you."

That's a relief, Allison thought. She could hear the biting sarcasm in her own internal voice. Brutus began licking Allison's bare feet. Allison pushed him gently away—it tickled—and tucked her legs up under her. She wasn't getting anywhere with Denise Carr other than a new appreciation for the skill of passive aggressiveness.

"When she returns home, please let me know," Allison said.

"Wait. How did things go, anyway? With the image consulting?"

Allison debated what to say. Anything positive would sound contrived at this point. She decided to stick with vague.

"We made progress. She's a sweet girl. Painfully shy, but then, you know that."

"Do you feel like we could have her ready for September?"

"All things considered, Denise, that's something we can talk about when she comes home."

Denise didn't respond. From the other room, Allison could hear the low murmur of Jason's voice as he spoke with someone on his mobile. She listened, feeling a sudden and overwhelming tenderness for her lover. Despite this mess, despite the craziness that had marked the last year, he was here. She still felt the warm, lingering whisper of his fingers against her face.

Just days ago, he'd asked to move back in. Afraid things were moving too fast, she'd said no. Allison watched Brutus lick the top of one paw with long, lazy strokes. She squeezed her eyes shut. Was she a fool? Perhaps.

"Did Tammy mention running away, Allison? Or being angry with her parents?"

Allison blinked, focusing back on the here and now. "Nothing at all about either."

"Was she sullen?"

"I'd characterize her as quiet, but not sullen. Why do you ask?"

"Oh, I just wondered if she resented working with you. Not that we blame you, of course. Or that assistant of yours. Vaughn."

"No, of course not." Allison un-tucked her legs and stood up. "Look, Denise, be a dear and call me when she returns, okay?"

"Yes, yes. No worries, Allison. I have your back."

Allison hung up, all too happy to end that call. She tried Mrs. Edwards one more time. Still no answer. She left another voicemail.

Two clients. Two disappearances. Too much of a coincidence?

Vaughn's apartment was hot and stuffy, as though the heater was battling it out with the air conditioner—and winning.

Allison followed Mrs. T, Jamie's favorite nurse/caretaker, through the living room, past the kitchen and into Jamie's bedroom. Paralyzed from the neck down since age nineteen when he'd received a bullet meant for Vaughn, Vaughn's identical twin had been sentenced to life inside these four walls until last spring when Jamie's research helped nail a killer. The local police force hired him as a consultant and, finally willing to journey outside the apartment, Jamie spent three days a week in the police precinct in a specially-equipped office.

Now he looked drained. When Allison walked in, she instinctively looked at the large computer monitor by Jamie's bed. Jamie couldn't speak. He used a special mouthpiece that caused his words to appear on the screen.

HELLO, ALLISON. I HOPE YOU'RE FARING BETTER THAN MY BROTHER TODAY.

Allison smiled her hello. She glanced to the back of the room and saw Vaughn propped on the couch. His tight facial expression said it all.

"I'm holding up okay, Jamie," she said. She kissed his forehead before joining Vaughn. She plopped down on the couch and patted

Vaughn's leg. He managed a half-hearted hello. "Unlike this guy."

HE BLAMES HIMSELF.

Allison nodded. "Looks that way." Clearly Vaughn was going through something. She had never seen her colleague, her rock, her friend, look so down.

She could understand why. Two missing clients, and Vaughn was the last to have seen both. But last night, Allison asked him to walk through the details of his day, through every excruciating word that had been uttered and every minute gesture made by each of her clients, until they were both cross and exhausted, and still she could see no point at which he'd demonstrated poor judgment.

Either it had been a day of bad luck, and both women, for their own reasons, had left of their own accord—in which case one or both women would likely return with some plausible story regarding their whereabouts—or foul play was at hand.

Vaughn said, "I should have gone in there with Francesca."

"To the bathroom, Vaughn? Listen to yourself. Francesca is a grown woman. And before you even mention Tammy, let me remind you she's eighteen. Legally an adult. She works, babysits...and will be headed off to California on her own soon enough. You did nothing wrong for either client. Period."

Vaughn nodded, but he didn't look convinced. The truth was, until they knew who or what caused each woman to disappear, they couldn't really say whether Vaughn might have prevented it. Or whether she might have. Had she done or said something to trigger a flight response in either client? But as experience taught her, hindsight was not only 20/20—it was absolutely worthless.

IT'S NOT EVEN BEEN 24 HOURS.

Vaughn wasn't looking at his brother's screen, so Allison read the words to him. Vaughn shook his head. He sat up and glanced over at Jamie. "Gut sense. Something happened to Francesca. I feel it in my bones. And it's driving me...well, I need to *do* something."

HER FAMILY SEEMS A LITTLE ODD, VAUGHN. SHE'S BEEN COOPED UP IN THAT HOUSE FOR DECADES. MAYBE SHE WANTED HER FREEDOM.

"No. She was too concerned about the family business to leave."

Allison said, "Concerned in what way?"

"She was clearly anxious. She spent most of the ride with her eyes closed, regulating her breathing."

"Probably because she was leaving the Benini property for the first time in years."

AGORAPHOBIC?

"Not necessarily. Her behavior might have been an attempt to calm her anxiety. And anxiety under those circumstances would be a normal reaction."

Vaughn said, "But when she talked about Benini Enterprises, there was determination in her voice. Anger. Maybe even a little desperation."

IF SHE WAS AGORAPHOBIC, THE DESPERATION COULD HAVE BEEN A REACTION TO LEAVING THE SAFETY OF HER HOME.

"I don't know," Allison said, thinking of the woman she'd spent time with during those first fateful encounters. "I worked with an agoraphobic in graduate school. Although it would be hard to say for sure unless I saw her outside her safe environment, Francesca didn't exhibit the anxiety levels I would associate with an agoraphobic. To stay there for so long, her disorder would have been quite advanced. There would be more...symptoms."

SO WHAT IF HER FEAR WAS CAUSED BY SOMETHING ELSE?

"You mean what if she was in some kind of danger?" Vaughn asked.

YES. MAYBE SHE'S BEEN HIDING ALL THESE YEARS.

Allison looked sharply at Jamie. "If she was in hiding, perhaps coming to me wasn't just about learning the skills she'd need to lead Benini Enterprises."

I *AM* WONDERING ABOUT HER MOTIVATION FOR CONTACTING YOU.

Vaughn sat up straight. "She could have been escaping to us for safety. Maybe the danger was in her house. Contacting us was a way to get out of the house."

ALLISON, DID YOU GET THE SENSE FRANCESCA WAS BEING FORCED TO STAY THERE AGAINST HER WILL?

Allison considered her stay at the estate. The tension between Francesca and family members. Alex's scorn over his aunt's choice to remain a recluse for so long. That large, lonely old house. The odd sense of being lost in time.

"No, I didn't get the sense she was forced to stay. She talked about vultures, though," Allison said. "At the time, I assumed she meant it metaphorically. You know, that without someone manning the ship the sharks would start circling, that sort of thing. But what if she was referring to someone specific?"

CREDITORS?

"Or other family members. I keep coming back to her family."

Vaughn sat forward. "She was pretty clear that she disliked her family when we talked in the car."

VAUGHN, DID SHE SAY ANYTHING ELSE IN THE CAR THAT MAY SEEM IMPORTANT NOW?

"She talked about growing up in Italy, about a cruel grandmother and an overly-passive mother. I told Allison all of this. Francesca was sent to boarding school at five years old, by her grandmother."

Allison pondered that. Five years old. A childhood spent at a school, away from family, away from home. How would that affect a person?

HOW ABOUT AFTER SHE FINISHED SCHOOL? DID SHE GIVE YOU ANY CLUE ABOUT HER LIFE AS A YOUNG ADULT?

"No," Vaughn said, agitated. "Actually, maybe she did, in a roundabout sort of way. I'd forgotten about that. She talked about Seligman's experiments."

"Learned helplessness?" Allison said, recalling the research from her days as a graduate student in psychology. She'd thought the trials cruel then. Now, just thinking of them in the context of her client made her legs feel weak.

Vaughn nodded. "Compared herself to those animals."

THAT COULD MEAN ANYTHING.

"She said life was unfair," Vaughn said. "That she'd learned to endure and to stop trying to change things."

MELODRAMATIC?

"No. If anything, understated." Vaughn looked at Allison. "You met her. Francesca seem the dramatic type?"

"Not really. More like quietly enduring." Allison remembered their conversation in the library, the way Francesca evaded questions about her family life and her past. "Although at one point, she said some would view her as dramatic. She didn't say how or why. Told me she'd share more when we met."

They all sat in silence for a moment. Vaughn was the first to break the spell. He stood up and headed toward the door.

"Where are you going?"

"I need to *do* something."

"But what?"

"I'm going to look for her."

"Vaughn, she could be anywhere by now."

"Then what do you suggest? I can't just sit here. She disappeared on *my* watch. I feel like a caged animal."

A caged animal...like Francesca?

Maybe that was it, something they could both do. It was a Saturday. Allison could cancel the few weekend plans she had scheduled.

"How about we head north for the weekend, Vaughn? I'll ask Jason if he wants to join us. We can stop in Scranton and talk with Tammy's parents, if they'll see us. And then go up to Ithaca, to the Benini estate. We still have Francesca's suitcases anyway. And I'd like another opportunity to meet the family. Ask some questions. Try to figure out whether Francesca really was a willing houseguest for all those years." Or a caged animal, waiting for escape, Allison thought.

Vaughn's eyes searched hers. His jaw clenched, then unclenched. He nodded. Allison understood his need for action. She wasn't sure what they were doing would help, but it seemed more productive than sitting here.

Vaughn walked toward Jamie's wheelchair. Allison knew he wished his brother could join them, and while Vaughn had made strides in increasing Jamie's mobility, the equipment Jamie needed for everyday survival still made overnight travel nearly impossible without adequate planning.

"Mrs. T will be here for the weekend, Jamie. Will you be okay?"

I'LL BE FINE. ANYWAY, SOMEONE SHOULD LOOK INTO FRANCESCA'S PAST AND BENINI ENTERPRISES. I'LL EMAIL YOU WHATEVER INFORMATION I CAN FIND.

Vaughn squeezed his brother's shoulder—a gesture Jamie could see but not feel. "That would help."

Vaughn and Allison were out the door of Jamie's bedroom when they heard a loud, shrill shriek. Vaughn turned, panicked. But Jamie still had something to say and had gotten their attention the only way he could.

Allison read the words on the computer screen.

PLEASE BE CAREFUL. IF—BIG IF—FOUL PLAY WAS IN-VOLVED, SOME BAD PEOPLE MAY RESENT YOUR INVOLVE-MENT.

Allison, another set of murders still weighing heavily on her mind, didn't need reminding. "We'll be careful, Jamie." She walked back in and hugged him. His body felt so frail, like her mother's. "You be careful, too."

But even as she made her way back out to her car, Allison couldn't shake the feeling of foreboding Jamie's words had awakened. She prayed there wasn't a killer out there this time.

Because if there was, her client's fate had already been decided.

SEVEN

Allison and Vaughn were on the road by two o'clock that afternoon. The sky had darkened to the color of overripe plums and small lightning explosions lit up the distant horizon. Allison drove, the coolness of her Volvo's interior a marked contrast to the suffocating humidity outside.

Next to her, Vaughn was quiet. Jason couldn't go—he was preparing for a trial—so it was just the two of them. Although Allison still had not heard back from Tammy's family, the Edwards' residence was their first destination. They arrived at 4:30 p.m., accompanied by the storms that had been threatening for hours. Allison parallel parked in front of Tammy's home and climbed out of her car, careful to avoid the raging river next to the curb.

"Full house," Allison said, pointing to the three cars in the driveway—a full-size van, a smaller sedan and a Cadillac that Allison recognized as belonging to Tammy's manager, Denise Carr.

Vaughn led the way up the steps and onto the broad porch. He knocked twice. Almost immediately, a man opened the door. He was tall and hulking, with thinning reddish hair, a neat mustache and a curdled expression on his face. He stood in the doorway for a few moments before opening the screen door to let them in.

"Is it Tammy?" a voice called from somewhere in the back of the house.

"No, Jane. I'm sorry, it's not. It's that image consultant. And her driver."

The man nodded at Allison and Vaughn and, without another word, turned to walk toward the voice. They followed him inside, entering what appeared to be the family's living room. An L-shaped brown couch stood against the wall to the left, on top of stained beige carpeting, its fibers long past their prime. To the right, a large entertainment center, its wood nicked and scarred, housed an old-fashioned television and a VCR.

Next to the entertainment center stood a rocking chair. Scattered toys lay claim to the center of the room, all seven or eight feet of it. Legos, blocks, plastic baby books and small green soldiers arranged in elaborate army battles.

Behind the living room was the dining room. No table, just more toys, a desk with an old computer and a sewing machine on a card table. The carpet, in noticeable contrast to the living room rug, was a navy blue shag. Allison and Vaughn glanced at one another before following Tony Edwards through both rooms and into the kitchen beyond. There, two women, one large-boned and brunette, the other, Denise, petite and blonde, sat at an oval wooden table. A baby gurgled contentedly from its nest in the brunette woman's arms.

"Allison." Denise Carr stood and shook Allison's hand, then Vaughn's. "We were just talking about you." Denise turned toward the other woman. "This is Jane Edwards, Tammy's mother. And you met Tony."

Jane nodded but didn't stand. Her eyes were swollen and red-rimmed. Allison felt her stomach clench at the sight of this mother's pain.

"We don't want to intrude," Allison said. "We were just hoping...well, we were hoping that Tammy had come home."

Jane shook her head. She placed her cheek against her daughter's downy head and started to sob.

"Not yet, but she will," Tony mumbled. He knelt next to his wife and patted her back awkwardly. "Jane's having a hard time. Lizzy here is only three months old, so Jane's still pretty hormonal."

Jane gave him a caustic look. He stood, removing his hand from her back. Hastily he said, "Not that she doesn't have a right to be upset. Tammy's never done this before. Leave, I mean."

"Do you want to sit?" Denise asked Allison and Vaughn.

"Oh yeah," Tony said. "Sorry." He pulled a chair from against a wall and pushed it toward Allison. He slid another chair from underneath the table, wiped crumbs from the seat, and handed it to Vaughn.

Denise said, "Is there anything else you can tell us, Vaughn, about what happened when you dropped her off?"

Vaughn shook his head. "Nothing, I'm sure, that Allison hasn't already told you."

"Once more, so Tammy's parents can hear it themselves?"

So Vaughn recounted the entire trip, from the time they left Villanova, to Tammy's "bye" when he left her Scranton home.

"Hmmm," Denise muttered. "Was she texting anyone while you were driving?"

"No. She never even took out her phone. Maybe you can use her cell to find her."

Denise glanced at Jane before shaking her head. "Tried that." She frowned. "Was anyone here when you arrived?"

"Not that I could see. Mr. Edwards' car was in the driveway, but Tammy said he'd gone to work."

Denise looked from mother to father and back again. "What time did you get home, Jane?"

Tony spoke for her. "Nine-thirty. My mom was watching the kids. Jane had a funeral to play for." He turned toward Allison. "My wife plays piano and organ for the church. They pay her to do weddings and funerals, right Jane?"

Jane nodded. Her face was turned toward the kitchen's only window and, in profile, she resembled Tammy. Her hair was stale brown, like Tammy's, and had been pinned into a neat bun. She wore an old-fashioned satin blouse in jade green, its neck bow serving as a toy for the infant in her arms.

Allison would have called her handsome rather than pretty, but there was something distant and unreachable about her. Grief? Or her normal persona?

Tony said, "Do you want coffee?"

"No, thank you." Vaughn looked at Jane. "Does Tammy have a boyfriend, Mrs. Edwards?"

Denise cleared her throat.

Allison looked up in time to see Denise trying to make eye contact with Vaughn in a way that said *don't go there.* Tony's pale skin flushed a bright crimson and Jane was looking cuttingly at Vaughn now, the dazed expression supplanted by something hard.

"Did Tammy say she had a boyfriend?" Jane spoke for the first time. Her voice was high-pitched and nasal—no hint of her daughter's honeyed vocals.

"No, she didn't. I was just wondering."

Allison threw Denise a questioning look. The other woman mouthed "later" and shook her head slightly. Allison changed the subject.

"Tammy sang for me. Her voice is magnificent."

Tony smiled. Jane looked back down at the baby's head.

"Did you know she can sing opera?"

Tony nodded. "It's something, huh? I don't know where that came from. Opera. Imagine. She once asked to go to college in New York." He shook his head, but the look on his face hinted at pride, not judgment. "Wish we could afford it."

Abruptly, Jane stood. "New York is too far away." She threw a condemning glance at Denise and said, "California is *really* too far away."

"We talked about this, Jane." Tony threw a pleading glance at Denise. "This is her big chance."

"She's too young. Too naïve. And Hollywood is a gussied-up name for Gomorrah. You know that as well as I." Jane busied herself mixing formula while she spoke, the baby still spooned in one arm, against her hip. Jane wasn't as tall or skinny as her daughter, but she was close. Thin ankles peeked out beneath a calf-length black skirt and ended in flat black loafers. She pulled the skirt up slightly now, spun around and said, "The baby needs to eat."

The accusation in her voice—aimed at her husband—said they'd overstayed their welcome. Allison rose to leave. Given the dissension between her parents, perhaps Tammy *had* run away. Her heart clearly was not set on the reality show. Maybe she'd decided to find another way to get to Juilliard. Teenagers were not known for their sound judgment or their impulse control.

But why now? They'd made progress. Or at least Allison thought they had.

"Thanks for your time," Allison said. She shook Tony's hand, then Denise's. Jane continued shaking the baby's bottle, her back toward them, shoulders squared in a posture of dismissal.

Denise walked them to the front door. "I'm sorry they aren't more hospitable."

"Their daughter's missing," Allison said. "We can certainly understand."

"Maybe," Denise said. "But this is how they always are. He can be overbearing and she's not very warm."

Allison heard the angry murmurs coming from the kitchen. Were they arguing over Allison? Or had the mention of a boyfriend rehashed old battles? Feeling like an interloper, Allison hurried outside. Denise followed.

At the Volvo, Denise said to Vaughn, "If you think of anything else...anything...please call me. This kid has a real future ahead of her. Why she would run now, I have no idea. It doesn't make sense." She arched her eyebrows inquisitively. "And if there's anything you want to share, Allison. Anything she may have told you...not that we're blaming you, of course."

Enough already, Allison thought. Standing tall in her black Ferrigamos, she said, "Denise, if you have something to say to us, please just say it."

Denise tossed her hair. "I don't know what you mean."

"You keep saying that no one is blaming us. Clearly you're blaming us."

Denise took a step back. She smiled sweetly, but the smile failed to reach her eyes. "The kid is money to a lot of folks. Her voice, her naiveté, it's a fabulous ugly-duckling-to-swan, rags-to-riches story. One we all can be a part of, if you know what I mean."

Allison knew all too well what she meant.

Vaughn said, "She's not a commodity." He made no attempt to hide the disgust in his voice.

"I'm not saying she's a commodity. I'm saying she represents opportunity. Everyone likes a winner, especially if they start out a loser. She has potential written all over her. And now she's missing."

Allison kept her voice even. "You think I said something to make her go?"

"I think it's odd that she spends five days with you and bolts. Why would that be? It was your job to stick to the message. To help her become more social, not less."

"My loyalty is to my clients. I want what's in their best interest. I didn't realize I was hired to spin a message."

"If Tammy wins, we all win. The message is about winning. That's best for Tammy, and for the rest of us. Including you, Allison."

Allison shook her head. Denise Carr was a manager, used to brokering deals and selling entertainment, whatever the cost to the artist rendering it. She would tell herself that her interests and her clients' interests were aligned because it no doubt let her sleep at night. But the truth was even those paid to represent others could have their own selfish interests at heart. And although Allison didn't know Denise Carr well, she was pretty certain that she was of that ilk. And no amount of discussion was going to change that.

"How did Tony Edwards find you?" Vaughn said.

Denise held Allison's stare a moment before moving her gaze to Vaughn. She was short, and even in stilettos, she didn't come up to Vaughn's chest. But Denise had a street toughness to her that seemed to bring out the street in Vaughn. His hands clenched at his side, his scarred face was a mask of anger.

Denise shrugged. "How would I know? The record label? I manage other artists." She ran through a list of somedays and has-beens, a few of whom Allison recognized.

"So Tammy could be your big break, too." Vaughn sneered. He looked menacing when he sneered and Allison didn't like where this was headed. She put her hand on Vaughn's arm.

"Let's go."

"Tammy could make you rich. She could help her parents out big time"—Vaughn gestured toward the house—"and all the while, who's looking out for the kid?"

Denise compressed her lips into a frown. "It certainly wasn't First Impressions, now was it, Mr. Vaughn?"

Allison watched as Vaughn took a deep breath, clearly gearing up for a showdown. The tension of the last two days was surfacing and Vaughn, with a conscience too finely honed after years of atoning for his perceived sin against Jamie, seemed ready for battle.

Allison stepped between Vaughn and Denise. She held up a hand. "We're all on the same side here. We want Tammy home, safe and sound. Let's stay focused on that goal. Arguing won't help Tammy."

With a frustrated harrumph, Vaughn shook his head and walked away. He climbed into the car, stony face forward. Allison said a brief good-bye to Tammy's manager and joined him. She started the vehicle and pulled away from the curb without another glance at Denise or the Edwards' home.

After a few minutes, Allison said, "What the hell, Vaughn? It's not like you to let emotion win."

"I don't like that woman."

"Clearly."

"That kid means nothing to her."

"She's her manager, not her aunt."

"And something's off about that family."

"They seemed nice enough to me. Salt of the earth sort." But then, who am I to judge when it comes to odd families, Allison thought.

"Ugh-ugh. The father, he's not too bright. And that mother...friendly as Newt Gingrich at a feminist rally."

"Her daughter *is* missing."

Vaughn shook his head. "There's more going on. It felt like we walked smack into the second act of a play."

Allison thought about that.

What could be hiding under the surface? Working class family with seven kids has child with amazing voice. Child is discovered and family connects with a manager. In the midst of preparing for the kid's big shot, she disappears.

Teenage opposition? Or something more sinister?

"What about the boyfriend?" Allison said. "I meant to ask Denise why all the tension when the topic came up, but I got distracted." She gave Vaughn a gentle punch. He responded with a half-smile.

"There's that, too. The kid's eighteen, after all. Why shouldn't she date?"

"Unless she was dating and they just didn't like the guy."

"Maybe." Vaughn looked troubled. "Something just doesn't compute. I'm telling you, Allison. Tammy may have run away. It could be that simple. But my radar is up."

Allison sighed. "I hear you, Vaughn. If she ran away—and until we have reason to suspect otherwise, I'm going with that—what can we do about it? Like her family, we need to wait for her to return."

Vaughn didn't respond. Allison knew that meant he was thinking. And that he didn't necessarily agree.

But there really was nothing else they could do at this point. *Right?*

She had two missing clients and one giant headache. It seemed to her that there was at least a likely logical explanation for the missing teen. Boyfriend, anger at her parents, fear over competing...all plausible reasons for her disappearance. A missing sixty-something eccentric, on the other hand? Different story.

"For now, let's put our energy into Francesca. If something changes with Tammy, we'll re-visit, okay?"

Vaughn nodded, but something told Allison it was a battle cry, not a gesture of agreement.

EIGHT

The storms that plagued them in Pennsylvania continued to follow them through the foothills of the mountains and into the Finger Lakes region. By evening, a heavy dusk had given way to night. Lightning like unwelcome fireworks accompanied veils of biting rain. Visibility was poor. Allison wanted to greet the Benini family early on Sunday, and so they kept going until they were near Ithaca, close to the estate. They pulled into the parking lot of the only motel they could find with a vacancy—a tiny motor court that advertised rooms by the night, week or month.

"At least it doesn't say by the hour," Vaughn said.

Allison smiled. She was thinking of bed bugs and other creepy crawlies and wondering why she hadn't packed her hotel sleeping bag.

Neither she nor Vaughn was particularly hungry, so they'd opted for a handful of granola bars from a convenience store during the last gas run. Vaughn yawned. It was only 8:32, but they were both operating on empty after the previous night's vigil.

"Turn in?" Allison said.

Vaughn nodded.

"You hear from Jamie?"

"Not yet. I'll call when I get in the room."

Allison grabbed his hand. She gave a squeeze. "It'll be okay, Vaughn. They'll both turn up."

"That's what I'm afraid of."

Allison gave him a quizzical look.

"*How* will they turn up? Alive...or in a pair of body bags?"

* * *

An hour later, Allison finally reached Jason on the phone. He sounded tired and cross, not typical for her laid back ex-husband.

"Don't forget that Brutus needs his skin medicine," she said. Her Boxer was still recovering from a nasty bout of allergic dermatitis he'd gotten while living as a stray. Hard to believe that was five months ago. The dog had become such a part of her life.

"Covered."

"And he likes a treat before bedtime."

"I know, Allison. I'm here often enough when he goes to bed, remember?"

"What's with the grumpies?" Allison asked. She'd changed into a pair of cotton pajamas and was flipping through the channels on the television, the sound on mute. "Everything okay?"

"Sure."

"Are you going to make me pull it out of you?"

He sighed. "Really, Al? Where to start? My girlfriend, who was nearly killed a few months ago, is off playing Sherlock again."

"I invited you to come along."

"Not the point, Al."

Allison took a calming breath. "Then what is the point?"

"You know what the point is. I want to move in. I want to get married again. I want us to—"

"Don't say it."

"Have children."

Allison turned off the television and tossed the remote across the bed. "Now you did it."

"Did what?"

"Started an argument."

"We're not arguing."

Allison lowered her voice. "But we're about to. Listen, sweetheart. I'm not ready. We went through a lot before the divorce. I couldn't be happier that we're back together, but we need time. I need time. We've only been dating again for a few months. Let's move slowly."

Jason said, "I think we—" but before he could finish, there was a loud knock on Allison's door. "Saved by the bell?" he said instead.

Allison smiled, despite her frustration at her ex-husband's insistence they move into domestic bliss at what felt to her like warp speed. "Hold on." She looked through the peep hole in the motel room door and was greeted with a fish bowl view of Vaughn's face. He was scowling.

"It's Watson. I'd better go."

Jason said "wait" without the sharp edge of anger, and Allison felt herself softening.

"Yes?" She unlocked the door and let Vaughn inside.

"I'm mostly cranky because I'm worried. I thought I was going to lose you last spring. I never want to go through that again."

"Oh, Jason." Allison sighed, remorse washing over her. What happened last spring had been terrifying for them all. The Main Line murders. The accusations against her client. And those final moments when she didn't think she would live through the ordeal. But she couldn't sit by now without doing something. Anyway, she told herself this was different. No one had died. At least not yet. "I love you," Allison said. "Don't worry about me. I have no desire to repeat history."

"I love you, too," Jason whispered, but Allison heard the hurt in his voice and it made her ache. She looked at Vaughn and wondered why men needed to be so damn complicated.

Vaughn sat down on the spindly arm chair tucked into the corner of the room, next to an old tube-style television. He still wore jeans and a Temple University t-shirt, and his handsome face was lined with worry.

"Jason?" he asked.

Allison nodded. "He's not too happy with me right now."

Vaughn shook his head. "I don't know how he puts up with you at all." He smiled.

"You're funny." Allison sat on the bed and wrapped her arms around her knees. "News from Jamie?"

"Something like that." Vaughn pulled out his mobile, tapped the screen a few times, and began to read. "Benini Enterprises: layoffs in three countries spark shareholder conflict. Benini Enterprises management accused of misappropriating funds. Stop toxic waste dumping: local companies must take responsibility."

"Headlines?"

Vaughn nodded. "Italian press. Jamie found quite a bit on Benini Enterprises, not much of it good. Francesca was truthful when she said the company has been declining steadily for some time now."

"Yeah, she made it sound as though they're on the edge of bankruptcy. Did that ring true?"

Vaughn tapped a few more times. "It's a private company, so only so much is publicly available. It has a fair amount of market share in the specialized food industry."

Allison considered the list Vaughn had read aloud. "What about the toxic dumping? Seems odd for a food exporter."

"I asked Jamie about that. He couldn't find anything beyond a reference to Benini in a long list of other offenders. It was related to Greek yogurt."

Allison sat up. "Greek yogurt?"

"They manufacture it. One of the byproducts is acid whey. They were allegedly dumping into streams. In large quantities, it can be toxic to aquatic life."

"Hmm. Was this in the States?"

"No. Italy."

"How about here? Anything touching the Ithaca headquarters?"

"Nothing directly about Ithaca, but he's still looking. Mostly some allegations of fiscal mismanagement by board members. No charges were ever brought, though."

"Against Paolo?"

"He's the brass, but nothing specifically pointed to him. Even if it was Paolo, or Dom, why would Francesca be the target?"

"Unless someone doesn't want her in charge." Allison stood, walked to the window, and peeked outside between heavy striped curtains. The harsh glare of a parking lot lamp illuminated sheets of driving rain. "Who would stand to benefit with Francesca out of the way?"

"Her family."

Allison nodded. "First people I think of, too. Specifically Dom, the most likely to take over if Francesca is out of the picture."

"Too obvious."

"Is it? Mentally unstable aunt panics and runs. Potential suicide. With no body, there are a million ways he could spin this. Simone is already planting those seeds with her talk of Francesca's depression."

Vaughn looked skeptical. "But with no body, they could spend time in court, fighting over who is in charge. Wouldn't it be cleaner to kill her? Make it look like an accident?"

"I guess. But she's always at home. Killing her there would dirty the pen. If she's kidnapped and simply disappears, they can say she ran. Try to prove that even if she returns, she's too unstable to run the company. Years of being a recluse would certainly back that up. It's not like she's been a pillar of her community."

"But who is *they*? The whole family?"

"Dom?"

"I don't know." Vaughn stood, paced. "You mentioned that Simone is planting the seeds about Francesca's mental health. But Francesca mentioned that Maria also aspires to run Benini. And Simone is *Maria's* mother, not Dom's. Maybe Simone and Maria are in on this together."

"Maria? She doesn't seem like the corporate type."

"Maybe not, but Francesca told me Maria's ambitions are transparent. She wants to run that company. She's young, aggressive and sneaky."

"Sneaky?"

Vaughn reminded her about his ascent to the Benini estate, the woman on horseback, the woman with a gun.

"Why would Maria be spying on you?"

"I don't know. I never mentioned it to Francesca. I didn't think much of it at the time. I was too worried the BMW was going to lose its undercarriage on that damn driveway. But the more I think about it, the more certain I become that she *was* stalking me. In the woods. On horseback."

Allison recalled her initial meeting with Maria Benini. The dead hawk. The rifle. The cold way she bagged the bird. Her insolence at dinner. Maria's insistence that the estate was haunted.

She said, "Speaking of Maria, did Jamie find anything about Gina Benini, Paolo's first wife?"

Vaughn smirked. "The ghost?"

Allison smiled. "Yes, the ghost. I can't imagine she has anything to do with any of this, but I'm still curious."

"Other than the small mention I'd found? I don't know. I'll ask him in the morning."

Allison yawned. The day was catching up with her, and from the tired set of Vaughn's eyes, it had caught up with him long ago.

She said, "I'd been planning to call Alex Benini, give the family notice that we're coming. I'm rethinking that."

"Want to catch them by surprise?"

Allison nodded. "The more I think about it, the more I wonder who Francesca's vultures are."

Vaughn put his hand on the doorknob. He turned before leaving and said, "But vultures only come in after the kill is made. I wonder if we're not looking for a different kind of bird. One that does the killing."

Like a hawk.

Allison thought about her conversation with Jason, her promise not to repeat history. Outside, thunder boomed, rattling her nerves. So much damn rain. "Let's remain optimistic," she said without enthusiasm. "Everything will seem brighter in the daylight."

NINE

Only nothing seemed brighter in the morning. Instead, Allison was greeted by another rap on the door. She opened it, bleary-eyed and with a hopeless case of bed-head, to find Vaughn waiting, hands clenched, anger pinching his features into an ugly scowl.

"The police want to talk to me." He brushed past her into her room.

"Sure, come on in," Allison said. She blinked, trying to wipe the sleep from her eyes and the cobwebs from her mind.

"Damn it, Allison, you know what this means."

"Calm down, Vaughn. It makes sense that they'd want to talk to you. You were the last person to see Francesca. That doesn't mean a thing."

He paced. "You and I both know that's bullshit. They'll take one look at my history and suddenly I'm gonna look real good as a suspect."

"A suspect in what? There are not even allegations of wrongdoing at this point."

"Does that matter?"

Allison grabbed his arm and led him to the chair. "Sit. And listen to yourself. What in the world would you have to gain by kidnapping Francesca?"

"What about Tammy? She's still missing."

"What about Tammy? Even her parents think she ran away."

"Fuck, Allison, don't be so naïve." He handed her his phone. On it was a web article from *The Philadelphia Inquirer* drawing a link between two sudden disappearances. And that link was Vaughn. "Someone must have alerted the media. The two events were too distant. How else would they know?"

Allison sat on the bed, heavily. Her stomach broiled. "Oh, man. I'm sorry, Vaughn."

He turned away and said, "No, I'm sorry. I don't mean to take this out on you. It's just...well, I've spent a long time putting myself on the straight and narrow. But the past doesn't just go away. And I've been racking my brains trying to figure out what the hell happened last Friday, but I keep coming up blank." He buried his head in his hands. "This is a damn nightmare."

Allison let him have a moment. As a kid, he did time in a juvenile delinquent center for everything from assault and battery to dealing drugs. When his twin brother took the bullet meant for him, Vaughn was snapped rudely into reality. But he, more than anyone, could not forgive his past transgressions. Allison put a hand on his broad shoulder and squeezed gently. He reached up and laid his hand over hers.

Allison stood. She whispered in his ear, "We *will* work this out."

She pulled a pair of gray pants and a French blue sleeveless wrap blouse from her suitcase and disappeared into the bathroom. There, she tamed her hair into a ponytail, washed her face, brushed her teeth and got changed, concentrating on these everyday actions so she wouldn't have to think about their predicament. When she came back into the hotel room, a different Vaughn was sitting on the edge of the bed, scratching notes on a yellow legal pad.

He said, "Let's stick with our initial plan. Today the Benini estate. On the way back, we'll stop by the police station."

"Will they wait?"

"I called the detective who contacted me this morning and told him I couldn't make it there until later today. He said as long as I show up by five that was fine. They want to show me some pictures." He took a deep breath, let it out slowly. His dark eyes searched hers. "It doesn't sound like I'm a suspect at this point."

"Of course you're not. I suppose it makes sense that they'll wait until later." But did it? Allison wondered. Wealthy Italian heiress disappears in their jurisdiction. Time may be of the essence. Wouldn't they want to push things along? "We can go there first, Vaughn. If it will help the investigation."

He shook his head. "It's early. If we leave soon, we can be at the police station well before five." He shrugged, his face back to an impassive mask, his shoulders squared in a posture of power. "Besides, I want to approach the Benini family now, before they have more time to come up with reasons and excuses. Catch them off guard."

Allison packed her few belongings back in her bag. She slipped two silver bangles on her wrist and glanced in the mirror. Tired eyes stared back.

"Let's go, then. Another trip to Ithaca. I like the Finger Lakes, but this is getting to be a bit much."

As Allison and Vaughn made their way north, the constant drizzle stopped, giving way to heavy fog and impenetrable gloom. Shifting, morphing clouds cast an ominous feeling on the day. Nature's melancholy was echoed in the interior of the Volvo.

Allison and Vaughn drove in silence, the quiet whir of the air conditioner and the occasional growl of distant thunder the only sounds. They grabbed breakfast from Dunkin' Donuts—coffee and a sesame bagel for each, although both bagels sat nearly untouched in a bag in the center console. It was 8:48 when they arrived in Ithaca, and another thirty minutes to the Benini home. At the mouth of the driveway, Vaughn was the first to break the silence.

"Game plan?"

Allison shrugged. "Guess it depends what we find."

Vaughn gave her a long look. "Chances are we'll find nothing."

"Ah, what happened to optimism?"

Vaughn smiled. "That was your word, not mine." He checked his mobile.

"Anything else from Jamie?" Allison asked.

"Not yet." He looked up, toward the house looming on the hill in the distance. "Ready?"

Allison said, "Sure."

The winding driveway seemed friendlier today, despite the low-lying mist. The Volvo crawled along the path, rounding the switchbacks with only faint complaining. Allison watched for movement, anything that might suggest Maria was out there spying. But she saw only the browns, greens and grays of a stormy summer day in the country. They found the iron gate open. A single car—a cherry red Porsche—sat in the driveway in front of the double-doored entranceway. It was parked several feet from the curb, blocking anyone from leaving without backing down the circular driveway.

"Do you know whose car it is?"

"I assume the older brother, Dom. Arrogant bastard," Vaughn mumbled. "Even parks arrogantly."

Allison assumed it was Dom's, too. Maybe she'd finally get to meet him.

Allison pulled up behind the Porsche, jammed on the emergency brake and killed the engine. The two climbed out, back into stifling humidity. Overhead, clouds gathered at an alarming rate, their watercolor edges a wash of angry black. She hoped the rain would hold off.

Vaughn followed Allison up the steps. They rang the bell and waited several minutes before the cook answered, her gray hair mostly hidden under a crisp white kerchief, eyes like dark hollows. A simple silver crucifix lay against her chest. She glanced down at the red suitcases, surprise and recognition registering on her sun-weathered features.

Allison introduced Vaughn. "We'd like to speak with Simone. We're returning Francesca's things and, well...we were hoping you'd heard from Francesca."

"I'm afraid not." Jackie kept a wary eye on Vaughn and said, "Last I saw Simone, she was headed out by the grotto. I suppose I could take you there."

"We would appreciate that."

Jackie glanced down at Allison's shoes, strappy leather sandals not made for walking. "It's a bit of a hike—"

"I have sneakers in the car."

The cook nodded. She looked at the watch on her wrist, and then turned to look back in the direction of the kitchen. She seemed to be mulling something over. "Go outside and get your sneakers. I hope the rain waits, but I'll grab some umbrellas just in case. I'll meet you out there."

The path turned out to be a hiking trail that started by the western corner of the house and hugged the edge of the flower gardens before leading into the woods. Allison and Vaughn followed Jackie, who managed the pathway like a pro, skipping over the roots and detritus that rose up like rocks in a creek bed. The morning air was still damp and hazy, and only the loud buzz of a chainsaw interrupted the silence.

They walked for fifteen minutes before the grotto came into view. Easily ten feet tall, it had been built with rough stones, and the rocks, worn smooth over time, were crisscrossed by green moss that traced intricate tracks across their surface. Statues of Jesus, Mary, and Joseph stood inside the grotto, near a half-buried wooden platform topped with a rusty iron ring. The statues were protected by a low wrought iron fence, its rails twisted into ornate pillars that ran along its width and served as the resting place for plastic flowers—Easter lilies, chrysanthemums, sunflowers and something that looked like a Poinsettia with petals washed to a splotchy pale pink.

The air smelled sharply of pine and humus. Jackie stood in the center of a bed of cedar chips, which made an eight-foot ring around the grotto. Two wooden benches had been placed on the outer edge of the ring. An empty koi pond, fed by a small creek, formed a semi-circle behind the benches. The area was accessible by a twenty-foot wooden bridge that crossed a small stream and the koi pond. On the other side the vestiges of an old stone foundation, reclaimed now by the forest. The forest was hushed by the gentle sounds of nature, deadening even the insistent churn of the chainsaw.

Jackie turned in a circle, scoping out the area, before facing Allison. "It looks like I was wrong. I could have sworn she said she'd be here." Face pinched with worry, she said, "Frannie loves it here. That's why I thought it was odd that Simone would come."

"They didn't get along?"

"They're not close. And no one comes out here, really. Just Frannie."

It was strange to hear such a familiar version of Francesca's name. "Do you have any idea where Francesca might have gone?" Allison asked.

"None whatsoever."

"She didn't say or do anything unusual in the days before she left?"

"She did a lot of things that were unusual. For her."

Vaughn had been scanning the grotto area as though searching for a sniper. He turned his attention to Jackie and asked, "Such as?"

"She left, for one thing. I've been in this house for nine years and I've never seen Frannie go anywhere, not even when Paolo fell ill."

"So she didn't visit him in the hospital?"

"Not once."

"Why do you think she stayed here all those years?" Allison asked.

Jackie poked a white-sneakered toe at something on the ground. After a moment, she said, "Fear? Contentment? I don't know. It never came up in conversation."

Allison didn't believe her. "Did you talk often?"

Jackie nodded. "Of the family, she was the only one who took the time. The others are very self-absorbed. Maria comes into the kitchen, but only to make requests or to steal food from the cupboards. She's like a wild animal, that one. No manners. Which is why she prefers the animals, I suppose. She's always out there with the horses."

"But Francesca's not like that?" Allison asked, careful to use the present tense.

"No, Francesca is always kind. She asks about me, my family."

Vaughn said, "What do you know about Gina Benini, Jackie? Is what Maria told Allison true? Was Paolo's first wide murdered?"

Jackie looked away, toward the bridge. "We need to get back. By now, Dom will have seen your car. He'll want to talk to you."

And we'll want to talk to him, Allison thought. "Just one more question. How about the family? Did Francesca get along with everyone else?"

Jackie's mouth hardened until all that was left was a slash of crimson. "Does anyone get along with everyone in their family?" She moved quickly toward the trail that led back to the house. "I've been here for nine years, Ms. Campbell," she said over her shoulder. "I know enough not to talk ill of my employers. I will say this, though. Ghosts, skeletons, demons...they are all part and parcel of the same thing. People hiding things, things they shouldn't have done, secrets that need the cleansing light of day." She skipped over a puddle and onto the wooden bridge. "This family is no exception."

Back inside the house, Jackie, all business once again, led them into a small parlor, where they waited for Dom. But it was Alex, not Dom, who came into the room fifteen minutes later. He shook Allison's hand with a warm but regretful smile, and then shook Vaughn's hand before saying, "What brings you back here, Allison?"

"Francesca. We brought her things."

Eyebrows raised, Alex said, "The police didn't take them?"

"No. They said she was an adult, and until there was evidence of a crime, they seemed uninterested in searching her belongings."

"Who has them now?"

Allison said, "We left them with Jackie. But we'd still like to talk to you, if you have a few minutes."

"Yes, yes, of course. Where are my manners? Please. Sit."

Allison and Vaughn sat on the two armchairs facing the door. Alex remained standing. He looked fresh today, clean-shaven and smart in black dress pants and a white button-down shirt. His gaze seemed more guarded than before, but when their eyes met, Allison saw that same amused half smile.

"Have you heard anything?" Allison asked, irked, for some reason, by his easy manner. "Anything at all?" With sudden insight, she realized she wanted him to look bereft. She wanted one family member she felt she could trust.

"I'm afraid not. We filed a missing persons report, of course, and the police have been here for a chat, but beyond that, we have no clue where she could be."

"You must be worried sick."

"We're all concerned. Francesca must have wandered off and lost her way. Perhaps gotten confused. She's not used to being out in the real world." Alex's brows drew closer, and he looked at Vaughn. "It would be easy to lose track of her."

"She didn't seem remotely confused to me," Vaughn said, tight-lipped and tight-fisted.

"No need to get defensive, Mr. Vaughn. That was Francesca's gift. She could hide it."

Just then, the door slammed open and in stormed another man. He had a full head of cropped graying hair, a bulbous nose and a neatly-trimmed beard. Unlike his handsome brother and beautiful sister, his looks hinted at peasant, not patrician. But for his contemptuous manner, he could have been just another visitor—but his cocky bearing gave him away. He was shorter than Alex, five-foot-nine or ten at most, but carried himself with an angry energy that demanded attention.

"Why are they here?" he said to Alex.

"Dom, I don't believe you've met Allison Campbell and her colleague, Christopher Vaughn."

Shoulders still squared for battle, Vaughn held out his hand. "Call me Vaughn."

Dominic Benini looked at Vaughn's outstretched hand for a pregnant moment, his contempt written in the snide turn of his mouth. Allison found herself holding her breath, for she knew Dom's next action would decide the tone of this meeting. Finally, he shook Vaughn's hand, but said, "You're the man who lost our aunt?"

Alex looked at his brother sharply. "As you can see, Dom's upset."

Vaughn seemed calm, his eyes taking in the scene unfolding before them with a detached intensity. Allison said, "We're not the enemy, Mr. Benini. My colleague did nothing but wait while your aunt used a restroom. I'm sure you didn't want him to follow her in."

Dom said, "I would have never encouraged her to leave this house."

"She contacted us, not the other way around."

"She was an emotional invalid. Not fit to make decisions."

Vaughn said, "She seemed perfectly sane to us."

Through clenched teeth, Dom said, "I never said she was crazy. I said she was an emotional invalid. My aunt was unstable, depressed...naïve to the world." He hung his head in a gesture that, to Allison, seemed contrived. "And now she's gone."

Vaughn said, "Leaving you to run Benini Enterprises. Convenient."

Dom inched his head up a notch and stared at Vaughn through hooded eyes. "Is that your assessment?"

Allison laid a warning hand on Vaughn's arm. Arguing would get them nowhere, and with everyone's nerves shot, both men seemed primed for a fight. She said, "We don't think anything, Mr. Benini. We want Francesca back as much as you do."

Dom shifted his gaze from Vaughn to Allison. He started at her feet and made his way up, resting his gaze on her chest, then her mouth. When he finally made eye contact, it was with a degree of surprise, as though he were seeing her for the first time. With his focus still locked on her, Dom said to Alex, "Maria's in the dining room with her mother. Simone wants to talk to us."

Dom started to walk out of the room. He paused at the threshold. "If the police have not contacted you already, they will soon enough. Perhaps Alex has already told you, but we've hired our own private investigator in the hopes of finding our aunt. Despite what you may want to believe, we want Francesca back. We're going to find her."

Dom left the room. His heavy footsteps could be heard in the hall as he receded into the bowels of the estate. Allison looked at Alex, trying hard to control her anger. "You set us up for that."

With a rueful shake of his head, Alex said, "No, that's Dom. Charming, isn't he?" Alex grasped the heavily carved door and motioned for Vaughn and Allison to go out before him. "But he's right in this instance. We need to find Francesca. If the police can't help us, we'll do it on our own. Our man's name is Burr. Reginald Burr. He's an old family acquaintance. Don't be surprised if you hear from him."

"Think this Reginald Burr is legit?" Alison asked. They were back in the car, about two miles from the Benini estate. Allison watched the woods go by through the driver side window, taking in this area, lush with old trees and dense foliage. Across the street, Cayuga Lake churned, its deep waters choppy and unwelcoming today. Thick tree trunks, roots covered in moss, blocked the little light emanating from the torn sky. So many places to hide, Allison thought. If one were inclined to hide in the forest.

Allison forced her thoughts back on Reginald Burr. It was no surprise that the family hired a private investigator. In fact, she would expect a wealthy family with nothing to hide to do just that. Which is exactly why it felt suspect.

"An old family acquaintance?" Vaughn said. "I don't believe a damn word they say."

"It does seem a little too convenient. But a family kidnapping its own..." Before the words were out of her mouth, Allison knew how silly they sounded. More preposterous things happened every day. And blood did not necessarily equate to loyalty. Allison pulled over and punched an address in her phone. She watched as her GPS pinpointed the location she wanted. She made the next right.

"Where are we headed?" Vaughn asked.

"The hospital. To pay a visit to Paolo Benini."

Vaughn looked over at her, surprised. "He's in a coma."

"I know," Allison said. "But the people around him can still talk."

TEN

The hospital corridors had the despairing antiseptic feel that Allison associated with her youth and her mother's illnesses. She stood in the lobby next to Vaughn, ignoring the quickening pace of her heartbeat and the little, niggling, rational voice inside her head that said she was out of her element.

"Just how do you plan to get in that man's room?" Vaughn asked.

He, too, had apparently heard the little niggling voice inside her head because he was looking at her with a healthy dose of *you must be crazy.*

"I overheard Francesca and Simone talking when I was here last week. Paolo is back in the Intensive Care Unit." She glanced at the hospital directory, written in square white typeset on a black background. "Fourth floor."

"Only immediate family are allowed into the ICU."

Allison took a belly breath, doing her best to calm her nerves. It wasn't working. Should have paid more attention to my yoga instructor, she thought. Mustering conviction she didn't feel, she said, "Follow my lead."

They rode up the elevator next to a tall, narrow nurse in blue scrubs. She looked at Allison and Vaughn but glanced away before decorum would have required a polite hello. They all got off on the fourth floor.

Allison walked with confidence to the U-shaped nurse's station in the center of the small ICU. The lights were bright over the station, a sharp contrast to the darkened patient rooms, all of which had open doors. Allison heard the whirs and beeps of a hundred different machines. She thought of Jamie, of the machines helping him survive each day. She put her hand on Vaughn's arm, wondering whether he was thinking of Jamie, too. He shot her a grateful smile.

The nurse behind the desk had raspberry-red hair and freckles so numerous they became the predominant color of her skin. She looked at Allison through tired eyes and said, "Can I help you?"

"We're here for Paolo Benini."

"And you are?"

"His niece, Barbara. This is my husband, Lou."

"Driver's license, please."

Allison rooted around in her purse, pretending to look for her wallet. Her mouth dry, she said, "I'm sorry. We came in a rush. I must have left it at home." She glanced at Vaughn, silently willing him to play along. "Sweetheart, do you have your wallet?" He shook his head.

The nurse glanced over her shoulder. She was alone. She looked back at Allison and Vaughn, biting her lower lip, clearly deciding what to do.

Allison said, "I'm Francesca's daughter. But if you can't let us see him..."

The woman's face relaxed. She grabbed a chart from the desk behind her and made a notation. "I didn't realize Francesca had a daughter. Such a doll! I spoke to her a few times last week when she called about Paolo." She smiled. "Your names again?"

"Rich. Barbara and Louis Rich."

The nurse scribbled something else on the paper. With a weary smile that pulled at the nugget of guilt in Allison's gut, she said, "Your uncle is in room 416. As I'm sure your mother told you, he's comatose."

Vaughn started to walk toward Room 416. Allison didn't follow, but chose to linger by the counter. "Tell me," she said, "has my Aunt Simone or any of my cousins been here today?"

"I haven't seen them, and I've been here since six this morning."

"When was the last time he had a visitor?"

The nurse shuffled through a few pages of the chart in front of her. "We don't always have a record, especially when we come to know the family. I don't see anything written in here for a while. But I remember seeing them over the weekend. His son, his daughter and Simone, at least."

"Which son? Alex?"

The nurse smiled. Clearly she, too, had been the target of the attractive man's charms. "No, the other one."

"Ah, Dominic."

The nurse nodded, put the chart down on the counter and straightened her uniform. "Is there anything else? If not, I have patients to attend to."

"That's it. Thanks for all you do for Uncle Paolo," Allison said.

The nurse nodded. "I wish we had better news."

"No change, I guess? My mother seemed pretty certain that he would not make it."

"Here, we never say hopeless. But..." She let her voice trail off.

An alarm went off, causing lights to flash in the nursing station. "If you'll excuse me—"

"Of course."

Allison watched the nurse disappear into another room. Before heading into Paolo's room, she took a furtive glance around. Chiding herself for breaking patient confidentiality, she grabbed the chart and hastily perused the visitors' names for Room 416. Not many entries. Alex was listed three times early on. Same for Maria. It looked as though they'd stopped recording the family's comings and goings about a week ago. Allison was about to put down the chart when an entry caught her eye. It was dated a week ago. A neat hand had written "Reginald Burr" in red ink.

Allison recognized the name of the private investigator Dom and Alex had hired to look into Francesca's disappearance. *Odd.* Alex mentioned he was a family friend, so maybe a visit made sense. But Allison decided she wasn't going to wait for Mr. Burr to visit her. Before they left Ithaca, they'd go looking for him.

Allison found Vaughn sitting in a red vinyl chair next to Paolo's bed. The drapes were closed and the interior of the room was dark and warm. Sickbed smells of antiseptic cleaner and urine filled the air. Allison's gaze fell to the figure on the bed. Tubes and wires extended from Paolo's emaciated body and connected to monitors and fluid-filled bags hung on silver carts around the bed. Paolo had a chiseled face, aged and pale and dotted with fine white whiskers. Despite age and illness,

Allison saw Alex's height, Dom's broad shoulders and muscular build, Maria's high forehead and patrician nose. He must have been a handsome man in his prime, Allison thought. Handsome and intimidating.

Vaughn stood up and grabbed a smaller chair, pulling it closer to the bed. Allison sat down on the edge. She felt jittery, nervous. The room was hushed by the stillness of dying, only the occasional beep breaking the unwritten code of silence. Allison became aware of her own breathing. She closed her eyes. When she opened them again, a feeling of urgency overwhelmed her. They needed to leave. Now.

She stood, clutching her purse, and walked quickly to the door, motioning for Vaughn to follow. Allison gave the man on the bed one last look before heading out the door, toward the elevator. She felt childish, impulsive and a little bit crazy. She jammed a finger on the lobby button three times, waiting impatiently for the doors to close and the elevator to begin its descent. In the lobby, she hastened silently toward the automatic entry and rushed toward the parking lot. Once safely at her car, she handed Vaughn the keys. "You drive."

She put her head back against the seat and allowed herself to exhale.

Vaughn said, "What the hell was that all about?"

Allison shook her head. "I can't explain it, Vaughn. Something told me to get out of the hospital. It was a compulsion like I've never felt before."

Vaughn laughed, but there was no humor in it. "Did you learn anything new from the nurse?"

Allison scanned the parking lot, looking for what, she wasn't sure. Three cars over, a mother walked hand-in-hand with a little girl and pointed her key fob at a red Chevrolet. The toddler sang happily to herself. The mother looked disheveled and grim, her hair in a greasy ponytail that said she had bigger things on her mind than bathing.

"That private investigator has been here. Reginald Burr."

Vaughn's eyes widened. He pulled out of the parking space and headed toward the exit. "The family friend? Was this *before* Francesca disappeared?"

"Yes. Last week."

"Interesting."

"You know what else is interesting?"

"Talk to me."

"I told the nurse I was Francesca's daughter."

"So?"

"The nurse didn't bat an eyelash. If your aunt or sister-in-law was missing and you were worried about her, what would you do?"

"I'd tell the hospital where her brother was admitted. In case she showed up there."

Allison nodded. "Especially if you were distraught, as they claim to be. You'd call everyone, look everywhere."

"Yet the hospital knew nothing. I'll be damned." Vaughn took a right out of the hospital parking lot and gave the Volvo some gas. "Where now?"

"Can Jamie locate Reginald Burr?"

"He sure as hell can try."

"Then get him on the phone. I'm betting Mr. Burr is local. Let's see if we can out-sleuth the sleuth."

Only there was no listing for a Reginald Burr, in Ithaca or the surrounding area. And any Reginald Burrs that Jamie could find anywhere in the eastern half of the United States seemed unlikely candidates: a seventy-two-year-old blind man from South Carolina, a ten-year-old in Washington D.C. and a ninety-one-year-old man from Pittsburgh. So who was Reginald Burr?

"Guess we'll have to wait for him to come to us," Vaughn said.

Allison stirred her coffee with the thin plastic straw and put the dome lid back on. They were at a ubiquitous Starbucks near Wilkes-Barre, Pennsylvania and a low-fat blueberry muffin was staring up at her from atop a paper bag. She had no appetite. In twenty minutes, Vaughn was due to meet with the detective assigned to Francesca's disappearance.

Allison shook her head. "Something is off. Not only didn't the family bother calling the hospital about Francesca, but Reginald Burr, the private investigator they hired to find her, has no official presence. How does a PI make money without at least some advertising?"

Vaughn said, "Maybe Reginald Burr is an alias and he works under his real name."

"Maybe," Allison said without conviction. She took a sip of her coffee and wiped her mouth with a brown napkin. Her low-fat blueberry muffin still sat, uneaten. She stared at it, willing her stomach to unclench long enough to consume the pastry. "Or maybe he only works for the family."

Vaughn arched an eyebrow, considering this. "Maybe." He glanced at his watch. "Ready?"

Allison rose, walked over to the trash bin and threw away the remainder of her coffee and the muffin, feeling guilty at her wastefulness.

"I would have eaten that," Vaughn said.

"Well I'm glad *you're* not anxious."

Vaughn laughed. "Never said that, but since when have I let a little case of the nerves kill my appetite?"

ELEVEN

Detective Butch Razinski had a sandy blond crew cut and a boxer's nose, pummeled and misshapen into a flattened snub. He peered at Allison and Vaughn through bright hazel eyes, his expression that of a man with more responsibilities than resources. They were in the reception area of the police station near the truck stop where Francesca had last been seen. The room was drab green, with a worn beige linoleum floor mottled with black scuff marks. A bored-looking receptionist sat behind a shatterproof sliding window.

The detective held out his hand and made brief eye contact with Allison, then Vaughn. They shook. The detective's gaze was piercing to the point of intrusiveness.

"Thanks for coming by," Razinski said. His voice was low-pitched, his tone reserved.

"Of course. I'd like Allison to join us, if you don't have an objection."

Razinski said to Allison, "Have you met Francesca Benini?"

"Yes. She's my client."

The detective shrugged. "Suit yourself, then." He turned and started to walk toward a door next to the receptionist's window. "This way."

Allison followed the detective through the doorway, down a poorly lit hallway and into a hundred-square foot office. Like the reception area, the room was painted drab green. Fluorescent lights cast a sickly glow in the windowless interior. A desk sat against the rear wall, covered by an over-sized computer monitor, stacks of files, and a half dozen reference books. The walls were bare of decoration. No pictures adorned the desk top, although a child's crayon rendering of a man and boy had been pinned to an otherwise bare bulletin board on the wall over his desk. The only other furniture in the room consisted of a desk chair on wheels, two brown folding chairs and a filing cabinet. Detective Razinski sat in the desk chair and pointed to the two folding chairs.

Vaughn was barely seated when the detective said, "So tell me again exactly what happened. I know we took a statement, but I'd like to hear it myself."

Vaughn took the detective through the events of that night from the time they arrived at the truck stop until the police were summoned.

When he was finished, the detective sat quietly, fingers strumming on khaki-clad legs. "How about before you got to the rest station?"

Vaughn looked startled. "Before?"

"Yes. Did you stop anywhere with Francesca Benini in between Ithaca and Pittston?"

"No."

"What was her mood like on the drive?"

"We've been through this, Detective. I told the police when they arrived at the truck stop—"

"Tell it again."

"She was quiet, but seemed fine. But hey, I don't really know her, so I have nothing to use as a basis for comparison."

The detective turned toward Allison. "But you met her before. How did she seem to you?"

"Like Vaughn, I don't know her well enough to say. She seemed...reserved. But I couldn't tell you whether her mood was depressed or suicidal."

"You said depressed or suicidal, Ms. Campbell. What made you choose those descriptors?"

"The family. When I spoke to Simone Benini after Francesca disappeared, she said Francesca was depressed. She seemed...uh, concerned...that Francesca had done something to harm herself."

Razinski stood, his mouth set in a grim line. He walked over to his desk and grabbed a file from the top of a short stack.

He sat back down, his expression never wavering, and pored through several pages from the file. He handed Vaughn a small stack of photographs. Head shots. All men.

Vaughn looked through them, one by one. "I don't recognize any of these men." He cocked his head. "Should I?"

"Just checking."

He slid the pictures back in the file, made a few notations on a piece of notepaper stapled to the inside cover, and then looked up.

"What can you tell me about Tammy Edwards?"

Allison fought to maintain a neutral façade. The newspaper article should have alerted her that Razinski would ask the question. Still, she felt unprepared. But Vaughn was smooth as Italian gelato while he recited, again, the circumstances surrounding his farewell to the eighteen-year-old.

"There was nothing between you? No flirtation? No...interactions of a sexual nature?"

Vaughn's eyes narrowed. "No."

"And that was it, Mr. Vaughn. You said good-bye, she disappeared into the house, and you left?"

"Yes."

"I see."

Razinski's words gave no comfort. Indeed, Allison was certain they were meant to instill the opposite. Silently, she admonished herself for not asking Jason to meet them here. He was at least a lawyer. With his experience in the DA's office, he could talk the talk. And make sure they didn't say anything incriminating.

Razinski placed his file back on his desk, adjusted the edges so they lined up with the corners of the desktop. "Do you have any travel scheduled over the next few weeks, Mr. Vaughn? Anything that will take you out of the country?"

Vaughn shook his head.

"Good," the detective said. "That will be all for now."

But Vaughn didn't move from his chair. "Am I a suspect?"

"I didn't say that."

"What about the travel?"

"Routine. If something changes, we may need to talk with you again. We want to make sure you'll be reachable."

Allison glanced from her friend to the police detective, not liking the tone of Razinski's voice or the detachment in his demeanor. "How can we help the investigation?"

"There is no official investigation, Ms. Campbell. At least not at this point. Francesca Benini is an adult, free to come and go as she pleases. And Tammy Edwards is eighteen. As long as there is no suspicion of foul play—" he glanced ever-so-briefly in Vaughn's direction "—there is no reason for the police to get involved."

"Then why the need for today's meeting?" Allison said.

"Routine. I wanted to tie up some loose ends, meet Mr. Vaughn in person, show him the pictures of local known felons to make sure he hadn't noticed them in the area where either woman was last seen." He clapped his hands together and started to rise out of his chair. "But I think we're finished." The phone rang. The detective said "just a minute" and picked up the receiver. "I see...yes, of course." He fixed his stare on Vaughn. "What time? Interesting." After another minute of uttering phrases that made no sense on their own, Razinski hung up the receiver.

"That was Simone Benini," he said.

Allison's heart raced. "They found Francesca?"

The detective shook his head. "No, unfortunately. She was calling about Francesca's brother, Paolo Benini. He died this afternoon."

Allison was speechless, the implications barreling over her like a tsunami. This afternoon. They had just been there this afternoon, and while Paolo was comatose, he'd been alive. The detective wouldn't share details, but he made it sound as though Paolo had died in his sleep. Expected, perhaps. But her premonition, combined with the timing, made her scalp tingle, her legs go numb.

Another coincidence?

Allison looked at Vaughn. His face was a mask of indifference, but Allison saw the rigid posture and slight tremor in his hand that gave away his unease. He must be thinking what I'm thinking, Allison thought. We very well may have been the last people to see Paolo Benini alive.

Tammy. Francesca. Now Paolo. One link: Vaughn.

TWELVE

Jason met her at the door with a cool hello and a stack of messages. "I'm beginning to feel like your personal assistant, walking your dog and taking your calls."

Allison brushed his cheek with her lips. He smelled of spicy musk and wood chips. "It's called a relationship. And you've been at your mother's."

"Yeah, well, I wouldn't mind so much if I *felt* like I was in a relationship." He wrapped his arms around her. "And yes, I helped her take down a tree. We put it through the chipper. She's home now, mulching her perennial beds."

"How is Mia?"

"She seemed agitated. I didn't ask why. If I didn't know better, I'd say it was a full moon. All the ladies in my life are out of balance."

Allison laughed and spent a moment petting and reassuring an ecstatic Brutus. The dog's severe under bite caused his tongue to get caught between his jaws so that the pink end stuck out. He wagged his tail stub wildly with a look of comical madness on his jowly face. He'd been a stray when Maggie, a former client, found him. Maggie had begged Allison—who was, back then, terrified of dogs—to take him in. Over time, Allison had come to love the big lug of a dog. Now, she wiped the drool off her pants and walked back to the kitchen, Brutus in tow.

She scanned her messages. With Vaughn along for the road trip to Ithaca, her messages had come through a service, and so there was none of the context and opinions Vaughn would typically include. The call from her client, Midge—normally marked with a "she's just worried about you" or some other notation next to the number—said simply, "call immediately." Likewise, the three media inquiries were not ranked in order of importance, as Vaughn would have done. And so Allison was left with a stack of messages, all of which she would have to handle today because she had no sense of how to best prioritize.

Another reminder of why she so valued Vaughn.

And you should tell him that, she chided herself.

"Did you look through all of them?" Jason asked.

"Enough to know that I'll have to spend an hour or two returning calls this afternoon."

Jason had pulled two cans of tuna out of the cupboard and was washing a tomato. "Did you see that one of the Beninis tried to reach you?"

That stopped her. "No. Which one?"

"It's on there. Alex, I think." He grabbed a knife from the drawer and examined its edge. "I'll make tuna sandwiches and you can fill me in on your trip. I want to hear how things went."

Allison watched Jason slice the tomato with slow, firm strokes. He was tall and slender, with longish brown hair combed back from his face. He watched the world through eyes that shone with compassion and intelligence. But Allison loved his hands best. Jason had broad, masculine hands and neatly trimmed, square nails. Hands that, despite his law degree and the years he'd spent in white collar jobs, weren't adverse to hard work. Suddenly, she wanted those hands on her. She wanted to feel the warmth of his body...and to forget about the Benini clan for a while.

Allison tossed the messages on the counter. She walked up behind Jason and wrapped her arms around his waist, from behind. Pressing her body against his, she kissed his neck, feeling the muscles in his broad back tighten at the caress of her lips.

"Umm," Jason said. "I *am* handling a knife."

Allison put her hand over his knuckles and gently placed the knife on the counter. She reached one hand underneath his t-shirt and ran her nails softly down his chest and abs, letting her fingers linger at his navel before dropping them to his waist, feeling his excitement. She tugged at his belt.

"Don't start something you can't finish," Jason whispered. His voice was thick with desire.

"Come upstairs." She felt him shudder.

Jason spun around, grabbing Allison's waist and kissed her, hard. Coming up for air, he said, "I'll take you to bed, Ms. Campbell, on one condition."

"What's that?"

He kissed her again. "You give me a full two hours of your time. No phone, no Nancy Drew detective talk. Just us." Slowly, he unbuttoned the top two buttons on her blouse and stroked beneath. "Deal?"

Allison lifted his shirt, lowering her gaze to his toned stomach and chest. "Two whole hours?"

Jason gave her a mischievous smile. "Sweetheart, I can make this last all afternoon if you want."

Allison laughed. She wanted to give in—she had initiated it, after all. But a collage of events from the last two days played like a slideshow in her head: the message from Alex Benini, Paolo at the hospital, Vaughn's sad expression. She pushed the thoughts away. Two hours. Jason unclasped her bra. She moaned. She could give him two hours. He deserved that and more. The world would wait.

Alex Benini had been calling to apologize. "While you were here, my brother was very rude. I realize that Francesca's disappearance has nothing to do with you. But you have to understand...we are all very much on edge. Especially since..." He hesitated. "My father died today. Shortly after your visit."

"I'm so sorry," Allison said. She was sitting at her desk at First Impressions. It was after six on Sunday, and her lovemaking with Jason was still on her mind.

Her body felt languid, sated, but as the conversation with Alex progressed, anxiety replaced satisfaction. She came crashing back down to Earth.

Allison toyed with whether to mention the visit to Paolo's hospital room. She decided not to—it would do nothing but increase whatever suspicions the family already had. Instead, she decided to ask about the private investigator. His name on that hospital check-in sheet continued to bother her.

"Reginald Burr—we haven't heard from him."

"Ah, yes," Alex sighed. "Eventually, you will. He's another personality, I'm afraid."

"A friend of your father's?"

Alex hesitated. Only for a second, but Allison caught it. "More like Dom's friend. My father never cared much for him. Dom hired him to find Francesca."

"Is he local to Ithaca?"

Alex laughed. "Are you investigating my investigator, Allison?"

"I did try to look him up. Hey, I'm an image consultant. We always come prepared."

"And you found nothing on him? That would be the case. Reginald is very...careful. Actually, I called for another reason as well. In addition to apologizing."

She knew he was changing the subject, but, curious, she said, "Yes?"

"Before Francesca disappeared, did she give you anything?"

"Such as?"

"I don't know, and I'm not sure it matters. To you, at least. To us, it may."

"She didn't give me anything that would hint at her current whereabouts, if that's what you mean."

Alex was quiet for a moment. Allison heard a car pull into the parking lot of First Impressions, then a door slam. The first arrivals of her Recently Divorced Group? At their request, Vaughn had rescheduled them for seven this evening. But they wouldn't be arriving *this* early.

Alex said, "Can we meet?"

The front door opened, then slammed shut. Allison couldn't see who it was from her office. She rose, her visit from a killer just a few months before still alive in her consciousness. But that was then, she told herself, and you can't let your fears—or the past—dictate your behavior, however understandable it would be.

"I'm afraid I have to go. I'm expecting clients."

"Tomorrow, perhaps?" Alex said. "In the evening? I'll take you to dinner."

Footsteps on the stairs. Women's footsteps, light but with the unmistakable *click, click, click* of heels.

"I don't think so, Alex," she said.

"It's important."

Allison thought of Vaughn, of Francesca and Tammy. No doubt Alex Benini wanted information from her, but that didn't mean she couldn't learn something, too. What could a dinner hurt?

"Fine. It will have to be late. Say seven?" She told him where to meet her.

"Thank you, Allison," he said before hanging up. She hated that she liked the deep caress of his voice, especially now, with the ghost of Jason's touch on her skin. Face it, he's an attractive man, she thought. And that's clouding your judgment. She walked toward the reception to First Impressions to see who had arrived. Work came first. When you focus on work, she reminded herself, there's no time for nonsense.

The heels belonged to Mia Campbell, her former mentor and Jason's mother. She'd apparently left her farm for the 'burbs this evening, and transitioned from crunchy country dweller to chic urbanite for the trip. Her long, gray curls had been pulled into a twist. Sparkling diamond-studded earrings showcased sharp cheekbones and a full mouth. Her slim body was silhouetted by fitted black pants and a black sleeveless blouse, very Coco Chanel, very expensive-looking. Her only nod to color was the rubies in her pendant necklace. Black wedges completed the transformation. Allison greeted her with a hug.

"I couldn't be happier to see you," Allison said. "That is you, right? I didn't recognize you without hemp and cotton."

Mia laughed. She'd moved to the farm a few years back, after losing her daughter in a car accident and her husband in a nasty divorce. She'd given up her home and business in one wink. It was only recently that she and Allison had reconnected, but it was as though the lost years had never happened.

"I have a group session in a few minutes, Mia, but if you can wait around, we could have dinner afterwards—"

Mia shook her head. "I'm here for Vaughn. Can you spare a few minutes? I'm on my way to his apartment, but knew I'd find you here."

"Sure." Allison said slowly. The topic of Mia's relationship with Vaughn had been a secret for the past two years. It was odd for Mia to show up, unannounced. It was really odd for her to want to talk about her younger lover.

"It's about the girl. And the woman—the Italian heiress who disappeared. Jason told me what happened. And then I saw this." Mia laid the *Philadelphia Inquirer* article on the desk. She'd highlighted Vaughn's name and any references to First Impressions. Allison skimmed the article. It had been written in a very straightforward manner and dealt largely with the facts of each disappearances. No assumptions or hypotheticals. The last two lines caught her eye, though:

While police have no indications of foul play, missing persons reports have been filed on behalf of both women. Christopher Vaughn, the last individual to see each of the women in question, will be interviewed by police.

Allison looked at Mia, eyes wide. "Vaughn knows about this article. He saw it this morning."

"Did the police question him?"

"They spoke with him. But he was the last to see each of these women, so who else would they talk to?" Allison tossed the article back onto the table. "I wish they hadn't mentioned Vaughn's name. It seems...unfair."

"We're lucky it's a procedural piece and not a human interest piece. If it was the latter, every Tom, Dick, and Nosy Nancy who has it in for you would be swooping in for the kill."

Allison had no words. Mia was right. Tried and convicted in the court of public opinion. She'd seen it happen before. The public loved an underdog, but by and large, the public disliked success. People liked to see giants fall, and although she considered herself a minor player in the wide world of consulting, she knew she'd developed an almost cult following in and around Philly. And that could mean trouble.

Allison said, "Mia, you're not concerned that Vaughn actually had something to do with it, are you?"

Mia spun around. Her eyes widened in horror. "Oh, no! Never that!"

"Then what is it?"

A pause. "Do you know what Vaughn's number one fear is?"

Allison shook her head. Given all he'd been through—the beatings as a kid, the poverty, his time in juvenile detention, and then the horror of seeing his brother struck down—she didn't know what was left for Vaughn to fear.

"Not being around for Jamie."

"Understandable, but—"

"*The police*, Allison. *Jail.* Being blamed for something he didn't do. He is terrified of having something happen to him, something that will result in him having to leave Jamie in the care of strangers."

"Ah." And now it made sense. Vaughn's sadness, his anxiety over these disappearances. It wasn't simply paranoia. It was the terror of a single parent caring for a child alone. It was the gnawing fear of anyone shouldering total responsibility for someone dependent and vulnerable. "But no one is accusing Vaughn of anything."

"Not yet, Allison." Mia wagged her finger. Her knobby knuckles and short, squared-off fingernails contrasted with her clothes. Indicators of Mia's new life. "But just wait. A black man from West Philly? A black man from West Philly with a criminal background? If things don't clear up, fingers will be pointed, connections made. And Vaughn was the last person to see both of these women. God help him if either turns up dead."

Allison didn't want to believe that his skin color or the mistakes of his youth would matter. Didn't want to but...well, she'd been around town enough times to distinguish idealistic poppycock from reality.

Mia said, "I'm headed over there now, to make sure he doesn't do anything stupid. But I don't like this, and I am here to help. Whatever I can do. Anything."

THIRTEEN

It was well after eight when Allison finally finished with her clients from the Recently Divorced group and had a chance to sit and think. Her mind felt cluttered. She wanted a warm bath and a glass of wine, but she couldn't help but mull over Mia's visit. Mia had been right, all of this would be even more stressful for Vaughn because of his brother. Not that Jamie couldn't find a way to care for himself, he was brilliant and resourceful, but Vaughn felt responsible...and they were the only family each other had.

She thought about Tammy "Swallow" Edwards. Had the girl run away as her parents and manager believed? Was there any way her disappearance could be connected to Francesca's?

Allison sat down at her computer and navigated to Google. She tried a few searches, linking the Edwards family and the Benini name. Nothing of significance came up. She tried a number of other combinations, using any grouping of Scranton, Ithaca, Benini and Tammy Edwards as search terms. Still nothing.

Frustrated, but not surprised, she thought about teenagers and the things they did online. She typed in Tammy's name by itself and came up with a host of hits, including her try-out video and Tammy's photos for the upcoming talent competition. In every picture for the talent show premier, Tammy looked lovely: hair tastefully coifed, appropriate clothes, just enough makeup.

No doubt the television producers had a hand in the makeover, but nonetheless, the pictures gave Allison pause. She considered how awful Denise Carr had made her client sound. Yet these photos seemed at odds with the portrait Denise had painted. *This* Tammy didn't look like a train wreck of a client.

Allison clicked on the link for Tammy's Facebook page. Her profile shot showed a grinning girl sitting on a mountain bike, hair pulled back in a messy ponytail, no makeup on her face. She had a slight sunburn and her nose was a healthy pink. One hand was gripping her handlebars, and the other was extended toward the camera as though she were telling the photographer to stop taking the picture.

It was a shot that spoke a thousand words. It showed a happy teenager comfortable in her own skin. A kid who liked to be outdoors and who was capable of having fun. A girl who, perhaps, felt more at home in sweats and a t-shirt than a party dress.

A girl who loved opera?

Tammy's privacy settings wouldn't allow Allison to dig much deeper on her page. Next to "Relationship," there was a link to a boy named Kai Berger. Allison clicked on Kai's name and Facebook linked her to his page, which was not restricted.

Allison sat forward in her chair and tried to swallow her excitement. She knew the chances were slim that Kai Berger's Facebook page would lead to Tammy's whereabouts, but it was at least a window into her life. She thought about Jane Edwards, her reaction to the mention of a boyfriend. Was Kai the reason?

Kai was an undernourished teen with a hawk nose and a mop of straight muddy-blonde hair. In his profile picture, Kai wore jeans and a flannel shirt. He didn't list Tammy as his girlfriend, but she was in a half dozen shots posted to his wall. In most of them, Tammy was balled up on an ugly tweed couch, wearing a black hoodie, with her hair in her face. In one shot, she was holding a half-empty plastic cup of what looked like beer.

Kai's wall was littered with quips from friends, things like "Hey TB, u goin 2 K's tonight? Party out back." The most recent had been posted two days ago, the day after Tammy disappeared. "Bro—try calling once in a while" had been written by someone named Nicky D. There was nothing on his Facebook homepage about a missing girlfriend.

Nothing at all.

Allison typed Kai's name into Google and found what appeared to be an address but no phone number. Was he living on his own? His birthday would make him nineteen. It was possible. The satellite view of the house showed a posh neighborhood in the Scranton area. It seemed unlikely that a nineteen-year-old would be able to purchase a house in that neighborhood on his own.

Allison opened her calendar and studied her schedule for the next day. Other than a meeting with an Allentown company in the late afternoon, her day, like the days after, had been blocked for Francesca. She could reschedule the Allentown meeting. She scrawled a note to Vaughn and left it on his desk. She'd take a ride up to Scranton first thing in the morning and see what Kai Berger had to say about Tammy. Vaughn could cover the office. She would have sent him an email, but he checked his email constantly and would insist on going with her. Allison figured it was best if he stayed on the sidelines.

Allison locked the door to First Impressions and started down the steps that led to the parking lot on the ground floor. The air was heavy and humid, the stars hidden by a mask of smoggy haze. Allison's watch read 9:42. The small parking lot, surrounded by shrubbery and partially hidden by a neighboring property's fence, was bathed in shadows.

Allison made her way to her Volvo, her mind reliving her conversation with Mia. On impulse, she texted Mia and invited her to join her for a trip to Scranton the next day. Tucking her phone back in her purse, she'd just clicked the fob to unlock the doors when a sound startled her. It was faint—the echo of a car door closing—but in the quiet heat of this summer night, Allison noticed. The street leading into the parking lot was empty. On the other side of the shrubs was a larger parking lot used for a bank headquarters. That's all I'm hearing, she told herself. Someone leaving work late.

On a Sunday?

Allison re-locked her door and walked toward the row of azaleas that separated First Impressions from its neighbor. Sure enough, over the bushes she saw a white Honda Accord in the lot, a man in a suit, sitting in the driver's seat, was looking at his phone, face hidden.

Allison murmured to herself under her breath, "Now you're paranoid, too." She climbed back into her car and locked the door for safe measure. She turned on the radio—WXPN—and pulled out as Dar Williams crooned about a past love. Three blocks down, she saw the Honda pull out behind her. She increased her speed, opting to skip the back roads and head straight for busy Route 30. Once on the main drag, she looked in her rearview mirror and saw a green Tahoe and, behind that, a moving truck. No sign of the Honda. Relieved, she eased into the right lane and coasted to a stop at the next light, convinced that she was letting events from the last few days get to her.

When the light turned green, she made a right onto a street lined with oaks and maples, stately fences and tennis courts. At the cusp of her street, she made a left. Just a few houses more and she'd be home, wine in hand, soaking in candlelit water.

As Allison slowed to turn into her driveway, she looked up in time to see a car pass the mouth of her street, the vehicle slowing as it passed the turn. Her heart raced.

The white Honda Accord.

FOURTEEN

"What do you mean by followed?" Mia asked. They were turning onto Kai Berger's street—at least the address given on the Internet—at 7:51 the next morning. Mia had agreed to accompany Allison on the drive to Scranton, and Allison was happy for the companionship. She'd finally told Mia about the white Honda, a fact she'd hidden from even Jason. But Mia's reaction was the reason she'd kept mum in the first place. Her friend was irate.

Allison said quickly, "It's not a big deal. It could have been a coincidence."

"Did you see the driver?"

Allison shook her head. "It was dark. I could tell it was a guy, though."

"I don't like this." Mia looked out the window, jaw rigid. "You need a gun."

Allison laughed. "A gun? Are you kidding?"

"I'm not kidding. Something's going on here, Allison. Wake up. Two clients? And now someone's following you?

Allison pulled up outside of the address she had for Kai. She considered Mia's suggestion. No gun. She hated guns. Hated the mere thought of them. But last spring, when faced with a killer with a gun, all she'd had was a can of pepper spray. A lot of good *that* had done her. Maybe she'd start small. Nunchucks. Or a Swiss Army Knife.

"Did you say this kid lives alone?" Mia said, interrupting Allison's thoughts on the matter of weapons.

Allison took in the house, one of two dozen in a newer development on the outskirts of Scranton. Two- and three-thousand square foot Colonials on half-acre lots. Manicured lawns, Home Depot lawn furniture, even an in-ground pool here and there. It confirmed her original assumption that this was not a place a nineteen-year-old could afford on his own.

"I wasn't sure. Seems unlikely, though."

"You're certain this kid is only nineteen?"

"No. I'm not even sure he's dating Tammy. Or, if he is, that this is the right address." Allison unbuckled her seatbelt. "But there's one way to find out."

After three hard raps on the door, a woman answered. She was trim, with thin, straight brown hair, and round brown, heavily made-up eyes that gave her a perpetually surprised look. She wore white dress pants and a blouse in jeweled shades of green, blue and ruby, tucked in and belted with a swath of black leather. Behind her, Allison could see an immaculate foyer and living room: white carpeting, white furniture, matted prints on the walls. In those few seconds, Allison's immediate impression was that this woman craved order.

"We're looking for Kai Berger," Allison said.

The woman's eyes clouded with fear. She gave Allison a once-over and shifted her gaze to Mia. "What has he done?" Although she didn't say "now," the word was implied in her tone.

"Nothing that we're aware of. We just want to talk to him about Tammy Edwards."

The woman seemed momentarily confused.

"His girlfriend," Allison said, and the woman said "ah" under her breath. "Would it be okay if we came in for a few minutes? I'm Allison Campbell and this is Mia Campbell." Allison handed her a business card. "Tammy's my client."

The woman glanced at her watch. "I'm Kai's mother, Joanne, but I'm on my way out, so I'm afraid I can't help you." She shrugged, hands up in a what-can-you-do gesture. "Life of a real estate agent. I have a client who wants to see a house before work."

"Look, Joanne," Allison said. "Tammy's missing. We're hoping Kai can shed some light on the places Tammy hangs out, her friends. Her family's worried sick and we're trying to help them find her. I'm sure you understand? We'll only take a few minutes of your time." Allison waited. When Joanne still didn't respond, Allison said, "Is Kai here?"

Joanne shook her head. With a sigh, she finally stepped back. "Come in. But I only have a minute." They followed her through the foyer, past the dining room and into the kitchen. Granite counters, oak cabinets, a generously-sized stock island. Here, too, everything was spotlessly clean and smelled of lemon disinfectant.

Joanne stood next to the island. A stack of mail—envelopes and circulars—had been placed in a neat pile on one corner. The mail shared the space with a bowl of what looked to be ceramic fruit: pears, oranges, bananas, and apples. No dust on the fruit.

"Kai doesn't live here. At least not right now." Joanne walked over to a small desk built into country French cabinetry and removed a pen from a glass holder. She scribbled something on a Post-it Note and handed the pink paper to Allison. "That's his father's address. Kai's with him."

Allison glanced down at the paper. A Scranton address. "Thank you."

Joanne walked back to the island and pressed the edges of the mail pile, readjusting what was already a perfectly neat and perfectly straight set of documents. She frowned. "Don't expect Kai to be of much help."

"You don't think he'll talk to us?" Allison asked.

"Depends on his mood. But even if he does, he won't tell you anything useful. He'll just dance around the topic. Just like his father."

"Have you met Tammy?"

"No, but Kai has mentioned her once or twice."

"Typical teen, keeping secrets?" Mia asked.

"Sometimes I wish he'd keep *more* secrets. His judgment is not always the best."

"Does he get into trouble frequently?" Mia asked.

"Not really." Joanne glanced at her watch again. "He just gets odd ideas. Like I said, he's a lot like his dad, Scott. Now, if you'll excuse me, I really do have to go."

After Allison and Mia were through the front door, Joanne yelled after them, "If you do see my son, please tell him I'm still waiting for my key. He can't have it both ways. It's my house or his father's!"

* * *

"A little Type A?" Mia asked once they were back in the car.

"Definitely compulsive." Allison took out her phone and punched in the address Joanne had written on the pink slip. Her GPS gave her a location about four miles away. "She was so cold when talking about Kai that I would have mistaken her for a stepmother if she hadn't said otherwise. Not to stereotype stepmothers, of course, but, well, that was not a mother's love I saw in her eyes."

Mia nodded. "Maybe it's her feelings toward his Dad showing through. Stereotypical divorce?"

Allison shrugged as she pulled away from the curb. "I don't care what their story is, as long as they lead us to Tammy."

The address Joanne Berger gave them led to a bar in downtown Scranton. Allison parked on the street, a block away from the flashing pink neon sign that read "McNally's." The bar was wedged between a pizza take-out joint and a consignment shop.

Across the street were a series of derelict row houses and a check-cashing place. A convenience store with a gas pumping station sat on the corner. The dark wooden door to McNally's led inside to an enclosed foyer. At one end of the foyer was the entrance—a glass door inlaid with a set of security bars. Through the door, Allison could make out four people sitting at the bar top and a long-haired bartender wiping down the counter. All eyes were turned toward the television hung on the wall. Baseball. The Yankees were winning, three to one.

Allison glanced around the foyer. Right inside the entry were two mailboxes. One was marked "McNally's" and the other "2A."

Mia pointed to the "2A" and then to a doorway on the right side of the room. "An apartment? That door must lead upstairs."

Allison reached for the knob. It was unlocked. Mia followed her through the door and up a narrow staircase. At the top was another door, painted an obnoxious shade of fuchsia.

"Not quite what I was expecting," Mia said. She knocked on the door.

"It is a Monday morning. Maybe they're at work. Or school."

"Maybe." But Mia looked skeptical.

After a few more tries, Allison said, "Let's try the bar. See if anyone there knows where we can find father or son."

At the bottom of the staircase, back in the foyer, they were met by the bartender.

She looked to be in her twenties, but if her appearance was any indicator, it had been a hard two decades. Her skin had the loose appearance of someone who'd spent way too many hours in a tanning booth, and tiny wrinkles were sprouting from a full mouth and dull brown eyes. A rose tattoo bloomed from beneath a black tank top. A fading bruise marred her left cheekbone. Three piercings graced her nose.

She said, "Are you ladies lost?"

"We're looking for Scott Berger."

From behind her, a deep voice said, "Found 'im."

The bartender turned around abruptly. Allison caught her wary glance at the man who'd spoken. He was standing in the doorway, and Allison recognized him as one of the men who'd been sitting at the bar, watching the baseball game. He was short, with a wiry build and a head of straight brown hair, slicked back with the aim of hiding a blossoming bald spot. He had a youngish face, reminding Allison of a worn-out Davy Jones.

"I've got this, Vicky."

Allison said, "Mr. Berger, is there somewhere we can chat for a few minutes?"

"About?"

Allison handed Berger a business card. "We're looking for Tammy Edwards, and as I understand it, she's dating your son."

"So?"

"So, we'd like to talk to you. A lot of people are worried about Tammy. We were hoping Kai—or you—could shed some light on where Tammy might be."

Scott Berger gave one longing glance through the glass door toward the television before giving a resigned nod. "I figured it was only a matter of time before someone came calling." He looked at Vicky. "Back to work. And make sure Curtis pays." To Allison, he said, "Come upstairs."

*   *   *

Upstairs consisted of a tiny two-bedroom apartment with wood paneling, an efficiency kitchen and enough dirty laundry on the floor to double as a carpet. Allison choked back a gag at the smell—part Italian hoagie, part smelly feet. It was a bachelor pad without an ounce of charm.

Scott sauntered over to a brown plaid couch, tossed a pair of running shorts onto a nearby table and sat down. He pointed to a matching loveseat. Mia flicked what looked like a flannel shirt to the side and sat on the edge of the fabric, her face one of practiced neutrality. Allison chose to stand.

"I have no idea where that girl is, if that's what you're wondering." Scott tapped one loafer-clad foot on the ground as he spoke. He looked at Allison but glanced at Mia every few seconds as though he was afraid she was planning an escape. "I don't even think Kai sees her anymore."

"He's listed as her boyfriend on Facebook."

Scott shrugged. "Wishful thinking?"

"How long have they been together?" Mia asked.

"They hung out for four, five months. Kai gets around. I doubt she was the only one he was hanging with. Good looking boy."

"Mr. Berger, Tammy's been missing for several days. No one has heard from her. Is there anything you can tell us about where she likes to hang out?" Allison kept her voice soft, non-threatening, but still Scott glanced at Mia.

"You the cops?"

Allison smiled. "Look at my card, Mr. Berger. I'm the farthest thing from it."

He pulled her card from his pocket and glanced quickly at the front. His foot stopped tapping. "An image consultant? I don't even know what that is."

"Like a life coach."

"Then why do you care about Tammy?"

"She's my client," Allison said. "I want to help find her."

When he didn't respond, she said, "Can you at least tell me where to find your son? Maybe he knows something."

Scott glanced at his watch, grimaced and stood. "You asked for it."

He disappeared into one of the bedrooms. Allison heard grumbling followed by the screech of a chair scraping against the floor, then a loud, "Fuck!" before Scott finally emerged looking sullen.

"Kai's not a morning person. He works the nightshift, so he's pretty tired. Go easy on him." He walked toward the apartment door, the saunter gone now, and paused before leaving. "You should talk to that girl's parents. That mother's a holy roller. A wackadoodle holy roller. I got nothing against religion, but don't go forcing it down other people's throats, know what I mean?" His shoulder twitched and he made a fist with his left hand. Allison caught a whiff of barely-controlled rage.

"What do you think the mother's religious views have to do with her daughter's disappearance?" Mia asked.

"Who the hell knows? A cult? Some sort of honor thing? I'm just saying some people have funny ideas, and Mrs. Edwards is one of those people. Talk to her. Get her alone."

He left, shutting the door with a bang. Mia looked at Allison, eyebrows arched, as if to say, *who's the wackadoodle?* Allison barely had time to shrug before Kai Berger stomped into the room, dressed in a soiled gray t-shirt and a pair of plaid pajama bottoms. Unlike his father, he was tall. His face had a fresh rash of pimples across the chin and cheeks, but when he looked at Allison, she saw a flash of intelligence that gave her hope.

Kai sank into the couch. "Yeah?"

Allison explained who they were. "We want to help find Tammy. Any idea where she might be."

"Why would I know?"

"You're her boyfriend."

Kai shrugged, a gesture that echoed his father's. "Damn if I know where she is."

"Has she contacted you?"

Kai's gaze darted toward the door. "Not since last week, when she was down in Philly."

Allison said, "With me."

"Yeah, I guess." Another shrug. "Look, she called me from the hotel all full of ways she could tell her parents to go fuck themselves. Next thing I know, her mother calls me accusing me of hiding her. She's always hated me."

Allison sat on the edge of the couch, across from Kai and as far from a pair of dirty socks as she could get. "Why?"

"Damn if I know. Dad owns a bar, maybe that's offensive."

Mia said, "Your father suggested we talk to Tammy's mother. He said she's religious. That maybe she had something to do with Tammy's disappearance."

"Dad's crazy. Has been ever since Mom left him."

"When was that?" Allison asked.

"Three years ago."

"Do they fight a lot?" Mia asked softly.

"Nah, they just don't talk. Dad slept with Vicky, his bartender. Mom found out and left him. He's pissed because she got the better end of the bargain. Lives in a new house, has a new boyfriend. He lives in this shithole. Give him enough time and he'll tell you all about it himself."

Allison decided on a different tact. "Have the police contacted you, Kai?"

That made him perk up. "No, why would they?"

"Your girlfriend's missing. I'd think they would talk to people close to her."

"Didn't talk to me. I only heard from Tammy's mom."

"What do you think happened to her?"

"How would I know?"

"Do you think she ran away, Kai?" Mia asked.

He looked away. "Nah, why would she?"

"I don't know. But if she didn't run," Allison said, "then something bad may have happened to her. Doesn't that possibility scare you?"

Kai shifted in his seat. "Yeah, I guess. When you put it that way."

Mia stood. "Kai, where did Tammy like to hang out? Mall? Clubs?"

"None of those places. She was either singing—choir, studio, at home—or hanging out with me."

"Where?"

He shrugged. "Wherever. We liked to mountain bike on Snow Mountain. Sometimes we'd hike."

"Did you come here?" Allison asked.

Kai snorted. "Would *you* take a girl here?"

He had a point. "Any other friends?"

"My friends were her friends. Sometimes she hung out with her neighbor, Kellie with an 'ie.' She'll tell you that when you meet her. 'I'm Kellie with an ie.'"

It was clear he didn't think much of Kellie with an "ie." "Where does Kellie live?"

"A few blocks from Tammy. Green house, orange shutters. Hard to miss." He yawned. "Done with me? I gotta go back to bed. Working tonight."

"Where do you work?"

"Pizza delivery. A few other odd jobs." His eyes fluttered, blinked twice. "Saving money to go back to school."

Allison stood carefully, taking pains not to touch any of the soiled laundry. "We appreciate your time, Kai. Good luck with work and school." Allison pulled another business card from her purse. "If you hear anything at all about Tammy, call me."

"Yeah, sure. Whatever."

Back downstairs, Allison exhaled in relief. She wanted to be outside, away from that cramped apartment and the smells and bullshit of the Berger boys. She took one more look through the glass door that led to the small bar and saw Scott Berger's leering face through the window. She nodded, and he gave her a smile that sent a chill down her spine.

"What do you think?" Mia said back out in the humid summer air.

"The boy's lying. They both are."

FIFTEEN

Jamie was still asleep when Vaughn snuck out of the apartment that morning. Angela was scheduled to be there until eight and then Mrs. T would relieve her, so he knew that his brother would be okay. He scribbled a note for both women. While Jamie hadn't said anything directly, Vaughn could tell that these disappearances were weighing on him, making him worry, and that only increased Vaughn's anxiety. Like he'd told Allison, he needed to *do* something. He'd texted Allison and told her he'd be late for work. She wouldn't care. She was the one always urging him to work less and play more.

He started with the boxing gym. A ninety-minute-long workout and a cleansing hot shower helped him clear his mind, get some perspective. Then he headed toward the office so he could clear out the pile of crap he'd been trying to get finished for the last few days. Work and discipline were called for now—and while his mind was occupied with other things, maybe he would remember something that would help, something that would trigger a lead.

Vaughn turned the BMW onto Route 30, which led to Villanova. Traffic had picked up and the roads were congested.

He slowed to a stop by a traffic light near a Starbucks and toyed with whether or not to stop for coffee. He generally avoided alcohol and caffeine, but today felt like it warranted an exception. When the light turned, he figured *what the hell* and made a quick right into the parking lot. Iced coffee. That's what he wanted.

He pulled next to an old Acura Integra, grabbed his wallet and mobile from the center console and opened the door to the BMW. His wallet fell to the ground. *Damn*, he muttered under his breath, and reached down to pick it up. It was then that he noticed the white Accord making a u-turn at the traffic light. The car pulled into the parking lot at the hair salon next door and sat idle, facing the Starbucks but barely visible from this angle. Vaughn wouldn't have thought much of it—guy waiting for his girl or something—but when he glanced back at the car on his way into the coffee shop, he could have sworn he saw someone inside watching him. The back of Vaughn's neck prickled.

You're a crazy bastard, he said to himself, and shoved open the door.

Tammy's neighborhood was quiet this time of day. Allison parked at the end of the street, a block and a half away from the Edwards' property, and killed the engine. Kai was right: the house was hard to miss. Kellie's home was a standalone in a neighborhood of twins. A coat of fresh orange paint graced the door, a shade or two off from the peeling orange shutters. A red, white, and blue wreath hung from a nail in the wood. The house itself was a seashore mint green. The forced cheerfulness of the exterior contrasted with a rusty Ford pick-up truck that sat flat-tired in the driveway.

"Holy kaleidoscope, Batman."

Mia laughed. "Why don't you go alone? It might be less threatening that way."

"You'll be okay?"

"I want to check on Vaughn anyway."

"I got a text from him earlier. He was going to the gym before work and then going into the office late."

Mia looked troubled. "Does he know you're in Scranton?"

Allison felt a stab of guilt. "I left him a note at the office. I was afraid if I told him ahead of time, he'd insist on coming. That didn't seem like a great idea."

Mia didn't say anything. She pulled her phone out of her leather purse. "I'll wait here."

Allison climbed out of her car and walked up the steps to the porch. She knocked once. Someone pulled open the door with gusto, and then looked disappointed to see Allison standing there.

"Oh," said the girl in front of Allison. "I thought you were someone else."

Clearly, Allison thought. "I'm Allison Campbell. I was hoping to talk to Kellie. Is she home?"

"That's me."

The girl didn't budge from the doorframe. She was average height and maybe fifty pounds overweight. Her ample frame had been poured into skin-toned spandex pants and a clingy print blouse cut low enough to expose a deep valley of cleavage. Her hair was dyed a shade of red that did not exist in nature. Her makeup looked professional: smoky brown shadow and mascara that opened up almond-shaped green eyes. She had beautiful eyes.

"Do you have a few minutes to talk about Tammy?" Allison asked.

She squinted. "Tammy?"

"Tammy Edwards? Your friend?"

"What about her?"

"Can I come in, Kellie?"

Kellie glanced back over her shoulder. She shook her head. "My mom's sleeping. It'd be better if we talk outside."

The girl walked out onto the porch and closed the door behind her. She stood with her back against the siding, one pedicured foot against the house. "Tammy's missing."

"I know. That's why I'm here. Do you have any idea where she might have gone?"

"What's it to you?"

Allison explained her role. "Have the police met with you?"

"No one has met with me. Tammy's mom called, but that was it."

"How well do you know Tammy?"

"Pretty well. We've been neighbors since elementary school. She's quiet, but we hang out sometimes."

"Does she have a wide social circle?"

Kellie looked down at her feet. "Neither of us has many friends. I guess that's why we hooked up." She looked up, shyly. "Misfits, you know. Safety in numbers and all that crap."

Which aligned with what Kai Berger had said. "How about Kai? Do you know him well?"

Kellie made a face. "Kind of. What of it?"

"Do you think Tammy might be with Kai, Kellie?"

"Who the hell knows? Kai and I don't really hang out."

"Not at all?" Allison asked the question with kindness in her voice. It was clear from Kellie's body language that she disliked Kai. Maybe because he bullied her. Maybe because he symbolized something she felt she couldn't have: a love interest. Either way, Allison wanted to know more about Tammy's circle of friends. And she had very few avenues from which to glean that knowledge.

"He thinks he's cool. All intellectual and shit. Doesn't want to be seen with someone who goes to cosmetology school." Kellie scowled. "Even though he can't hold a steady job or manage to stay in school. Doesn't seem all that intellectual to me. But Tammy really likes him. Yin and yang, maybe. Who knows."

Allison smiled. She'd taken a liking to Kellie. The girl seemed honest and a little lost. If Allison had to guess, home life wasn't too easy on Kellie. Sleeping mom probably translated to sleeping-one-off mom. And if there was a paying job in the household, that broken-down Ford truck said it was a thing of the past.

"And anyway, cosmetology school's not that easy."

"Did you apply your own makeup?" Allison asked on impulse.

"I did." The hint of a smile gave life to a pair of sweet dimples.

"Nicely done." Allison dug a card out of her purse. "Maybe you can come work for me when you're done with school."

"Really?"

"Really."

The front door opened and a disheveled woman in a velour sweat suit stumbled out onto the porch. "*Kel-lie?*"

"Mom, go back inside."

"Who's that?"

"Go back inside. *Please.*"

The woman, hair a helmet of platinum blonde spikes, shot an unfocused look Allison's way. "Kellie in some kind of trouble?" Her words slurred together in one intoxicated mélange.

"No. I'm just here to ask about Tammy Edwards."

"Oh." And like that, she slammed the door.

Kellie resumed her interest in her own feet. "Sorry," she mumbled. "My mom's not well."

Allison leaned down to catch Kellie's eye. "Nothing for you to apologize about. Now keep that card. Let me know if you hear from

Tammy. And don't forget to look me up when you've finished school."

Kellie gave her a sideways smile, one that made Allison feel the ache of her own lonely childhood. "I promise. On both counts."

From the car, Allison caught a glimpse of Tammy's mom, Jane Edwards, sitting on her front porch, baby in her arms. Allison climbed back out of the Volvo and with a quick explanation to a pensive Mia, headed toward the Edwards' residence. She approached cautiously, wary of the reception she would receive. It took a moment before Jane noticed her. When she did, alarm distorted her plain features into a mask of wary anger.

Allison held up a hand. "I was in town and thought I would check in."

Jane Edwards pulled the baby closer to her chest. "Check in for what?"

"To see whether you have any news? And to find out if I can help in any way."

"You've done enough."

Jane tugged at the waist of her navy blue skirt. She wore another frilly blouse, the off-white collar tied at the throat with a bow. In contrast, the baby was wearing a bright floral dress with ruffled panties and matching pink socks. At the sight of Allison, the little girl stuck her fist in her mouth and sucked contentedly, drool dripping down a chubby chin.

"Have the police been in contact, Mrs. Edwards?"

"Why would they?"

"Tammy's missing. I'd think they'd want to search for her."

"I called the local hospitals and morgues. No sign of her. I don't think this is police business."

Jane spoke without affectation. Allison watched her face closely. Was she lying, still in shock—or did she really feel that little emotion?

"I could contact local government officials for you, unless you've already done that."

"Please stay out of it, Ms. Campbell." Jane's voice was high-pitched, her words coming quickly. "Tammy's run away. The more I think about it, the more certain I am. No need for the police."

"Just in case, wouldn't it be a good idea to search for her? Have the police search?"

"I'm a woman of faith. And no one knows Tammy better than I do. My daughter is rebelling. She'll turn up eventually. It's all this nonsense about music and Hollywood. I told my husband that she needs school, marriage, but in the end, he makes the decisions." Jane stood. The baby reached for her hair with one spit-soaked hand and she pushed the girl's fist away with a harsh, "Stop that, Isabelle."

"I need to get Isabelle down for her nap. Please stop worrying about my daughter. She'll come to her senses eventually, and when she does, we will see to it that she receives the appropriate consequences."

Allison watched Tammy's mother go back inside, little Isabelle gurgling happy baby talk over her shoulder. As her mother pushed through the door, the baby opened and closed one chubby fist in Allison's direction, waving good-bye.

Back in the car, Allison found Mia sitting in the passenger seat with her head against the glass. She wore a dazed expression. Allison felt her stomach twist into ropes. Something bad had happened.

"What is it?" Allison asked.

Mia continued to stare straight ahead. "Vaughn called. He's been taken in for formal questioning. In the disappearance of Francesca Benini." She blinked, and Allison saw tears pooling under her eyes.

"Oh no."

"It gets worse."

"How could it get worse?"

"Paolo Benini. Someone at the hospital identified a young black man who visited Paolo with his wife just hours before." Mia shook her head. "They know it was you and Vaughn."

SIXTEEN

They didn't wait for a call. Allison was on the horn with Detective Butch Razinski before she'd pulled away from the curb. He wouldn't tell her anything, but she had to believe that the police had little against Vaughn other than circumstantial evidence—he'd been in the wrong place at the wrong time. Three times over.

Allison's second call was to Jason.

After explaining where she was, she waited for his rants against her amateur sleuth antics. Instead he surprised her by saying, "I'm coming up there, Allison."

"You don't need to, Jason. Although I appreciate the offer. We just need the name of a good defense attorney. Just in case."

"Look, I'll talk to the detective. See what's going on. Then we can decide whether Vaughn needs a defense attorney."

Allison had to admit Jason made sense. "If you're sure." She gave him directions. "How soon can you be there?"

"Give me three hours. And in the meantime Allison, please don't say anything. Wait for me."

While they waited for Jason, Allison called Alex Benini, determined to cancel their dinner appointment.

"I'm afraid something's come up."

"I'm sorry to hear that." And he did sound sorry. "It's become even more imperative that I talk to you."

"I really can't. I couldn't commit to a time."

"Look," he said, "I'm already down here. I drove down this morning. Just call me when you're free and I'll meet you."

She felt her resolve wavering. What could be so urgent he would leave his family now? Surely there were funeral preparations, family matters to attend to. The business. And the search for Francesca.

With a sigh, Allison said, "It will have to be late. But if you can live with the uncertainty, I will call you when I'm done."

"Thank you. Truly. We'll talk tonight, Allison. Until then, stay safe."

Allison tried to decipher if his words were a wish—or a warning.

Allison and Mia sat in the parking lot at the police station until Jason arrived. He strode purposefully over to her car, looking all-business in a summer-weight charcoal suit and crimson tie. He leaned down to give Allison a kiss, then noticed his mother climbing out of the Volvo.

"Really, Mom? Not you, too."

Mia frowned, waving away his concern. "Just do your job, Jason. And bring Vaughn home."

Jason and Vaughn were with Detective Razinski for almost an hour. Afterwards, they entered the lobby of the police station alone, their expressions unreadable.

Allison's mind flitted to twenty different scenarios. They were arresting Vaughn. They wanted to question her, too. Francesca had been murdered. Based on the blank looks on their faces, any of these could be true. Or everything could be fine.

"Ready?" Jason said.

The two women stood. Mia reached out and took Vaughn's hand. He held it for a moment before letting go. Mia shot a worried shrug in Allison's direction and Allison shrugged back. Damn if she knew what was going on.

In the parking lot, Jason said, "We need to regroup. I know you have a lot of questions, but let's meet back in Villanova. It would be better to talk there." He looked at Vaughn. "Why don't you ride with me? We can discuss what just happened while it's fresh." To Allison, Jason said, "Meet you at home?"

She nodded, at a loss for words.

* * *

See you at *home*. Allison mulled over those words the entire drive back to Villanova. Jason had said it without thinking. The house *had* been *their* home, once upon a time. Could they wash away the years since the divorce, start fresh, build a new life together? Was either of them capable of the kind of compromise a healthy marriage required?

Allison wasn't so sure. She was pretty damn sure that Jason wanted safe, predictable, and normal. Although Allison spent her days teaching social norms, her life—at least lately—had been anything but. Could he live with that?

Maybe she was underestimating him.

And herself.

Mia was lost in a world of worry and said barely three sentences the entire drive.

They pulled up to Allison's house before Jason and Vaughn got there. Inside, Allison clipped a happy Brutus to a leash and took the dog for a brisk walk while Mia made tea.

In times of crisis, Mia always made tea.

By the time Allison and Brutus returned, Jason and Vaughn were installed in her kitchen, tea mugs in hand. Allison noticed the bottle of rum on the table. In times of real crisis, Mia felt tea deserved rum.

"How did it go?" Mia asked.

Jason looked at Vaughn, who nodded his permission for Jason to continue.

"Obviously they didn't hold him, but he is on the watch list."

Mia rose from her chair. "But—"

Jason held up one hand. "But is right, Mom. There is no indication of foul play in either instance. Tammy is outside Razinski's jurisdiction, but he's cooperating with the Scranton police in case there's something larger going on here. But for now, all they have are two missing adults who could have very well left of their own volition. But no one seems inclined to investigate the disappearances." Jason paused. "My opinion? The police are papering their files."

"Which is in line with what Mia and I learned today." Allison turned to Vaughn. "Tammy's mom doesn't even *want* the police involved. How strange is that? If it were my daughter and she was truly missing, I would be looking for help from anyone who was willing. And if the police weren't onboard, I'd be screaming my head off."

"If your daughter was truly missing," Vaughn said.

"Are you saying she's not?"

Vaughn stood up, walked to the window overlooking Allison's backyard. "I'm saying that's how a typical parent would react if they didn't know where their kid was. What if this kid has done it before? If the mother has reason to believe—or even knows—she's run away."

Jason nodded. "Vaughn has a point. I'm actually more worried about the Benini woman."

"I don't know," Allison said. "Tammy didn't seem like the type to run away."

"But she did have a conflict with her parents," Jason said.

"Not really. There was no actual conflict. Tammy did what was expected of her. Even when it wasn't what was best for her. She wanted to please her parents." Allison wasn't buying the runaway theory, at least not for the normal teen reasons. After their initial conversation, Tammy never brought up opera or Juilliard again. She didn't seem to be scheming, sullen, or upset. Allison had been surprised that she ran. Could it have been anxiety and turmoil over California? Sure. But Allison's gut said that wasn't the reason...as easy as it would have been to just accept that premise and stop worrying.

"How about Paolo?" Mia asked.

Vaughn remained standing with his back to the table, still staring out the window. Allison watched him, concerned. His spine was rigid, his shoulders tight. She waited for him to answer.

But it was Jason who spoke. "After Paolo died, the nurse in charge called Simone. She mentioned a visit by Paolo's niece and her husband. She told them the husband was black."

"So knowing that Paolo had no niece, that I was in Ithaca, and that I am black, the family put two and two together." Vaughn's voice was as tight as his spine. "They watched the security tapes and there we were."

"I'm so sorry, Vaughn," Allison said. "It was my idea to go there in the first place."

Jason held up a hand. "There was no evidence of foul play. If there had been, you'd have been hauled in, too, Allison."

Allison remembered the sudden feeling of dread, the urgent need to escape the hospital. "Is it possible Paolo was drugged? Or suffocated?"

Jason chewed at his bottom lip. His eyes darted to Vaughn. "Either of those scenarios is possible. Paolo died without regaining consciousness. The family has refused an autopsy, so frankly, we may never know."

"Then why question Vaughn?"

Vaughn spun around. "Isn't it obvious, Allison?"

"Stop." Jason held his hand up to Vaughn. "Thinking that way isn't productive. You were the last to see all three people. Like I said at the outset, the police are papering their file at this point, in case something goes down. They couldn't very well ignore the connection. But they haven't charged you."

"Yet." Vaughn rubbed his eyes. "Paolo died within forty-five minutes of our arrival, Allison. You knew something was going down, you had that damn premonition."

"I did." Allison relayed her reaction to Mia and Jason. "But how could someone else have snuck in after we left? And if it was a family member, he—or she—would have been noticed by the nursing staff."

"Unless that someone was impersonating a doctor or nurse. Or an orderly," Mia said. "Hospital staff might not be noticed by the nurses or stand out on the tape."

Jason nodded. "Good point. The security tape doesn't record patient rooms. They caught Allison and Vaughn on the elevator. It's possible someone had his or her face covered. Dressed like a hospital employee, a nun, a priest. Who the hell knows?" He stood. "If the old guy was even murdered. He'd just had a stroke. He was already on borrowed time."

Jason bent down and kissed Allison on the lips. He waved to his mother and Vaughn. "I have to head back to work for a while." Looking at Allison, he said, "Dinner tonight?"

She almost said yes and then remembered her promise to meet Alex Benini. "Not tonight. I have dinner plans. I'm sorry."

Jason nodded. He didn't look happy.

When Jason had gone, Vaughn said, "Thanks for calling Jason. I felt a hell of a lot better having him there."

"No problem." Allison forced a smile. "Are you going to be okay?"

"Hey, I'm a survivor, right? And like Jason said, they have nothing at this point." But the look on Vaughn's face didn't match the bravado in his voice. "I asked Jason to meet here instead of my house because I'd rather Jamie not know too much. Not now. It will only make him feel frustrated that he can't do more to help."

"You shouldn't keep this from him," Mia said. "Let him help."

"The less he knows, the better."

But Mia held her ground. "He's your identical twin, Vaughn. He'll sense something is wrong. Don't do that to him. Tell him. Let him help."

Vaughn and Mia looked at each other, the language of lovers and friends spoken without the utterance of a single syllable. Finally, Vaughn relented. "What do we need him to do?"

Allison gave him the names of the people they had met today along with a rundown of the conversations they'd had. "Anything he can find out about Tammy's boyfriend, Kai or Kai's family would be helpful. And I'd like to know more about the Benini finances. How in the red are they?" She also wondered who served to profit upon Paolo's death, but decided she'd try to get that information from Alex later tonight.

"Anything else?"

"That's enough." Lists of issues were collating in her mind, but she didn't want to overwhelm Vaughn, not until she had a better sense of the direction she was headed. "For a start."

SEVENTEEN

It was 8:14 when Allison finally arrived at The Village Pub, a large, noisy restaurant near her house. She wanted noisy and casual. What she did not want was any intimation that her dinner with Alex Benini was to be anything other than an informational exchange. She didn't trust him, pure and simple.

Alex sat across from her looking elegant in a dark gray European-cut suit, no tie and a collared white shirt, unbuttoned at the throat. The suit's tailoring was impeccable, and it paired nicely with his slightly ruffled hair and the five o'clock shadow on his face. If he was aiming for European model/playboy, he was spot on. If the image he wanted to portray was grieving son/worried nephew, not so much.

They occupied a booth at the back of the restaurant, attended to by a twenty-something waitress with a surly attitude, too-short bangs and buck teeth. Like all of the wait staff, she wore a yellow and red striped rugby shirt. A three-person band played music in the far corner of the restaurant. In the span of five minutes, they covered Springsteen, the Clash, and Van Halen.

"Eclectic bunch," Alex said. His smile, for once, did not reach his eyes. Allison wondered if perhaps she'd been wrong. That he was in mourning. And trying to hide it.

The waitress took their orders—Caesar salad and iced tea for Allison, a burger and a beer for Alex. After a few moments of informal chit-chat, Alex said, "I won't beat around the bush, Allison. I had a reason for driving down here."

"I'm sure you did."

The corners of his mouth pulled up in a half smile. "But it's still nice to see you. Even under these circumstances."

"I would think, considering the circumstances, it wouldn't be so nice." She kept her voice light, but she meant what she said. His aunt disappeared while traveling with *her* employee. By now, he had to know they visited Paolo before his death. How could he be so nonchalant? Even if she knew there were no connections between events, he didn't.

"Allison, I don't hold you or your assistant to blame. Francesca will turn up, I'm sure of it. As for my father...his time was coming. He smoked, ate rich food, and drank much too much *grappa*. He was a time bomb, ready to explode."

"Perhaps, but I don't imagine all of you are so willing to forgo blame, deserved or not."

"If by that you mean Dominic, true. To Dom this all looks very bad, I'm afraid."

Allison took a long sip of water, eyeing him over the glass. "If I may be blunt, you don't *look* worried, Alex. Or particularly grief-stricken. Why is that?"

He spoke without hesitation. "In my line of work, you have to look good. Play the part. Always. Regardless of the circumstances." He shrugged. "Maybe I'm too used to hiding how I really feel."

Confused, Allison said, "I thought you worked for your father's company?"

"I'm on the books, of course—we all are. But I'm a musician, too. Sax player."

"Professional?"

"Well, I try. But the truth is, I mainly play for fun."

Allison looked at him with heightened suspicion. Musician? Could that be the connection to Tammy? Would a singer from Scranton and a sax player from Ithaca travel in the same music circles?

The waitress came with their drinks. Alex thanked her and took a long swallow of beer. Putting the mug down, he let his head fall to the side and gave Allison a wry smile. "You look surprised."

"I'm just surprised no one mentioned it before now."

"Why would we? What does it matter?" He looked over at the band in the corner, now playing Eric Clapton's *Layla*, and said, "I still have a role in Benini Enterprises. I'm the so-called resource manager." He shrugged. "It keeps me on the payroll and gave my father a reason to include me in the succession plan. I show up at the office, review our only HR person's reports, make a few recommendations. It's all good."

Alex smiled, but his smile had that same wistful quality that Allison had seen back at the estate, when she'd first broached the subject of Alex and Benini Enterprises.

She wondered whether it really was "all good," or whether Son Number Two had gotten the short end of the stick and resented it. A musician and a human resources manager? Not what she would have picked for Alex Benini.

Allison said, "Speaking of the business, Francesca mentioned that it's not been doing well. She seemed hopeful that she could turn that around, but I never did understand the reason for the decline."

He sat back in his chair. "Simple. The company had been declining for some time. When the market tanked, it led to even less demand for our products, especially the specialty food goods. They tend to be higher-end and expensive. As consumer discretionary income decreases, so does the demand for luxury foods. But my father was an optimist. He refused to cut expenses and overhead in line with the decline. And he was stuck in his old ways. Dom and I had ideas for new lines that could perhaps have increased sales, but he would hear none of it."

"What kind of ideas?"

"Products that would seem a better bargain, more accessible. Sold under a subsidiary, if Father didn't want to change the perception about Benini. And maybe some higher end products marketed to the very rich, people whose discretionary income didn't change when the market fell." He searched Allison's eyes for understanding. "And we considered branching out into other avenues all together."

"Such as?"

"I don't want to bore you with all this business talk."

"You're not boring me at all. In fact, for a sax player, you sound pretty knowledgeable about the inner workings of Benini Enterprises."

"You can't grow up in our household and not be."

"So why not dive head first into business? Why music?"

Alex stroked the handle of his beer mug and watched the waitress as she placed their food in front of them."Anything else?" she said.

"Another beer," Alex said. "You, Allison?"

"Another iced tea would be great. Thank you."

A few minutes later, the waitress arrived with their drinks. Alex waited while she placed the glasses in front of them. When she was out of earshot, he said, "Dom was always the golden child. I guess I didn't want to compete with that. Maybe a psychologist would say I couldn't compete, so I went a different way all together. But you can't really escape Benini Enterprises, so I have my music, and I have a piece of the action, so to speak. Albeit a small piece."

Mulling this over, Allison asked, "And Francesca, was she involved, too?"

"Francesca's not directly involved in the business."

"Directly—or at all?"

"She doesn't participate in the decision making."

"Francesca told me that she often counseled your father."

Alex smiled. "There you have it, then. If she was counseling him, she had no more business savvy than he did. Or we wouldn't be in the predicament we are today." He leaned in closer to the table. "Which brings me to the reason I wanted to see you."

"And here I thought it was for the pleasure of my company," Allison joked.

Alex didn't react. "Did my aunt give you anything at all, Allison? Anything that may give us some indication of her whereabouts?"

"Such as?"

"I don't know."

"That's a bit broad."

He sat back, gestured with open hands. "I'm sorry, but I'm being honest with you. I just don't know. And if you do have something, and it's something related to her disappearance, then you could be in danger, too."

"But I thought your family believes Francesca bolted."

Alex regarded Allison, as though deciding what to say next. "We don't know what to think. We haven't received a ransom note. And even you must admit that staying locked up in a house for forty years is very odd behavior. So no one would be surprised if she ran."

"But something is making you question that. And you have reason to believe there is information out there, information that could lead to finding her." Allison met his stare with a direct one of her own. "Something you seem to believe I have."

The waitress returned with their check. She looked from Allison to Alex before tossing the check in front of Alex's half-finished plate. She walked away without another word.

Alex's eyes followed the waitress before returning to Allison, his expression pained. Play acting? Allison wondered. What the hell did he think she had?

Allison thought of the white Honda the night before. Maybe she wasn't imagining things. Maybe she *was* being followed. And maybe things were worse than she'd considered. She studied the man in front of her. Should she tell him about the Accord, about Tammy? Could she trust him?

She remembered her night in Ithaca, at the estate, and the odd family dynamics. While she had chalked it all up to the tension of the night and the haunting atmosphere of the Benini household, she decided to be her own best counsel and keep these details to herself.

She said, "We brought you her suitcases. Maybe whatever you were looking for is inside?"

"We searched. Clothes. Only clothes." He gave Allison a sideways glance. "But I'm sure you know that already."

Allison took a drink of iced tea and tried to ignore the flush creeping up her neck. Of course they had looked through the bags. But she and Vaughn hadn't found anything, either. "You must have some reason to believe there's something else out there, or you wouldn't have bothered driving down here."

"Her safe."

"Francesca had a safe?"

Alex nodded, looking suddenly exhausted. "It was left open and empty. We noticed after you called last Friday night, after Frances-ca...left."

"Do you know what she kept in there?"

Alex shook his head. "But if it had been locked in her safe, we're assuming it was important."

"She didn't give anything of importance to me."

"Check with your colleague, Vaughn, please?"

"He'd have mentioned it, but I will. What about Maria? Or Simone? Could one of them have accessed the safe and taken its contents?"

"No one at our home had access to that safe."

"The man you've hired to investigate Francesca's disappearance? Reginald Burr. Has he had any luck?"

"Not so far." Alex speared a French fry with a fork, examined it, and put it back down on the plate. Eyebrows gathered, he said, "So you have nothing, Allison? I'm sorry, then, to have wasted your time."

Allison thought about the file folder of papers Francesca had handed her the day Allison left Ithaca. Francesca hadn't said a word about safekeeping or privacy, and a cursory glance had shown some marketing brochures and Internet print-outs about the company. There were a lot of documents, but nothing that seemed controversial. Certainly nothing that would raise an eyebrow, much less cause a kidnapping.

Allison said, "The things your aunt gave me were taken from the public domain. I don't know what you think she may have had in her possession that would have triggered her disappearance, but whatever it was, she didn't give it to me."

Alex didn't try to hide the disappointment on his face. He picked up the check, pulled his wallet from his pocket.

"So who will be CEO now, especially with Francesca missing? And your father...passed on."

Allison pulled open her purse, but Alex waved her away before she could get to her wallet. He placed a platinum American Express card in the faux leather folder with the bill.

"I asked you to dinner, the least I can do is pay. And to answer your question, that remains to be seen."

"Is the succession plan defined after Francesca?"

"No. It will be Dom, I suppose. But right now, we're in limbo."

"And you?"

"Would like my aunt to return."

Allison smiled. "But I thought you said the notion of her running Benini Enterprises was absurd. Ridiculous was your word, if I remember correctly."

"It is ridiculous. But until Francesca's back, we have no leader...and that's even worse."

"Who is acting CEO? Surely someone's in charge."

"Dom. But only because he assumed the role. My sister and Simone also believe themselves to be in line for the throne, so to speak."

Alex handed her a card with several names and numbers scratched on it in blue ink. "That's my hotel address and some additional contact information. If you find anything, or if you notice anything strange, or even if you just want to talk, please call me. Despite what you may think about my family, I want my aunt back."

Allison took the card. But she wouldn't be calling.

EIGHTEEN

Allison thought about her conversation later that night while she went through the materials Francesca had given her. It felt surreal. A saxophone-playing Italian businessman with a dead father and a missing aunt. But then, what about this arrangement *hadn't* been strange?

She was in her home office, comfortably dressed in cotton pajamas and the slippers Brutus most liked to steal. The dog was curled next to her, head on his paws, sights set on her feet. Allison reached down absentmindedly and scratched him behind the ears. His focus never wavered, but Allison's mind kept drifting to Alex Benini and his amused smile. Pragmatic, grieving musician...or shyster? Damn if she knew.

"You're not getting them," Allison mumbled to Brutus. "So stop with the pathetic face."

Brutus wiggled a little closer.

"Nice." If it hadn't been for her last client fiasco—the former Congressman's daughter, Maggie McBride—she wouldn't have this canine beast living with her. She smiled. So good could come from tragedy. That damn dog tugged at heartstrings she hadn't even known she had.

Allison paged through the stack of photocopies Francesca had given her, reading through each piece of paper, deciphering its significance. She needed some order to the mess, so she began sorting: marketing materials in one pile, financial summaries in another, family-related articles in a third. She remembered the moment Francesca had handed her everything. She hadn't seemed upset. But had Allison missed some cue, some hint that there was a hidden message? At the time, it had simply been another engagement. An unusual one, but an engagement nonetheless.

When she was finished sorting, Allison counted five piles. In addition to marketing, finances and family, she'd added two categories: Italy and miscellaneous. Then she paged through each piece of information again. She stopped when she got to family. The first two articles were simply promotional pieces about the Benini family: photo ops of Paolo and Simone, snippets about each of the boys. Nothing about Maria other than a mention buried in a PR piece. Maria wasn't even in the family photograph. And neither was Francesca.

The third piece of information in the family category was an old newspaper clipping about Tommaso Benini, Francesca's father, and his launch of Benini Enterprises. He was a small, dark-complexioned man with a thick head of white hair and a thin mustache. He had kind eyes, though, and Allison saw in the grainy photograph the same amused look Alex often wore. And she saw echoes of his frame in Dom: stout, short stature, broad shoulders.

Allison scanned the remainder of the article. Tommaso credited his success to his mother, Antonia Benini, and her keen business prowess. Allison recalled Francesca's description of her grandmother as a shrew, a woman who disliked other women. Including Francesca's mother. Including Francesca.

Francesca had been sent to boarding school when she was very young. And then she was sent to live in the United States. Had Antonia Benini disliked her granddaughter that much? And if so, why? Or had Francesca been escaping the limiting expectations of the family matriarch.

But then why arrive in the States and live like a hermit? What freedom was there in that?

Frustrated, Allison turned to the stack of papers about Italy. An article from Condé Nast about Calabria. A piece about Francesca's hometown village printed off an Internet site that Allison didn't recognize. Both were written from a travel perspective. One snippet about the Benini home town caught her attention. It was a veiled reference to family feuds and one family's failed efforts to broker a truce.

Francesca had mentioned that theirs was one of the prominent families in town.

She'd also mentioned that Benini Enterprises had shareholders in Italy they needed to please.

Could Francesca's disappearance be related to a family feud? Could some of those rival family members be Benini shareholders? She made a note to ask Jamie to research Benini board members and large shareholders. Just in case.

Quickly, Allison jotted down the name of the Internet site. Travel Suspense—"A dot com with a story." Hmm, she thought. Again, she questioned Francesca's reasons for including the article. Suddenly everything seemed ominous. Remember Al, she chided herself, small villages in Calabria are probably not the most sought after vacation destinations in Italy. So there could have been no reason other than availability of information for including this article. The feud reference could be meaningless.

Curious, Allison ran a Google search. Besides Wikipedia, the search engine turned up forty-two references to Francesca's home town, and thousands on Calabria. So there was plenty of material to choose from. Why this piece?

Finally, Allison turned to the miscellaneous pile. In it was an article on wine-making, a piece on Ithaca vineyards and Gina Benini's obituary. This she read with a heavy heart:

Giovana (Gina) Benini, nee Pittaluga, beloved wife of Paolo Benini, died on January 8, 1976. She is survived by two sons, Dominic and Alessandro (Alex) Benini, her parents, Pietro and Rosalia Pittaluga, and nine brothers and sisters. Services will be held at St. Anthony's Catholic Church in Ithaca. Mrs. Benini, a devout Catholic, was a longtime member and patron of St. Anthony's.

Allison found the last line interesting, especially considering the manner in which Gina died. *Thou protest too much*, she thought. Perhaps. Or perhaps Gina Benini was a depressed woman who took her own life—*and* she was also a devout Catholic. End of story.

Allison clicked off the Internet and shut down her computer. It was well after midnight, and had been an incredibly long and exhausting day. She was ready to retire. Beside her, Brutus snored and his paws twitched, his fixation on her slippers traded for the unknown recesses of the canine dream world. She hoped his dreams were better now that he had a warm home and two square meals a day.

Allison began clipping together the various piles of papers when she heard the sound of glass breaking and then the shriek of her alarm. Like a Greyhound after a rabbit, Brutus was up and running downstairs, barking furiously, before Allison could even stand.

Allison yelled after him, grabbed her cell and dialed 9-1-1 as she chased her canine friend.

Pulse racing so that it felt like her chest would explode, her eyes took in the shattered dining room window. A large white rock lay in the middle of the floor. She ran into the kitchen and grabbed a knife, then stood, back to the wall, so she could see all angles. Brutus continued barking, running from the broken window to the front door and back again. Afraid he was going to cut his paws, she called him to her and held his collar, her own jaw clenched to the point of pain.

Fighting a rising sense of panic, Allison thought about the white Honda. About Alex's admonitions to be careful. With a glance at her shattered window and the white rock that, she was certain, didn't stand for truce, Allison was suddenly certain that two client disappearances were not a coincidence. Whoever had taken them was warning her away.

She hoped the cops arrived quickly.

"Pro'ly kids," said the officer who took Allison's report. His name was Bert Solomon. He and a back-up had walked around her property, looking under bushes and in the neighbors' yards. Finding nothing, they stayed while Allison searched her house, Brutus by her side. She also turned up empty-handed.

Officer Solomon was medium height, with a black uni-brow and a thick mustache. He seemed unconcerned about the rock until Allison mentioned the disappearance of her clients.

"Huh," he said. He looked at his colleague and then back at Allison. "I don't like coincidences."

Allison said, "I don't either."

"Could be some kind of warning," Solomon said. His colleague nodded. "You live alone?"

"Yes. Except for Brutus."

"That's one ugly dog," the other officer said.

Allison scowled at him. Officer Solomon took another glance around the room, then at her left hand, before landing his gaze on Brutus. He chewed at his lip, causing the mustache to move like a fuzzy caterpillar along his face.

"Any friends or family you can stay with?" Solomon asked.

"I'll be fine."

The officer looked around. "Maybe a boyfriend? Your father? I'm not so sure you should stay here alone, not with that window broken." He spoke with an air of strained and practiced patience.

Allison was quickly losing her own. "Look," she said. "I'm fine. I told you about my client so you wouldn't dismiss this as a silly kid prank."

"Prank or no prank, you really shouldn't be alone," Solomon said again.

"I said I'll be fine. Besides, I'm not alone." Allison reached down and stroked Brutus. She hated the suggestion that she needed a man to be safe. She also hated the nervous energy that made her fingers shake and her mind whirl.

She'd patch up the window, reset her alarm and let Brutus do what he did best—protect her. What else could she do? She'd be damned if she was going to call Jason. If he came over for this, he'd never let her out of his sight. No, it was better that he not know about the rock. She'd get the window pane replaced first thing in the morning.

Anyway, maybe it had been a kid's prank, she told herself.

But no comfort came. Because she knew in her gut that it wasn't.

The next morning, Allison arrived at the office before eight o'clock. She'd spent the entire car ride looking over her shoulder for a white Honda—or any suspicious vehicles. Happy to get to work, she trudged into the building and up to First Impressions. She found Vaughn already in his office.

Allison debated how much to tell him and finally decided on the whole truth.

If the rock had been someone's idea of funny, then no one had anything to worry about. If it was more, Vaughn could be in danger, too.

Vaughn listened to the details of her dinner with Alex and the ordeal with the broken window without a trace of emotion. When Allison was finished, he stood up from his desk and disappeared into the kitchenette for a moment. He came back with two mugs of coffee and handed her the caramel-colored one.

"You don't drink coffee," Allison said.

"I do these days." He reached in his top desk drawer, pulled out a file and handed it to Allison. "Look what Jamie pulled together last night."

"Already?" she replied, taking the packet.

She wasn't surprised, though. When she said Jamie could help, she meant it. Earlier that year, he'd been instrumental in solving two murders.

His mind, not to mention his understanding of computers, was nothing short of amazing.

Allison was staring at a rap sheet. Two pages worth of petty crimes spanning three decades. All for one Scott Berger.

"Kai's dad," Allison said. "A criminal?"

"Yeah. Breaking and entering, assault and battery, harassment. Drugs. Crazy shit."

"Did he do time?"

"Here and there. Nothing like what he deserved. Must have had himself a very good lawyer."

"Or a patient and forgiving judge. Wink, wink."

Allison thought about her visit the day before, the bruise on his bartender's face. Could Scott Berger be violent? Could he have done something to Tammy?

She handed the sheets back to Vaughn, who said, "And this." He passed Allison a list of properties owned by Joanne Berger.

In addition to the house in the Scranton suburb, she owned a rental property in Mount Pocono and a beach house on the Jersey shore.

"Notice the dates of purchase," Vaughn said.

All three properties had been bought in the last two and a half years. "And they divorced three years ago?" Allison asked.

Vaughn nodded.

"Anything on Joanne? How long has she been a realtor?"

"Sixteen years. She's won awards for being one of her agency's top sellers."

"Hmm. She's been in the biz for sixteen years, and just now has the funds to buy three new properties? I smell fish." Allison frowned. "How about Scott's bar? Was Jamie able to get any info on how well it's doing financially?"

"He's still working on it."

"Has Scott owned that bar for long?"

"About four years. Bought it six months after his last jail stint for harassment and intimidation of a material witness." Vaughn smiled. "Interesting, huh?"

"Let me get this straight. Scott Berger has been in and out of jail for decades. He was married to a successful real estate agent who was clearly the bread winner in the relationship. They divorce, and suddenly he buys a bar and she has enough money for three properties."

Vaughn nodded. "So your next question is—"

"Where the hell did the money come from?"

"Don't know."

"What did Scott Berger do before he owned the bar?"

"He worked at the Kremsburg landfill, about twenty miles from Scranton."

"The same place Tammy's father works?"

"Yep."

"Possible they knew each other back then?"

"Possible and probable. Scott worked security. Tony Edwards, maintenance."

Allison looked down at the papers, her mind turning over the possibilities. She knew the jail sentences, the petty crimes and lenient judges suggested one thing.

"So Scott Berger is on a Mafia payroll?"

Vaughn nodded slowly, eyebrows arched. "Looks that way."

"Who owns the landfill?"

"Gretchko and Sons is registered to Andrei Gretchko. But it's his son, Nicholas Gretchko, who runs it now."

"Anything obvious there?"

"Nothing so far." Vaughn picked up the file. "I don't know what the Berger family's connection is to Tammy's disappearance, if anything. But I will be damned if I'm going to leave a single stone un-turned."

Allison didn't say anything. She was too busy thinking of the bar-tender's bruised face. And of all the places you could hide a body at a landfill.

Later that morning, Allison was working on intake for a new client when Vaughn popped his head into the client room. "I'm sorry to both-er you, Allison, but you have an urgent call."

Allison looked from him to the man in front of her, a fifty-six-year old former vice president in the position of having to reinvent himself after being laid off. She felt for him. It wasn't easy to admit that the very thing you allowed to define you—your business success—was now gone.

Having given up so much to get where he was, he was grieving his former life. And Allison didn't want to leave him in the middle of his first session.

But Vaughn knew only to interrupt her in the most dire of circum-stances. So she gently excused herself and followed Vaughn into his office.

"My mother?" Allison said, nearly choking on the words. Ever since her mom's Alzheimer's had taken a turn for the worse a few months back, Allison lived in fear of getting *that* call. But it wasn't Alli-son's sister, Ann, who was on the line.

Vaughn shook his head. "Maria Benini."

Allison took the phone. Why was Maria Benini calling her? But Vaughn just shrugged and said, "She wouldn't talk to me. She said it was urgent, though."

Allison put the receiver to her ear and immediately heard the whir of machinery in the background. "Hello?"

"About fucking time. Look, I can't stay on the line. I know where Francesca is."

Allison straightened. "Where?"

"I'm only calling you as insurance. In case something happens to me."

"Why would anything happen to you?"

"I don't have time to explain. Please just listen. There's an old abandoned building at the back of our property. It used to be a hunting cabin. They have her there."

"Who's they, Maria. And if you know she's there, call the police."

"I can't call the police."

"Why not?"

"They're watching me, too. I know it."

"The police?"

"No. Them."

"Maria, there has to be someone up there who can help. If Francesca is being held captive on your property, explain that to the police. They can send someone in undercover."

"Look, I'm going to get her myself. Like I said, calling you was just for insurance. I need someone who's not involved. If something happens to me, you'll know why."

Allison caught Vaughn's eye, but he looked as confused as she felt. "Maria, who is *they*? *Who* is holding your aunt captive?"

"There was a tracking device on his car. That's how they followed him. That's how they nabbed Francesca. I saw it."

"Who, Maria? Who did that?"

"I don't know who. I tried to tell Dom and Alex, but they don't believe me. I was in the woods. I couldn't see who did it, but I saw the device." Through the phone, Allison heard a door slam. Maria whispered, "I have to go." The line went dead.

"Shit," Allison said. She looked at Vaughn. "Is the BMW here?"

He nodded.

"Come with me. And bring your cell."

Before heading outside, Allison asked her client if she could reschedule. She explained that it was urgent and offered him two free sessions. He agreed, but she still felt guilty. But not as guilty as she would feel if something happened to Francesca because of her. They waited until he left before heading outside.

On the way, they called Detective Razinski. He agreed to contact the local police, but he sounded skeptical. It did sound far-fetched, even to Allison, and she had been on the receiving end of Maria's call.

Vaughn's car was parked near the fence. Allison took off her shoes and got down on her hands and knees. If they could find a tracking device, that would be a concrete lead. It would also help to clear Vaughn's name.

"I don't even know what I'm looking for," Allison said. "I'm an image consultant, not a damn investigator."

Vaughn was on other side of the car, examining the wheel well. "Anything unusual. A small box, most likely. It'll probably be under the car. My car was locked while I was there, so it couldn't be on the inside."

Allison felt under the vehicle. She mimicked Vaughn and felt the inside of the wheel wells, around the front bumper, anywhere that looked like a potential hiding spot. Other than dirty knees and grimy hands, she had nothing to show for it.

Neither did Vaughn.

"Damn," he said, clearly disappointed. "That woman is nuts."

Allison stood. She looked across the fence toward the bank beyond, remembering the white Honda. "Maybe not," she said. She told Vaughn about her stalker a few nights prior.

His eyes grew wide. He leaned one arm against the car. "A white Accord?"

Allison nodded. "Have you seen one, too?"

"I thought I was going crazy. Three times now. And the first time, I could have sworn the guy inside was watching me."

"Did you get a look at him?"

Vaughn shook his head. "No. Couldn't get the license plate either." He arched his eyebrows. "Are you thinking the driver of the white Honda took the tracker off my car?"

"If Maria's telling the truth, then that would make sense. Whoever put the tracker on your car is happy to have Francesca viewed as a flight risk. It wouldn't do if the police knew you'd been followed. A tracking device would lend credence to the argument that they should be searching for a kidnapper. Or a killer."

Vaughn started back toward the office.

"Where are you going?" Allison called after him.

"We're heading to Ithaca. To talk with Maria Benini in person."

NINETEEN

But Maria wasn't there.

Allison and Vaughn couldn't find a convenient flight that would get them to Ithaca before the next day, so they drove. They made the trip in record time, arriving at the Benini estate before nightfall. As they snaked their way up the long driveway and around the circular portion in front of the house, Allison realized she'd been holding her breath. She half expected to see police cars and detectives searching for Francesca. Instead, they were met at the door by Jackie, the chef. It took Jackie a moment to register who they were before she opened the door and let them inside.

"Paolo's funeral is not until Friday," she said.

"Actually," Vaughn said, "we're here to see Maria. Is she around?"

Jackie's eyes widened. "I haven't seen her since this morning. She comes and goes like the wind, sometimes I don't see her for days."

"Is it possible she's in her room?" Allison asked.

"I doubt it, but I'll double check."

While she was gone, Vaughn and Allison stood looking at one another, enveloped in heavy silence. Allison glanced around the house. It struck her again how much like a museum this home was, as though nothing had been disturbed for a hundred years. Was that because it hadn't? Was it possible that time had stood still once Gina Benini died?

Jackie came back down the marble steps, shaking her head. "I'm afraid Maria's not there."

"Could she be down at the barn?"

"Probably." Jackie glanced at her watch. "I have a soufflé in the oven." She lowered her voice. "Why don't you two take a walk down. Just don't go in the horse stalls, okay?"

Allison nodded. She was about to head out the door when she stopped the cook. "Were the police here today, Jackie?"

"Not that I'm aware of, but I just arrived this afternoon."

Allison studied the older woman, trying to determine if she was being truthful. Jackie looked sad, tired and a little rushed—but she gave no indication that she was lying. "Maria mentioned an old hunting cabin on the property. Do you know where it is?" Allison asked.

"Past the grotto about a quarter mile or so. I haven't been back there in years. It's rundown and hard to get to, covered by brambles and fallen trees. Why would you want to go there?"

Allison and Vaughn exchanged a glance. "We don't," Allison said. "Just curious."

Jackie still looked perplexed, but she didn't push. Afraid the cook would change her mind about letting them walk down to the barn alone, Allison thanked her, said, "We'll see ourselves out," and left.

Vaughn practically sprinted toward the barn to check for Maria or any clue regarding her whereabouts, a man on a mission. Allison struggled to keep up, wishing she'd brought sneakers. When would she learn to give up style for comfort in these situations? Instead, she looked down at her open-toed wedges and muttered "damn" under her breath. Her feet ached already.

"What the hell, Allison. No police? Nothing? What's going on around here? I feel like we're in the goddamn twilight zone."

The barn and chicken coop were visible over the hill and across a pasture. They'd have to go all the way around the fence to the gate, which was on the far side of the barn, or climb over the railing to get there. Allison glanced down at her work outfit for the day: brown linen pants and white summer sweater. She was happy brown was the color of dirt, because it looked like they were about to get dirty.

"I know. I have no idea what's happening. Let's see what we can find before Jackie has an unfortunate change of heart."

"Maybe she thinks they're as strange as we do."

"Or maybe she's in on it. Whatever *it* is."

Vaughn took the split rail fence in one quick leap. Allison stood facing it, every tortuous, humiliating gym class from her youth replaying in her head. It was an understatement to say she hadn't been athletic. The only sport she'd played willingly as a kid was Kick the Can, and even at that, she was always last.

She looked into Vaughn's eyes and recognized a sense of urgency.

"I'll help you," he said, and held out a hand.

Allison shook her head. "I can do this." She hopped up and swung one leg over the railing, straddling the fence. She teetered for a moment before hopping down onto the other side.

Vaughn smiled, eyes kind, before striding ahead in the direction of the barn. Allison followed. The inside of the hulking structure was dark. The sweet-sharp smell of hay mingled with musty animal smells, reminding Allison of Mia's farm. In their stalls, the horses stood placidly watching Vaughn and Allison as the duo walked the length of the building. Allison stopped in front of a chestnut-colored colt with a white star splashed across its long face, the same horse she'd seen her first day at the estate. The horse nuzzled its head against her shoulder. Unsure of herself around large animals—she was just getting used to dogs—Allison ran a hand along the top of its head, feeling the smooth hair that ran between its eyes, and down to its nose. The horse closed its eyes and leaned in toward her caress.

"You've made a friend."

Allison looked up to see Vaughn staring at her, tenderness in his eyes. She gave the horse another stroke, pausing to tickle the soft spot under the horse's chin, and said, "What if we misjudged Maria? What if she was the sane one in this house?"

Vaughn looked at the horse, then at Allison. He seemed tired, his body posture a little wilted, his dark skin a little ashen. "What if we misjudged Maria and she's a killer?"

He was right, of course. There were so many *what ifs* in this case. Nothing was as it seemed. It was like a house of mirrors, with each passageway leading off into a thousand directions—or nowhere at all.

Reluctantly, Allison left the horse and made her way toward the far end of the barn where four empty stalls were doubling as storage sheds. Objects covered in tarps, a cedar chest, rows of standing tools—shovels, pitchforks, and rakes—crammed into small spaces. The barn was quiet, and tendrils of dread crept down Allison's shoulders and crawled into her belly. Lots of places to search.

Where to start?

Vaughn began pulling a tarp off a large, oblong object. A small tractor that had been left in the back corner of the barn to rust. He recovered it quickly before moving on to a multi-pronged farm tool Allison didn't even recognize.

"Two city folk. We could be looking at anything." Vaughn turned to her and smiled.

Allison returned the smile. "I was thinking the same thing."

They worked together to peek under every tarp, look behind every stack of hay bales, every bundle of tools. Rakes, scythes, boards, old saddles...no animate objects other than a mouse that made Allison spring backwards.

"Not a damn thing," Vaughn muttered.

"Not sure what we expected. She did say the hunting cabin, not the barn." Allison glanced at her watch. They'd only lost a half hour, and she didn't think either of them was anxious to head into the woods.

"Well, I expected the police. So either Razinski didn't call the local cops or the local cops didn't bother to check this out. Which is it?"

"If I had to guess, I'd say Razinski made a half-hearted call to the locals and they dismissed it."

"Why would they do that?"

"Maybe they thought she made this up." Allison had a thought, not a pleasant one. Considering Maria's hysteria at dinner, her allegations that Gina Benini's ghost still prowled the halls of the estate, what if this wasn't the first time the police had heard her name? "Maybe Maria has made calls in the past. The local cops could have her pegged as a girl who cries wolf."

"But even if that's the case, in this instance, her aunt's missing. They'd have to do something."

"True. Maybe they called Simone and she told them not to come. Or maybe they've come and gone—Jackie arrived late, so she may have missed them." Allison shrugged. "Who knows." She glanced at the horse, now standing against the wall in his stall, her mind spinning with possibilities. Such a calm animal. Calm and well cared for. Maria had clearly loved her horses. "Maria kept saying 'they.' They put a tracker on your car. They were holding Francesca. I wish to hell she'd said who *they* were."

Vaughn looked at Allison. "You gave Razinski the number that showed up on your cell, right? The number Maria was using to call you?"

"I did."

"Did you do a reverse phone number check to see where she was calling from?"

"I did. It was just a mobile phone. That's all that came up." She saw the frustration in Vaughn's eyes and said, "Let me try it again now."

But out here, in the barn, Allison's phone had no reception. And neither did Vaughn's.

"Dead zone," he muttered.

"I heard machinery in the background when Maria called. Francesca mentioned that Benini had a bottling factory in the area. Maybe Maria had been calling from there."

Vaughn studied his watch. "We'll never get there and get back here in time to search the hunting cabin."

Ugh. Allison had been dreading this. "Do you want to head out on our own? Before we look for Maria? For all we know she could be there."

"We have no idea where we're going. This property is huge."

"Jackie said it's a quarter mile past the grotto. We've been to the grotto."

Vaughn started pulling aside tarps, searching for something. After a second he muttered "gotcha" and pulled a long, heavy flashlight from a cabinet.

"Saw it earlier." He looked at Allison's outfit, gaze lingering on her shoes. "You know, if you're going to play detective, you'd better start dressing the part."

Allison smiled. "I had the same thought earlier. Although frankly, I think this is just a short career detour."

The chickens and sheep had been fed, the garden weeded and her afternoon chores completed. Mia pulled off her gardening gloves and closed the door that led from her front porch to the small kitchen. The bungalow was warm in the summer heat, but the stone walls kept the kitchen cool—as long as she didn't light up the AGA stove. So she'd have salad for dinner, and maybe a glass of white wine. The French bottle that she'd been saving.

Mia walked through the kitchen and into the short hallway that led to the living room. Off it, one door opened to her bedroom, and the other, stairs into the basement. The original owners of the house had set up a second canning kitchen down there, so it was spacious and cool. She used it as a wine cellar and a place to store winter vegetables.

As she made her way down to the basement now, her thoughts drifted to Vaughn. They needed to end their affair. She hated the thought, but it was the right thing for both of them. But not now. Now, he had bigger things on his mind. He needed her support. Mia pulled her cell phone from her jeans pocket and called his mobile. When she got no answer, she tried First Impressions. A cordial answering service employee told her that the office was closed for the day. Concerned, Mia dialed Allison. No answer there, either. Even Jason was a dead end—his secretary said he was in court.

Frustrated, Mia decided to forgo the wine and the salad. She ran back up the cellar steps and grabbed her purse from its resting place on the dryer.

Maybe Jamie would know where they were.

TWENTY

The grotto seemed farther than Allison remembered. Once again, she and Vaughn started down the path by the house, where the trail was just a wide swath of wood chips winding its way toward the woods. Once in the trees, the path changed to packed dirt and then, eventually, to loose humus and fallen leaves. The canopy of trees overhead blocked most of the remaining daylight. Unfamiliar sounds like a cacophony of animal noises assaulted Allison's anxious ears. The forest would come alive in the night, and while Allison was grateful for Vaughn's surefooted presence, she didn't think her city boy was any more used to dealing with wild animals than she was.

They trudged along in silence, neither Vaughn nor Allison saying much until they reached the grotto. There, Allison sat on the bench to pull a twig out from inside her shoe and Vaughn tried his mobile again.

"Still no service?" Allison asked.

"Nah. We're screwed."

But Allison knew the worried look on his face had more to do with Jamie than their situation. He didn't like being unreachable in case there was an emergency. She didn't blame him. And under current circumstances, their inability to communicate made her feel especially vulnerable. She hadn't told Jason where she was going.

And they couldn't even call 9-1-1 if they *did* find Francesca.

"Ready?" Vaughn said. He eyed the sinking sun. They had maybe an hour of daylight left. Maybe.

Allison stood. She tried to get her bearings. "I think the old cabin must be that way." She pointed to a spot where the flattened path re-entered the woods, behind the small koi pond and over the bridge.

Vaughn nodded. "Lead the way," he said. "Let's do this."

* * *

Jamie was awake when Mia arrived an hour later. He grinned, happy to see her. Using his mouthpiece, VAUGHN'S NOT HERE appeared on his screen.

"I figured as much, Jamie," Mia said. She sat on the couch. "Do you know where he might have gone?"

BACK TO ITHACA.

"Why?"

Jamie showed her an email that contained a brief summary of the phone call from Maria and their subsequent attempts to contact police.

"So they went to talk with Maria?" Mia asked.

IN THE HOPE THAT FRANCESCA HAS BEEN FOUND. Jamie's handsome face darkened. ALTHOUGH THAT SEEMS UNLIKELY.

"Why?"

WE WOULD HAVE HEARD SOMETHING BY NOW.

"True." Mia felt her anxiety level rising.

She crossed her legs and leaned forward. She really wanted someone to talk to, and Jamie was always logical, but she didn't want to betray Vaughn. How much did Jamie know?

Vaughn was trying to keep some of this from him, to lessen Jamie's worry, but she also knew he was damn smart and he'd probably figured out more than he was letting on.

"So," Mia said, deciding to trade coy for pointed, "Anything new about Tammy?"

Jamie ran through the information he'd discovered about Tammy's boyfriend's father, Scott Berger—the petty crimes, the connection to Tammy's father via the landfill.

Mia interrupted him, "Wait a minute, Jamie. Did you say the landfill in Kremsburg?"

YES.

"Who owns it?"

NICHOLAS GRETCHKO AND HIS FATHER, ANDREI GRETCHKO.

Mia searched sideways in her mind for a connection. Why did the Kremsburg landfill ring a bell? And that name seemed familiar. An alarm went off in her head at the mere mention of the dump.

MIA.

Mia looked up to see Jamie staring at her, his face stern.

"Yes?"

DON'T WORRY ABOUT MY BROTHER. HE'S SMART AND RE-SOURCEFUL. AND HE DIDN'T DO ANYTHING WRONG. SOON EVERYONE WILL REALIZE THAT.

Mia stood. She walked over to the bed and held one of Jamie's lifeless hands. His skin was dry and papery. She felt a surge of love for this boy—for, God help her, she viewed him as a boy—and wanted to keep him safe.

"You really believe that, don't you? That the world is just?"

As soon as she said it, she regretted the words. Because wasn't Jamie's motionless body evidence that the world was a very unjust place?

But he simply smiled.

IT MAY TAKE A WHILE, MIA, BUT JUSTICE DOES PREVAIL. IN THE HERE AND NOW...OR THE HEREAFTER.

When Mia got home, she gave Buddy a quick head pat and sprinted for the living room. There, against the back wall, sat an antique Mission desk and her computer. She turned the machine on and waited for it to come alive, regretting her decision not to upgrade. The damn thing was slow.

Kremsburg Landfill.

Gretchko. Benini.

Two ethnic names with no obvious connection. But she couldn't ignore that worm of doubt wiggling its way through her brain. She was missing something, some clue that existed in the farthest recesses of her memory.

Years of image consulting, hundreds of clients. She couldn't be expected to remember every one of them. But, damn it, she was wishing she'd taken her gingko or ginger or whatever the hell was supposed to boost memory. She felt the clock ticking on this one.

When the computer was finally booted, Mia typed in Google and searched for "Kremsburg" and "Gretchko." She pulled up references to the landfill, a few business-oriented links, and two or three 5-K times, races that the younger Gretchko must have participated in. Nothing ominous, and nothing that triggered her memory.

She tried "Andrei Gretchko." Still nothing.

Buddy ran into the room, and Mia rubbed behind his hound ears, the way he liked it. He leaned into her and gazed at her with adoration. He'd been a stray, showing up weeks after she moved to this property, after her daughter had been killed at the hands of Mia's drunk-driving husband. At first she'd resented the dog's presence. Buddy needed care and attention, and she'd had little will to provide either. But now she realized that the dog had saved her life as much as she had saved his.

"What do you think, Buddy?"

The dog opened one eye, hoping, Mia was sure, that if he ignored her, she would keep on rubbing.

"Andrei Gretchko? Kremsburg Landfill?" She said the names over and over to an oblivious Buddy. And that's when it dawned on her. She stood, pulse racing, the veil of a memory hanging over her eyes like moth-eaten silk. A woman. Tall, broad, blonde. The landfill rang a bell because Mia knew the woman who had inherited the business. The only daughter of the prior owner. A woman who went by a different last name. Not Gretchko.

Katerina Tarasoff. A former client.

And the only child of a certain mobster.

Vaughn and Allison reached the cabin fifteen minutes later. The trail led from the grotto, through the woods and into what once must have been a clearing, but was now so overgrown with weeds and brambles that Allison could only make out the ghostly remnants of a wooden fence and a dilapidated outhouse, a crescent moon carved high on one side. An uprooted tree crossed the trail, its roots leaving a crater-size hole in the earth. Allison stepped carefully over the trunk, making her way quietly toward the hunting cabin. Its front fascia torn and mottled so that it resembled a child's depiction of a haunted house, the building itself teetered on the edge of viability at the back of the ragged clearing.

The cabin was small, not much bigger than a child's playhouse. Another uprooted tree had fallen against the roof on one side, and green moss ran a carpet-like line along the side of the debris.

"Man," Vaughn mumbled. "I really do not want to go in there."

They stayed crouched in the brush, out of the line of sight of anyone who was in the cabin. An unnecessary precaution, Allison thought, because the windows and only door were boarded shut. Unless there was a peephole, she thought. All good kidnappers need a peephole.

Allison glanced up at the darkening sky. Considering the meandering path they had taken to reach the cabin, she didn't think they had much time. Even if they hurried, they might not make it back to the house before night fall. And if someone was in there...well, they needed a plan.

Although most of the windows were shuttered, the one on the right corner looked accessible. Its wooden cover was broken and hanging from two hastily-placed nails. Unless they wanted to pry the front door off, noise and all, it was the best option.

"Come on," Allison whispered.

As they got close, Allison slipped her shoes off. She pointed to the narrow window opening, which sat about four feet off the ground. "Hoist me over."

"No way, Allison. I'll go." Vaughn whispered. He started to climb in, but Allison placed a hand on his chest.

"You won't fit without pulling more boards off and that will make noise. Let me go. I'll be fine. Be my look-out." When he shook his head, Allison said softly, "Francesca could be in there, Vaughn. If she is, we're wasting time. I'll be fine."

Vaughn frowned. He glanced up at the sun, now an orange ball nestled behind the trees. Finally, he said, "Fine. Hurry." He handed Allison the flashlight. "One peep and I break in."

Before Vaughn could change his mind, Allison ducked through the window opening and squeezed herself through, dropping down on the other side as quietly as she could. The inside of the cabin was dark. Allison braced herself against the wall and waited for her vision to adjust to the light, alert for any sounds that would indicate movement. Other than a faint scratching noise coming from the ground near her feet, she heard nothing. A mouse?

She forced herself to stand still. What was a tiny rodent when your feet were bare? As long as it *was* a tiny rodent. Stop, Al, she said to herself. Pull up those big girl panties and get a move on.

After her sight finally adjusted to the murky light, Allison studied the room. A wreck of broken furniture and cobwebs.

"Are you okay?" Vaughn hissed through the window opening.

"Yes," she whispered. She felt her way around the room, hands against cool walls, toward the doorway that led to the front portion of the small house. She gritted her teeth against the sensation of sticky cobwebs on her face and tried not to think of creepy-crawlies that hid in corners of places like this. There could be a kidnapper, and you're worried about spiders, she thought. Sheesh, Allison.

Momentarily disoriented, she closed her eyes and pictured the layout. From the look of the place on the outside, the cabin had two rooms and maybe a kitchen and/or a bathroom. She wouldn't pull out the flashlight until she was sure no one else was inside.

Her heart raced. Sweat trickled down her face and between her breasts. Allison's bare foot touched something cold and furry. She stifled a scream, shuffled two steps to the left, and forced herself forward. The room smelled of rot. Her stomach lurched. If Francesca was being held captive here, she must be terrified. The thought propelled Allison forward, toward the other room.

The door between the front and rear rooms was closed. Night was quickly closing in and Allison had to squint to see anything at all. No flashlight, though. Not yet. Her head began to pound, the pressure a vise on her forehead.

Conscious of her own breathing, she made her way to the door. She pressed her ear up against the scarred wood, but heard no sound coming from the other side. With a deep breath, slowly, carefully, she opened the door a crack, every cell in her body bracing for an explosion of sound or violence. But there was nothing.

Encouraged, she opened the door further. She raised the heavy flashlight, the only weapon she had, and swung the door wide, hoping like hell that Vaughn had her back.

The room was empty.

Allison felt first a wave of relief, then a stabbing disappointment.

Had Francesca ever been here? It seemed like Maria was nuts after all.

A square hole where a stove vent had once lived allowed the last remnants of daylight to seep into the room. Allison glanced around.

She was facing a small area, about 10' x 10'. Like the back room, its windows and only door were boarded up. A kitchenette had been situated against the far wall. A single set of kitchen cabinets, doors ripped off, insides empty, stood next to an old-fashioned once-white refrigerator, its hinges sagging. A gaping spot in the cabinetry, like a missing tooth, marked the spot where the stove once stood. A stained basin must have been the sink at one time. There was no faucet.

An old metal bed frame leaned up against a filthy wall. Its mattress was on the ground, stained and torn. A single table was wedged next to the kitchen cabinet. Otherwise, the room was bare.

Allison let out her breath. She was about to yell for Vaughn when a sound startled her. She jumped, clutching the flashlight. The sound was coming from one of the boarded up windows at the back end of the room. Vaughn coming in?

Allison stepped gingerly across the torn wooden floor. The sound was scratchy, more like birds or rodents than a person. Allison flicked on the flashlight and ran the light along the perimeter of the board. It was nailed from the inside, but, when she looked closely, it seemed like two corners had been recently disturbed. With one finger, Allison pulled at the corner of the board. It came away easily. She did the same to the other side. The board fell sideways, exposing a small area. The stink emanating from the space made her choke.

Allison trained her flashlight beam into the room, her heart beating wildly against her ribcage. Please don't let it be a body, she thought. Please don't let it be Francesca.

"Allison!"

She jumped, swirled around and came face-to-face with Vaughn.

"What the hell is taking you so long? I was worried."

Allison nodded toward the small cubby. Vaughn moved closer. He put his hand to his mouth. "Oh, man. That stench."

Allison swept the flashlight across the interior. It was a bathroom, the source of the smell was a broken toilet ripped from its mooring.

"The hole"—Vaughn pointed—"raw sewage."

Allison tried not to breathe in. She started to back away, then thought of those loose nails. Could someone have been using this space? For what? No person could stay in there. The smell was simply overpowering. But someone could hide something in there. A package.

A small body. A clue. She decided to do one more sweep of the small room. That's when she saw it.

She pointed to the wall next to the broken toilet. "Look!"

Vaughn leaned in, his hand still across his mouth and nose. In small block letters, the word "GINA" was written in blue marker. Other words, written in the same blue pen, had been smeared to illegibility. Vaughn turned, eyes wide. "Think Francesca wrote that?"

"Maybe," Allison said. She looked again, aiming the light directly over the word. The writing was fresh, letters painted on top of the grime.

Allison said, "But if she did, Maria was telling the truth when she said that Francesca was being held here against her will. We need to find Maria."

"But why would Francesca write 'Gina'?" Vaughn said. "What the hell does a dead woman have to do with Francesca's disappearance? Wouldn't you just write the name of your captor?"

"I don't know." Allison took a picture of the wall with her camera phone, about all the damn thing was good for out here, and started back toward the other room and the open window. "But it certainly seems like the past is connected to the events of the present, doesn't it?"

"I guess," Vaughn said. That was all he got out before the sound of approaching voices shut him up.

TWENTY-ONE

The voices got louder, rising above the sound of Vaughn's whispers and the blood rushing rapidly through Allison's veins. It sounded like three men. Startled, Vaughn closed his mouth, eyes wide, body tensed like a wild cat sighting prey. "Come on," he mouthed. "It's coming from the front."

Allison didn't need prodding. She flicked off the flashlight. Night was complete now, and the only solace was the glow of the moon flowing through the hole over the cabinets. Quietly, she started toward the back room, finding her way with a combination of memory and groping. Then she thought of the bathroom.

"Shit, Vaughn, we need to close that door again."

"I'll get it. Just get in the back room."

Allison waited, her back up against the wall near the door to the rear of the cabin. Vaughn moved like a cat, gliding back to the broken board that had covered the bathroom entrance. He worked silently while Allison strained to hear what the men were discussing. Their voices were only a low murmur, though, competing with the chorus of crickets and her own barely-controlled breathing.

Finally, Vaughn was back by her side. "I did my best. One of the nails is missing, but it should hold for now."

Allison nodded, aware even as she did so that he probably couldn't see her. She led the way back through the door and into the rear room, Vaughn's hand clasped in her own. Once in the back room, she heard the unmistakable sound of the board that covered the front door coming down. Whoever it was wasn't worried about being heard. The boards gave way with a loud crack just as Allison and Vaughn were climbing back through the window, into the humid night air.

Still barefoot, Allison stayed against the dilapidated cabin and made her way toward the front of the building. She could feel Vaughn behind her. From their hiding spot behind the bushes, they watched the cabin. Light glowed from flashlights bigger than their own. The men were inside the cabin, sweeping the interior with powerful beams. Allison started to move toward the light, but Vaughn put a restraining hand on Allison's shoulder. "This way," he whispered.

Allison followed Vaughn, back around the rear of the cabin, through the brambles shrouding the side of the building that faced the woods, and around the side where the kitchen stove had been. There, from their perch on a small hill, they could see inside the cabin. One man was walking around the rear room, his bobbing flashlight all that was visible. The other two were standing in the middle of the front room. One was talking.

"Oh, Lord," Allison said.

"Who is it?"

"Looks like Dominic and Alex."

"Francesca's nephews?"

"The very same."

"Why would they be here?" Vaughn asked.

"I don't know. Maria said they didn't believe her. Maybe they had second thoughts."

"Or they're searching for us."

The thought gave Allison pause. "You're right. Vaughn, your car is at their house. All they would have to do is ask Jackie, and she'd point them to this cabin. They know we came here. They probably saw the glow from our flashlight."

Vaughn took a deep breath. "Who is the third man?"

"I don't recognize him."

Vaughn was silent for a minute. "What do you want to do? We can make a run for it, but in the dark, without being able to use our flashlight, we could get lost."

"No," Allison said. "We confront this head on."

"Where are you going?"

"Back inside."

* * *

Katerina Tarasoff died six years ago, at her home in Kremsburg, surrounded by family. Mia found an obituary in a Russian-American newspaper, but it told her little other than the woman's age at the time of death (68) and the fact that she was survived by a husband, three sons, one daughter and twelve grandchildren. No mention of the landfill. No mention of the Russian Mafia, either. But then, Mia mused, there never is.

Mia was sitting in her living room, Buddy at her feet, reading the obituary online. Outside, the sun had dipped below the horizon, all that was left, a thin orange line, helpless against the pressing darkness.

The chickens had been tended to and the sheep were in the barn for the night. Mia toyed with what her next step should be. She still hadn't heard from Allison or Vaughn, and Jason hadn't called her back.

Mia printed off the information she'd found on the Internet. The location of the landfill, the number for its corporate offices. And a series of articles tracking the history of the Mob in Scranton, including a statement by one local official that after the death of Vladimir Tarasoff, Katerina's father, the Mob's connection to the region had died, too.

It certainly *seemed* like the family kept a lower profile these days. Katerina's oldest son, Nicholas, along with his father, Andrei, ran the family business. The rest of Katerina's children had moved away. The daughter lived in New York City, one son was living in California and the youngest, Benjamin, resided near Allentown, Pennsylvania with his wife, where he was a professor of engineering. She'd make a visit to his university tomorrow morning. Maybe Mr. Benjamin Gretchko could shed some light on the true nature of his father's business.

Allison watched the three men as they finished casing the cabin. Alex looked genuinely worried, Dom seemed angry, and the third man had a take charge demeanor that rivaled even Dom's domineering persona.

After psyching herself up, Allison took a deep breath and walked through the front entrance. Vaughn agreed to stay behind, watching from outside in case anything happened.

"Looking for me, gentlemen?"

All three turned toward the door, taken momentarily off guard.

"We thought we might find you here," Alex said. "Jackie said you were asking questions."

Allison nodded. "Maria called me. She said Francesca was being held here against her will."

Dom and Alex exchanged a glance. "Then you haven't heard," Dom said.

"You found Francesca?" Allison asked, feeling suddenly breathless.

Alex shook his head, slowly, back and forth. "No, Allison. Francesca is still missing."

"But Maria said—"

Another look passed between the three men. In the light of Alex's flashlight, Allison got a better look at the third man's face. He was old and wrinkled, with skin like a Shar-pei. His eyes, his nose, his lips—all drooped downward, as though they had given up on the fight against gravity. But there was a cruelty in his hooded eyes that made a chill run down Allison's spine. He stared at her like her father used to, as though he were judging her and she was coming up wanting.

She pushed the negative thought away and said, "Tell me what happened, Alex. I got a call from Maria saying Francesca was being held captive in this cabin. But she's not here. And it doesn't seem like the police have been here, which is odd because I called them."

"So it was her who called them," the third man said to Dom.

"Who is this?" Allison asked. She directed her question to Alex, but it was Dom who answered.

"Reginald. He's helping us look for Francesca."

The man with no online record, Allison thought. The family friend.

"Are you here alone?" Reginald asked.

Allison debated what to say.

She didn't think these men meant her any harm, but it would be better for them to know she wasn't alone. Just in case. "Vaughn is here, too. He's outside, looking around."

Reginald stared first at Dom, then at Alex. He seemed to be weighing something in his mind. Finally he said, "Let's go back to the house. There's nothing more to see here."

As the men walked toward the door, flashlights drawn, Alex shook his head. He looked worn and apologetic, his dark eyes shadowed in the weepy light. She felt an unwelcome jolt when their eyes met.

"I'm sorry you've been pulled into this, Allison," he whispered. "I really am."

"Me, too. I just wish I understood what *this* was."

"Maria is dead. It happened this afternoon at the processing plant." Dom spoke with a steady coldness that made Allison wonder whether it was controlled grief lying under the surface or if he was glad to see his sister gone. "When we saw your car, we thought you might know something."

"The police believe it was an accident," Reginald said. "There was an explosion at the bottling plant. She was trying to fix an industrial steamer and was...well, steamed to death." Reginald spoke the last words with disdain, as though dying in such a manner was somehow uncouth.

"Do you believe it was an accident?" Vaughn asked. He'd been quiet the entire walk back to the house, a quiet that Allison recognized as distrust and suspicion. Now he made no attempt to hide the contempt in his voice.

"We don't know what to believe," Alex said. They were in one of the Benini estate's parlors. Formal furniture. Lace doilies, urine-colored from age. Family portraits lined up along the wall, tributes to ghosts from the past. Allison sat on a Queen Anne chair next to Vaughn who, like a bird of prey on the cusp of flight, balanced on an ottoman. Alex paced by the window. Dom and Reginald sat on the couch, on opposite sides, and Allison noticed that neither looked at the other. The tension in the room was thick.

Somewhere a clock chimed nine o'clock. It was late and Allison was tired. Her head throbbed, and her right food stung where she had stepped on a bramble.

She was trying to process this new piece of information. First, Francesca disappears while traveling with Vaughn. Then Paolo dies within an hour of their visit. And now Maria was dead, having been killed accidentally after speaking with Allison? First Impressions had become an angel of death. The thought spooked her, and she wrapped her arms around her chest, warding off the thought.

"Why aren't the police here?" Vaughn asked.

"They were here earlier. They searched the cabin." Dom said. "Before you were busy trespassing on our property."

"Jackie gave us permission," Vaughn said.

Dom's hand curled into a fist. "Jackie didn't have the *authority—*"

Vaughn matched Dom's body language, stare for stare.

"Gentleman, *please.*" Alex spun around, features twisted in exasperation. "Allison, what, exactly, did my sister say to you when she called?"

Allison relayed the gist of the conversation with Maria, leaving out the bit about the tracking device. Some things were better left untold.

"Did she sound afraid, rehearsed?"

"She sounded," Allison searched for the right word, "rushed. Insistent."

Alex ran a hand through his hair. "What phone number did she use?"

Allison pulled her phone from her bag. Here at the house, she had reception again, and noticed three missed calls from Mia and one from Jason. She gave Alex the mobile number. "I assumed it was Maria's cell. When I attempted to call back, no one answered and there was no voicemail."

Alex peered at the number. "That's Maria's cell." He looked at Dom. "She called at 10:14."

Reginald said, "That answers that question. She must have made the call from the plant."

Vaughn, posture still rigid, said, "Would she even have reception from inside the manufacturing facility?"

Alex nodded. "Good point."

"She could have been outside," Dom said.

"I don't think so," Allison said. "I heard factory-type noises. I'm certain she was inside somewhere."

Allison watched a look pass between brothers. Reginald stood. "I'll check with the police to see if they have any additional information. In the meantime, they may want to talk to you, Ms. Campbell. You should remain in town."

"I was only too happy to talk to them earlier. Remember, it was me who called the police. No one seemed to take me seriously then." She looked from Dom, to Alex and back to Reginald. "Why is that?"

"We have no idea," Dom said.

Without another word, Reginald lumbered out of the room and down the hall. Dom followed. When the other men were gone, Alex finally sat. "I'm sorry, Vaughn. Again. For my brother's behavior."

"He's upset."

"Perhaps. That doesn't excuse his words or his tone." To Allison, Alex said, "Reginald is right, though. You should probably stay in the area in case the police want to talk to you. They seem to think it was an accident, but you know how these things go."

She didn't really, but she was quickly learning,

"You're welcome to stay here," Alex said. His eyes were an open invitation. He seemed to catch himself, though. He looked at Vaughn and said, "Both of you."

That was the last thing they needed: another night at the haunted mansion. Allison replied, "Thank you, but no. If the police want to find us, they know where we live."

Vaughn jumped from the chair and walked to the other side of the room, lingering by a portrait of a younger woman. Plain features. Somber expression. Dead eyes. "Tell me, Alex," Vaughn said, "Now that the others are gone, do *you* think Maria's death was an accident?"

Alex mulled the question. When he spoke, his voice had an ache to it that told Allison there was love between the siblings, despite the apparent conflicts. She believed Alex's current turmoil, wanted to believe he was a good person. His aunt, his father and now his sister. Almost against her will, she found herself wanting to comfort him. But then she reminded herself that everyone in this crazy family was suspect, even the handsome man sitting before her, looking like a young boy whose first dog had died.

"Maria knew her way around animals and machines. If something was broken, Maria could fix it. Do I think she was in there trying to fix the steamer? Absolutely. But if it was ready to blow, she would have known that. So she was either trying to stave off a disaster, or she was set up." He looked at Vaughn and then quickly looked away. "I'd like to say yes it was an accident, because that would be easier. But I'm afraid the answer is no. My sister was shrewd, smart, and very mechanically-inclined. She kept our machinery in top-notch shape."

"So you think she was murdered?"

This time, Alex didn't look away. "I don't know what to think anymore."

It was almost eleven when Allison and Vaughn drove back down the winding Benini driveway.

"You tired?" Vaughn asked.

"Strangely, no."

"Me, either. I saw a twenty-four hour diner about five miles down the road. You in?"

Allison looked down at her grass-stained feet and her soiled clothes. She wanted Brutus's greeting, Jason's shielding embrace, and a good night's sleep. But that would never come tonight anyway. It was too late, and home was three hours away.

"Absolutely," she said, suddenly certain that she wouldn't be sleeping in her bed for a while. "Greasy diner food would be a fitting end to this day."

TWENTY-TWO

The diner was a Greek mom and pop joint named Opa, situated on a busy throughway. Allison and Vaughn arrived at half past eleven. The restaurant had three large dining rooms, but other than a group of rowdy teenagers and a pair of tattooed truckers, the place was empty. An older waitress with a bored smile showed them to a booth.

"Coffee?"

"Hot chocolate," Allison said. "And soup. Whatever you have."

Vaughn said, "I'll have the same. With French fries. And a piece of pie. Blueberry, if you have it."

The woman nodded absentmindedly and walked away, still writing.

Vaughn yawned. "Hot chocolate and soup. Comfort food."

Allison smiled. "My mom used to make hot chocolate when we were little. It was one of her few nods to processed foods. And instead of mini marshmallows, she'd add marshmallow fluff. When my sisters weren't looking, she'd put extra fluff in my mug. She knew how much I liked it." Allison shook her head at the bittersweet memory, one of the few good ones she had of childhood. She felt the tears well up at the thought of her mom, and she smiled apologetically. "It's late and I'm getting sentimental."

Vaughn didn't say anything, but he didn't need to—the warmth in his eyes was enough.

She studied her friend. He always wore an armor of reserve, but this current bearing was different.

Tough. Determined. Edgy. This was Vaughn the fighter, and, if she had to guess, it was this Vaughn who'd survived the years in juvenile detention and his time in a gang.

"I want to get a hotel for the night. If you need to go home to Jamie, I understand. I can rent a car."

"He's fine. I texted Angela. She'll stay."

"She'll tell him what's going on?"

Vaughn's eyes darted toward the truckers. "I'll email him."

"You're keeping him in the dark."

"I'm trying to keep him safe."

"Hiding this from him only makes it worse. He can help."

"You don't get it, do you?" His eyes flashed with anger. "My brother can't run away, Allison. He's a fucking sitting duck, prey for any jackass who wants to make a point. There is only one thing I can do. Understand?"

Allison held his stare and after a moment his gaze softened. "I'm sorry," he said."I guess I'm tired, after all."

"You're not in this alone. We'll figure it out. Together."

He let out a bitter laugh. "Do you believe even one of these people? Because I sure as hell don't. Reginald is a fucking PI? I don't buy that for a second. And those brothers? Dom with his jacked up attitude. And don't think I don't see the way the other one looks at you, like he's itching to score and you're a whole pile of the white stuff. And now that crazy sister is dead. *Dead*, Allison, as in the sun will *not* be coming out tomorrow." He shook his head. "What the hell are we mixed up in this time?"

What *were* they mixed up in this time?

Allison had to think, despite the haze of exhaustion. She combed through her purse until she found a notebook and a pen. "Let's go through what we know so far."

"What we *know*? Jack shit."

Allison flinched. She could feel her blood pressure rising. Not because Vaughn wasn't right, but because this wasn't productive. He needed to focus. And she needed to stay calm. She thought about the questions Jamie would ask, his rational way of dissecting a situation, getting to the crux of what was important.

"One," Allison said, voice firm. "Francesca Benini contacted us because her brother had a stroke and she's next in line to run the business. Two, we learned she hadn't left the house in decades. Three, her family doesn't want her taking over Benini Enterprises."

"Four," Vaughn said, with only the slightest eye roll, "Tammy Edwards' manager calls days after Francesca signs on."

"Which could be totally unrelated," Allison said.

"You said we're just reviewing the facts. And that's a fact."

"Okay, true. Let's go through Francesca first, then Tammy." Allison said, relieved that Vaughn was at least humoring her. She finished writing the first four points in her notebook. "Five, Francesca hinted at family strife and maybe even conflict with shareholders abroad. She referred to 'vultures' on several occasions. She seemed to like, or at least respect, Maria. She was less positive about Dom. I sensed mixed feelings when it came to Alex."

Vaughn nodded. "Six, when I arrived to pick up Francesca, I was late. And I spotted Maria in the woods, spying on me as I drove up the driveway. Francesca didn't like Simone, but seemed okay with Maria." He paused, unraveling his paper napkin from the fork, knife and spoon around which it was wrapped. "How about you? Did you notice anything strange between Maria, Simone, and Francesca?"

Allison thought back to the dinner at the Benini estate. "There was definitely something going on between them." She toyed with the edge of the butter knife, running a finger alongside the dull blade. "And Simone seemed overly...seductive. She gave Alex the Chippendale once-over, was dressed pretty provocatively for a family dinner."

"Think there could be something to that? Maybe an affair?"

"Maybe, but Simone seems to be the one person whose name doesn't keep cropping up."

"That doesn't mean anything."

The waitress arrived. Allison eyed the whipped cream overflowing the mug of hot chocolate and decided that calories didn't count when you were in the midst of a murder investigation. Because suddenly this had become a murder investigation.

When the waitress was gone, Allison said, "Seven, Francesca disappeared from a truck stop near Wilkes-Barre. She gave no indication to you beforehand that she was scared or upset. And she didn't have a mobile phone."

"Right," Vaughn said between mouthfuls of minestrone soup. "And no one we spoke to admitted seeing a woman who fit Francesca's description."

Allison glanced down at her notes. She was bothered by Francesca's disappearance for a number of reasons, but one thing really stuck out to her. "You never discussed stopping at that particular truck stop beforehand? No one at the house knew you were going there?"

"We didn't even know we were going there until we did."

"And you don't think you were followed?"

Vaughn put down his spoon. "I wasn't expecting any problems, so I suppose we could have had a tail and I didn't realize it."

"Do you remember seeing a white Honda?"

Vaughn shook his head. "Even if I had been followed, whoever was following me would have to be pretty savvy. The truck stop was crowded, and Francesca is small and nondescript. Unless there was a tracking device on my car, like Maria said. Or on Francesca."

"Or in her bags. What if someone had put a tracking device in her purse or her suitcase. Did she have a bag with her when she went into that rest area?"

Vaughn considered this. "I think she took her purse."

"Can you describe it?"

"Square. Black, plain. Not too big." He gestured with his hands. "And stuffed. She kept it by her feet in the car."

"Something that could hold papers?" Including whatever papers Alex had been looking for.

Vaughn shrugged. "You think she was bringing more stuff?"

"Maybe," Allison said. "And maybe someone didn't want her to pass papers along. Someone who put a tracking device on your car or one in her bag."

Vaughn's brow creased. "That would mean someone in the Benini family is involved."

"Not necessarily. That's a big property, and it abuts state game lands. It's possible someone could have hiked in and put a device on the BMW."

"But what about her purse? That would have to be an inside job."

"A device in her purse is just a hypothetical. If one had been on your car, whoever was tracking you could have followed Francesca to the bathroom."

"Especially if they already knew what she looked like," Vaughn said. "Like a family member."

"You seem stuck on the family."

"My dad was an abusive alcoholic, Allison. I know dysfunctional. But the Beninis are *weird*. Yes, I'm stuck on the family."

Allison thought of Alex and his innocent-sounding questions. She thought of Dom and his demeaning personality. She thought of seductive Simone and cantankerous Maria. What a cast of characters. "Yeah," she sighed. "Me, too."

Vaughn ate a French fry, chewing slowly, clearly thinking about something. He snapped his fingers. "There was one more thing about the day I picked up Francesca. She had that purse and the three large suitcases—the suitcases we dropped off when we came here last time."

Allison looked at him questioningly over a spoonful of soup. "So?"

"So I forgot about the fourth bag. It was small, probably a toiletries case. Black, unlike those red bags—which is why it stood out. I don't remember seeing it when we pulled the big cases from the car."

"Could Francesca have taken it with her?"

"It's possible. She brought it out to the car. I'm not sure what she did with it after that."

"Worth checking your car again. Maybe you missed it."

Vaughn nodded, still looking pensive. The waitress returned to check on them. When she was gone, he said, "And then there's Gina, Dom and Alex's mother. Her name scrawled in that bathroom. You never told the Benini boys about that."

"No, and I won't. If someone in the family is involved, that will set off an alarm. Francesca—if it was Francesca—wrote that for a reason. Although I wish we knew what the other words were."

"Here you go." The waitress returned with Vaughn's pie. He stuffed a few French fries in his mouth and, without waiting for the waitress to leave, said, "And you didn't even list the white Honda, Maria's call, or Paolo's death."

Allison jotted them in her notebook. "And Reginald Burr, the PI."

"Him, too."

Allison considered what she'd written. "I can't shirk this feeling that the present situation was linked to the family's past. Gina's name has come up multiple times. Why? And who are these vultures Francesca was talking about? We need to understand the history of not just the company, but the family."

Vaughn stared down at his now-empty plate. "You want Jamie to do it." It was a statement, not a question, and Allison could hear the pain in his voice. Her resolve softened.

"Not if you don't want him to get any more involved, Vaughn."

Vaughn nodded, but didn't commit. "And what about Tammy?"

What about Tammy? Events of the last few days were catching up with her, and her whole body longed for bed. Allison put cash on the table next to her notebook, then forked a bite of Vaughn's blueberry pie. "That's the million dollar question. Is Tammy Edwards connected at all?"

TWENTY-THREE

Benjamin Gretchko was listed on Middletown University's website as the Department Head of Biomedical Engineering. When Mia called to obtain his summer teaching schedule, she chose not to mention the real reason for her call, preferring to insinuate that she was a benefactor with a desire to help out the Engineering Department. With that as her altruistic goal, Mr. Gretchko's administrative assistant was only too happy to accommodate her request.

And so Mia found herself at the University on Wednesday morning waiting outside of a lecture hall amidst a sprinkling of young men and women in wrinkled cotton clothes and athletic shoes. For her part, she'd dressed for the role.

She took a certain pride in the fact her black Gucci pants suit, long forgotten in the back of her closet, still fit. If anything, it was a little loose around the waistline.

Mia sat on a wooden bench in the solarium, next to a bespectacled teen wearing micro shorts, a fuchsia tank top and flowered flip-flops. The girl gave her only a cursory glance before returning to the e-reader she'd been staring at.

Within seconds, Mia flashed to thoughts of her own daughter, Bridget, and felt anger wash over her. Who decided this girl should have a future, that she should graduate and go on to work and have kids, when her Bridget was denied all of that? The cruel die cast by a random universe? Or the act of a higher being, made even crueler because it was intended?

Damn it, Mia, she thought. This girl is someone's daughter. And here you are thinking thoughts that you should be ashamed of. Mia looked at the kid again. She noticed a baseball-size bruise on her calf, the way her foot shook up and down as she read, a pimple next to her left ear. And like that, Mia's anger was gone.

But not the ache. The ache, she was sure, would never go away.

She didn't have time to dwell, though, because in the next second, Professor Gretchko's class let out. Mia waited until the thin crowd of students had disbanded before walking into the lecture hall. It was set up stadium style, and one lone student was still collecting his notebooks, an eye on the teacher. For his part, the teacher seemed lost in thought, a binder in front of him, a frown on his face.

"I don't know, Jacob," Gretchko called to the student. "I don't think your equation will work. Maybe if you replace—" He stopped when he saw Mia standing there. His face registered surprise, then wariness.

He wouldn't know who I am, Mia thought. But I know he is Katerina's son.

He looks just like her.

"So how did you say you knew my mother?"

"I didn't," Mia responded. She'd dropped the façade when she noticed the look of distrust that immediately clouded Benjamin's open face. He had his mother's thin, blonde hair and hooked nose, but his eyes were kind, lacking the squint of spitefulness that, to Mia, had been Katerina's trademark. Mia asked to treat him to coffee. He said no at first, but, perhaps sensing her resolve, eventually nodded and said he could spare fifteen minutes.

Mia took a sip of tea—a lukewarm Earl Grey that required an extra packet of sugar to give it any flavor at all—and glanced around the cafeteria. Other than a few students and one pot-bellied man who was wolfing a Hot Pocket down with fervor, they were alone.

"Katerina was my client. In a former life, I was an image consultant." Mia looked up from her tea and found Benjamin studying her intently with a mix of curiosity and guardedness. "Your mother went through a mid-life crisis. Your father hired me to help her. He thought she needed a job. That perhaps she was bored."

Some unwelcome emotion flashed in Benjamin's eyes. He half-smiled wistfully, looked away in the direction of two Asian students across the room. "That was my mother. Nothing was ever enough. When life was its most peaceful, she would create a problem. Just to add some drama." He took a swallow of coffee and wiped his mouth daintily with a white paper napkin. "She never did get a job."

"No, she didn't. For three months, your father paid a driver to bring her to me. Every week. My office was near Philadelphia, so it was a hike for her. At first she was excited about the possibilities. She especially loved the fashion consultations. Back then, much of my business was about fashion. How to dress more glamorously, that kind of thing."

"My mother was always fashionable."

"Indeed, she was. But I think she liked being able to tell her friends that she was working with a professional, someone from the big city. It made her feel different. Special. Wealthy." Mia regarded him, to see if she'd caused offense. "I don't mean to disparage your mother, Benjamin—"

He waved her concern away with a flourish of his hand. "Please. I know how my mother was."

Mia nodded, took a sip of tea. Maybe this man had perspective on his parents. Not everyone did.

"You said 'at first.' I'm assuming that eventually my mother became bored, even with you."

Mia sighed. "Don't be too tough on her. Making over your image, and I think deep down that's what your mother wanted, can be hard. Very hard. It's not about putting lipstick on a pig, as my son used to joke, but rather about digging deep, identifying the beauty inside and bringing that forward."

"My mother wanted to slap lipstick on the pig?"

"Perhaps."

They sat in edgy silence for a moment. Mia was remembering Katerina, with her blond twists and her jealous streak. What would it have been like to grow up under her rule? She was probably as capricious and cruel a mother as she had been a client. More so. Mia could walk away. And walk away she had. When it had become clear that Katerina was no more interested in real change than she was in ending world hunger, Mia let her go.

She'd tired of Katerina's tart tongue and hellacious mood swings. Suggesting to Andrei Gretchko that Katerina needed a psychologist, not an image consultant, she'd quit. And for months she'd been nervous. It was never a good idea to piss off the Mob.

Oh, Mia had known who she was dealing with. When Katerina was feeling mean, she'd often let Mia know of her connection to the Russian Mob. Mia looked at the man across from her now, wondering how much he knew.

The sad tilt of his eyes, the defeated set of his mouth, the shoulders hunched by weight and worry...maybe he did know. Family could be a blessing—or a burden.

Finally, Benjamin said, "So why are you here, image consultant from the Main Line?"

"*Former* image consultant."

He smiled sadly. "*Former* image consultant. What could you possibly need from me twenty years later?"

"Information."

"More specifically?"

Mia toyed with how much to say. She'd been playing this in her mind all morning and half of the night before. Sleuthing was not her forte, but getting people to talk was. "Your family's business."

"I don't have any connection to the business."

"That's fine, Benjamin. I don't want to know about you. I want to know about them."

Benjamin sighed. "Look, if you want information on the landfill, call my brother or my father, I'm sure they'd be only too happy to talk to you."

Ignoring the sarcasm, Mia said, "I don't want to talk to them. I don't even know if the landfill is relevant." She hesitated, then decided to trust her instinct, which said that Benjamin had no family loyalty left. "A friend's daughter is missing. Her father works at the landfill. There are other connections to your parents' business, too. I remember your mother telling me—"

"That it was run by the Russian Mob." His face had hardened, but it was fear, not cruelty, that narrowed his eyes and set his jaw. "That was then, Mrs. Campbell. Now it's a legitimate business."

"Really?"

Benjamin Gretchko stared right into Mia's eyes and said, "Really." But it was the defiant look of a little boy trying to fool a narcissistic mother. Mia was neither narcissistic nor easily fooled. And a man with eyes as kind as Benjamin's could not readily lie.

After the deed was done, Benjamin's gaze shifted to the left. He squirmed in his seat, balled his napkin. "Is there anything else?"

Mia didn't move. "I got what I needed."

Without looking at her, Benjamin said, "I remember you, you know. I didn't at first, but I do now."

Mia smiled. "Really?"

He nodded. "I was off from school one day, sick with a bad cold. I was ten. Mother brought me with her to the appointment. You ordered me hot soup and gave me a couch to lie down on."

Ah, yes. Mia vaguely remembered the tow-headed boy, so beaten down by life already. She hadn't realized it was this son. Those were Katerina's early meetings, when she was still enthusiastic and on her best behavior. Still, she had dragged a sick child to Philadelphia to talk about dressing for a job she never intended to get.

Mia smiled warmly. "I remember. You were a good boy."

Benjamin's look was melancholy. He stood, turned to go, and then thought better of it. "Thomas Svengetti. Look him up. He lives in Gouldsboro now, in the Poconos. Don't tell him I sent you. Don't tell anyone."

Mia thanked him. "Will you be alright?" she said. Suddenly, he looked unsteady on his feet. She was worried he would topple over.

"I'll be fine, Mrs. Campbell. But take of yourself, okay?"

Mia watched the man walk out of the cafeteria, the professorial air replaced by hunched shoulders and an awkward gait. Again she wondered at the vagaries of fate. How could such a good kid be born to a tyrant like Katerina Tarasoff?

Injustices never ceased.

It was ten o'clock before Allison met Vaughn in the hotel's small dining area. She'd taken advantage of the free breakfast and was picking at a banana, a strawberry yogurt, and a cup of coffee. She'd spent the last two hours rearranging client appointments and arguing with a very angry Jason. He'd taken care of Brutus the night before but was irate that she and Vaughn had headed to Ithaca once again.

"Really, Al, you didn't learn your lesson the last time when you were nearly killed?" he'd said, referring to her brush with the Main Line murderer earlier that year. "Leave this one to the professionals."

"Tried that. The professionals didn't seem too interested."

"Try again." He'd slammed the phone down after an exasperated, "My God, Allison, you're impossible."

He had a right to be angry. They were on dangerous ground. But she'd come this far. She really didn't think she had a choice.

Vaughn sat down across from her. He was wearing the same khaki pants and button-down blue shirt he'd had on the day before. At least his clothes look clean, Allison thought. She was also wearing the same outfit—something she intended to fix as soon as they could stop at a store—and her clothes were filthy. The hotel had no cleaning service and a rinse in the sink clearly had not been enough.

"Good morning," Vaughn said. He dove right into a plate of reconstituted eggs. He'd had a stack of papers next to him, and these he pushed across the table toward her as he chewed. "From Jamie."

So he had contacted Jamie after all, Allison thought. She accepted the stack with a smile. "Anything good?"

"I haven't had a chance to read everything. He sent me the email a half hour ago. I just printed these papers in the hotel's excuse for a business office."

Allison sipped hot coffee and paged through the documents. "These are mostly on Benini Enterprises. Tax forms, corporate filings."

"You wanted information about the Italian shareholders. And the board members."

"Yes, thank you. Anything of importance?"

"A lot of numbers. Jamie said he would scour everything, too, and he's still looking at the company. But he wanted to give us these in the meantime."

Allison turned to the last few pages. One was a photocopy of a wedding announcement for Gina and Paolo Benini. It was in Italian. An old, grainy photograph showed a cherub-faced, very young and very plain woman wearing a simple white gown and a white veil, her hair peaking from beneath in smooth tendrils. Paolo stood next to her, tall, thin and dapper in his tuxedo. Although it was a formal portrait and old-fashioned, even for the early 1950s, their bodies touched in a way that suggested they were happy about the union. Allison stared at that photo. Again, she saw Dominic reflected in his mother's eyes and slightly bulbous nose. She saw Maria and Alex in Paolo's intelligent and defiant stare.

This was the same woman in the portrait that graced the Benini parlor, although that woman had looked solemn, serious. She wondered what happened to Gina between the time this picture was taken and the day she decided to end her own life. What could have been so bad?

The last paper was simply a print-out of an email from Jamie to Vaughn. It said, "Gina Benini, nee Pittaluga, originally from Genoa. Married at 18 (Paolo was 26). Moved to the United States two years later. Dominic was born in 1963 when Gina was 25. Alex was born three years later in New York State (at home). Gina died on January 8, 1979 at the family's home in Ithaca, New York. Death ruled a suicide."

Allison looked up. "Do you know where Jamie found that?"

"He didn't say."

"Hmm. When did Francesca move to the United States?"

"I don't know the year, but she was young. Still a teenager. Seventeen or eighteen."

"Interesting." Allison looked at the information again. Her mind sidled sideways, assembling bits of information, creating a story she wasn't yet ready to posit aloud.

"There's more." Vaughn took out his phone, tapped it a few times and handed it to Allison. It was a text from Angela sent at 2:46 that morning. It said: "John and Enzo Pittaluga" and gave an address.

"Relatives?"

Vaughn nodded. "Gina's brothers. Her parents had ten kids, nine boys and Gina. Two of her brothers immigrated to the United States shortly after Gina did. They were older than Gina and are very old now. One is eighty-eight, the other ninety-two, but they live together on a small farm not far from here."

"Our first stop, then," Allison said. "After I read through corporate paperwork." She looked down at her grass-stained pants. "And after we buy some new clothes."

TWENTY-FOUR

As they drove through the farmland region of the Finger Lakes, Allison stared out the window like a child seeing the countryside for the first time. Her family never vacationed. Her father had worked two jobs most of his adult life, and her mother suffered from debilitating migraines and then Alzheimer's. As a result, there was never time or money for something as frivolous, in her parents' view, as a family trip. But from a young age, Allison would pore over books, reading about faraway lands and interesting locales, and one of the places she had always longed to visit as a kid was a farm. A real, working farm. Seduced, perhaps, by books like *Charlotte's Web* and *Anne of Green Gables*, she'd envisioned farm life to be idyllic, a place where fathers didn't beat kids, mothers weren't always sick, and there were plenty of secret hideaways.

The Pittaluga farm looked like the farm of her childhood fantasies.

Situated on a hundred acres twenty-two miles outside of Ithaca, the property was a patchwork of mowed fields and corn crops. A barn, freshly painted a deep red, sat on a hill overlooking a pasture. The house itself was a white Victorian.

Not large, but neat and well-maintained, with a wrap-around porch. A porch swing hung from two I-hooks on one end, next to two white wicker chairs. Flowerpots dotted the porch, their ceramic interiors overflowing with festive red, pink and white geraniums and trailing vines of vinca.

"Wow," Vaughn muttered. "Either these guys have found the secret to longevity or they are paying someone a lot of money to take care of things."

Allison had to agree. The grass around the house was a well-manicured green. Perennial flower gardens had been planted along the walkway from the driveway to the house, and waves of brightly-colored perennials lined the front of the home, against the porch. The trees surrounding the house, now in full summer glory, provided restful shade. As they climbed the porch steps, Allison admired the view. Farmland in every direction, hills in the distance. Overhead, the sky was blue and the sun, vibrant. Here, it was almost possible to forget that two clients were missing and one woman was dead.

Almost.

Vaughn knocked on the screen door. After a few moments, a woman in her early sixties answered the door.

She said, "Can I help you?"

The woman was slender, with wispy white hair and hard eyes that stared at them with suspicion.

Vaughn said, "We're looking for Enzo or John Pittaluga."

"For what purpose?"

"Just to talk," Allison replied. "We have a few questions about a relative of theirs."

The woman continued to stare at them through the screen door. She had one hand on the storm door, which she looked ready to close, when a deep, thickly-accented voice behind her said, "Let them in, Carol."

The woman pursed her lips in disapproval, but she opened the door and moved aside. Allison entered an immaculate foyer. The walls were pristine white, the floors, gleaming oak. Behind Carol was a stairway, its risers also white, the center lined by a rich Persian runner. To Carol's right, the foyer entered into the dining room. An antique-looking walnut table and matching buffet took up most of the room. The walls were painted ecru, a crystal chandelier had been hung over the table. To Carol's left, blocking much of the entrance to a nicely appointed, albeit old-fashioned, living room, stood a short but very rotund—and very old—man. He had white-yellow, bristly hair, cropped short, a sallow complexion and eyes so dark they looked like pools of ebony.

"Who are you?" he said. He was holding a cane, despite impeccable posture.

Allison introduced herself and Vaughn. "We'd like to talk about your sister, Gina Benini."

The man looked at her for a long time, shifting his gaze back and forth between her and Vaughn. Carol had moved to the dining room, and Allison caught her staring at the man, her eyes searching for some indication that she should show these strangers out. But he surprised Allison by saying, his voice hearty, "I'm Enzo Pittaluga, Gina's brother. Come into the parlor. Carol, some iced tea for these people, please."

Carol nodded, a sour expression still on her face. She gave them a distrustful once-over before heading toward what Allison assumed was the kitchen.

Allison and Vaughn followed Enzo. He made his way slowly but steadily to a pair of deep green loveseats in the living room. The couches were positioned across from one another, in front of a stone fireplace, with a floral Queen Anne chair at the end between them. Enzo sat on one couch, Allison on the other, and Vaughn on the chair. Carol returned a few minutes later with three glasses of iced tea on a tray. She placed the tray on a black coffee table and disappeared quietly into another room.

"Our nurse, housekeeper, security guard. Carol does it all. But she can be overly protective. She means well." Enzo smiled. Allison saw capped teeth, gleaming white. He took a sip of tea, put the glass back down and said, "So you want to talk about Gina? All these years and someone wants to talk about Gina." He looked at Allison. "What do you want to know, my dear? And if I might ask, why do you want to know?"

Allison debated how much to say, but realized there was little point to being coy. "I'll start with the why, Mr. Pittaluga. Francesca Benini is my client. Francesca disappeared last week under suspicious circumstances. Her niece, Maria Benini, died yesterday. While Maria's death looks like an accident, it seems awfully coincidental. Anyway, both ladies mentioned your sister. We don't know if there is a connection, or if there is, what it could be. We're just trying to understand what happened to Gina. Her life in the States and the circumstances surrounding her passing."

"Passing. Such a euphemism, Ms. Campbell. And you can call me Enzo, by the way." He looked at Vaughn. "You both can."

"She took her own life?" Vaughn asked.

"She did, indeed."

"Any idea why?" Allison said.

Enzo toyed with his cane, passing it back and forth between two meaty hands. "Gina moved here first. She was our younger sister. Our parents thought maybe she needed some family, so they sent John—my brother—and me to the States, too. When we arrived, we found our sister had aged considerably. She was only eighteen when she married Paolo, in her twenties when we saw her next. She and Paolo had tried for years to have a child and it didn't work, she was upset. She felt like a failure, a bad wife."

"But she did conceive. Twice," Allison said.

"Ah, eventually, yes. But imagine the pressure, Ms. Campbell. Paolo was a good man, but his grandmother was a tyrant. She wanted an heir. It was only Francesca and Paolo and when it became apparent that Francesca would never marry—not that the daughter was as important, especially back then—the responsibility fell to Paolo." Enzo shook his head. "And in the ways of many families, it was the wife, not the husband, who was blamed when no child was produced."

Vaughn looked skeptical. "But Gina was only around forty when she took her own life. By then, her youngest at least ten. She'd achieved her goal—heirs for the Benini estate. Not one, but two male children."

"The years in between had taken their toll. They'd tried for seven years to have their first child, Mr. Vaughn. Do you have any idea how much abuse she took in that interim?"

"Physical abuse?" Allison asked.

"No, subtle abuse. Mental, emotional."

"By Paolo?"

"I believe he loved Gina. In fact, I think Gina was his true love, if you believe in such things. He was a weak man." He let out a sad sigh. "He just couldn't make her happy."

Vaughn said, "But Paolo's grandmother was in Italy. How could she have affected her here?"

Enzo turned his body to look at Vaughn. "My sister was a child when she married. My parents were old-fashioned. Peasants, really. They brought her up to believe she was good for one thing: child-rearing. Her sole purpose in life was to marry and bear children." He turned toward Allison, smiled apologetically. "I'm sure that sounds absurd by today's standards, but back then...well, it was the norm. Have you been to the Benini home?"

Allison nodded.

"Then you know how big it is. It would be easy to get lost, to feel lonely in that house. And she was there by herself, feeling dejected and like a failure, for seven long years. Constant questions, constant pressure. No one to confide in. And she was young. So young."

"She had you and your brother," Allison said.

"We were close enough, but not in that way. And Paolo was growing the business here in America. As a consequence, he was rarely home. I'm sure my sister felt restless, a caged animal used for breeding and failing even at that."

A caged animal. Like Francesca?

"Still," Vaughn shook his head, skepticism in his eyes. "She killed herself more than ten years later."

"She was depressed. She hadn't received treatment. It happens."

Allison said, "Enzo, when Francesca arrived, did that help alleviate her loneliness? Were they close?"

"Yes and no." A look passed over his face. "Francesca was very young. Barely seventeen when she showed up at the Benini estate, another casualty of Antonia Benini, the grandmother. Francesca helped care for the two boys, but in the beginning, especially, she was yet another burden on Gina, who by then was older and used to being in charge. Of the house, at least."

The look on Enzo's face, one of unspoken stories, made Allison say, "There's more."

"You're very perceptive, Ms. Campbell. There's always more, of course. These are stories passed through the filter of an old man's brain. And don't let this handsome façade fool you. I'm almost ninety."

Allison smiled. "I'll keep that in mind. And it's Allison, please call me Allison."

"Allison, Francesca was hated by her grandmother, but adored beyond belief by her father and her brother, Paolo. In their eyes, she could do no wrong. And in her younger years, she was quite lovely."

A sudden glimmer in Enzo's eye made Allison wonder if there had not been more there. Perhaps a love affair between a younger woman and a debonair older man, for she believed Enzo was probably quite the catch in his younger years. Allison's mind flashed to Alex and she felt a flush creep across her face. She looked down before Vaughn or Enzo could notice.

"So Gina was angry and jealous?" Vaughn asked.

"No." Enzo sighed. "That was not Gina's way. Her way was to internalize, play the role of the martyr. My sister could be very passive aggressive. I'm sure she did her best to show Francesca she was neither welcome nor wanted."

Allison thought about that. A big, isolated house. Sisters-in-law vying for the attention of one man. Nothing to do but wander those halls and dote on two small boys. Such a limiting life.

"And you," Allison said. "Were you there often?"

"John and I went when we were invited. Not frequently, I'm afraid."

"Did you get along with Paolo?"

Enzo smiled. Suddenly, he looked tired. Tired and old. "Everyone got along with Paolo. That was his gift."

His words echoed those spoken by Alex about his aunt. Allison didn't have time to ponder that because Carol came into the room, a striped apron tied around her waist. "Excuse me for interrupting, but John's awake."

"Ah, yes." Enzo struggled to his feet with the help of the cane. "I'm afraid this visit will have to come to a close. My brother is not well. I need to attend to him. Carol will see you out."

Allison watched him disappear through the dining room and into whatever rooms existed beyond. Carol followed them back out onto the porch, shooing them along like she would an unwanted stray dog.

Once on the porch, Vaughn pointed to the corn fields. "Do Enzo and John take care of the fields?"

Carol shook her head. "No, no. The land is subleased to a local farmer. The brothers used to do a little farming themselves, but not much."

"What else did they do? For a living?" Vaughn asked. "This is an impressive piece of property."

"They owned a local bakery. John was a genius in the kitchen in his time. Enzo, a keen businessman."

"A bakery, huh?" Vaughn said.

"Fireside Bakery," Carol said. While it was clear she wanted to end the conversation, she couldn't keep the admiration out of her tone or her eyes. "Best bread for thirty miles. And Italian pastries like you wouldn't believe."

"And they never married?" Allison asked.

Carol's eyes stormed over. That stern expression was back. "Never. The brothers are devoted to one another." She frowned, started to close the door. "I have food on the stove. Enjoy your day."

As they climbed back into Vaughn's BMW, Allison took one last look around. Carol was watching from the dining room window, waiting for them to leave in spite of her cooking. But it was another face that caught Allison's attention.

Upstairs, curtains had been pulled aside, and a man was watching them pull out of the driveway.

An old, old man with a face like a mask.

TWENTY-FIVE

Thomas Svengetti had gone to some lengths to stay out of sight. Mia would have tried calling first, but Svengetti's number was unlisted, so Mia had relied on a paid background check, which only provided an address. She wasn't even sure it was the correct address. Google Maps led her to the top of a mountain in the Poconos, to a long dirt driveway that snaked from a rural route into the woods.

Mia idled her truck and debated what to do. She'd come this far, although no one—not even Jamie—knew she was here. And did she really know whether Benjamin Gretchko was trustworthy? But if the landfill and the Gretchko family were dead ends, she wanted to know that up front. Based on Benjamin Gretchko's reactions, she was pretty certain that the family still had Russian Mafia ties. And she wasn't sure who Svengetti was, although she had a hunch, but if the dearth of public information about the man's current whereabouts was any indication, he was keeping a low profile for a reason.

After a few minutes, Mia shifted from neutral to first and started up the driveway. The trees formed a canopy so dense that all light was blocked, making the dirt road nearly impossible to navigate. She flicked on her headlights and sat forward in her seat, trying to watch the winding path before her for fear she'd derail into the woods. She was thankful that the Toyota had four wheel drive.

At the top of a steep embankment, dirt gave way to pebbles and the driveway entered a small clearing. A turnaround and a wood pile the size of a small house, its contents neatly stacked, were on one side of the clearing.

On the other side stood a trailer home. Its vinyl exterior, once white, was now a mottled gray. A white Toyota pick-up, not much different than her own, was parked next to the house, facing the road. Ready for a quick getaway?

Mia noticed the hum of a window air conditioner. She looked at the turnaround. No fresh tracks. So Svengetti's home, Mia thought. Or someone is.

She took a deep breath, willing herself calm, and climbed out of the car. She'd worn jeans and a plain black sleeveless blouse, and her wild curls were pulled into a tidy twist. Neat and nondescript. She pulled her bag closer to her body and made her way toward the door. Mia was three feet away when the front door slammed open. She stopped, frozen.

A male voice said, "What do you want?"

He stepped into the light. In his early sixties, the man had a neatly-trimmed beard and full head of graying brown hair, also carefully cut. Fit and tall, he wore a plaid flannel shirt, despite the summer heat. But most noticeable of all was the pistol he held in his hand, pointed at her.

"Who are you?" he demanded. His voice was rough, hoarse, with the raw edge of someone who didn't spend much time talking. "Goddamn it, answer me."

With incredible effort, Mia found her voice. "My name is Mia Campbell. I'm here to talk about the Kremsburg landfill and the Gretchko family."

"Go away." The man started to slam the door, seemed to think better of it, and pulled it open again. "Who sent you?"

"Nobody."

"Nobody? Then how did you find me?"

"I was researching the Gretchko family. Someone mentioned your name. I can't tell you who. I traced you here."

"I don't talk to journalists."

"I'm not a journalist." Mia dropped her purse and held up her hands palms down and open, heart hammering. "Please. If you could put the gun down, Mr. Svengetti. Truly, I want nothing from you other than to talk. A girl is missing. Only eighteen. I know what it is to lose a daughter, I just want to help." Mia's words came out in a tumbled rush. She saw Vaughn, the echoes of past terror in his eyes. She thought of Jamie, of the fact that justice did not always serve those most deserving of its salve. And she forced herself to hold this man's stare even if every nerve in her body said *run*.

And when she looked up at Thomas Svengetti, she saw distrust and fear, but also pain. This was a hurting man, and that tugged at the part of her that was irreconcilably wounded, too.

"Please," she said again.

Svengetti sighed. "Fine, I've got nothing else on my social calendar today. Your purse stays outside. And you need to open your shirt. I want to make sure you're not wired."

Well, that's a new one, Mia thought to herself. But she unbuttoned her blouse and pulled it to the side, showing him a lavender bra and a bare midriff.

He nodded brusquely. "If you know anything about me, *Mia Campbell*, you know that people around me tend to drop like flies. You're taking a risk just being here."

Svengetti swung the door out, then followed her inside. The trailer was tiny. Mia entered the living room. One brown recliner, a small folding table, and a flat-screen television on the wall. A brownish rug covered the floor, its piling rubbed bare in spots. A half-wall separated the living room from the dining area, which consisted of a small table and one chair.

A galley kitchen looked scrubbed and outdated. That was her overall impression of the trailer: clean, drab, and old.

Svengetti pulled the dining room chair into the living room. "Sit down." He motioned to the recliner, but Mia opted for the dining room chair. He sat on the edge of the recliner, alert and poised to move. "So, what brought you here? You don't look like a lady from these parts."

Mia smiled. "I'm helping a friend, Mr. Svengetti. Her client is eighteen years old. She disappeared last week. No one has heard from her. Her parents don't know where she is."

He shrugged. "So what does that have to with me? With the landfill?"

"Her father works there. And so does her boyfriend's father."

"So?"

Mia pulled out the papers Jamie had given her on Scott Berger's record. She handed them to Svengetti. "So something smells. The parents don't want police involved, the boyfriend's father has a mile-long record with minimal time spent in prison, and things keep leading back to the damn landfill."

Svengetti raised an eyebrow. "What do you know about the landfill?"

"Its prior owner, Katerina Tarasoff, was my client once upon a time."

He smiled, but his look was bitter, not happy. "Katerina."

"A real bitch," Mia said, and they both laughed. "So, I know of the family. I know that Katerina's father was a Mob affiliate, and it makes me wonder what, if anything, this girl's disappearance has to do with the Kremsburg landfill operation or the family's business."

"And someone gave you my name?"

She nodded. "Someone no longer connected to the family."

"So you think."

Svengetti stood. For a moment, Mia thought he would ask her to leave. Instead, he went to the refrigerator and pulled out two Michelobs. He opened both, came back into the living room, and handed one beer to Mia. The other he placed on the folding table. Mia thought it a girly choice of beer for a guy like Svengetti, but she decided to keep that particular opinion to herself.

With his back to Mia, he said, "You should stop asking questions, go home, and be done with this nonsense."

"I'm afraid it's too late for that."

"Then you are either very brave or very stupid." He turned back around. "But I am neither. So I need you to tell me three things about yourself that I can verify online using public records."

Mia smiled. "First I need to strip, then I need to give you personal information?"

Not so much as a smirk. "You're free to leave at any time."

Mia glanced out the window, then back at Svengetti, deciding how far to go. "One, I own a fourteen acre farm in Sunnydale, Pennsylvania. The property was sold to me almost five years ago by Mark and Louise Birch. Two, I used to own an image consulting business on the Main Line. If you look, you will still find references. I sold it to Allison Campbell, my then-daughter-in-law, four years ago."

"And three?" Hard eyes bored into Mia's. Unconsciously, she brought her hand to her neck. "My daughter died in a car accident almost five years ago. She was with her father, Edward Campbell. He was drunk. You'll find news articles. It was a human interest story." The last words burned like bile.

"Stay there. But understand I can see you."

Svengetti disappeared into a rear room and came back seconds later with a laptop. He placed it on the dining room table. After a few minutes of painful silence and constant keyboard tapping, he snapped the computer shut.

"You sold the business almost *five* years ago, not four. Otherwise, you check out." He sat back down on the recliner, looking a hair more relaxed. Mia's eyes strayed to an old dog cushion, wedged behind the recliner, against the wall.

Svengetti followed the direction of her stare. "I had a German Shepherd. Rocky. Big, smart dog. He stayed with me at night, but during the day it was everything I could do to keep the damn dog inside. He had an independent spirit. Liked to roam."

Svengetti rubbed his face with one beefy hand. "Rocky's dead, ma'am. He was poisoned. Convulsed to death right outside my house, where that woodpile is."

"I'm so sorry."

"Not as sorry as I. Rocky was my third dog. All poisoned. I have no neighbors for a mile in any direction, no businesses nearby, no factories or streams that would have run-off. How have three of my dogs been poisoned?"

Mia wasn't sure he expected a response. She stayed quiet.

"But that was nothing compared to my Emily. She died three years ago. Car accident. Hit and run. The perp was never found. Know why?"

Mia shook her head.

"Because it was the same fuckers who killed my dogs. Them. The Russians."

"The Russian Mafia?"

He nodded, eyes clouded with grief. Mia said softly, "Were you a police investigator?"

"Retired from the U.S. Attorney's Office. Organized Crime Strike Force."

"Tell me what happened."

"I can't. I can tell you this, the Russian Mob continues to operate in Northeastern Pennsylvania. Don't believe the official bullshit—excuse my French—that the Mafia has been eradicated from the area. The Mob may be keeping a lower profile these days, but they're still around."

"Gretchkos?"

"Gretchkos and any number of others. The landfill is still a money laundering hot spot, I'm sure. It's one of the things the Russians do well, even better than the Italians."

"If the Gretchkos or others are still operating in the region, why is the official bullshit, as you say, that they're gone."

"Because if there is no crime, Ms. Campbell, then there are no criminals to go after."

"And no one wants to mess with the Russians?"

"It's not that simple."

"Then how simple is it?"

Svengetti stood. His tall, broad frame strode across the room, toward the picture window. He kept his back to her. "There was a big clean-up operation years ago. Tarasoff was arrested, his men jailed. After Tarasoff died, his widow and daughter swore that connections to the Russian Mob in New York were finished. Nevertheless, the daughter, Katerina, had married Andrei Gretchko, a wealthy businessman with ties to mobsters in Russia, some of whom go back to the old Soviet Union hierarchy. Since Tarasoff's death, they've kept their noses cleaner. But that just means they've gone further underground."

"In what way?"

"I'm still trying to figure that out."

"I thought you were retired."

Svengetti walked toward the rear of the living room and disappeared into what Mia assumed was his bedroom. During this short conversation, he'd dropped the hick façade and she was now talking to a learned and sharp federal employee. But she smelled desperation. And anger. And she was well aware of what a dangerous combination that could be.

He returned a minute later with a stack of file folders. While he sorted through them, he said, "Used to be just the Italian Mob. Now we have others—Asian, African, Balkan, Russian, Middle Eastern, even youth gangs. Everyone wants in on the action. The Russians often launder for other Mafia groups. The Italians, for one. It's my hunch that Gretchko is still dirty, but he's covered their dealings so well that they're virtually impossible to unearth."

"Is it possible the Gretchko family has gone straight?" Mia asked.

Svengetti snorted. "As likely as the Pope converting to Buddhism."

"Then why aren't the Feds on it?"

"Maybe they are. Maybe there is some tacit agreement to publicly say the Mob is dead in this area so that the Gretchko family and their henchmen will get lazy, soft." He shrugged. "I'm not part of that world anymore, so I don't really know."

Mia pointed to the files. "But you've been busy gathering information."

Svengetti stared at Mia for a moment. His eyes narrowed. "Know what separates the Italian Mafia from the Russians?"

Mia shook her head no.

"Boundaries. Believe it or not, the Mafioso has respect for boundaries, for honor. Generally, they don't go after journalists or prosecutors. There is usually some regard for conventional societal structure."

"Not so with the Russian Mafia?"

"They make the Italians look like nuns. My wife, my dogs? Retribution for my role in putting Tarasoff away. They waited until I was retired, until there didn't seem to be a direct correlation between what was happening to me and my role in the investigation."

"Were others targeted?"

Svengetti shifted his eyes. "Maybe. They're smart. It's hard to know what was an accident and what was connected."

Mia looked at the files, thought about the time that must have gone into researching and following the Mob's activity. She looked around at the tiny trailer, and the simple way Svengetti lived. Looked like Svengetti had a vendetta of his own.

"So, if the Feds have cooled their investigation, and if the Russian Mafia is so cruel and vindictive, why are you still after them?"

Svengetti smiled. His eyes took on a manic glaze. "I have nothing left to lose, Ms. Campbell. *Nothing*." He held up the files. "When I go, my last act will be to bring those fuckers down with me."

TWENTY-SIX

At one-thirty that afternoon, Vaughn received the call they knew was inevitable. They were on their way to the Benini factory where Maria had been killed the day before in the hopes that someone would talk to them. About a mile from the plant, Vaughn's mobile rang. Detective Butch Razinski. He wanted to meet with Vaughn and Allison as soon as possible.

"He's up here, in Ithaca. He suggested a coffee shop a few doors from Moosewood, that vegetarian restaurant. We're meeting at three."

"Did he say anything specific?" Allison asked. Although the look on Vaughn's face said the detective had said enough.

"Nothing that bears repeating." Vaughn glanced at her from across the BMW's interior. He shrugged. "Maybe the police are as stumped as we are."

Or maybe they're not, Allison thought. She gave her friend a reassuring smile. She wished she could do more.

Mia was on a roll. She'd left Thomas Svengetti's house with potential contacts. After an email to Jamie with her whereabouts and a call to a neighbor who agreed to feed the chickens and sheep and let Buddy out of the house, she pulled onto Route 380 and headed west, into Scranton.

First stop was Brian Frist, former IRS agent. A call from Svengetti had secured a thirty minute interview. With a head shake, he'd warned her that the man was surly on a good day. She'd said "thank you" and hugged Svengetti good-bye, surprising herself as much as him. But he'd hugged her back. Two veterans of heartbreak.

Mia found Frist at his office on Wyoming in downtown Scranton. Now a part-time accountant, Frist lived his days quietly helping taxpayers recognize the loopholes in the laws that he'd once enforced. But Frist and Svengetti had worked together on the Tarasoff case, and, according to Svengetti, no one knew more about the family's financial dealings outside of their own accountant.

The second she laid eyes on Frist, Mia knew Svengetti was right. Not a people person. The man mumbled a hello without meeting her eyes. He was a stoop-shouldered fifty-something with a ring of white hair that horse-shoed around a reddened, bald pate. Green checkered pants had been paired with a pressed white button down shirt and a brown tie. A rust-colored mustache hid a thin upper lip.

"Thanks so much for your time, Mr. Frist." Mia held a hand out but was rebuffed. Instead, Frist sat down at his desk. He didn't offer for Mia to sit in the chair across from him, but Mia sat anyway. Frist watched her, his expression taciturn.

"I promised Svengetti I'd give you a half hour of my time. I didn't promise I'd tell you anything."

"Then why bother to meet with me?"

"What do you want to know?"

"Getting down to business already?"

"Half hour, I told you."

Mia smiled. "Wow, once IRS, always IRS."

He stared at her. "What do you want to know?" he asked again.

Mia sighed. "Andrei Gretchko."

Arched eyebrows. Mia thought she saw a flicker of emotion cross those dead eyes. "What about him?"

"If, hypothetically, he still maintained connections to the Russian Mafia, what might Gretchko be doing?"

"Doing?"

"Hypothetically speaking, what could Gretchko—and the landfill—offer the Russian Mafia?"

"I have no idea."

"Svengetti thought you might."

"Svengetti's wrong."

"We're talking hypothetically, Mr. Frist. Where might the Gretchkos fit in the Russian Mob hierarchy?"

Frist sat back, sighed. He examined the precisely-trimmed nails on soft, smallish hands. Finally, he said, "The Russians aren't like the Italians. They don't have a family hierarchical structure, with a boss, underboss, soldiers, etc. It's a much looser structure. This means each unit profits and has a degree of autonomy that the Italian middle men might not enjoy."

"Meaning?"

"Meaning that the Gretchko family could be working autonomously. They don't need to be acting on orders from a higher power."

"Assuming they are still involved in the Mob business. They could have gone straight, right?"

Frist shook his head. "Hypothetically? It's not that easy to walk away."

Mia considered this. If the Gretchkos were still involved in Mob business, what did this have to do with Tammy Edwards? With the Benini family?

"Does the name Benini ring a bell?" Mia asked. "Benini Enterprises?"

Frist frowned. "No, should it?"

"A family-owned business out of New York State. Ithaca."

He shook his head, glanced at his watch.

"How about the name Edwards? Anthony Edwards?"

"Not sure. Don't think so."

Mia tried to remember the name of Tammy Edwards' boyfriend. It started with a K. Ken, Kris, Kyle...Kai. That was it. Kai Berger. "How about Berger? Scott or Kai Berger."

"That name I know. Scott Berger was one of Tarasoff's messengers. Started when he was just a kid. Took the fall for Andrei and Nicholas a few times, too, early on. Petty stuff. They set him up with a business. Feds were convinced that he was laundering. Probably is. But he's been playing it clean for the last couple of years."

"Laundering?"

"You must be familiar with the concept, Ms. Campbell."

"With the concept, yes. With the practice, no."

Frist spoke in a rote, mechanical fashion when he said, "It can take a lot of forms, but the end goal is always the same: converting dirty money into legitimate, clean assets. Organized crime is particularly adept at this. Sometimes mobsters use underground banking, crooked political regimes, or financial institutions. Often, though, they look for legitimate businesses. Or, if they can, they make cash transactions or real estate deals." Frist shrugged. "This has all been made easier by the advent of the electronic age. Transfer of funds across borders happens much more quickly. And once the Feds discover one technique, the bad guys have moved on to another."

"So Scott Berger's bar is a laundering operation?"

"Could be."

"Mr. Frist, a girl is missing. She's eighteen, and the girlfriend of Scott Berger's son, Kai." Mia paused, allowing Frist to follow the change in direction. "What would they want with a young girl?"

For the first time, Frist looked taken off-guard. "Kai Berger's girlfriend?"

Mia nodded. "She disappeared late last week. Friday. Her parents think she ran away, but that doesn't make sense. The girl is a singer, recently scored a spot on America's Next Pop Star. Why run away now?"

Frist stood up. He walked over to a bank of filing cabinets, reached into his pocket and pulled out a set of keys. He opened the bottom drawer of the farthest cabinet, and, squatting, sorted through folders and binders until he found what he was looking for. He pulled a red binder out of the drawer and stood.

Still standing, he read through the binder, stopped, and marked his place with his right pointer finger. "That's what I thought," he muttered. He looked at Mia. "Last year, Kai was arrested. He was caught dumping toxic chemicals into a local creek. Caught red-handed by a cop watching for speeders nearby."

It was Mia's turn to be surprised. "Where did he get the chemicals?"

"Good question. He claims someone paid him to dump them, some unknown guy he met on the street. Needed money so he agreed."

"Not true?"

"I made a note of it, not because I give a special damn about the environment, but because it sounds like someone did pay him to do it. Maybe someone who can make some money disposing of illegal waste."

"By dumping it in local streams?" The idea horrified Mia.

Frist shrugged. "Why not? Compliance with regulations can be expensive. If companies, especially small companies, can get rid of waste cheaper, some will do it. And where there's a market—"

"There's a buyer and a seller."

Frist nodded. "Exactly. You asked what the Gretchkos might be up to. Who the hell knows? When I was with the Service, the Tarasoff family was big into laundering, plus drug trafficking. We ultimately got Tarasoff for tax fraud. That's what landed him in prison."

"But the family could have diversified."

Frist smiled, the first smile Mia had seen since they began this discussion. "Good way to put it." He flipped through the red binder. Without looking up, he said, "But that doesn't explain your missing girl."

"You said you weren't sure if you recognized the Edwards' name. Is there a possibility you have records on Tony Edwards?"

"Nah, don't think so. I'd recall if that were the case." He raised one finger. "But you said this girl is a singer? With Hollywood connections?"

"Yes," Mia said. "America's Next Pop Star."

Frist looked up. He bit his lip, thinking. "Maybe she's worth something on the black market."

Alarmed at the awful implication, Mia said, "Trafficking?"

Frist shook his head, looking pensive. "Forget it. The Gretchkos are bad news, but selling the child of an employee—and that would be their most likely use for an eighteen-year-old girl, if she just disappeared like that—would seem low, even for them. And I never saw anything hinting at trafficking. Although it's not outside the realm of possibilities."

The thought made Mia nauseous. "Unless the Gretchkos were getting back at her father for something," she said.

Frist nodded, put the binder down on his desk. He chewed on his lip again. "I suppose she could have seen something she shouldn't have. Mobsters don't like loose ends." He shook his head. "If that's the case, my condolences. Your girl is a goner." He picked up the file in front of him, turned it over.

"Thanks," Mia said, barely managing to hide her fear and disappointment. She was terrified for Tammy. "I appreciate your time."

"You're welcome, Ms. Campbell. And I gave you an extra eight minutes because your questions were reasonable and you're an acquaintance of Thomas Svengetti. Use the information wisely."

TWENTY-SEVEN

The Benini bottling facility was on the outskirts of town, along a creek that fed into Cayuga Lake. Set back from the main road, its grounds were a rolling vista of green fields and manicured shrubbery, but the building itself was a nondescript vanilla rectangle surrounded by a nearly empty large parking lot. Vaughn pulled in between a silver Saab and an older-model Subaru Impreza. Allison counted nine cars in the lot.

"I guess they're not operating because of what happened to Maria," Allison said. "But someone's here."

Vaughn nodded. "Maybe the plant manager and a few office and maintenance crew."

Allison nodded. She'd been thinking along the same lines. She and Vaughn climbed out of the car and walked toward the front doors. Two empty picnic benches sat in front of the entrance, a metal garbage container with an ashtray lid between them. The ashtray overflowed with butts.

Allison eyed the mess. "Someone's slacking on the job."

"Or there are lots of raw nerves around here."

"Guess there would be." Allison pulled open one of two glass doors that led to the interior. Inside, a tiled reception area contained a half dozen wooden chairs.

A reception window with sliding glass doors faced the entrance. A bottled blond with thick tortoiseshell eyeglasses hanging from a black beaded chain looked surprised to see them.

She said, "Delivery?"

Allison shook her head. She closed the space between the entrance and the receptionist's cubby and held out a business card. "Allison Campbell. My colleague Vaughn and I were hoping to talk to the plant manager."

The woman eyed them with wary indecision. "The plant's closed."

"Is it normally shut down on Wednesdays?"

"No." The woman looked uncomfortable. "There's been an accident. The shutdown was precautionary."

Allison nodded in sympathy. "That's actually why we're here. I was hoping to talk to the plant manager, please, Ms.—"

"Stacy. I don't know if he's even in."

"It's important, Stacy. Please."

The woman's lips tightened into a rigid line. She picked up the phone, dialed five digits and waited. After a second, she said, "Lou, some people are here to see you." After a few seconds of listening and a sideways glance at Vaughn and Allison, she said, "No, not cops." She glanced down at Allison's card, still in her hand. "An image consultant." Looking confused, she said in answer to a question Allison couldn't hear, "I have no idea, Lou. You'll have to ask her yourself."

The woman hung up. "Well, he wasn't expecting that. Give him five. He'll see you."

Five turned into twenty-five, but eventually a thin-faced man in a red Polo shirt bounded out to meet them. He had tiny, beady brown eyes that danced around as much as he did.

"Lou Strickland." He held out a pale hand, knuckles covered in brown fur. "Plant manager." He looked around quickly, eyes shifting from spot to spot. "Plant's down today. Bad day yesterday. Real bad."

Giving the staring receptionist a quick glance, Allison said, "Mr. Strickland, is there somewhere private we can talk?"

"Yeah, yeah. Stacy, we'll be in the lunchroom."

The receptionist nodded as they passed behind reception and into a broad cafeteria-style space. Two refrigerators sat against one wall next to a cabinet with a sink, water dispenser, and two older-model microwaves. Another cabinet on an intersecting wall held three coffee machines, Styrofoam cups and boxes of sugar, artificial sweetener, stirrers, and cylindrical containers of artificial creamer. Three vending machines occupied the other wall. Rows of tables took up the rest of the room. Lou sat down at the table on the end, closest to the door, and gestured for Vaughn and Allison to join him.

"Want something to drink?" he asked, looking ready to spring up at any second.

Vaughn waved a hand. "No, thanks. We just want to ask you a few questions about Maria Benini. About what happened here yesterday."

Lou shook his head rapidly, a gesture of nervousness or habit, Allison wasn't sure. "Yeah, yeah, a tragedy," he said. "Never thought I'd see something like that."

"Can you tell us what happened?" Allison asked.

"Yeah, I guess I can." He shrugged again, the knobs of thin shoulders bobbing underneath his shirt. "I'll tell you what I told the reporters."

"You spoke to reporters already?" Vaughn said.

"Yeah, of course. Today. Small town. People want to know when an accident like this occurs. Bad for business, of course. But we're the main bottler in this area. Even Maria's death won't change that."

"So, the police are sure it was an accident?" Allison snuck a glance at Vaughn, who was looking intently at Strickland. "No sign of foul play?"

"If there was, no one has said." Strickland shook his head, grimaced. "Truth? I question how it happened. Maria is—was—almost a savant when it came to mechanical stuff. She knew how things worked around here. And even though it wasn't her job, she'd fix stuff if required. All kinds of stuff."

Vaughn said, "Was she here every day?"

"Not every day. She came when the mood struck her." He rubbed his eyes, looked away.

Vaughn raised his eyebrows. "Was she on the payroll?"

Strickland started to respond before clamping his jaw shut. He looked back and forth between Allison and Vaughn, grappling with a decision.

Finally, he huffed out a dramatic sigh. "Why are you here?"

With a darting glance at Vaughn, Allison said, "Maria was my client's niece."

"Francesca?" Strickland's eyebrows knitted into a perplexed frown. "Francesca was working with *you*?"

Allison nodded. "Maria called me shortly before she died. She had something to tell me, but she never got the chance. Vaughn and I were surprised to hear about her death."

"You and me both." Somewhere in the plant, metal clanged on concrete and Strickland jumped. "I can't understand how it happened."

Vaughn shifted in his seat. "Was there an explosion, Mr. Strickland?"

"No, not exactly. Maria was in the boiler room, checking out a gas leak. While she was in there, the boiler blew." He shuddered. "I'm afraid Maria didn't have a chance." Closing his eyes against the memory, he shook his head. When he spoke, his voice was heavy with regret. "She was basically steamed to death, Ms. Campbell. Which is why I have to believe it was an accident. Only a soulless being would do something like that."

"Were you here that day, Mr. Strickland?" Allison asked.

Strickland nodded. "I was in an employee meeting when it happened."

"Did you see anyone here who shouldn't have been here?"

"The alarms sounded, it was chaos." Beady eyes bounced between Allison and Vaughn. "I wouldn't be able to tell you if anyone out of the ordinary was here that day. Too crazy."

"How about the family? Dom or Alex?"

"They're usually at the corporate offices."

"So you didn't see them here that day?"

"Not that I recall."

Allison turned to Vaughn. "So no family, other than Maria."

"And Simone."

"Simone? Does she work here?"

Strickland gave a short, raspy snort. "Oh no, of course not!"

"Then why was she here?"

Strickland shrugged. He tried to look nonchalant, but red cheeks gave him away. "To see me, I guess. Sometimes she visits. Just to say hello."

Hammond's Coffee Shop was tucked between a used bookstore and a high-end clothing boutique. The interior was dominated by a large wooden bar with a cash register at one end. Tables sat too close together in the back, next to the bathroom. Allison ordered two coffees and she and Vaughn took a seat against the wall, waiting for Razinski. Next to them, four women chatted about kids, wine, men. Two dark-haired, one blonde and one curly-haired brunette, all forty-something, seemingly happy to be together. Allison tried not to listen to their conversation, but in the tight space, she couldn't help overhearing. It was a lot of talk about nothing, and Allison felt a stab of envy.

She wanted to curl up with Jason and talk a lot about nothing. Not kidnapping, murder, shady business dealings, explosions, just...nothing. But until they could put this one behind them, that wasn't to be. And now that Jason was angry with her, she was afraid it was never to be. So Allison sat, listened, and waited, trying desperately to shove aside her growing anxiety.

Razinski finally showed up fifteen minutes late looking like he'd just swallowed rancid milk. "What the hell do you two think you're doing?" He pulled up a chair, turned it backwards, and without ceremony, plopped down on the empty side of the table. "Talking to the family, traipsing around on private property, asking questions of infirm old men?" Seeing Allison's surprise, he said, "Yeah, that's right, I know about all of it."

Not all of it, Allison thought. She met Razinski's gaze, at the same time placing a calming hand on Vaughn's knee. "Francesca is my client. Last I checked, I wasn't doing anything illegal by asking questions. And as for the Benini estate, we had permission to be there."

"You're interfering with a police investigation."

Allison worked hard at not rolling her eyes. "Funny, when we last spoke, you weren't actively investigating Francesca's disappearance because there were no—and I quote—'suspicious circumstances.'"

Razinski looked down at his hands. Allison saw fingernails chewed to the quick, peeling cuticles. Something had Razinski on edge, something other than a disappearance lacking any hint of *suspicious circumstances*.

Vaughn said, "Perhaps something's changed, Detective?"

"Look, you two," Razinski sighed, running a hand through razor-short hair, "I'm doing you a favor, believe me. Go home. Leave this to the professionals."

"What about Maria?" Allison said.

"What about her?"

"She's dead. You don't think it's odd that she died shortly after that call to me?"

"Local police think it was an accident."

"Bullshit," Vaughn said.

Razinski held up a hand. "Don't start looking for conspiracies, Mr. Vaughn. The facts are pretty simple. Paolo Benini had a stroke, became incapable of running the family business. In the midst of the stress, the family loonies came out of the closet. Francesca, Maria. And now I'm dealing with that mother, Simone. Who the hell knows, or cares, what the family dynamics are? We checked out the cabin your Maria claimed—"

"She wasn't *our* Maria," Vaughn said.

Razinski ignored him. "The locals checked out that cabin on the property. Nothing. No sign of anyone held captive, now or in the past."

Allison thought of the reference to "Gina" scribbled in that bathroom. She considered mentioning it, but one look at Razinski's face, at his obvious determination to make this series of events into nothing more than a string of coincidences, and she decided to keep mum.

Apparently Vaughn had the same thought. He stayed silent, too—although he radiated an angry energy that Allison could practically feel in the charged air around them.

"So why are you here then, Detective?" Allison asked quietly. She kept her gaze locked on Razinski's, even when he tried to look away. "If this all amounts to nothing more than one crazy family's antics, or a series of coincidences, why drive all the way to New York? It's not even your jurisdiction."

"Paperwork. Follow-up. Administrative stuff."

His eyes shifted to the left and Allison knew he was lying. But why? And why bother to orchestrate this meeting?

Razinski said, "You'd better learn to live with coincidence, Ms. Campbell. Because there is an awful lot of coincidence surrounding your name." He looked pointedly at Vaughn. "And around your colleague here."

Allison tightened her grip on Vaughn's knee, both to quiet him and to control her own blossoming irritation.

"You think we have something to do with this?"

Razinski continued looking at Vaughn. "I think you should go home and let the professionals handle things."

"Is that a threat, Detective?" Allison's eyes narrowed. How dare he insinuate that he would focus on First Impressions, on Vaughn, if they didn't back down?

Razinski gave her a hollow smile. "It's not a threat, Allison. Your boy here has a past. Juvenile records might be sealed, but some of what he did happened when he was eighteen, nineteen. Did he tell you that?"

"I know what he did."

"Drug deals, theft, more than kid stuff. He may be all cleaned up now, but it doesn't take much for a jury to remember. Prosecutors have a knack for making sure the media digs."

Razinski didn't look like a man who relished bullying. In fact, he spoke with an almost apologetic tone. Nevertheless, Allison shook her head back and forth, anger giving way to rage. "More threats. Our involvement wouldn't bother you so much, Detective Razinski, if this was as simple as you'd like us to believe. But it's not, is it? And somehow our presence is complicating things."

"Only for the family. Let them be, Allison. You, of all people, should understand how hard this must be."

Allison took a long, hard look at the detective. Was he simply saying that she, as an image consultant, should bow to etiquette and leave the Benini family alone? Or had he done some digging on her, too? Did he know about her own family's past, her work with another teen, so long ago? Her dealings with the McBride family? Were his words a veiled threat, or was she seeing conspiracies where there were none?

Allison thought of Francesca, her determination to lead the family business back to health. No, she wasn't imagining conspiracies. Something was as fishy as a back alley in Chinatown.

Allison said, "Certain family members should be prime suspects."

"What proof do you have that the Benini family has done anything wrong?"

Allison opened her mouth to answer, then shut it just as quickly. For what real proof did she have? None.

"Just as I thought." Razinski stood. He studied Allison for a long second before turning his attention to Vaughn. "You should heed my warning, Mr. Vaughn," he said, his tone stern. "A man like you has a lot to lose. Stay out of this one. Go home." He pushed his chair backward, causing the legs to squeal violently against the flooring. The women at the table nearby turned around. Razinski didn't seem to notice, but when he spoke again, his voice was kinder. "Go home and return to your brother and your life."

After he left, Allison and Vaughn lingered. Allison's head hurt, the pain behind her temples quickly spreading to the rest of her skull and extending its grip around her neck. She pulled Excedrin out of her bag— all she had with her—and popped two capsules with the remainder of her coffee. She hoped the medicine would quell the coming storm.

"Razinski did his homework," Vaughn said.

"He's dealing with a disappearance and possibly a murder. Of course he did his homework."

Vaughn shook his head. "Doesn't add up, Allison, and you know that. Razinski acts like there really is nothing to investigate. But then he digs into our backgrounds?" Another head shake. "I want to hate the guy, but I really don't think Razinski's a bad cop. He's caught up in something bigger than him. Someone is pulling his puppet strings."

Allison thought about the difference between the Razinski she'd met originally and this Razinski. Vaughn was right. The guy seemed squirrelly, edgy even. That was not the calm detective they'd met immediately after Francesca's disappearance. His behavior today did seem odd.

"When I think puppet," Allison said, "the first thing that comes to mind is Mob."

"Which would explain a lot of things, including the detective's behavior." Vaughn rubbed his eyes.

"Problem is, we're drowning in facts with no clear connection between them, especially if you throw Tammy into the mix."

Vaughn nodded. "But if someone's pressuring Razinski, then the most likely candidate is organized crime. Who else has that much clout and span of control?"

"Politicians? Government?"

"Simplest answer, Allison. Mafia."

TWENTY-EIGHT

Allison was tired of driving back and forth between the Finger Lakes region of New York and her home in Villanova, so she and Vaughn found an inn near Ithaca. Ironically, it looked much like the Benini estate, with its neo-Gothic façade and sprawling interior, only newer and full of charm, no shadows. Allison paid for two rooms, thanked the very young and very pretty receptionist, and led the way down an interior hallway toward the guest suites. She wanted a hot bath and some time to think.

Not just about the Benini family, but also about Jason.

He was going to be irate. He wanted her home and out of this mess now. Hadn't he said as much? She'd had the window in her home repaired immediately, but if he found out about that, too, there really would be hell to pay. She couldn't blame him. Last year, her foray into detective work had nearly ended her life. He was still smarting from that. But what was she supposed to do now? Throw up her hands and let Vaughn take the fall for something he didn't do—if it came to that? Take the risk that something could happen to two of her clients?

Stop it, Allison, she thought. You're a big girl. You can make your own decisions. And Jason is not your husband anymore.

Ah, but he wants to be, she thought. And maybe I want him to be, too.

She placed the electronic key against the key pad and opened the door into a well-appointed suite. A bedroom flanked a small sitting room and full bath, both adorned in saturated shades of plum, khaki and green. Allison dropped her small bag on the desk and then headed for the bathroom. There, she turned on the water and started filling the oversized tub.

In the bedroom, she slipped off the jeans and simple brown t-shirt she'd purchased at Target, the most convenient shop they'd found. Naked, she was padding her way back toward the bathroom when her cell rang. Thinking it was Jason, she braced herself and grabbed the device. Denise Carr's number flashed on her phone.

Anxious for news, Allison said, "Hello?"

"This is Tammy's manager. Denise Carr. I'm just checking in to see whether you've heard anything."

Disappointed, Allison said, "No. Nothing. I was hoping...I was hoping perhaps you had something to share."

"We haven't found her, if that's what you mean." Denise's voice was a nasally mix of disappointment and frustration. "Are you in your office?"

"No, I'm up north. But if she'd tried to reach me, I would have known."

Denise paused. "If you hear anything, Allison, anything at all, I hope you'll call me. This is serious. No one blames you, of course, but the family...well, the family is broken up. If Tammy did run away, she owes it to her parents to come back. They're worried sick. We all are."

"Of course," Allison said, and hung up. But her mind was already elsewhere.

She turned off the spigot and sank down into a hot froth of bathwater, relishing the warmth that enveloped her skin. She thought about Tammy Edwards, the girl's ties to Kai Berger and Scott Berger. The Edwards' reaction to the mention of a boyfriend.

Denise said that Mrs. Edwards was bereft, worried sick. That wasn't how Jane Edwards seemed just a few days ago. Was Denise being honest?

Allison heard a knock at her door. Reluctantly, she climbed out of the tub, dried off quickly, and slipped into the white bathrobe thoughtfully placed on a hook in the bathroom.

"Coming!" she yelled. She wrapped the robe tight across her naked chest and did her best to wipe the water from her eyes.

She opened the door, expecting Vaughn. But it was Alex Benini who stood in the hallway.

* * *

Mia tried to ring the last contact, a journalist who'd written about the Tarasoff take down. His name was Michael Jiff and he was not answering at the number Svengetti had given her. She left her cell number on his voicemail and sat in the truck, neck against the head rest, contemplating her next move. It was early evening, and while the sun was still shining, it wouldn't be long before the shadows would lengthen. She didn't relish a drive home in the dark.

Mia knew she needed to talk to Allison and Vaughn. It was imperative that they trade notes, because she was certain that wherever they were, they were collecting information just as she was. She hoped something she'd discovered would mesh up with their findings. Because right now she had a whole lot of *so what*.

Mia dialed Jason's number. He picked up right away.

"Where the hell are you?" he said.

"Nice way to greet your mother."

"I swear, Mom, I think you've all gone insane. I stopped by your house after work. Your neighbor was there, feeding Buddy. She seemed to think you were going to be away overnight."

"Thank goodness for Mrs. Crumbly."

"Well, are you? Going to be out all night?"

Mia laughed. "Since when are you so worried about me?"

"Since you also decided to play detective. And don't tell me that's not what you're doing. Are you with my w—"

But Mia heard it. He'd started to say wife and stopped himself. Like that, the old heartache returned. Jason was still madly in love with Allison, and while Mia had forgiven Allison for the divorce, she was all too aware of the hurting the younger woman could put on her son if this relationship went south.

Her voice softer, Mia said, "I'm not with Allison. I have no idea where she is."

Mia heard her son's breathing, slow and steady, calming himself the way he'd done as a child. But he isn't a child, Mia reminded herself. He's an adult who needs to take care of himself—and manage his own relationships.

"Look," Mia said. "Allison is with Vaughn. I'm not sure what they're up to, but she'll be fine. You need to trust her, Jason. She can take care of herself."

"Like she did last spring?"

"Need I remind you that she came out of that fine? And people were jailed because of her efforts—and an innocent kid avoided prison. Stop thinking of Allison as something fragile that needs protecting. If she feels compelled to be part of this, then you need to support her."

Jason was silent for a moment. When he spoke, he sounded resigned. "What do you suggest?"

"Run whatever reports she needs. Take care of Brutus. Be there to talk through the facts. This is serious, not just for her, but for Vaughn. I'm terrified for him. And so is Allison."

Jason let out a sound like a low moan. "I don't want to lose her again."

"I know, baby," Mia said. "So don't."

It was a full minute before either of them said anything else. Outside, the temperature had cooled and the sun extended orange tentacles toward the horizon. The Scranton streets were pockmarked with bumps and bruises, and a haze of misty humidity wafted from the pavement. Mia turned her attention from the city to the paper on her lap. She glanced at Michael Jiff's number.

She said, "Are you at a computer, Jason?"

"I'm at Allison's house."

"Can you do me a favor? Run a name for me?"

"You still haven't told me where you are."

"I'm in Scranton, following up on something. I should be home tomorrow."

She heard another deep breath. With a sigh, Jason said, "What's the name?"

"Michael Jiff. He's a journalist."

"Okay, give me five. I'll call you back."

Mia hung up and waited. But it was only a minute or two before Jason rang her mobile.

"This guy has a ton of stuff on the Internet. What do you need?"

"His address."

"You can't just pop in on a guy like that." The suspicion had crept back into Jason's voice.

"Jason, you need to trust me, too. I did have a career handling people." When he didn't respond, she said, "An address, please."

Mia could hear Jason typing. "I have no idea if it's right, but I'm emailing it as we speak."

"Thanks, Jason," Mia said. "I love you."

"I love you, too." Another bout of silence. "Trust, huh?"

"Trust."

Jason sighed. "When you love someone, trust can feel an awful lot like letting go."

Vaughn heard the knocking. He'd been sitting on the bed in his room, staring at the wall. Worrying. Damn, what a waste of fucking time worrying was. He was starting to feel trapped, imprisoned in his own head. He needed to *think*. And it was so hard to think with all this adrenaline pulsing through his body.

So when he heard the insistent knocking out in the hallway, he sprang up, hands clenched. He leaned against the door, listening. He heard voices—one of which was unmistakably Allison's. Vaughn opened the door to his room in time to see a man walking into Allison's suite. Jason? He couldn't tell.

Better safe than sorry, and all that clichéd horseshit.

Vaughn grabbed his key off the dresser and made his way down the hall toward Allison's room. Outside her door, he leaned in, listening for voices. Hearing nothing, he raised his hand and knocked. His body felt coiled like a snake ready to spring. When no one answered, he knocked harder. He was starting to feel a little foolish, afraid it was Jason and he and Allison were...otherwise engaged.

But then he heard murmurs. Allison's voice said, "We're fine, Vaughn."

"Who's in there with you?"

She hesitated. "Alex Benini."

"I want to see you."

"I said we're fine."

"Just let me see you, Allison, and I'll leave you alone." He didn't want to admit it, but he was worried.

His brow felt moist with sweat, his pulse raced.

Were Allison and Alex Benini together? He hoped to hell not.

That would be too much. The Allison he knew wouldn't cheat on Jason. The Allison he knew wouldn't get physical with a kidnapping suspect. And in Vaughn's mind, all of the Beninis were suspects. Even Francesca.

"Allison!"

The door slammed open. Alex Benini stood in front of Vaughn, head cocked to the side, eyebrows raised in exasperation. But Vaughn didn't want to see Alex, he wanted to see Allison. And there she was on the bed, legs curled under her, a book spread open on her lap.

"Did he hurt you?" Vaughn asked.

Allison shook her head. "Relax, Vaughn. No one has hurt anyone."

"Then what are you doing?" He shot a look of suspicion Alex's way.

Allison glanced at Alex, who nodded. She said, "This is Gina Benini's diary. Alex brought it for me to read."

Confused, Vaughn said, "How did you know we were here?"

"Dom is having you followed." Alex said it so matter-of-factly that Vaughn couldn't react. Alex looked at Allison and Vaughn saw longing reflected on his face. Longing for Allison? Or longing for help?

"Let me come to your room later, Vaughn," Allison said.

"Do you hear this guy, Allison? They're having us followed. Two people are dead and one woman is missing. Missing, Allison. And you're in here alone with *him*." Vaughn stopped himself. He knew he was letting his anger and fear—yes, fear, although he hated to admit it—get to him. He needed the mask of calm that he wore every fucking day, now more than ever.

"Vaughn, I'm fine." Allison spoke slowly, signaling her displeasure at his outburst. "If I don't get back to you in an hour, you have my permission to burst back into my room." She smiled, softening her tone. "Okay?"

Vaughn stole one more look at Alex. The guy's face was as neutral as Switzerland, but as Vaughn walked out of Allison's suite, he could have sworn he caught the tiniest bit of a smirk. Bastard, Vaughn thought. Two can play at that game.

TWENTY-NINE

Alex closed the door. He stood with his back against the wood, a half smile playing on those lips. Allison wasn't immune to the wanting in his eyes, but despite what Vaughn might think—and she sure as hell saw the concern on Vaughn's face—she had no intention of allowing anything physical between Alex and her.

She saw Alex Benini's appeal. But she wasn't interested.

Alex had come in here full of explanations and apologies. Dom was having her followed while she was up here, he'd explained in a rush, for her benefit as well as his own. It would be harder to point fingers at First Impressions if their whereabouts were accounted for, he'd said. She would have been more angry if she hadn't half expected it.

And then Alex pulled out the diary.

"What's this?" she'd asked before starting to read. She'd excused herself and changed back into jeans. And those were the last words spoken by either of them until Vaughn showed up at the door.

Now the small leather book was burning her fingers. Gina's diary. She skimmed the last few pages, then put the book aside, tracing its roughened edges with the tip of a nail. Gina Benini had only been a few years older than Allison when she took her own life. Allison was plagued with questions, most of all, why would a woman with two children kill herself?

Alex walked across the bedroom, slowly. He pulled the chair away from the small writing desk and sat down.

"Satisfied?" Alex asked.

"Satisfied with what?"

"You've been asking questions, Allison. We know you visited my uncles, Enzo and John. We know you stopped by the bottling plant.

You obviously felt you needed to know more about my mother. Now you know." He looked away, the expression on his face all echoes of pain and sorrow. Allison knew true grief. She'd seen it painted in the lines of Mia's face, in the rage on her father's eyes when her mother was diagnosed with Alzheimer's, in the mirror whenever she thought about Violet, her former patient whose short life had been marred by abuse and violence. She wasn't sure what she saw on Alex's face *was* grief. She'd made a career of reading people, yet he was indelible.

"Alex, what could your mother's death possibly have to do with Francesca's disappearance?"

"Nothing. It has absolutely nothing to do with my aunt's decision to flee."

"How can you be so sure?"

"Because it happened years ago. You can stop asking about my mother because she has nothing to do with any of this. And that diary proves they weren't very close. In fact, my mother disliked Aunt Francesca. Read it. You'll see."

"You'd think two women of similar age living in the same house would be close."

Alex shrugged. "I don't know why they didn't get along. With no one else around, maybe they were fighting for the attention of my father."

"That's a rather chauvinistic view. Surely your mother wasn't jealous of Paolo's sister?"

"Think about it, Allison. Two women, alone in that house with two small boys and one man. Who else would Francesca talk to?"

"Gina. That's my point."

"For all her faults, my aunt is somewhat of an intellectual. My mother was not."

Allison studied Alex, the tension in his shoulders, the sudden coldness reflected in his eyes. "Were you close to your mother?"

"I was young when she died."

"That's not an answer, Alex."

He stood. "It's the only answer I have."

He held his hand out for the diary. "Please. I should be on my way." He glanced at the door. "And you don't want your personal knight to come looking for you again."

"When we visited Enzo, he seemed," Allison searched for the right word, "affected when he talked about Francesca. Is there any possibility that Enzo and Francesca were lovers?"

Alex laughed. "Doubtful. I'm pretty certain Enzo is gay."

"Then why would he react?"

"Maybe they are friends. The fact is, it doesn't matter."

Allison didn't buy his easy dismissal. She saw a flash of discomfort in Alex's eyes and believed that perhaps she'd hit on some nugget of truth, some tie that bound Enzo and Francesca, whether it was sex or love or shared history.

"Can I keep the diary, Alex? I'd like to read all of the entries."

"I don't think—"

"You said yourself that there's no connection between Gina and your aunt's disappearance. So how could it hurt?"

"Why do you want it?"

Allison shrugged. "I don't know." And that was the truth. She didn't know why, but she did know that she wanted to read it thoroughly. Maybe it would be a looking glass into the life and death of Gina Benini.

Alex shrugged. "I don't suppose there is any harm. I'd need it back before my brother realizes it's gone."

"I can bring it by tonight."

Alex seemed to think about this. After a pause, Alex said, "Dom is away tomorrow. Why don't you come by his house and I'll make you dinner? You can ask me whatever questions you want then. Seven tomorrow night? That will give you a full day with the book."

"Vaughn?"

"I'd prefer if you come alone."

"That doesn't sound like a great idea."

"Vaughn is protective of you, and he strikes me as a man who isn't thinking straight right now." Alex held up his hands. "No judgment, but if you want the diary, stop by alone." He smiled, eyes alit with amused intelligence. "I promise not to hurt you."

Allison flushed at the double entendre implied in his tone. His words left no room for debate. But Vaughn would balk if she suggested she go alone. She could tell him the truth, or she could make it impossible for him to insist on going too. Would that be foolish? Was this man dangerous? Recognizing that dangerous could have several meanings, she blushed again. Maybe the better question was whether she could trust herself.

Allison thought of Jason. His broad smile, his warm laugh, the feel of his muscular back against her fingertips when they were making love. Jason was her friend first. As lovers, they were rediscovering each other. It was an awkward journey, filled with all the little hurts they'd left littered in their wake like so many tiny landmines. But any relationship was work—and Jason had been a part of her life for so long. She cherished their friendship. And she didn't want to do anything to jeopardize their rekindled love affair.

Allison weighed all of this in a split second. In that same flash, she saw Francesca in her home the first day they'd met. She heard her say again that the vultures were circling. Those words had taken on new meaning. Had her client been aware of some undisclosed danger? Now, with the benefit of hindsight, it seemed likely. She could be suffering...or worse. All Allison and Vaughn had were data points. Lots and lots of random facts. They had to tie them together. They had to find the links.

Maybe Alex Benini—willingly or not—could help them do that.

Allison squared her shoulders. "Seven o'clock tomorrow night. Alone. On two conditions."

Alex nodded for her to continue.

"One, total honesty. I will come with questions, and you need to answer them candidly."

"And two?"

"Stop having me followed."

Alex sighed. "Those are complicated requests, Allison. More complicated than you know."

"Why? Why does all of this need to be so complicated? What the hell are you and your family hiding?"

"We're not hiding anything. The question is, what was Francesca hiding?"

That stopped Allison.

Was this all about protecting a secret that Francesca had held close? Were the vultures circling, trying to get a glimpse of whatever she was clinging to? Was it something worth dying for?

Allison heard footsteps in the hall. Vaughn? She glanced at her watch. The hour was almost up.

"Can you promise those two things or not?"

Alex looked at her with sad eyes, no hint of amusement this time. "It was Dom who had you followed. I can't make any promises there. He's a lone wolf. He doesn't answer to me, or anyone for that matter." He gave her a rueful smile. "I'll see you tomorrow night? I'll text you the address."

"What about my other condition? Total honesty?"

"I'll lay bare what I can."

Alex left, and Allison was left to ponder the meaning of those words.

"Wolf. Vultures. What is it with this family and predator metaphors?" Vaughn didn't look up from his bowl as he spoke. They were eating homemade chicken soup and biscuits in the inn's dining area, compliments of the manager. The soup was a bit salty for Allison's taste, but she welcomed its searing heat and the comforting flavor of something so familiar. It made her think of the rare times when she was a kid and her mother felt well enough to cook for them. Especially if her father wasn't home. Just Allison, her mom and her sisters. Those were the good days.

Vaughn cleared his throat, interrupting Allison's thoughts. "Vultures and wolves, Allison." He pointed his spoon at her.

Allison's mind traveled back to her first visit, to the hawk that had fallen from the sky. To Maria's rifle. Wolves and vultures, indeed. And here I am, sitting across from one of my closest friends, preparing to lie, she thought. I am no better than the vultures or the wolves.

But it was for his own good. At least that's what she told herself.

But now she was having second thoughts. And third.

"So what was in that diary?" Vaughn asked. He tapped at the bottom of his empty soup bowl, looking vaguely disappointed. "Was it worth Rico Sauvé's trip over?"

"I haven't had a chance to go through it yet."

"Why did he bother bringing it over?"

"He heard that we were talking to Gina's brother, Enzo."

Vaughn twisted the white cloth napkin around his hand. "When I heard Alex in your room, I figured as much. I'm glad he came clean about the tail. I'm not surprised they're watching us. Let them. In fact, maybe that explains how Razinski knew. And the damn white Accord." Vaughn looked down at his hands, then back up at her, clearly uneasy. "I was worried for a minute that you had called him."

Allison felt her color rise. "Do you really think that little of me?"

"I really think that little of *him*. I don't trust Alex Benini, Allison. I don't trust any of them."

"Well, you don't have to worry. I'm committed to Jason."

Vaughn's mobile beeped. He picked it up, stared at the screen, and scowled. "This can't be good. I'll be right back."

Allison watched as he walked toward the inn's entrance hall, his tall, muscular form lithe from all of the boxing he did to stay in shape. Once again, Allison felt a pang of admiration for Vaughn. His devotion to Jamie, his self-discipline. She hoped once this was over, it wouldn't scar him. He'd worked so hard to create this life for them. Nothing could be allowed to destroy it.

Vaughn was back a few minutes later looking glum. "I need to get back tonight."

"Jamie?"

Vaughn nodded. "Angela is sick and Mrs. T has family in town. Mrs. T is heading over for a few hours to stay with Jamie until I get there. But I need to get moving." He glanced at his watch. "I know we paid for the rooms already. If you want to stay—"

Allison frowned.

"I'm sorry," Vaughn said. "If I had another option, I'd use it. But on such short notice," he shook his head, "I just don't."

"It's fine, Vaughn. I just have a few more loose ends to tie up here."

"Like?"

"I wanted to head to the library and see what's available about the Pittaluga bakery on microfiche, for one thing."

She eyed Vaughn to gauge his reaction. "You could fly home," he said.

Allison tried to look like she was considering that as a fresh option. She hated lying. But this wasn't really lying. She had been trying to figure out a way to send Vaughn home alone, and now she had it.

"Maybe I'll do that. I only need another day or two. I'll be right on your heels."

Vaughn looked miserable. Allison cringed, knowing she was responsible for his unease. But she was a grown woman, absolutely capable of taking care of herself. "Stop worrying," she said.

"Jason will be pissed at me."

Allison stood. Her bowl was empty and her head was pounding. She wanted to get back to Gina's diary before the guilt overwhelmed her. But this insistence that she needed looking after was infuriating and she felt the guilt give way to anger.

"Jason will have to deal," she said. "I'll see him soon enough."

"Let me pack and get going." He studied her for a moment before turning to go. Thinking better of it, he spun around. "Francesca's other bag. It was stuffed in the back of my trunk, where she must have left it. I have it in my room. I'll drop it off before I go."

"Anything good?"

"Nah. Girly stuff. Underwear, toiletries. I felt like a perv going through it."

Allison smiled. "Leave it with me. I'll take another look."

THIRTY

Vaughn was gone by 9:30, and Allison was left alone with her thoughts—as well as Gina Benini's diary and Francesca's bag. She pulled on the blue pajamas she'd purchased at Target, brushed her teeth, and curled up on the settee, anxious to read.

The diary was small. When placed on her left hand, it reached only her fingertips and weighed just ounces. The cover may have once been a shade of rich purple, but it had faded to a washed-out gray. The material was silky, though, and perhaps even softer to the touch because of time's caress. Allison sat for a moment, holding the book, wondering where Gina had purchased it. Had it traveled from Italy? Or had it been a gift from Paolo?

She opened to the first page. The paper was a quality parchment, now yellowed from age. The writing was a heavy black, in a script so flowery that Allison struggled to decipher each word.

The first page contained a catalog of goods. Scarf, mittens, bonnet, Nona's blanket. Next to each item was a checkmark, straight and unadorned compared to the lettering in the list itself. Allison wondered if Gina had written the list and Paolo the checkmarks? Why was it in English, not Italian?

Did it really matter?

The next few pages looked to be a toddler's feeding schedule. At the top was the date, and underneath a recording of the time for each feeding. On the bottom were notations that Allison assumed were the time and consistency of bowel movements. The orderly recordings of a new parent? Clearly if Dom was eating green beans and sweet potatoes, he had been older than a tiny infant. So Gina must have been pregnant with Alex at the time. Or would be soon.

The next ten pages, written at intervals of days or even weeks, were similar. Lists and schedules and notations about toy preferences and food quantities and behavior. There was a tone to the list, a roteness that seemed out of step with the frivolity of the book itself. Why use the diary for such mundane content? Were these lists a diligent mother's notes—or a neurotic mother's obsession? Allison wondered.

About twenty pages in, the content changed. Gina began to include references to dinner dates with Paolo, picnic outings, luncheons with descriptions of magnificent spreads. On page thirty-eight, she mentioned a "gorgeous red silk dress, one he will have to love." Her words seemed lighter, as though a burden had been lifted. Why? And what had been the burden to begin with? Child rearing? Loneliness?

Allison kept reading. She was tired, and her back ached from sleeping in strange beds. She missed Jason and Brutus. But she was enthralled by the diary, by the lack of intimate details. Was Gina hampered by limited English? Was she afraid Paolo would read the book? Or was she simply uncomfortable putting thoughts and feelings on paper?

About fifty pages in, the book took another turn. Gina had gone back to cold lists and stark descriptions. Here were notes about Paolo's dinner preferences, her own caloric intake and reminders that she was getting fat.

Gradually, the new baby crept into the pages, although rather than the doting mother's lists that Dom's infancy warranted, Alex was mentioned in passing, as though he was a mild inconvenience or another chore to which she needed to attend.

Francesca was mentioned, too. But never by name. She was always a pronoun, or, at best, "Paolo's sister." Entries read like angry comments on a modern blog. "Dinner with Paolo. Why does she stare? I feel like she's stalking me. Every time I look up, there she is. Watching. Waiting. But for what? No wonder they sent her here. I wish they'd chosen the asylum." Or, "He is such a little pig, with those eyes that follow me everywhere. Dom can't sleep with him in the room, so Paolo and I have another challenge during the night. And she is no help."

The word asylum caught Allison's attention. Allison assumed Francesca had chosen to come to America. Had she been sent? Had a mental hospital been the alternative?

The entries went on, a litany of complaints and secret indignities. It came to an end on January 19. Gina Benini's final entry said simply, "Coincidence?"

Coincidence.

Allison paged back to take another look at the entries right before that final notation. On December 10th, Gina had written a reminder about a doctor appointment. On December 24th, the entry read, "Dinner for twelve tonight. Remind cook of food allergy. And bitter greens. Always bitter greens." Had she been planning a Christmas dinner? If so, who were the other guests?

Gina Paolo died on January 28. Because there was no year written in the diary, Allison didn't know whether Gina had time to start a new diary before her death. But based on her notes about the children, Allison's hunch was that the diary entries ended just weeks before Gina Benini took her own life.

Perhaps Alex could tell her tomorrow.

Allison stood, stretched. Why the hell had Gina's name been written in that latrine in the old hunting cabin? And had it been Francesca who'd written it?

First Francesca Benini disappears during a pit stop off the highway. Then Tammy Edwards is mysteriously missing from her home. Add to that an invalid's suspicious death, and an allegedly accidental steam leak that kills Maria Benini after a panicked phone call.

And all Allison had was a name and an old diary.

Allison placed the diary carefully in her purse. She double checked the door to her suite to make sure it was locked before settling in to call Jason. She was only mildly disappointed when he didn't answer. She knew he would be angry that she was here alone. She didn't feel like hearing it. Although she despised the guilt that knotted her gut, she wished he was here with her, but only if he would help. Because she could use the help.

She called Mia's house next, but her former mother-in-law didn't answer, either. Allison glanced at the clock. It flashed 10:14. Early, but Allison had a lot planned for the next day. She decided to turn in for the night.

She remembered Francesca's small bag. She unzipped the top and peeked inside. Everything was neat and orderly. Clearly Vaughn didn't get too far. Allison chuckled at the thought of Vaughn refusing to look through an older woman's underwear. For someone with such a tough exterior, he was a softie underneath.

Allison laid a towel on the bed. One by one, she pulled the items from the bag. Five pairs of white women's underwear, neatly pressed and rolled, sat on top. She placed them, still rolled up, on the towel. Underneath were jars of Olay, Noxzema face wash, a loofah, hand cream, toothpaste, an electric toothbrush, and a hairbrush. A small Bible, empty of any personalization, and a Rosary had been placed in a side pocket. She laid everything out on the towel and turned the bag upside down, searching for hidden compartments.

That was it. No papers. No secret diagrams or diaries or tracking devices. Nothing but an older woman's personal belongings. Allison felt a little guilty rummaging through Francesca's things, as though she were violating her privacy, however pure her motivations. She started to put everything back in the order she'd removed it. She was placing the second pair of underwear in the bag when she felt something hard inside the cotton. Slowly, she unfolded the garment. A small, silver key fell out.

Well I'll be damned, Allison thought. Could this be what Alex was looking for?

She might have felt smug, except that she had no idea what the key opened. No idea at all.

It was nearly eleven o'clock at night and Mia'd had no luck tracking down Michael Jiff. The address Jason had provided turned out to be a foursquare home in Kingston, Pennsylvania, only a half hour's drive from Scranton. It was a beautiful Mission-style house in a neighborhood of sprawling Bungalows on small but manicured lots. But when Mia knocked, the door was answered by an older woman who was quite adamant that no Michael Jiff lived there.

Not convinced, Mia had sat in her car, parked a few doors down, and watched the house. Through lace curtains, she saw the woman sitting on a couch, watching a cooking show on a large, wall-mounted television. At 10:22, the woman turned off the television. At 10:48, she turned off the downstairs lights and went up to bed.

Frustrated and tired, Mia sat in the darkened truck and scrolled through her emails. Nothing relevant, other than a note from Jamie reminding her to be careful. She called her home voicemail and heard Allison's message from earlier. It was too late to call her back now.

Mia rested her head against the seat. She thought about her call with Jason. She wished him the things every mother wished for her child. Love. Happiness. An end to his restlessness. Once upon a time, she'd blamed Allison for not soothing Jason's demons. She realized now that only he had the power to do that. And sometimes he was ignorant of his own blind spots.

Mia smiled. Like mother, like son.

Mia started the truck. She'd grab a hotel for the night and would try again tomorrow, before heading home. She was a retired divorcee, after all. She had all the time in the world.

Mia was pulling away from the curb when her phone rang. She glanced down, saw an unlisted number, and answered, "Hello?"

It was then that an old brown Audi pulled in front of the Mission-style house.

A voice on the phone said, "Mia?"

A guy got out of the car. The watery streetlight silhouetted a hulking man with a loping, tired gait.

Mia pulled the car up next to him. She held her hand over the phone and said, "Michael Jiff?" Even in the dark, she saw panic in the enlarged whites of his eyes.

The voice on the phone repeated, "Mia?"

The guy on the sidewalk shook his head.

Mia said to the man, "I really need to talk to you."

Another head shake. He started toward the house, his head tucked down as though to hide his face. Mia glanced between the phone and the stranger on the street.

Finally, she said, "Michael, please. There's a child's life at stake."

The guy stopped. The voice on the phone said, "You're being watched."

Mia froze. She looked at Michael Jiff, for she was certain that's who this stranger was, then at her phone. "Hold on," she said to the voice in the phone.

"Please," she said again to Jiff.

His shoulders slumped. He nodded.

"Who is this?" Mia said into the phone.

"They're watching you. I'll help you. But you have to do what I say." The voice sounded deep, echo-y, but she recognized it as Svengetti's.

Torn, Mia met Michael Jiff's gaze. "I'm listening," she said into the phone.

"Get the reporter into your car and head toward the Cross Valley Expressway. Route 309, north. I'll guide you from there."

THIRTY-ONE

Allison couldn't sleep. She lay in bed, thinking. Jason had called her back just minutes after she went to sleep, and his forced cheerfulness and lack of direct questions were almost as disconcerting as his previous over-concern. What was up with that? And where the hell was Mia?

Allison rolled over. She clutched one down pillow to her chest and breathed in the smell of fresh sheets, but even the feel of 400-thread count cotton against her skin couldn't ward away the creeping sense of disquiet. This inn was as large as the Benini estate, yet it felt warm and welcoming. The Benini estate had felt like a tomb. Was that part of the equation? That damn house?

Allison's mind hop-skipped to Gina's diary.

Asylum.

Gina said she'd wished they'd sent Francesca to the asylum. Who was *they*? And why an asylum? And what had Francesca done that she needed to be sent anywhere?

Allison considered Simone Benini's call soon after Francesca disappeared. Francesca's sister-in-law had theorized that Francesca bolted, maybe even killed herself. Had Simone had good reason to think that? Had Francesca been mentally ill, sent to America to live with her caretaker brother, an unstable woman with no prospects of her own?

What about Maria's call? And the word Gina written on that bathroom wall? How in the name of all that was holy did Gina's death—or life—fit into this equation?

And then there was Tammy "Swallow" Edwards.

Coincidence?

Coincidence. The last line of Gina's diary. Allison was caught up in a mystery, slugging through possibly unrelated clues to find the nugget of truth that tied everything together. Is it possible that Gina had been looking into a mystery of her own?

Reluctantly, Allison crawled from beneath the warm comfort of the blankets and flipped on the bedside light. The clock read 11:06. Her body felt tired, but her mind was suddenly alert to new possibilities.

What if Gina had stumbled across something? Something that led to a depression so severe that she took her own life? Or, more implausible perhaps, what if someone had been responsible for her death? The idea made Allison shudder. She reached for a throw from the closet and opened her laptop. While she waited for her computer to boot, she poured herself a glass of spring water from the complimentary bottle on the desk. She wished it were wine.

The glow from the computer cast shadows in the darkened room. Allison turned on every light, welcoming the sudden brightness. Even thinking about the Benini household was depressing. She pulled up a search engine. She did yet another search on Francesca Benini. Nothing new. No luck with Gina, either. She tried typing in Gina's brothers' names, John and Enzo Pittaluga. Then their business, Fireside Bakery. She found a reference to a fire that had happened not long before Gina died. It was a comment in a food blog dedicated to Ithaca's dining options:

Too bad Fireside's not still around. Best bakery between New York City and San Francisco. Never did catch the bastard who started that inferno. Guess there's irony in a name, after all.

So the Pittaluga's bakery had burned down? Allison made a note on the inn's letterhead to check into the fire when she visited the microfiche room at the library. This family seemed to have a cloud hanging over it, and Allison suspected that cloud was somehow related to her client's disappearance.

It was now almost midnight. Allison still didn't feel sleepy, so she decided to do another search. She plugged in Tammy Edwards' name and turned up nothing new. She logged into Facebook. Tammy's Facebook page hadn't changed. Same profile picture Allison remembered seeing the first time. And the girl's security setting still blocked Allison from further access. Allison navigated to Tammy's boyfriend, Kai's, page. As before, his page was open to the public. Today's status read: Insanity runs in the family. Thirty-six friends had commented; none of the friends was Tammy.

Kai had posted what looked like two or three new albums-worth of party pictures since Allison had last visited Facebook. Photo after photo of drunk teenagers. Some pictures had been taken in a wooded setting, some were in what she recognized as Kai's father's apartment, some were in a house Allison didn't recognize at all. Always, Kai had a half-grin on his face and a cup in his hand. The life of the party. Not a worried boyfriend, that was for sure. Assuming these had been taken recently.

After sifting through what felt like a million uploads, one of the pictures caught Allison's attention. A girl, laying on the couch, barely noticeable behind five teenagers hanging on each other in front of the camera. The other teens were grinning, arms entwined, drunken glazes on youthful faces. One was giving the cameraperson the finger. But behind them, the girl on the couch was looking down, her face shadowed by a blue baseball cap. Allison thought about Tammy that day at First Impressions, when she had escaped to the parking lot and sat folded up on herself, long arms wrapped around gangly legs. The girl on the couch was Tammy, Allison was certain. Same lanky body, same hair hanging from beneath that hat, and even the strong line of the jaw matched the Tammy of Allison's memory.

Allison opened a new window and pulled up the YouTube video of Tammy's television try-out. She paused, zoning in on Tammy's face. Yep, she was sure the kid on the couch was Tammy.

But so what, Allison thought. This picture could have been taken months ago and posted only recently. Again, Allison went through the pictures in this set. Stained beige carpeting, light-colored furniture. The pictures on the wall hung askew, which told Allison it probably wasn't Kai's mother's house. She remembered Joanne Berger as being an exceptionally tidy woman with compulsive tendencies. Stained carpeting and tilted pictures didn't seem her thing.

Allison went through each picture in the album several times, looking for nonexistent clues. Frustrated, she was about to close the window when another picture caught her eye. The cameraperson had taken a shot of a laughing, half-dressed girl standing in the threshold of the room. Behind her, Allison could just make out the edge of the white couch to the right. But what interested her was the small desk wedged up against the wall, on the left side of the picture. The girl had her hand on the desk, next to one of those Far Side daily calendars.

Allison saved the picture to her laptop. She opened it anew, using her own software, and enlarged the calendar page.

August 9 of this year.

After Tammy's disappearance.

So Tammy Edwards was alive. And Kai Berger knew where she was.

The man sitting beside Mia had coffee-colored skin and a mop of unruly black hair. He looked at her through drooping brown eyes, taking her in with the impartial candor of a camera. Mia guessed him to be in his late thirties, although he had an ageless quality that made his years hard to pinpoint. The intelligence in his expression said he was no fool; the slumped shoulders said he had a lot on his mind.

Mia said, "Thank you. For coming with me."

Jiff nodded.

Mia merged onto the Cross Valley Expressway and headed north, following the directions of the man on the phone. He'd hung up hastily, telling her which way to drive and promising to call back in a few minutes. Mia was surprised at how calm she felt given the situation. She thought of her daughter Bridget's death, the phone call that shattered Mia's world. She supposed that loss had marked her. She didn't fear death. She didn't fear much of anything these days. Other than harm to more loved ones. Including Vaughn.

And Allison.

But her concern for her own safety was limited. So she waited through the silence of the stranger next to her and waited for the call of another stranger, careful to drive the speed limit, watching for the deer that inhabited these roads late at night.

Mia felt oddly happy. In some ways, she hadn't felt this alive in years.

"Svengetti told me you'd be in contact. So your voicemail wasn't a surprise." Jiff's voice interrupted her reverie.

"But you ignored it anyway?"

Jiff grunted.

"You know Svengetti well?"

"Well enough."

"The woman at your house, is she your mother?"

"Doesn't matter."

Mia shrugged. She switched on her high beams and squinted at the road. "I'll cut to the chase. What can you tell me about the Gretchkos and their connection to the Russian Mafia?"

Jiff looked at her with jaded eyes. "Who wants to know?"

"Me."

"Why?"

"Didn't Svengetti tell you that, too?"

"Svengetti told me a well-coifed woman of a certain age would come asking questions about the Russians. He told me I could avoid her or talk, but he wanted me to be forewarned." Jiff raised neatly groomed eyebrows. "And to know that she was harmless."

Hmm. A harmless woman of a certain age, Mia thought. The description made her cringe. And then she wondered why she cared what Svengetti thought.

The phone buzzed. Mia answered with surprisingly steady hands.

Svengetti said, "Get off at the next exit. Go straight through the first stop light, whether or not it's green, and make the first right after that. Then the first left, and the first right. Sixth house on the right. Pull around to the back and park behind the garage. You'll see what I mean. Stay in your car. Tell the reporter to do the same."

Mia glanced at Jiff. He was staring straight ahead, lips pursed. He knows, Mia thought. He knows what's going on.

Before Mia could respond to the voice, the phone clicked off.

Mia took a deep breath. She got off at the exit. The roads were dark. Outside, it was starting to drizzle. Mia's headlights cut through a foggy haze. A traffic light loomed about three hundred yards from the exit. A car pulled onto the road behind her, from the same exit she had taken, and Mia accelerated, heading toward the intersection. As Mia approached the traffic light, it turned yellow, then red.

She gave a cursory glance each way and plowed through the light. Beside her, Jiff was still.

"Shit," Mia said under her breath. As she made it through the light, she saw another vehicle speed through, coming from the cross-road. It had the green light. The driver stopped in the middle of the intersection, though, rolled down the window and seemed to be yelling at her from inside his car, effectively blocking the car that had followed her off the Cross Valley Expressway. That driver slammed on the horn.

Mia didn't wait to see what would happen next. She focused on remembering the caller's instructions. *First right, first left, and then first right. Sixth house on the right.*

The increasing drizzle made visibility poor. Mia slowed before the last turn, half expecting a car to follow her through the haze. But she and Jiff were alone. She wondered for a moment what she'd gotten herself into. But only for a moment. Because as soon as she found the sixth house on the right, it was déjà vu.

Vaughn crept quietly through the apartment, more out of habit than necessity. Jamie kept odd hours and Mrs. T would be up, waiting for him. He stopped in the living room and listened to the sounds of his home. From here, he could hear the whir of Jamie's respirator and the hum of the dishwasher. Mrs. T must have started it before getting ready to leave. He and Jamie occupied the top floor of the building, but below them, someone was watching a movie. If he really concentrated, he could hear the sound of simulated explosions coming from his neighbors' surround sound.

But he couldn't hear anybody in the hallway outside his apartment, and that's what he was really listening for.

Vaughn walked to the window and peeked through the blinds. The living room was dark, so anyone watching from outside couldn't see him. His eyes flitted across the parking lot as he watched for movement, light, anything that would give away a tail. He hadn't seen a white Honda while driving home from Ithaca, but it paid to be careful.

After a moment, he was satisfied that even if someone was out there, he wasn't going to see him. As he let the blinds fall back into place, a voice behind him said, "Christopher, what in the good lord's name are you doing?"

Vaughn smiled. "Thanks for staying, Mrs. T."

Mrs. T flicked on a lamp. In its soft glow, she looked younger than her fifty-some years. Today her hair was held back in a bun. Around her neck, she wore a gold cross adorned with diamond chips that sparkled against her dark skin. A floor-length black skirt and apricot-colored blouse skimmed a curvy body. She pointed a manicured nail in his direction.

"That boy is sleeping. Let him rest, Christopher. He was up all night researching God knows what on that dang computer. Had the look of the devil in his eyes. I don't know what he's up to for those police officers, but he's driven to solve something." Mrs. T shook her head. "I'm sorry I had to make you come home. Cousin Frida and her brood are in and they're leaving in the morning. I couldn't very well not be there after they drove all the way up from Atlanta." She smiled. "You know how that is." Another head shake. "I hope Angela is feeling better. A stomach virus is no fun at all. But we can't have Jamie getting it."

Vaughn gave Mrs. T a tight smile, his mind focused on what she'd just said. Jamie on the computer all night, researching something. Only Vaughn knew it wasn't for the police. And if Jamie had the look of the devil in his eyes, that meant he wasn't happy about what he was finding.

Damn. Vaughn hoped to hell Allison was okay up there in New York alone.

Vaughn took a deep breath. He had three people in his life he loved. Jamie. Allison. And Mia.

He'd die to protect all three.

THIRTY-TWO

Allison shut down her computer. She debated what to do with this new information. If Tammy was, indeed, alive and fine, Vaughn should be told. He was busy beating himself up over her disappearance, and this would give him at least some relief. But something kept her from making that phone call just yet.

She had a visceral, whole body sort of intuition. There was a reason Tammy Edwards was hiding out. The boyfriend's father and his underhand dealings. Tammy's mother and her reluctance to call the police. That wacky manager, Denise Carr. Clearly, Tammy didn't want to be found. Which either meant she simply didn't want to be a star. Or she felt she was in danger.

Allison sat on the edge of the bed, nursing a headache. She needed to think. But first she needed to sleep.

Only with all the adrenaline coursing through her, with all the unanswered questions and loose ends, and free-floating anxiety, sleep just wouldn't come.

Mia recognized Svengetti's truck.

He'd led her to a boxy one-story house with ugly, asymmetrical windows. A paved driveway ran through a weedy front yard, around the side of the building, to a taller, boxier garage in the back. Between the house and the garage was an awning. Svengetti's truck was parked under the shelter, tucked up against the house, nose facing outward. Mia did a K-turn in the narrow lot and pulled her truck up alongside Svengetti's. The reporter continued to stare straight ahead, mute.

Mia found his silence unnerving.

A cursory look at Svengetti's truck said it was empty.

Mia glanced around at her surroundings. She'd tried to pay attention while driving here, in case she needed to get away quickly, but the darkness and her unfamiliarity with the town diluted her senses. They were in an industrial neighborhood. Coming in, she'd noticed plain houses and, interspersed between them, small factory buildings and concrete auto garages. But here, tucked back behind this house, nothing was visible other than the blocky garage.

"So how do you know Svengetti?" she asked Jiff.

"We traveled in the same circles once upon a time."

"Were you part of the Tarasoff bust?"

Jiff smiled. "Hardly. I just had the misfortune of being assigned the financial section of the paper."

"So you reported on the family."

Jiff turned his head slowly, weighing his words. "My name was on the byline."

"Did they go after you, too?"

"Nothing so blatant."

"Then what happened?"

"Let's just say I'm now covering pee wee football and neighborhood yard sales."

"So they ruined your career?"

"They made sure it never got started. Among other things."

Mia watched as a car pulled into the driveway. She tensed, the beat of her heart suddenly the loudest sound in the car.

It was the same vehicle that had pulled into the intersection just a few minutes ago, the car that stopped whatever tail was following her. With relief, she saw Svengetti behind the wheel. He held up a hand for her to wait.

"So why do you stay here? In the Wyoming Valley?" Mia asked Jiff quietly, keeping her eyes on Svengetti. "If they've ruined your career, if they've made it difficult for you to find a better job, why not move on?"

This time, Jiff's eyes flashed with the heat of a thousand hells. "That woman you met? That's my mother. She's alone now. Because of them." Jiff spoke mechanically, a man reciting news unrelated to him. "My father was seventy-two, alone and suffering from dementia. Two armed robbers on a December night. My mom, at Bingo. The police said the motive was theft. But Dad wouldn't have put up a fight. He was wheelchair bound. And my mom said nothing was stolen."

"A hit?"

"He was a sitting duck." Jiff's voice cracked. "Who *does* that?"

A sitting duck. Like Jamie. Mia swallowed. "So you stay for your mom?"

Mia watched as Svengetti got out of his vehicle, walked around the edge of the house, disappearing from Mia's sight. He had a gun.

He reappeared just as Jiff said, "No. I stay because *they* still exist." His voice cracked again. "Two can play the revenge game, Ms. Campbell."

It was almost ten minutes and two perimeter walks before Svengetti finally called for Mia and Jiff to follow him. He led them around the back of the garage, through a thicket of overgrown hedges, to a dilapidated shed. After opening the padlock on the shed, he slid the door aside and flicked on a small flashlight. Inside the shed were a lawn mower, several trimmers, and an assortment of shovels and rakes. The smaller tools had been hung neatly on the walls. Svengetti moved aside one of the trimmers and directed the flashlight's beam to the back of the shed. After a second, he located a small metal ring. This he pulled. The floor of the shed gave way to a trap door, beneath which was a set of stairs.

Svengetti vanished down the portal. Jiff went next. Mia hesitated. Once down there, what was to stop Svengetti from locking her in...or worse? How well did she know this man? Suddenly the outrageousness of her situation slammed her in the face like a rock.

Clearly sensing her hesitation, Svengetti said from below, "I didn't invite *you* into *my* life, Sunshine. You're free to go at any time. You want some answers, come down. You want to take your chances on your own, go ahead. Your tail is gone. Drive home and stay safe like I told you yesterday."

Mia had come this far. She started down the steps to whatever lay beneath.

* * *

It was an underground apartment. Thick concrete walls encased a three-room bunker. The steps led into the first room, a ten-by-twelve living space with a futon, mini-kitchen, and small table and chairs. The ambience was pure Man Den.

Room two was a tiny bathroom with a toilet, sink, and floor with a drain. Overhead was a shower nozzle that would convert the whole room into a shower. A red First Aid kit was attached to the wall over the sink. The bathroom smelled of disinfectant and menthol.

The third room was a twenty-foot supply closet. Mia got only a cursory glance inside before Svengetti closed the lead-lined door, but in those seconds she saw boxes of canned goods, freeze-dried foods, and bins of neatly stacked medical supplies: antibiotics, syringes, tranquilizers, allergy medication, iodine, and other Armageddon necessities.

The man was ready for anything. Mia looked at him sideways, doubt creeping along the edges of her mind again. This wasn't simply the doings of a man with a vendetta against the Mob. This was a paranoid person's fantasy home. Was Svengetti mad?

Her senses on high alert, Mia followed Svengetti into the sitting area. He pulled out a kitchen chair. Mia and Jiff sat on the Futon.

"Before you get any ideas about me, I didn't build this place. I bought it like this from someone far more paranoid than me."

"Killmore?" Jiff asked.

Svengetti nodded. "Another colleague in the fight against organized crime," he explained to Mia. "But he added a healthy dose of Book of Revelations crazy to the mix. Convinced America would be the target of a nuclear rogue state, he spent twenty years building this place."

"The supplies look new," Mia said.

"Some are mine, others I inherited."

Jiff spoke. "Killmore died in a car crash eighteen months ago."

Svengetti nodded. "Left his bunker and the game of chance took over."

"Mob again?" Mia asked.

Svengetti and Jiff both shook their heads. "Drunk. Hit a tree head-on," Svengetti said. "Paranoia fed by alcoholism. His widow sold me the house. She'd never bought into his theories. I paid cash. Zoning board doesn't know about this underground playground, and the little missus gets herself a nice condo in Boca. Win-win."

"So you hide out here as well as in the Poconos?"

Svengetti smiled. "Let's be clear, I'm not hiding anywhere."

"Then why go to the trouble and expense?"

Svengetti glanced at Jiff. Jiff nodded. "Because when the shit hits the fan, I will need somewhere to stay. And this is as good a place as any."

Mia raised her eyebrows. "When the shit hits the fan? Sounds like you're expecting something to happen."

Svengetti glanced at the clock on the microwave and Mia followed his gaze. 2:12 a.m. Svengetti looked back at Mia. "Oh, I'm expecting that something will happen. And you and your friends just may be the catalyst."

"What does that mean?"

Svengetti rubbed his face with two burly hands. Mia noticed the lengths of his fingers, the widths of his palms. Strong hands, steady demeanor. This was a man on pursuit and Mia, for one, wouldn't want to be in his way. At the same time, there was something incredibly masculine and safe about Svengetti.

She realized with a start that she trusted him.

Svengetti put his hands down, resting them on the wooden seat arms, and sank back into his chair. The air in the bunker was stale. Beside her, Jiff fidgeted in his seat, crossing and uncrossing his legs and eventually settling for crossed arms and a sour facial expression. Everything about Jiff screamed "leave me alone." But given what he'd been through, she could forgive his rudeness.

"When you arrived yesterday morning, I had a hunch that perhaps you were on to something. Young girl goes missing, boyfriend's father is an employee at the landfill. Did time in jail. A definite gopher for the Gretchko family. And why would they need a gopher unless they were back in the game." He stretched, yawned. "But none of that spoke to me."

"Then what did?"

"When I spoke to Frist, he told me about the son. The fact that he was caught dumping."

"That seems like kid stuff. Why would that be more of a red flag than anything else?"

Svengetti turned to Jiff, who was busy examining his nails. "Care to elaborate, Michael?"

Jiff looked up, bored. "The family is officially out of the business. On the books, they look clean. Even the Attorney General has dismissed them as a threat, for the most part. But if you wanted to stay in the business without risking any attention whatsoever, what might you do?"

"Something so underground that no one would catch you."

"Or?"

How, indeed? Mia's tired brain turned over the options. "Pay someone else."

"That's part of it."

Mia thought about criminals, about some of the worst offenders and how they got away with their crimes. Serial killers, child molesters, white collar embezzlers. She said, "Do it out in the open."

"Exactly."

Svengetti stood, paced the length of the room. "You see, the kid, his ties to the family, it all got me thinking. What if they'd branched out. Into something invisible."

"Something like toxic dumping?" Mia asked.

"Yes, exactly. Your boy's actions were small stuff. Meant nothing. But what if it had been a test. Would the authorities notice a little pharmaceutical waste in the local streams? How much could they get away with before some environmental watch group started screaming?"

Jiff nodded. "There are some incredibly rural areas around here. The people are poor, and there are no rich yuppies calling the EPA when their creek smells funny. Companies get away with shit. But most would rather not take the chance."

"So they hire a third party," Mia said.

"Exactly." Svengetti pointed up, toward the ceiling. "Companies can't have illegal dumping on their books. The Mobsters don't want anything traceable. Everyone wins."

"Except the environment." Mia stood, hands on hips. "It happens in plain sight, and no one's the wiser—unless they're caught in the act."

Svengetti said, "Yep."

"But what does this have to do with Tammy Edwards, her disappearance?"

Svengetti and Jiff looked at each other. Mia could have sworn Jiff shrugged, but the gesture was so subtle she might have inferred rather than seen it.

Finally, Svengetti said, "Probably nothing."

"Then why would someone bother following me?"

The two men exchanged another glance. "We're not sure it was the Mob following you."

"I don't understand."

Svengetti looked apologetic. "I was following you, hoping your questions had raised some interest. Something we could latch on to. Someone *has* been tailing you, only we don't know who."

Jiff said, "What else have you been doing, Mia? Who else might be following you?"

Mia thought about Francesca Benini. Could it be related? But she hadn't been involved with the Benini family. She'd stuck to the kid, Tammy Edwards. And anyway, she wasn't ready to mention Francesca to these men. They clearly had their own agenda, and she wasn't divulging more until she had a chance to talk with Allison and Vaughn.

She shrugged. "Nothing, exactly."

"That's a half-assed response, Mia. We've been forthright with you. We were hoping you'd be forthcoming, too. Whatever else you've been doing could be connected to the Gretchko family. That's why I wanted to talk with you." Svengetti glanced at Jiff. "That's why Michael finally agreed, too."

Jiff said, "You could be in danger. These aren't nice people."

Mia thought back to the events of the last few days. "Did you run the plates?"

"Registered to a rental company in Pennsylvania."

"If it's a rental, it could be the Gretchkos."

Jiff said, "Not really their style to simply follow you." He glanced at Svengetti, who nodded for him to continue. "When the Tarasoff family was around, accidents happened, if you know what I mean."

"But it's possible it's them. Especially if they were hoping I'd lead them to something." Or someone, she thought.

Svengetti said, "Possible, yes. Probable, no."

"Can you at least tell me the make of the car?"

Svengetti sighed. "Common vehicle."

"Just so I know what to look for."

"You're out of your element. Sometimes it's better to be oblivious. Like Michael said, you could be in danger. If I tell you, you'll start to see it everywhere." He sighed again. "Believe me."

Mia pleaded with her eyes. "Tell me."

Jiff said, "A white Honda Accord."

THIRTY-THREE

The local library was a plain brick building, tall and modern in its dimensions. Allison had found the online index and, notes in her pocket, asked for the microfiche room. She followed the young librarian through a cavernous reading room, past the children's section and into a small room at the back of the building. The room was warm, even with air conditioning, and had no source of outside light.

"Do you know what you want?"

Allison pulled out her notepad and handed the woman the list.

The woman raised her eyebrows. "All of them?"

Allison nodded. "'Fraid so."

Allison placed her purse under a chair and settled in at one of the machines. The innkeeper had driven her to the car rental shop first thing this morning. She'd wanted to be at the library as soon as it opened, so she'd have time to look into the key before her dinner with Alex this evening.

The librarian returned with sheets of microfilm. After a quick tutorial, Allison was left alone in the room. She took a deep breath and began reading.

After an hour, she looked up. Still alone, she pulled the notebook next to her and began to make notes. Nothing on Gina Benini. Benini Industries was mentioned in a number of local papers, especially when the bottling factory opened in 1982. Before that, the company was largely an importer and distributor, so the launch of the factory meant jobs, and the local media like stories about jobs.

But none of the stories discussed the Benini marriage, or Gina's suicide—which seemed odd, because the media liked a sordid story even more than a good news story about jobs. The Beninis seemed like an important family with a robust company and an interesting history. Francesca was related to royalty, after all. Why not write about them? Unless the Beninis didn't court the limelight, which, considering Francesca's eccentric refusal to leave the house, made sense.

One feature, written in 1983, after Gina's death, included a picture of the Benini family taken some years before, sans Francesca. In the photo, Paolo stood behind Gina. He looked handsome in brown pants, a crisp white shirt, and sports coat. A thin mustache graced his upper lip, and his patrician nose and serious, coal-nugget eyes stared straight into the camera. A man of his word, a man of business, proclaimed the photo. Gina Benini sat on a wooden armchair in front of Paolo, her arm around a young boy of about nine or ten—Dom. Both mother and son wore wooden expressions—mouths that smiled, eyes that remained flat and cold. Another boy stood several inches away, closer to his father than his mother, but apart from both. He had his arms pressed against his sides. His mouth was turned down, but his eyes were alive with mischief.

Young Dominic. Young Alex. Such a contrast.

Allison stared at that picture. Dom looked much the same. He had his mother's features and his father's serious demeanor, even at that fledgling age. Although younger, Alex was nearly as tall as his brother, and gangly. He held his face at an angle, away from the camera. But the camera caught a glint of those knowing, perpetually-amused blue eyes. No smile—just those eyes.

On impulse, Allison hit the print button.

She moved on to the bakery owned by Gina's brothers, Enzo and John.

She'd found several articles on the Fireside Bakery fire, short pieces that she picked through like a scavenger hunting for scraps of information. She pieced together what she could. The fire had devastated the bakery, the building burned to the ground, only the stone foundation remaining. And John had been hurt in the blaze. If authorities knew what had caused the blaze, the papers didn't say. In fact, circumstances were suspicious enough to warrant an investigation by the police and the bakery's insurance company. The news reporters didn't come out and say it, but it was easy enough to read between the lines. Suspicion of arson.

Allison read through the last few articles. Nothing more about the fire investigation. One piece discussed area restaurants and noted the permanent closure of Fireside Bakery. The other was a five-line notation in the real estate section about the purchase of the "old Crayton farm" by the Pittaluga brothers. A quick county check told her they paid $475,000 for the property, and that was years ago. Zillow said the property was worth $1.3 million dollars today. A small fortune then, a small fortune now.

How the hell had two destitute bakers from another country purchased a farm worth that much money? Had the brothers ultimately received a settlement? But the bakery couldn't have been worth a half a million dollars back then. Maybe Paolo had lent them money?

And then there was the fact the bakery burned down less than a year before Gina Benini's death. Related?

Allison was starting to see connections. And she didn't like where they were headed.

She printed off the articles she'd been reviewing. She tucked them and the photo of the Benini family into her purse. A glance at her watch said she had plenty of time to make another stop before her dinner date. The key would have to wait. She grabbed her purse and left.

It was eleven o'clock the next morning when Mia arrived at Vaughn's apartment. He answered the door wearing nothing but boxers and a gray t-shirt, sporting several days' worth of shadow. If it hadn't been for her sense of urgency and the forlorn look on his handsome face, Mia would have taken him to bed.

But clearly it wasn't sex on his mind.

Instead, Mia followed him into Jamie's room. Jamie was in his wheelchair by his high-tech desk.

A mouthpiece extended from the computer to his chin. He didn't look up when Mia entered.

Quickly, Mia read what Jamie had said so far:

I STARTED WITH THE COMPANY'S ASSETS IN THE STATES, THEN ITALY. IT'S A PRIVATE COMPANY, SO ONLY SO MUCH IN-FORMATION IS AVAILABLE. I FOLLOWED THE MONEY TO THE EXTENT I COULD. DUN & BRADSTREET, PRIVCO, BUSINESS IN-

SIGHTS—ANY RESOURCE I COULD TAP. FOUND SOMETHING IN-
TERESTING.

Mia said, "Hi Jamie, what was it?"

He looked at her with welcome surprise.

HELLO, MIA. I'M GLAD YOU'RE HERE. I DIDN'T HEAR YOU
COME IN.

"You were so focused," she replied. "Don't let me interrupt you."

IT'S MORE OF AN ODDITY. AS OF A YEAR AGO, BENINI EN-
TERPRISES HAS SEEN A FORTY-MILLION DOLLAR DECLINE IN
ANNUAL REVENUES OVER FIVE YEARS. IN A COMPANY THAT
TYPICALLY GENERATES 110-150 MILLION IN REVENUE EACH
YEAR, THAT'S A HUGE DECLINE.

Vaughn said, "Okay, but we knew that."

I'M NOT SURE WE KNEW THE DECLINE WAS THAT SEVERE.
THAT'S ABOUT THIRTY PERCENT. A LARGE NUMBER.

Mia frowned, "Okay, so the company was vulnerable."

RIGHT. AND THAT'S WHERE THINGS GET INTERESTING.
TAKE A LOOK AT THIS.

With a subtle shift of his jaw, Jamie used the mouthpiece to
change screens. Mia found herself looking at a Google Maps satellite
view of a portion of Calabria, in Italy. Lots of green with a few patches
of gray and one large area with concentric circles of white.

"What is it?"

Vaughn said, "The Benini property?"

Jamie flipped back and said:

YES. TWELVE MONTHS AGO, THE COMPANY PUT IT UP FOR
SALE. FROM WHAT I CAN TELL, AFTER REDUCING THE PRICE
TWICE, THEY HAD A BUYER THROUGH AN ITALIAN BROKER.
THE DEAL WAS SET TO CLOSE NEXT MONTH.

Mia pointed to the screen. "What are the circles?"

I THINK IT'S AN OLD QUARRY. FROM WHAT I CAN TELL,
THE PROPERTY HASN'T BEEN USED IN YEARS.

Vaughn said, "Marble?"

MAYBE.

Mia said, "What happened to the deal?"

BENINI PULLED IT.

Vaughn sat straighter. "Why?"

I CAN'T TELL YOU WHY. BUT THE TIMING IS QUESTIONA-BLE.

Mia considered this. "Did it happen after Paolo's death?"

A FEW WEEKS BEFORE.

Vaughn said, "Who pulled the deal? Could you tell?"

NO.

Mia turned the possibilities around in her mind. "Did they have a better offer?"

NOT THAT I COULD FIND. BUT IT'S POSSIBLE.

"Then why pull it if they needed the money? What else would they want to do with an old quarry?"

Vaughn said, "If it is a marble quarry, maybe they want to mine it again."

BUT TO GET IT UP AND RUNNING AGAIN WOULD TAKE CAPITAL THEY DON'T HAVE.

Mia thought about her conversations with Svengetti, Frist, and Jiff. A perfect place for dumping toxic waste?

"That may fit with what I learned last night." She shared her adventures, from her meeting with Svengetti to the time she left the underground bunker.

Vaughn looked at her, his eyes dark. "You took a lot of risks."

"I'm fine. I knew what I was doing."

Vaughn stayed quiet. Mia saw the clenched jaw, the tight fist. He glanced at Jamie, then back at her. He was furious with her, furious and probably at least a little scared, and trying hard to stay cool. Mia was deciding whether to be flattered or angry when Vaughn's mobile beeped. He glanced at the screen. "Right back."

Mia stared at the satellite view. Nothing for miles and miles. A perfect spot for a perfect environmental crime?

When Vaughn returned, he looked relieved.

"That was Allison," he said.

"Is she okay?"

"She's fine. She's still in Ithaca, wrapping up a few loose ends. She has some good news."

"Francesca turned up?"

"No, unfortunately. But she thinks Tammy's okay. Allison found recent photos of Tammy with Kai, taken after Tammy disappeared.

They'd been posted to Kai's Facebook page. Buried in the midst of other shots. But Allison recognized her."

"So, she did run away. Maybe she's not connected to Francesca's disappearance after all. Which means I asked questions about the Russian Mob for nothing." Making myself a potential target, Mia thought.

Mia glanced at the Google Map, now back up on Jamie's screen. He too was staring at the monitor, deep in concentration.

THAT'S GOOD NEWS, BUT I'M NOT SO SURE SHE'S OUT OF TROUBLE.

"But Allison said—"

I KNOW, VAUGHN, BUT I THINK IT'S TOO EARLY TO DISMISS A CONNECTION. GIVEN HER BOYFRIEND'S ASSOCIATION WITH THE GRETCHKOS, THE FACT HER FATHER WORKS AT THE LANDFILL, AND THIS—he nodded toward the monitor—YOU HAVE TO CONSIDER ALL POSSIBILITIES.

Vaughn hesitated, a battle between hope and reality taking place on his face. Finally he said, "At least she's okay." The longing in his voice made Mia yearn to put her arms around him. At that moment, he sounded so young.

YES, HOPEFULLY SHE'S OKAY. BUT LOOK AT THAT MAP AGAIN.

Mia and Vaughn directed their attention to the Google map, at the strange circles embedded in the Italian countryside like pustules.

"So what?" Vaughn said.

SO, IF WHAT THIS GUY TOLD MIA IS TRUE, AND THE GRETCHKO FAMILY IS LOOKING TO DIVERSIFY, THINK ABOUT THE POSSIBILITIES THIS PROPERTY OFFERS. REMOTE. AN OLD QUARRY. I THINK MIA'S RIGHT. THERE IS A HUGE MARKET FOR TOXIC WASTE DUMPING. NATIONALLY AND INTERNATIONALLY.

"Benini could also be a prime company for an organized crime outfit looking to launder money," Mia said, thinking back to her talk with Frist. "An otherwise legitimate business with an infrastructure abroad. If it's not dumping, the Mob could be financing the quarry's reopening as a means to launder money."

"And they have other properties, some of which are in developing countries," Vaughn said.

Mia looked at Jamie. "Are you suggesting that the Mob has Francesca?"

I'M SUGGESTING IT'S A POSSIBILITY. WHAT IF FRANCESCA DIDN'T WANT TO GO ALONG WITH THIS? WHAT IF SHE STOOD IN THE WAY OF A DEAL BETWEEN THE TWO FAMILIES, THE TWO BUSINESSES?

"Then what about Tammy?"

Mia put her hand on Vaughn's shoulder. "Tammy may have seen more than she should have and run."

RIGHT. IN HIS OWN MISGUIDED WAY, KAI COULD BE PROTECTING HER.

"But what could she have seen?"

Jamie met Mia's gaze over the computer mouthpiece. I GUESS THAT'S THE QUESTION.

THIRTY-FOUR

It was nearly noon by the time Allison reached the Pittaluga farm. This time, she studied the property from a different perspective. Namely, cost. How much income would a farm like this generate, and would it be enough to pay the taxes? Allison hadn't found any bank liens, so presumably the brothers owned the farm outright. But they would still need to pay the costs associated with keeping up the farm. And much of the land now stood empty.

As with the last visit, the house and grounds were immaculate. Allison pulled the car near the Victorian and climbed out. After all she'd been through last spring with Maggie McBride and the Arnie Feldman murder, she should be more accustomed to sticking her nose in other people's affairs. But it never seemed to get easier.

Allison heard a noise like a faint but high-pitched roar, followed by a sharp bark. The next thing she knew, the world's smallest dog came bounding around the side of the house, barking wildly. That was another thing that had changed. Before Brutus, Allison would have been terrified. Now she stood her ground, startled but amused.

"Bonnie, no!"

Allison looked up. An old man was standing by the porch. He had a shock of white hair centered in a strip down the middle of his head. The sides of his scalp and the skin on his face and neck were smooth, pink, and stretched to the point of shiny. His nose, a mere two slits in his face; his chin and lips, nearly nonexistent. The lack of eyebrows and eyelashes gave him a childlike, surprised look—as did his open, innocent gaze.

Allison had worked in a pediatric burn unit for a semester during graduate school. She knew the signs of extensive burn damage. The resilient spirit of her young patients came back to her now, along with a deep stab of sympathy for the man in front of her.

This must be John Pittaluga, she thought. The fire devastated him, too.

"Bonnie doesn't know you," the man said. His voice was heavily accented, thick and viscous, like he had a mouth full of cotton. He bent down and picked up the Terrier, cradling her in his arms like an infant. "Who are you? I don't know you, either."

"Mr. Pittaluga?"

"That's me."

"I'm an acquaintance of your brother, Enzo."

John looked at her blankly. "He's not here. He went to the store to get chicken feed. We have chickens." He tilted his head, seeming to make a connection. "Do you want to see the chickens?"

Allison smiled. With a glance at the big house, she nodded, wondering when the housekeeper would come out and chase her away. "I'd love to see the chickens."

John grinned. Allison followed him past the house, down a path through the flower beds, and over a small hill to the chicken coop. A large, red, shed-like structure on wheels occupied one end of a grassy yard, enclosed by a fence and dotted with mature trees. Inside the fence, about fifty chickens pecked at the ground. Others gazed down at them from lower tree branches, balancing fat bodies on thin limbs.

"We have forty-three chickens," John said. "We used to have forty-nine, but a hawk got some." John looked at the small dog in his arms. He tickled her under the chin and she closed one eye contentedly, keeping the other eye on Allison. "Bonnie here is not a good guard dog. I keep asking for a big dog, a Great Pyrenees or even a Labrador, but Enzo says they shed too much. And poop. He doesn't want to pick up dog poop. But I would do it."

Allison laughed. "Why is the chicken coop on wheels?"

John puffed out his chest, clearly proud of the chickens. "It's a chicken tractor. We can move the coop anywhere on the property." He pointed to a chicken, busily pecking at a patch of bare dirt. "See, the chickens eat bugs, which is good. And their poop produces compost, which is also good. If we move the chickens around the property, they help restore nutrients to the soil. Which is good."

Allison was impressed. She felt a wave of warmth for this man and his childlike candor. So refreshing after spending days trying to weed through half-truths and dubious motivations.

"Are you in charge of the chickens, John?"

"The chickens and Bonnie are my jobs. Carol, that's my nurse, doesn't like animals, which is just fine with me."

"How about your brother, Enzo? What does he do?"

John's expression darkened at the mention of his brother. He frowned, scratched at the dirt beneath him with one thick-soled shoe. "He takes care of the business."

"What business?' Allison asked. "I thought the bakery had closed down."

Another shadow passed over John's face. Allison felt bad, but, thinking of Francesca, of Vaughn, she pushed. "Didn't the bakery close years ago?"

John nodded. He patted the top of Bonnie's head and for a moment Allison didn't think he would say more. But after a long pause, he said, "Enzo takes care of the money. That was always his job. The money."

"From the farm?"

"From the bakery, from the farm." He smiled. "But I get to sell my eggs, and I take care of *that* money."

Allison walked over to the edge of the grassy hill and sat down under a tree, hoping that John would join her. The sun was heavy in the sky, and sweat glistened on John's face and ran down Allison's neck in tiny streams. She worried about John's skin in the sun. He followed her to the shade but didn't sit.

"What happened to the bakery, John?"

He touched his face, his arms. "There was a fire."

"Is that how you got this farm?"

John shrugged. "Maybe. I don't know. They wouldn't give us the money to make a new bakery. So maybe that's why we came here. To raise chickens and corn."

Allison looked at John Pittaluga. Clearly, he was mentally limited. Was that a result of the fire? Allison doubted it, unless something else happened that day, like a severe fall or asphyxiation. No, Allison was pretty sure that he'd spent his life this way. Perhaps his parents had sent him with his brother to keep an eye on Gina and to ensure they had one less mouth to feed. If Enzo agreed to mind his mentally-challenged brother, he got a ticket to the States. Or maybe the Beninis paid for their passage. She watched John now, nervously shuffling back and forth, anxious to please her yet put off by her questions. How to get the information without upsetting him?

"You were the baker," Allison said.

He smiled, nodded. "Bread is my favorite. My mother and grand-mother taught me. The trick is the fire. It has to be hot enough." Like that, the smile turned to a frown. John looked down at Allison and squinted. "They burned me with my fire."

"They, John? Who is *they*?"

John closed his eyes, rocked on his feet. When he opened them, he looked beyond her, at the house. "Enzo is coming. You should go."

"I don't think he's—" but suddenly she heard it, the low rumble of a vehicle coming down the driveway toward the house.

"John, did you know Francesca Benini?"

Allison could almost see the cogs turning as he shifted from thoughts of his brother to her question about Francesca.

"Francesca Benini? She knew your sister, Gina?"

The rocking began again. Bonnie licked John's hand and squirmed to be let down. He bent down and let her go, straightening back up slowly and with obvious effort.

"Gina is dead."

"I know, John. Do you know how she died?"

"In her sleep. She died sleeping."

He doesn't know she killed herself, Allison thought. "Do you like Francesca?"

"Her eyes are funny."

"Funny how?"

"Uh-oh. Here comes Enzo. Carol will be in trouble." He stared in the direction of the house. "You, too."

"For talking with you? But we had a nice conversation. And I got to meet the chickens."

"For being a snooper. Enzo says you are a snooper."

"Then you remember that I came before, John?" The mask-like face at the window, the shock of white hair.

His dark eyes stared into Allison's own, and she saw the echoes of the man he might have been had the inequities of fate or genetics not altered his course. He ran one unblemished hand across his brow, wiping away perspiration.

"You had better leave."

But Allison knew it was too late. She'd already heard the car door slam. Enzo would be down here any minute now. And John was right. He'd be pissed.

"Is there anything else you can tell me about Francesca? Was she your friend?"

"Not my friend, no. Not Gina's friend, either."

"Why not, John? Why didn't everyone get along?" She kept her tone soft, insistent.

John shook his head, touched his face again. He looked agitated, scared. Why? Why would the mention of Francesca Benini have him this frightened?

Allison heard the house door slam. "John!"

"John?" Allison whispered, the sense of urgency nearly overwhelming her.

He frowned, rocked some more. Allison knew he was not used to disobeying. She reached out and gently touched his hand.

"Please?"

"*An overflow of good converts to bad*," he said. The dog ran toward the house and John walked after her, his gait a slow, trudging lumber.

Allison recognized the quote from Shakespeare. An odd thing for a man like John to say, she thought.

Unless he'd heard it repeated many times before by someone else.

"I'm afraid you need to leave, Ms. Campbell."

"I'm sorry, Mr. Pittaluga. It wasn't my intention to upset your brother."

"You know what they say about the path to Hell." Enzo looked at her from across the yard, over small silver glasses, eyes narrowed in anger. He was dressed as impeccably as before, dapper in light wool pants, a blue button down shirt, silver cuff links and a bow tie, cane at the ready. He looked ready to beat her with that cane.

"Can we talk, Mr. Pittaluga? About Francesca and your sister? Please?"

"There is nothing more I can tell you."

"Francesca is missing. She could be in danger." Allison sighed. "Look, I won't mention you or John as the source of any information. I have reason to believe Francesca's disappearance is somehow related to your sister, as crazy as that may sound."

"Good day, Ms. Campbell."

Allison advanced another step. Enzo opened the screen door, started inside to join his brother. Allison decided to take a chance.

"Who set the fire, Mr. Pittaluga? Was it arson that destroyed your bakery and burned your brother?"

Enzo looked startled. "What did my brother tell you?"

"Nothing. I wouldn't have asked him that. But I am asking you."

She saw a flash of relief, replaced quickly by fear. "Leave him alone, Ms. Campbell. He's suffered enough."

"Then *tell* me. *Help* me to understand."

Enzo's eyes widened with exasperation. He raised his voice. "Tell you that John was born with an umbilical cord wrapped around his neck? That as an old man he has the developmental ability of an eleven-year-old? That the only things he likes to do are be with me, bake, and care for animals—and one of those things was taken from him?" He stared into Allison's eyes, seething. "My brother is my sole responsibility, my only reason for being. You are not the problem, Ms. Campbell. But you will be if you do not stop asking questions. You need to leave us alone."

He slammed the door, disappearing into the interior of the house. Allison started back toward her car, feeling awful. Enzo's words triggered thoughts of Vaughn, of his desperation to care for Jamie. At all costs. Of his ruthless determination not to let anyone stand in his way of that goal. But there were many ways to protect someone. Not all of them excusable.

Mia arrived home late that afternoon and collapsed on her bed in a fit of utter exhaustion. Vaughn was outside, walking around her property, checking for break-ins or other signs of trouble. Angela was feeling better, but to be safe, he'd hired a respite nurse to stay with Jamie for a few hours. It was just as well. He needed some escape.

Mia lay there, inert, letting her breathing calm her. After a few minutes, she rose and peeled off the jeans and blouse she'd been wearing since the day before. Naked, she walked to the bathroom and turned on the shower, making it as hot as she could stand. She stepped under the spray, relishing the soothing feel of the heat against her back, her legs. So many things to think about, but her mind still felt cluttered and useless.

She lifted her face, let the dirt and tension of the last twenty-four hours run down the drain. She soaped her hair with honeysuckle shampoo, took a razor to her legs, and scrubbed her skin until it felt smooth and clean. She was reaching for the shower handle when she heard Vaughn come into the bathroom. She peeked out from behind the curtain. He was sitting on a stool, facing the shower.

"See anything out of the ordinary?"

He shook his head, looking surly.

Mia softened her voice. "What's the matter, Vaughn?"

He raised his eyebrows.

"I mean, besides the mess we're in."

Vaughn huffed out a sigh, twisted in his seat. He crossed his arms over his chest. "You're going to leave me." His voice was flat, resigned, without even an edge of accusation or self-pity.

"I love you."

"That doesn't change anything."

"Oh, but it does." Mia opened the curtain, water still running. She stood before him, nude, and held out her hand. "Join me."

Vaughn looked away, but not before Mia caught the hurt in his eyes. That should have mattered, but it didn't. Somewhere along the line, they had broken the rules of engagement. She cared, he cared. Too much. Right now she was strong and independent, but that wouldn't last forever. Twenty years his senior, she refused to be dependent on him. She refused to have the love and lust she felt reduced to something needy and, she hated to admit it, unattractive.

But now, in spite of everything, they had this moment. That's all she could offer. It was all she had a right to ask for.

Mia stepped out of the shower. She knelt on the floor in front of Vaughn and took his face in her hands. Dripping, still a little soapy, she didn't care. She kissed him. He pulled away at first, but then he gave in, matching her need with his own.

Mia reached up and under his shirt. She felt the rise of his chest, the hardness of his back and stomach. Slowly, gingerly, she traced a nail down the length of his torso, stopping at his belt. She looked up at him and smiled.

He didn't smile back.

Instead he picked her up, pushed her against the wall, wrapped her legs around his waist. She felt his hand on his buckle, the tug of his zipper, his mouth on her breast. The thrust of him inside her. His clothes remained on, fueling her hunger.

They finished like that, an animalistic need overriding any sentiment. Spent, exhausted, Mia relished the ache in her bones and the bite of his teeth marks on her bruised flesh. She reached down, stroked him, and pulled him toward the still-running shower for another round.

He obeyed, the hurt in his eyes replaced with desire.

Desire, Mia wanted.

But the hurt would not wait forever.

THIRTY-FIVE

Dom's house was a handsome but unassuming Cape Cod in a neighborhood of older, stately homes. Modest by Benini standards, the
house sat upon a half acre of sloping lawn dominated by ivy and hun-
dred-year-old trees. Stone exterior, white wooden shutters, a detached
garage mini-version of the main house. The house to the right of Dom's
was a three-thousand-square-foot Colonial. The house to the left, a
slightly smaller Dutch Colonial. All were well-maintained, ivy-covered
and just old enough to be charming. Professors' homes, if Allison had
to guess.

Professors...and Dom Benini?

Allison climbed out of the rental car and glanced around, half expecting the white Honda, or some other tail. But the street was quiet,
which, she supposed, was odd in and of itself. A hazy summer night,
she would expect to see kids running about. Skateboarders, bikers,
small tots on Big Wheels with parents scurrying behind. But other than
the steady hum of air conditioners, the street was barren.

Allison saw Alex's Audi parked next to the house. She made her
way across the driveway, a bottle of good French Chardonnay under
one arm, her purse and Gina Benini's diary under the other. Allison
rang the doorbell. It was only a moment before Alex answered. He
smiled when he saw her, a smile that lit up those captivating blues.

"Allison, so nice to see you. Come in."

Alex placed his hand on Allison's back, between her shoulder
blades, and led her through a narrow vestibule, past a steep set of
steps, and then into a vaulted-ceilinged living space. She looked
around, trying to ignore the heat of Alex's hand through the thin material of her blouse.

If the outside of Dom's house was conservative East Coast, the inside was contemporary New York City penthouse. Large, open spaces. Chrome and black leather. Modern art in bold colors. Sleek lines and absolutely no clutter. The only nod to the house's past consisted of two-inch quarter sawn oak flooring, refinished to an un-scuffed shine.

Allison pointed to the high ceiling over the family room area. "It's unusual to see two-story ceilings in a Cape, isn't it? Custom work?"

Alex nodded. "My brother had the house gutted, modernized. The stairs lead to a bedroom and bath, which is where I stay when I'm here. The other half of the upstairs was sacrificed to create this space."

Allison looked around the open family room/dining area/ kitchen in which they were standing. The kitchen ran the length of the outside wall. A three-foot-deep island ran parallel to the cooking space and served as a divider between the kitchen area and the family room. A small but expensive-looking dining room table, dark wood, sat off to one side, a sleek, modern chandelier dangling above it. The couches were black leather. They faced each other across a lacquered coffee table, its surface inlaid with an intricate marble design.

"It's...impressive."

Alex laughed. "It's not everyone's taste, but it suits Dom. A true bachelor. Hates clutter, in his home and his life. I guess a psychiatrist could have fun with that."

Allison smiled. "And you? Do you hate clutter, too?"

"Maybe if I found the right...clutter." Alex smiled. "But for now, I keep it simple." He pointed at Gina's diary, still tucked under Allison's elbow. "As you probably gleaned from that book, I wasn't what you'd call a wanted child."

Allison gave him an empathetic smile. She handed him the wine.

"Chilled white. Lovely. I'll get two glasses."

"I wasn't sure what to get a man whose family owns vineyards."

"You can never go wrong with French."

"Spoken like a man of the world."

"Spoken like a true Italian. We appreciate fine anything, no matter where it comes from." He gave Allison a long look. "Even the Philadelphia Main Line."

Allison swallowed, and found somewhere other than Alex's face to rest her gaze. "It smells heavenly in here."

"And it's going to get better." He pulled out a bar stool for Allison before heading to the stove. "You sit. Relax. Would you like anything to drink besides the wine?"

"Ice water, please. Tap is fine."

He poured them each wine, filled a tall crystal glass with ice and water from the refrigerator dispenser, and handed her a glass of each.

Allison sat back against the stool. She tucked her purse and the diary on the bar stool next to her and watched as Alex pulled a head of radicchio from the Sub-Zero. He chopped the vegetable like a pro, long, tapered, masculine fingers flying over a Global chef's knife. Next up, a chiffonade of Swiss chard. He pushed the thin strands of chard to the side of a large, wooden cutting board and minced garlic, then onion.

"Mmm. What are you making?"

"Pan-seared trout. With a sauté of radicchio and Swiss chard. So white wine was a perfect choice."

Allison sniffed, savoring the aroma of chocolate. "I smell something sweet, too. Cake?"

"You have a good nose. Chocolate soufflé. For dessert. With Italian coffee."

"Do you always cook like this?"

Alex looked up from the lemon he was slicing. "Only when I like the company."

Allison flashed him a caustic smile. She wasn't that easy. "Where's Dom?"

Alex looked down, sliced lemon with swift, smooth strokes. "I don't know. He just said he'd be out."

"I'm so sorry about your sister, Alex. I—"

"Don't, Allison. It's okay. Really. We are all a little crazed, with Francesca, my father, now Maria. Dom, he doesn't react well to things generally. He's like a grizzly bear, just waiting for a reason to attack." He frowned. "The truth is, there is only so much one family can endure."

"Have there been any new developments in Maria's death?"

He glanced down at the knife in his hand, twisted his wrist. "They seem convinced it's an accident."

"You still don't believe that?"

"I don't know what to believe. What would you think?"

"That someone wanted Maria dead."

Alex bit his lip, nodded. The gesture held little boy echoes and Allison pictured the boy in the family photo, on the outside, alone. Was it possible that Alex had no part in any of this? That he was simply a victim, caught up in his family's issues through no fault of his own?

Or maybe you just *want* him to be innocent, Allison thought. Get a grip. Tall, handsome, dark and mysterious played well in romance novels. In real life, such men spelled trouble.

Problem was, Alex was distracting. And she couldn't afford to be distracted right now.

"Tell me," Allison said, pulling the diary onto the island's marble surface, "what do you remember about your mother? You were so young when she passed."

"You mean when she killed herself."

"Alex, I—"

"It's okay, Allison. I've had a lot of years to come to terms with what happened."

Do you ever come to terms with something like that, Allison wondered, thinking of her own parents.

She watched as he walked to the end of the counter and pulled a glass dome off a cheese dish. He wore khaki pants and a dark gray Polo shirt that hugged the muscular width of his back and the slim line of his waist. His hair was combed back, away from his face. Those blue eyes shone bright with intelligence, and he focused them on her now, drinking her in, as he placed the cheese and olives in front of her, along with a freshly sliced baguette.

"You look like you could use some refreshment, Allison. Eat, drink." He poured himself a fresh glass of wine. "Let's sit outside. The sun is going down, and Dom has a deck he built specifically to capture the sunset. Come. I'll answer all your questions."

Alex picked up the cheese plate and his wine and Allison followed. Off the back of the house, behind the kitchen, a wall of windows and a set of modern French doors looked out onto a three-tiered deck. The decks fanned an amoeba-shaped in-ground pool, outlined with stone. A spa graced one end, a fountain the other.

Each tier of the deck had its own elaborate seating area, and Alex chose the highest platform, resting against a chocolate-cushioned chair, and placed the food and his drink on the small glass coffee table. Allison sat on the chair next to him.

"This spot has the best view of the horizon. I sit out here often when I need to think. Or be alone."

"Why do you stay at the estate if you enjoy it here so much?"

He let his head fall to the side. With a half-smile, he said, "The estate is my home," as though she'd asked a silly question.

"But not Dom's?"

"Dom is a complicated man."

"And you're not?"

He laughed. "Not as complicated as my brother."

"In what way?"

"Did you come here to talk about Dom?" A bristle of jealousy crept into his voice.

"I came here to understand your family."

"Why, Allison? Why the insistence on getting involved?"

"Your aunt is missing. She's my client."

"This has nothing to do with you."

Allison tilted her head, tried to gauge his honesty. "Let's see. Francesca disappeared while with Vaughn. Maria called me just hours before she died. Vaughn has been questioned by the police multiple times. I've been followed, and someone broke into my house. Isn't that enough?"

"Sounds like someone's trying to warn you away. Maybe you should listen."

"Someone as in you and your brother?"

"I don't know what you're talking about."

Allison shook her head. "Who has more to gain than you and Dom? With Francesca gone, Dom can run the business. He doesn't have to share the power." She gave him a pointed look. "Except with you."

But Alex didn't take the bait. "Allison, you have a very active imagination." He cut into a piece of Gruyere, placed it on a slice of baguette, and ate it with a cured Kalamata olive. "Have some food."

"Why do you think Francesca and your mother were at such odds?"

"You picked up on that."

"Gina was pretty clear in the diary. She disliked Francesca."

"And she resented me." No hint of self-pity, just the same matter-of-fact tone one would use to describe the weather.

Allison looked at the man across from her. So handsome, yet so...unknowable. Was he a bad guy, or simply a guy who'd learned to deal with dysfunction by limiting his emotional reaction?

Or was she seeing what she wanted to see? Was this just a show? Allison reminded herself that he was a musician, an entertainer. He was paid to make people want more of him. In fact, perhaps of all the Beninis, he was the one who required the most caution.

"Why would your mother resent you, Alex? She tried for so long to have a child. Then she had two. Two sons in an Italian family. Surely that was cause for celebration."

Alex picked at a piece of bread, but didn't eat it. "Ever since I could remember, she was like that. Moody. Distant. She adored Dom. He was the golden child, could do no wrong. Me, on the other hand," he gave Allison a bittersweet smile, "with me, she had a short fuse. Personally, I think she resented having a second baby. She never wanted me because it was another anchor, weighing her down and tying her to the Benini family."

What a sad thing for a man to believe about his own birth, Allison thought. She considered the diary, Gina's reaction to Francesca. "You were right. In your mother's diary, it was almost as though she felt Francesca was competing for your father's attention. Jealous of any time Paolo spent with his sister."

Alex took a sip of wine, examining Allison over the rim of his glass. "Want the truth?"

Oh, if only, Allison thought. "Please."

"I think Francesca had her own issues. One of which was an unhealthy infatuation with my father."

"You think she had inappropriate feelings for her own brother?"

"I'm not saying they were sexual in nature. I'm simply saying they were unhealthy." He put his glass down on the table between them and leaned forward. "Think about it. My aunt moved here when she was only a teenager. Paolo was older, a man. Suddenly she knows no one, has only my parents for company."

"And Dom. And you."

"Ah, but I wasn't born yet. I arrived months after she did."

"Didn't your grandparents visit?"

"Not that I can recall."

"How about your great-grandmother? Francesca told Vaughn that she was quite a...pip."

"If by pip you mean bitch, I've heard the same stories. No one from my father's family visited. It was just the triangle—my mother, my father, and Francesca. In Italy, Francesca had been the apple of my grandfather's eye. She didn't have that here. It was...disruptive."

"So you're saying she transferred those feelings to your father?"

"Dom has memories of a happy, loving mother. I have memories of a doting, if erratic aunt and a sullen, resentful mother. What else could have caused that change? I think Aunt Francesca and my father were inordinately close, causing a rift between my parents."

Alex stood, walked to the banister and looked out at the pool and the setting sun. A cacophony of color—red and orange and violet—spread like lava across the horizon. When Alex turned, that same heat was reflected in his eyes.

He said, "Too bad you didn't bring a suit. We could swim."

His narrowed, laughing eyes said he had more than swimming on his mind. Allison held his gaze, her mind imagining, just for the briefest moment, what it would be like to kiss him in that beautiful pool, wait until dark, and make love by the water. Pushing the thought away, she said firmly, "You were telling me about your mother and your aunt. Were you and Francesca close?"

"You are an amazingly focused woman. I can understand why Francesca chose you." He walked back to the sitting area and folded himself on the edge of a chair. After slicing a piece of cheddar, he said, "Francesca and I were quite close. The odd thing is, after my mother committed suicide, Aunt Francesca changed. She no longer doted. She'd never gone out much, but now she stayed in all of the time. She moved downstairs, physically separating herself from the rest of us. She seemed depressed. It was as though she'd swapped places with my mother." He popped the cheese into his mouth, chewed and swallowed. "I was no longer the favored child."

Maybe Francesca felt guilty, Allison thought. She pictured the "Gina" written in that bathroom in the hunting cabin. Thought of Ma-

ria's accusations the night Allison had stayed for dinner. Had Francesca had more to do with Gina's death than anyone suspected?

Allison said, "Maybe your aunt was simply mourning your mother."

"But they despised one another!"

"But you said yourself, Paolo and Gina were all she had."

"But then she had my father to herself."

"That didn't last long. He married Simone soon after, didn't he?"

"Oddly enough, my father's marriage to Simone seemed to bring
my aunt some peace. Not that they got along. Frankly, Simone is not
very bright, and Francesca treated her like the hustling money-grubber
I suppose she is. But Francesca liked Maria. She'd spend hours watching my sister, playing with her, in a way she never seemed to do with
Dom."

"And still she never left the house?"

"Never."

"Why?"

"I don't know."

"You must have some educated guesses about your aunt's behavior?"

"Agoraphobic? That's the easy answer, but it's wrong. She never
seemed particularly anxious. Never had panic attacks."

"But if the source of her anxiety is open spaces, people, then she
wouldn't necessarily demonstrate anxiety in her own home."

"She wasn't agoraphobic, Allison. I know my aunt. She chose to
stay there. Why, I don't know. As a kid, it embarrassed me. Now, I feel
sorry for her. What would keep a woman willingly locked in a virtual
prison for forty years?"

Allison shook her head. She had no idea.

THIRTY-SIX

Dinner was delicious. The fish perfectly moist and flaky, the vegetables tender, and the second bottle of wine, a vintage from the Benini family's Italian vineyard, superb. Alex refused her help with the clean-up and she sat again at the island, watching him put away the last of the dishes.

"Where did you learn to cook like that?"

"From watching Francesca in the kitchen."

Surprised, Allison said, "Francesca cooks?"

"Really well. I think she was rather disappointed when my father hired Jackie. But they became fast friends, and Francesca's cooking got even better." He smiled. "What else would she do with all that time?"

"I figured she was busy getting her MBA on the sly."

The smile faded. "Did she tell you that?"

"No, I was joking."

He looked down at the glass in his hand, trying to recover. But it was too late. Allison had seen the chink in his armor. She decided to prod.

"She did say she'd read an MBA's worth of books, though."

"That doesn't make her an expert."

"And she used to counsel your father on business matters behind closed doors."

"He humored her, I'm sure."

"Why are you so against your aunt running Benini Enterprises?"

He put the glass in a cabinet, turned to face her, his handsome features twisted with indignation. "It's not in her best interest."

Allison thought of Francesca's vultures. "That sounds bad, Alex. Especially considering what's happened."

"It wasn't meant to. She's old, eccentric. The shareholders would never accept her."

"Maybe they would. She's also bright and, from what I saw, very knowledgeable. And motivated. Don't forget motivated."

"It will never happen. If she decides to return, she will have changed her mind."

"You sound awfully sure that she left of her own volition."

Alex met her gaze. His look was penetrating. Allison felt her stomach tighten. She blamed the wine, the sunset, the glorious meal. She looked away.

"You read the same diary I did, Allison. My mother painted a picture of a woman with nothing to live for."

"I'm not sure that's true."

Alex pulled up a chair and sat close to Allison.

Close enough that she could feel the warmth of his body, smell the scent of his spicy aftershave. "Why do you think Francesca came to the States, Allison?"

His voice was low, melodic. Allison played with her half-empty glass. "Adventure? To see a new country?"

He smiled, that look of perpetual amusement back in his eyes. "No. It was a marriage gone wrong. I'm surprised she didn't tell you."

Alex had her attention.

"She never mentioned being married."

"I don't even know his name. My great-grandmother traded Aunt Francesca the way you would a cow or goat. A local family with lots of land, rivals of the Benini family dating back to my great, great, great, great grandfather, the duke. She wanted to increase the Benini wealth and stature, thought her sixteen-year-old granddaughter could do that for her."

Allison recalled the news article Francesca had given her—about an ongoing family feud. "An arranged marriage?"

He nodded. "The man was older. Controlling, mean. I don't know what he did to her, exactly, but it was bad enough that she went running home to Daddy. For the first time in his life, my grandfather defied his mother."

"He didn't make her go back?"

"He shipped her to America. To my parents."

Allison thought about this. Rather than answering questions, it raised even more. She remembered the diary. "Your mother mentioned an asylum in her diary."

"I don't know any details. I think they needed to do something with Francesca, and it was a convent, an asylum, or America."

Interesting. "You'd think a woman who escaped a fate like that would embrace her new-found freedom in a new country."

"You'd think," Alex said.

"Unless…"

Alex leaned closer. He touched Allison's chin, pulled it forward. Her head spun. She felt his breath on her cheek, his shoulder against her shoulder. Those blue eyes searched her own, held her. His mouth was inches away.

She wanted to give in. She knew he was a player, but somehow, that made him more attractive. No worry about relationships, commitment. Just a little fun. The stress, the alcohol, there were a hundred excuses for impulsive longing.

None of them forgivable.

Allison pushed back against the island, moving away from Alex. She saw a momentary flash of disappointment, then anger. He's annoyed he can't have me, Allison thought. He thinks I'll eventually give in. And he's probably very used to getting what he wants.

"Unless?"

Allison found her voice. "Unless she'd suffered something so terrible that she couldn't recover."

Alex stood, flicked on the living room lights, his attempt at seduction over. "My aunt is no more capable of running Benini Enterprises than Simone, though for different reasons. She ran away. I am quite sure of it. Let's hope that when she returns, she's come to her senses."

Allison remained seated. She fingered the edge of the diary. "You promised me answers if I came here tonight."

"Haven't I delivered?"

"I'm curious about two things."

He waited, arms crossed.

"One, I understand that Francesca gets control of the company upon your father's death, but who gets the house and the rest of his assets?"

"I don't know."

"Bullshit."

"Ms. Campbell, I wouldn't expect that language from you."

"You promised me the truth."

"Very well." With a weary glance in her direction, he said, "Simone gets a life estate in the house and a tidy sum of cash. Enough to see her through to the beyond. The rest of my father's assets will be split between Francesca and his kids."

"How about the company?"

"We haven't seen the will yet."

"I'm sure you knew his estate plan before he fell ill. With all that money and power at stake, you were sure to know."

"Francesca gets the controlling half of the company. She also has a life estate in the house, and one-fourth of the remainder of his cash and stocks." He looked down at his hands, examined his nails. "She's a very rich woman, even in the company's current state. And at the helm of Benini Enterprises? Very powerful, too. Powerful enough to ruin us."

Allison paused, considering what he'd just said. "And you, Dom, and Maria?"

"We share equally in the remainder of his cash and stocks. And we each get an eleven percent ownership in the business."

Allison arched an eyebrow. "Only eleven percent?"

"My father owned sixty-six percent of the business, outside shareholders the other thirty-four percent. Half of his portion went to Francesca, along with control. We share the rest."

Allison thought about this, yet another piece making sense.

With thirty-four percent of the business in the hands of outsiders, and no one family member holding the rest, the family risked losing control.

The other shareholders could act in consort, taking over control of Benini Enterprises and ousting the Benini family—unless a majority of the Beninis acted together. No wonder Francesca had so desperately wanted help. She couldn't risk that. And neither could the rest of the family.

Allison said, "Eleven percent. That must feel like a slap in the face."

"Why? What did we do to deserve more?"

"Dom has been working for Benini Enterprises for years. Even you and Maria have a role."

"It was my father's company to do as he pleased." Alex shrugged, then sat. "Besides, his hands were tied. He agreed to those terms for Francesca when he took over the company from my grandfather."

"Despite your great-grandmother's displeasure at the failed marriage?"

"By then, she was gone."

"What about Maria's portion? What happens now?"

"I don't know. Maybe Simone."

Allison believed him this time. "If something happens to Francesca, do you know who gets control of the company?"

"Dom and me."

"What about Francesca's other assets?"

"That I don't know. I'm not privy to the terms of her will."

She looked at him, skeptical. "Really? You have no idea?"

"Really, Allison. I have no idea." He smiled. "Are you done?"

"My last set of questions." Allison pushed back a stray tendril of blonde hair and tucked it behind her ear. Alex was watching her from his perch on the couch. She knew she was testing his patience. "Tell me about your uncles, John and Enzo."

"That's awfully open-ended. Can you narrow it down?"

"Why did they come to the States?"

"As I understand it, they were sent by Gina's parents."

"Your mother came from a wealthy family?"

"Quite the opposite. They were peasants with too many kids. Clearly they believed the Catholic Church's edict against birth control."

"Then how did they buy the bakery?" Allison finally gave voice to the question that had bothered her all along, but watching Alex now, she wasn't sure he knew the real answer.

"Like any immigrants, I imagine. They scrimped and saved."

"There was that horrible fire. Your poor uncle. Was its origin ever discovered?"

"If you mean was it arson, I don't think so."

Allison hesitated. "The brothers, did they get a large settlement?"

"I imagine. Enough to buy the farm, at least." Alex looked genuinely perplexed by Allison's questions. "Why do you want to know?

What could this possibly have to do with my aunt's disappearance?"

Allison shook her head. Her gut said it was connected, that some-one was paying off the Pittaluga brothers, with both the bakery and the farm. She just wished she knew why.

Allison was back at the inn before ten o'clock. She peeled off her clothes, set the shower on its highest setting, and stood under the hot spray until her body felt clean and the evening had receded to its prop-er place in her mind. She felt confused, angry, but also, oddly ener-gized. Whether Alex realized it or not, he had given her some im-portant information.

She needed to digest it, figure out what was a red herring—and what could yield results.

After drying off, she traded the hotel towel for her Target pajam-as. Hair still wet, she sat on the bed with her notebook in hand. She made notes, continuing the list she and Vaughn had started.

Something was niggling at her, tickling the edges of her con-sciousness.

Something about the family dynamic.

Francesca's failed marriage, her relationship with Gina. Alex and those eyes, amused one moment, forlorn the next. So expressive. A boy rejected by his mother, growing up in a home so large and opulent, but ultimately claustrophobic. A brother and sister sharing a manor, one protecting the other. And a family cursed by suicide, fire, disfigure-ment.

And bubbling beneath was the family business. Once a true enter-prise, now a failing company with thirty-four percent of the stock owned by non-family members. Demanding change. Valuing tradition. Rejecting a female leader.

Shareholders in a foreign land?

The phone rang. Mia. Allison picked up right away, thrilled to be talking to someone from home.

"You should come back," Mia said. "I'm beginning to think it's too dangerous for you to be up there alone."

"Now you sound like your son."

"Maybe my son has a point."

Allison sighed. "I'll be on my way tomorrow night. My flight's at seven."

There was a pause followed by the sound of a dog barking. Mia said, "There's some information you should know."

With Buddy still barking in the background, Mia recounted her discussion with Benjamin Gretchko, her encounter with Svengetti, the strange Michael Jiff, and the underground bunker. She spoke quickly, words spilling from her mouth as though she were in a race to get them out.

When she was finished, Allison said, "Holy hell, Mia. You want to talk dangerous, you've had a far more adventurous run than I have."

"Look, Allison, adventure aside, we think Benini Enterprises is involved with the Mob. The Russian Mob." Mia explained the land in Italy, their theory that Benini Enterprises and the Gretchko family could be connected.

Allison considered what she was hearing. On some level, it fit—and she and Vaughn had wondered the same thing. The secrets, Razinski's odd behavior at the coffee bar in Ithaca. An organized crime family would have friends in high places. Police could be compromised, or at least silenced. Or an upright cop, like she believed Razinski to be, might be unwilling to act without proof. Afraid of the repercussions for being wrong.

Allison thought about the land deal pulled at the last minute. Because something more lucrative was at hand? Something that had the potential for pulling Benini Enterprises from potential ruin? If the Gretchko family had connections overseas, Benini Enterprises could be a perfect target company. Land for dumping, plus, with the variety of Benini's legitimate business operations, the opportunity for money laundering. The Gretchko family maintains respectability. The Benini family keeps its shareholders—and the corporate bottom line—happy.

Allison saw the business as the thread, the thing that seemed to weave together a few of the pieces of otherwise disparate cloth.

But whole squares of cloth in this odd patchwork mystery still remained. Like how did Tammy fit in? And what about Gina Benini? What did she have to do with any of this? And what about the Pittaluga brothers?

And where the hell was Francesca?

Allison told Mia about the ownership structure of Benini Enterprises. "Things are starting to make sense. Someone in Benini could
have made a deal with the devil to save Benini Enterprises from financial ruin and to maintain control. The most likely candidate is Dom.
And he has the most to lose if Francesca heads the company."

"Especially if she's against this deal."

"Exactly. But we have some missing pieces, and we can't go to the
police without a clearer picture. One of the main things we need is
something tying Benini Enterprises and the Gretchkos. That is, anything, other than me." She took a breath, thought about her list of open
questions. "Can you ask Jamie to look into a few things?"

"Shoot."

"One, ask him to see if there have been any large influxes of cash
into Benini Enterprises. Money that may have been given to seal a deal
with the Gretchkos."

"Two?"

"Get me what you can on the Gretchko family. Articles, bios, anything. Scour for a connection." Allison thought about Tammy, music,
Alex's saxophone. "And it may be a long shot, but see if you can find
anything that ties Alex and Tammy within the music world."

"We tried that angle and came up empty."

Damn. Allison thought of her dinner with Alex. Of the easy way he
slipped between business persona and playboy. "How about the Benini
family? Can you check out each one? Simone, Alex, even Jackie? Especially Dom. What are his vices? Criminal history, gambling, drugs,
prostitutes. Anything you can dig up that could make him vulnerable."

"Anything else?"

"Not for now."

"Allison?"

"Yes, Mia?"

"Stay safe."

Allison smiled. "I intend to. Call me tomorrow?"

"First thing," Mia said. "We'll get on this stuff tonight."

THIRTY-SEVEN

Morning couldn't come quickly enough. Allison tossed and turned her way through another night, high on adrenaline and the feeling that they were on the cusp of a breakthrough. She lay in bed, thinking about Jamie's discovery and Mia's information about the Gretchko family. They were connected. Tammy on the run, Francesca missing, these were not coincidences.

She wished there was a way to find Tammy. Maybe there was.

At 6:19, Allison pulled open her laptop and did a search. She remembered reading about metadata, the information imbedded in photos to pinpoint the location the photo was taken. Maybe they could home in on Tammy's whereabouts that way.

Energized, Allison took a quick shower and got dressed. At 6:48, Allison's phone rang. It was Vaughn, calling to fill her in on what they'd found and to hear firsthand what she'd been doing in Ithaca.

She told him about her side trip to the Pittaluga brothers' farm and dinner with Alex Benini and he'd reacted just as she expected. With barely-disguised rage. "Allison, I'm coming there. This has gone far enough."

"No, I'm fine. You need to stay there." Allison pulled on one shoe, then the other. "Anyway, there are a few things I need you and Jamie to do. And I'll be on my way home later today."

"This isn't up for debate."

"You're right. It's not. I'm fine. I have a few loose ends to tie up here, and then I'll be home." She softened her voice. "Look, I know you're worried. I promise to be careful, Vaughn. I don't want any history repeats, either. But this thing is bigger than any of us. Let's put it to bed. At least our part. We're finally getting somewhere."

"Maybe." Vaughn hesitated. Exhaustion seemed to have won out over anger, because next he said, "Let me tell you what we found."

"Please."

"You were right about the cash. A shell company in the Bahamas paid a years' cash up front for lease of the land in Calabria. Payments began before the other deal was revoked. Care to guess how much?"

"Twice what they would have gotten for the land if they'd sold it outright?"

"Three times. And that's not all. We checked out Dom's personal credit. Your hunch was right."

"Player?"

"Gambler. In debt for half a mil this year alone."

"Sheesh."

"It gets better. He's been paying off debts, one by one, in increments less than ten thousand dollars."

"They're paying him off, too?"

"Looks that way."

"Alex? Simone? Maria?"

"Nothing on Maria or Alex. Paolo was Simone's fourth marriage. First one was at eighteen, lasted three months. Other than a crappy history with men, she checked out."

"So Dom, huh?" Allison thought about recent circumstances, how this could have gone down. "He's in bed with the Mob?"

"Looks that way."

"So you think the Gretchko family took Francesca? And killed Maria?"

"We think so."

"Do you have information on the Gretchko family members yet?"

"Jamie and I are working on it. When we come up with some, we'll email it to you."

Allison told Vaughn about the key she'd found hidden in Francesca's underwear.

"You can pursue that, Allison, but I think it's another dead end. If the Russians have Francesca, we won't find her. That's a job for professionals." He hesitated. "I really think you should come home."

But Allison wasn't listening. Something else was bothering her. "Vaughn, if the Mob took Francesca, who's been following us?"

"The Benini family?"

"They've been here. And anyway, why would they follow us?"

"Maybe they think we took her."

"I don't believe that." She paused, making connections in her mind. "What if the family kidnapped her, as we originally thought? And the Gretchkos are following us because they think we have her. If that's the case, you and Mia could be the ones in danger."

Vaughn remained silent. Allison stretched on the bed, feeling the tug on tight, unused muscles. "And what about the connection to Tammy? Even if the Gretchko family is involved with Benini, how did *we* end up with Tammy and Francesca? Something's missing."

"What are you going to do next?"

"Talk to Simone, figure out what the hell this key is for." Allison opened the laptop. "And I think I may know a way to locate Tammy." She told him about the metadata.

"You want to pinpoint Tammy's location based on the Facebook page photos? That won't work. Facebook erases the metadata. The location coordinates won't be there."

"I did some reading on it, Vaughn. You may know more, but some social media sites don't erase the metadata. Try some of the newer sites. Maybe Kai will have an account. And if Jamie can scour the Net for more pictures, maybe he can start to home in on Kai and Tammy's hangouts."

"Create a scatterplot map?"

"Exactly. With the right picture posted to the right site, he can get the coordinates of the places they frequent. From what I saw on Kai's Facebook, there aren't many. Maybe one will be the place where Tammy is hiding."

"Find the coordinates, plug them into Google Maps, and find the kids. Simple enough." Vaughn gave a strained laugh. "We'll give it a try. But then what? If we can locate Kai's hangout, or even get something close, what do you want me to do? We do have paying clients, Allison. I can't hold them off forever."

Allison took a quick look in the mirror. Her hair had air dried and was flat and lifeless. She wore no makeup. And her shirt was wrinkled.

She picked up her purse and said into the phone, "One more day, Vaughn. That's all I need."

*   *   *

On the way to the Benini estate, Allison called Jason. He answered on the first ring.

"I won't even tell you how worried I've been."

"I miss you," Allison said. "I know this is hard for you. Letting me do what I need to do, coming here. But I want you to know...I appreciate it. And I love you the more for it."

"Yeah, well—"

"Yeah, well, what?"

"This patience won't last forever."

Allison's stomach knotted. "What does that mean?"

"Nothing, Al. I know you've been keeping me in the dark because you're worried I'll try and talk you out of whatever cockamamie plan you have up your sleeve. If this is what you feel you need to do, fine. But let me help you."

Allison pulled to the shoulder near the Benini home. Out of habit now, she glanced behind her, looking for a tail, but the road was empty. It was nearly eight, and she wanted to be mentally prepared before she drove up the long driveway that led to the estate. But even more, she wanted to give Jason her full attention. This trip had made her realize how much she cared for him. And how badly she *did* want him. But on terms they both could live with.

"Truce? We table all of this until I'm home and we can talk face-to-face?"

Jason didn't speak for a moment, and Allison found herself counting the seconds. Finally, he said, "Truce. But I'm going to hold you to that."

"You're a lawyer. I'd expect nothing less."

He laughed. The sound was sunlight. "Tell me what's happening."

Allison relayed bits of what she, Mia, Vaughn, and Jamie had learned over the last few days, ending with their theory about the connection between Benini Enterprises and the Russian Mob.

"Why the Russian Mob? Why not the Italian Mob? Not to stereotype, Allison, but they are from Calabria."

"I don't know. I've been wondering that myself. The only thing I can think of is supply and demand. The Gretchko family needs to keep their collective noses clean, and they have a demand for cheap land and a legit company that can help them launder money. Benini is going under. That's no secret. The Beninis have a need for cash, but what they have is a legit business and vast amounts of acreage in Italy and developing countries in the Balkans." She paused, thinking. "I wish I knew who did the matchmaking."

Jason was quiet for a moment. "If it is the Russian Mob you're dealing with, Al, you can't handle that alone. You'll end up in the bottom of a river somewhere." His voice got tight.

"Despite what Vaughn and Jamie think, I don't believe the Mob took Francesca. A deal with the Mob may be the motivating force, but kidnapping without ransom doesn't seem their style. They'd just kill outright, dump the body."

"Then what do you think's going on with Francesca?"

"I have a hunch it's a family affair, rooted in the past. And this creepy Benini mansion." She looked out the window at the house looming on the hill. "I think the answers lie here."

"I assume that's where you are now?"

Overhead, dark clouds gathered, portending more storms. Allison studied the woods that hid the Benini property from view. A dark, tangled mass of vegetation, full of shadows. Funny how it could look beautiful one day, ominous the next. And today, with the darkened sky and the tasks ahead, those woods looked downright menacing.

"Yes, I'm here. I have a flight home at seven tonight. I'll call you before then."

"You'd better, Allison. If I don't hear from you by tonight, I'm going to come looking."

Allison's rental car, a blue Ford, stumbled its way up the Benini driveway. A tomb of gloom enveloped the vehicle, a thick blanket of mist left over from the awakening day, trapped by the canopy of trees overhead. Allison patted her purse and, in it, the Swiss Army Knife she'd tucked within its depths. She hoped that Simone would be awake, alone—and willing to talk.

The mixture of gravel and chipped pavement under her tires felt bumpy and coarse, the headlights a weak foe against the fog. Simone's

Land Rover was parked in the circle, a few feet from the door. Allison climbed out of her car, remembering the first time she stepped foot on this property, only two weeks ago. A lot could happen in such a short time.

Shoring her shoulders, she rang the bell. It was Jackie who answered. Her eyes were red-rimmed, her normally rigid shoulders, stooped.

"Is Simone available?"

Jackie ushered Allison inside. She made her wait in the central hall while she fetched Simone, which only took a few minutes.

In contrast to her employee, Simone was impeccably dressed in a black suit, black veil, black pumps. The grieving mother? Or playing a part? Allison wondered. It was hard to decipher the difference anymore.

"Allison, please come in." To Jackie, Simone said, "Two hot teas, please."

Allison followed Simone into the sun porch, the room in which Allison had first met with Francesca. She took the seat she'd occupied before and watched Simone perch on a chair with a line of sight to the barn.

"They'll miss her, you know." She turned to Allison. "The horses. She loved them, but oh, how they adored my Maria."

"I am so sorry for your loss, Simone."

Simone nodded, dabbed at her eyes with a lace hanky. "She was a wild child from the beginning. Smart. Oppositional. She didn't deserve to go this way, though." Another dab, another long glance outside. Allison could feel the pain washing off Simone in waves. While she might be playing a role, there was sincere emotion at her core, and it tugged at Allison. She understood loss.

"Do you believe it was an accident?"

Simone shook her head slowly, back and forth. "No, I don't. Maria was too smart for that, too good with machines. But the police seem convinced." She rubbed her hands together, clearly agitated. "I hate that this happened. Everything's changed." Simone flipped up her veil, revealing features contorted by rage. "With their constant bickering, and their insistence...their insistence on..." Like that, the rage dissolved into grief and Simone broke down into sobs.

Confused by the shift in topic, Allison said, "Who is 'them?' Dom and Alex?"

She nodded. "They gave Paolo that stroke."

"How did they do that?"

"More arguing, fighting. The business." Her words were slurred and choppy. "I hate them."

"Simone, this is important. Did you see either of them at the plant the day Maria was killed?"

She looked at Allison with horror. "How did you know I was there?"

Because you're having an affair with the plant manager, Allison thought. Instead she said, "It doesn't matter. Did you see your stepsons?"

Simone buried her head in her hands. "No."

"Did you see anyone?"

Simone was quiet for so long that Allison thought she'd lost her. Finally, she whispered, "Just that man. Dom's friend."

"Reginald Burr?"

Simone looked up briefly, eyes watery pools, face streaked red. "Him. He must have been meeting with someone. I saw him leaving the parking lot."

Jackie never came with the tea, which was just fine. Allison left the grieving Simone and headed through the labyrinth, to the Alice in Wonderland door and up to the library. There, the air was still, the books silent witnesses to years of family secrets. If only you could talk, Allison thought.

She scanned the room, searching for anything that might fit the key. But she came up empty.

She turned, disappointed, ready to head back downstairs, when she spied the large Bible, still on its resting spot where Francesca had left it just two weeks ago.

Gingerly, Allison lifted the book, feeling the worn pages that had given Francesca comfort.

Comfort? Or penance? And that's when she saw the inscription. *To Frannie. Blessings, Jackie.*

Her next stop became clear. She sprinted for the steps and headed down to the kitchen.

She found the cook there, sitting on a stool, looking out the window.

Without turning, Jackie said, "She wasn't a monster, you know. Neither was Paolo. They're the ones who should still be alive."

"I'm sorry, Jackie. I can see you're upset."

The woman wiped her hands on her white apron and stood. "What do you need?"

Allison held out the key she'd found in Francesca's underwear. "Where can I find the receptacle that fits this key."

Jackie touched her neck, looked away. "I'm sure I don't know."

"And I'm sure you do." Allison moved so that she was in front of Jackie, but the cook turned again, avoiding eye contact. "Look, Francesca's life's in danger. You don't want her to end up like Maria."

Silence.

"Jackie, this key was in a bag that Francesca was bringing to me. She told me she had things to share, secrets about her past and the family. Please, I am truly begging you. If you care for your friend, and I know you were her confidante and possibly her only friend, tell me."

Jackie turned, looked at Allison, eyes wide and liquid.

"Alex mentioned that you used to cook together, that Francesca learned from you. You told me yourself that she was the only one who took the time to come down here, to chat. And Francesca never left this house. Who else would she have trusted with secrets, things she may have even hid from Paolo?"

Jackie stood, motionless. Finally, with a sad shake of her head, she said, "Francesca wanted to protect Paolo. Once she found out what Dom and Alex were up to, she tried to keep it from her brother. She loved him. But—"

"But what?"

Jackie swallowed.

"But they cornered him," she said. "Pushed for him to sign papers, first relinquishing control of the company, then going along with their scheme. He refused, they pushed more." Full blown tears now, streaming like raging creeks down her face. "And he had the stroke."

Allison lowered her voice. "They were selling parts of Benini Enterprises to the Russian Mob, weren't they? Until Paolo and Francesca found out."

It was barely a nod, but Allison caught it. Jackie moaned, a long soft moan that spoke of bottled up secrets and the cancer of hate. "He built this business on honor, despite...well, he did his best. Francesca, too. And they sold his honor. For what?"

"Did they kill him?"

"Dom and Alex?" Jackie looked horror-stricken at the thought. "I hope not."

Allison pictured Reginald Burr's name on the hospital registry. It would have been so easy to smother a comatose man, delay the alarms connected to the monitors, slip in and out of his room dressed like a hospital employee. It could have been Burr. It could have been one of the sons. If it happened at all. They may never know for sure.

"Jackie, what does all this have to do with Gina?"

"I don't know." Eyes wide, she said, "I really don't. There were some secrets Francesca wouldn't share, even with me."

"Tell me what the key is for."

Jackie glanced around the kitchen. She seemed to be thinking, weighing. Finally, she pulled off her apron and threw it down on the counter. "I can't leave. But I'll write you directions."

Vaughn and Jamie sat, staring at the computer monitor in Jamie's room, in stunned silence.

Jamie said: ARE YOU SURE?

Vaughn nodded, sweat soaking his t-shirt, heart thumping at his ribcage. There was no way he could get to Ithaca before Allison had to leave for her flight. But they needed to get this information to her as soon as possible. She needed to know.

THIS ALL MAKES SENSE NOW.

"Yeah, I knew something was up with both of them."

They were looking at pictures of the Gretchko family.

It had taken Jamie an hour to find a good shot of Andrei Gretchko's daughter. But there she was, Denise Gretchko Carr. Tammy's manager. Mob boss's kid.

It had taken Jamie five hours to find a picture of Andrei Gretchko, and he'd finally had to get Jason's help. The guy was damn good at avoiding the media.

But he couldn't avoid his mug shot photo.

Andrei Gretchko. Reginald Burr.

"No wonder we couldn't find anything on Burr."

SO THE GRETCHKOS HAVE BEEN BESIDE THE BENINIS THE WHOLE TIME. IN PLAIN SIGHT.

"Denise called me after we started the engagement with Francesca. She knew. And she was using Allison to get to Francesca." Vaughn's mind spun with the implications. "The Gretchkos went through either Tony Edwards or Kai. Somehow they knew about Tammy and her burgeoning musical career. They used Tammy to get access to Francesca."

BUT SOMEONE THWARTED THEM.

"You think Allison's right? That Dom or Alex has Francesca, not the Gretchkos?"

I DO NOW. THINK ABOUT IT. IF THE GRETCHKOS WANTED BENINI, AND PAOLO BALKED, THEN HAD A STROKE, THEY WOULD NEED FRANCESCA'S COOPERATION. THEY FOUND OUT THROUGH DOM OR ALEX THAT SHE'D BEEN DOWN HERE. THEY NEEDED HER OUT OF THAT HOUSE. AND OUT OF THE WAY.

"So they arrange for a second client, Tammy Edwards. Denise has an excuse to be here, to snoop, to ask questions." Suddenly nauseous, Vaughn said, "And a way to kill her." He let that sink in.

RIGHT. ONLY FRANCESCA NEVER MAKES IT DOWN HERE.

"Because someone else placed that tracker on my car. Followed me. Took Francesca."

BUT DID THEY TAKE HER TO SAFETY...OR DID THEY WANT TO GET TO HER FIRST?

Allison listened to Vaughn's information with a heavy heart. She'd just left the post office with a manila envelope of materials from Francesca's post office box, and she was anxious to go through them. But when Vaughn told her about Denise, she had to pull over.

"There's only one way Denise knew about me, knew to connect me and Tammy."

Vaughn had the sense to stay quiet.

"Alex," she continued. "She must have been his manager. He was using me from the start."

"I'm sorry, Allison. You don't know that for certain."

"I'm pretty sure, Vaughn. Think about it. How would the Gretchkos and Beninis have connected in the first place? I suppose the Gretchkos could have approached Benini Enterprises, but why that company? No, I thought from the beginning that this was more personal than that. I think Alex and Denise knew each other. That's what started the corporate courtship."

"And he and Denise used Tammy to get to you. To Francesca."

Allison started to nod before realizing he couldn't see her. "Poor Tammy. She must have figured it out, been frightened. Did Jamie have any luck pinpointing the location of that picture?"

"He's working on it now."

"Let me know what you find."

"Where are you headed? You should take the package and get to the airport. Come home. We can figure out the rest from here."

She pulled out the family photo she'd gotten at the library and studied the picture. She thought of Francesca's determination, Alex's playboy charm, Dom's serious demeanor, always looking at the world through his mother's dark eyes.

And then it hit her. Gina Benini. Trying forever to get pregnant. Then having not one, but two sons. Number two born soon after Francesca arrives.

Francesca, married off to the highest bidder. A family rival. A bad man.

Abused, frightened, she runs back to Daddy. But Daddy has to send her somewhere. A convent. An asylum. America.

Not because she's mentally ill. Because she's pregnant.

"Allison? Are you still there?"

"Oh Lord, Vaughn. There it was all along. The key."

"What are you talking about?"

She turned the key in the ignition, started the Ford. "Alex Benini. Those damn striking blue eyes. He looks nothing like Gina. That always bothered me, that one son looked so much like his mother, the other not at all. It's because Alex is Francesca's child."

"From her marriage?"

"Yes." Quickly, Allison explained her theory, thinking of Gina's diary. "It makes sense that Gina rejected Alex. She didn't want to have to live that lie, resented Francesca and her son for intruding on her life and marriage, the tidy world she'd created for herself. But she was forced to play along, pretend Alex was hers."

"But why the façade once Francesca got to the States?"

Carefully, Allison opened the envelope. As she suspected, inside was a binder clip of documents outlining the Gretchko-Benini alliance. Real estate transactions, shipping instructions, bank deposits. Things that, by themselves, meant nothing. Together they could bring down the whole arrangement.

"I have a hunch, Vaughn, that this all ties back to organized crime. From the time of Alex's conception. Jackie, the cook, mentioned Paolo's honor, his honest efforts to grow this business. And his sons' betrayal."

"You think the boys have Francesca?"

"Yes."

"But where?"

"I think I know that, too."

THIRTY-EIGHT

Allison's first call was to Jason. She left a message at his office, giving him a bare bones account of what was happening and telling him where he could find the incriminating papers, which she'd left in the safe back at the inn. Then she called Razinski. She hoped to hell he was clean, because she had no real choice but to trust him. She didn't know who else to turn to. He listened quietly, reacting only when she said she had hard evidence. "I'll see what I can do," he'd said at that point. She gave him Jason's number. Then she called 9-1-1 and reported a kidnapping at the Benini estate.

When she arrived back at the Benini home, no cars sat in the circle. Jackie let her in immediately. "Simone and Dom are at the funeral home," she said. "You probably shouldn't be here."

"I need your help." Allison told Jackie about the police and where she was headed. "If I'm wrong, it's a false alarm. But I don't think I am."

Jackie gave a grunt of assent. "Hurry." She gave Allison a flashlight from a kitchen drawer. Allison rummaged in her purse until she found the Swiss Army knife. Then she placed the knife in her pants pocket.

"You remember the way?"

"Yes. But my phone won't work out there."

"I'll watch for the police." Jackie made the Sign of the Cross. "Just be quick."

It was hard to be quick in the rain. The muddy path slowed Allison's progress, and made it hard to see clearly. But rain had its advantages, too. It would hide her tracks if anyone came searching. After all, she reminded herself, Dom and Simone were accounted for, but Reginald and Alex were not.

It took her fifteen minutes to find the grotto, another ten to locate the trap door in the ground. She remembered seeing the platform and the metal ring, but when she tried to visualize where it was, its distance to the statues, she couldn't remember. She tapped along the muddy ground, listening for a hollow sound, but the rain and wind muted whatever echo there was.

Allison dropped to her knees. She searched the area with slick fingers, feeling her way along the dirt and grass, hoping to feel wooden boards, metal, an edge, anything that would indicate the door, for she was certain now that's what it was. Water streamed down her face, into her eyes. Her shirt clung to her, wet cotton against raw skin. Fingernails caked with mud clawed the earth. Frustrated, she made pass after pass. She started to wonder if she'd imagined the whole scene at the grotto.

Bingo.

Her hands finally brushed something hard underneath a section of mud. Allison followed the edge of the wood, looking for a handle. She found a small ring on one edge, smaller than the original. They'd changed it, she thought, to hide the entrance. With one mud-streaked hand, she pulled. The door wouldn't budge. She tugged harder.

The door came up slowly on rusty hinges. The sweet smell of rotting vegetables mingled with human excrement hit her, even with the wind and driving rain. Allison tried to listen. She thought she heard noises like a human grunting. Excited, terrified? She turned on the flashlight and aimed it carefully into the hole. She saw a rope ladder extending into the darkness, and began her descent into the depths of the hiding place, flashlight between her teeth.

"Nooks and crannies," Alex had said when describing the Benini estate. Nooks and crannies, for sure. Allison figured this was an old root cellar, a place to store vegetables over the winter.

Now it was the den of a kidnapper.

She reached the last rung and hopped down, onto a dirt floor. Letting her eyes adjust to the dark, she stood for a second, getting her bearings and listening for sounds that might indicate a trap. When her vision was clearer, she swept the room with the light from the flash-light, searching for Francesca. There she was, tied to an old armchair, gagged.

Allison ran to her, pulling the knife from her pants pocket. Quick-ly, carefully, she sliced the ropes holding Francesca's legs together and the ones binding her arms to the chair. Francesca pulled the gag from her mouth, coughed. When she could breathe, she said, "We have to hurry! He went to get food. He'll be back soon."

"Who, Francesca?"

But it was too late. Another form started its descent into the blackness. Before Allison saw who it was, she caught the unmistakable silhouette of the gun.

"Really, Allison," Alex Benini said. "You're more tenacious than I thought. And it was downright amusing watching you crawl around in the mud."

Alex walked across the small cavern, gun aimed at her, not Fran-cesca. He was carrying a bag, which he thrust toward Francesca. "Eat."

Francesca took the bag, dropped it to the ground. "Alex, let her go. She has nothing to do with any of this. I don't even understand why she's here."

"Andrei was having her followed. They can't figure out who took you, Aunt Francesca. They thought maybe Allison was hiding you."

Francesca looked at Allison with a mixture of pity and sorrow. "I'm so sorry you're involved. And that young man, the one who was driving me. I felt so bad when Alex nabbed me. I was afraid he would be blamed." To Alex, she said, "Let her go."

"No, Aunt Francesca. I don't think we can."

Francesca sat down on the chair, rubbing her leg. Calm. Stoic. Not quite the reaction Allison had anticipated.

"You used me for information," Allison said. "Played the part of the grieving son, worried nephew. When all along, you were lying." Allison shook her head. She twisted her hand behind her back, adjust-ing the knife in the shadows. "It was you who placed the tracker on Vaughn's car. You didn't come to Philadelphia to see what Francesca had given me. You wanted to remove any evidence that Vaughn had been followed. But Maria knew. She saw you place the tracker on Vaughn's car—"

"Allison, Allison, Allison." He gave her a tired smile. "I was never using you. I enjoyed our conversations, would have enjoyed even more. But for the life of me, I couldn't figure out what kept you going, despite the danger. I knew Andrei and his people were following you, trying to scare you. And I said as much. I figured," he shook his head, let the gun fall a hair, "that you were playing some angle yourself."

"No angle, Alex. Just trying to find your aunt." She had the knife in the right position now, so she kept talking, back against the wall. "Tammy Edwards was your idea? So Denise is your manager?"

"I wanted her to be. Instead, she's fucking my brother."

"Always with the competition between you two," Francesca said.

Alex turned to his aunt. "And the competition continues." He looked back at Allison. "I never wanted to hurt my aunt. I was trying to save her."

Allison glanced at Francesca. The older woman ran a dirty hand down a haggard face. Francesca said wearily, "I haven't changed my mind."

"Dom is getting antsy," Alex replied. He did sound regretful. Whether it was sincere or not, Allison had no idea. "Andrei is pressuring him, he suspects we have you. Dom never wanted to do this in the first place, he wanted to let the Gretchkos work things their way. And I'm afraid I'm losing the battle. If you don't agree soon, he'll put you back in the hunting cabin and let Andrei find you."

"Then let him! I told you before, I won't let you two ruin what your father and I worked so hard to build."

"It's only money."

"It's never only money!" Francesca stood, pointed a finger at Alex. "You have no idea what you're talking about."

"No, I don't. So why don't you tell me."

"Because you're her son, Alex."

Francesca and Alex turned to Allison, both horrified. And in that instance, Allison once again saw the resemblance. Not in stature, but the eyes. His were blue, hers brown, but they reflected the same world-weary, lively intelligence. No wonder they were never together in pictures, Allison thought. That should have been a dead giveaway.

"Yes, Francesca, I finally pieced it together. Your marriage, it was arranged by your grandmother. You escaped, but not before you got pregnant with your husband's child. His family had to be rich, powerful for the marriage to be worth it. A rival family. If I had to guess, I'd say he was Mafioso. You didn't want to be tied to him, and a child would bind you."

"More than that," Francesca said. "He would own that child. Control him. Turn him into a monster like he was." She shook her head. "That could never be allowed to happen."

"So you lived a lie. Came here, pretended Alex was Gina's, stayed in this house, guarding your son and your secret."

Alex was staring at Francesca with a mixture of hurt and betrayal. "She despised me. All those years, you let me believe I was her son?"

"I despised her for despising you. But she was fragile, jealous. Paolo forced her to go along, but she couldn't be trusted. There was nothing I could do." Francesca's voice was burdened by years of guilt. "When Gina died, I thought it would all die with her, but then your uncles..." She put her hand out, pleading. "I couldn't tell you."

Alex lowered the gun. He shook his head, dazed. "You set the fire?"

"Paolo had it set. As a warning. They were threatening to tell your father. Enzo thought he could get more from us." To Allison, Francesca said, "We bought them the bakery. A gift. For their silence. You understand, right?"

"You and my father knew John was in that building? You tried to kill him?" Alex said, backing toward the ladder.

"No! We only wanted to remind them not to get greedy, to take back what we had given. We didn't know anyone was in there." Sobs now, deep, throaty sobs. "The farm...we repaid them."

"You can't repay someone for disfigurement, *Mother*."

That's when Allison heard the distant wail of sirens. And footsteps, right overhead.

Francesca heard it, too. "Shhh," she said. "Dom."

But Alex was standing by the ladder, visibly shaking. Despite what he had done, Allison felt a frisson of sympathy. His whole childhood, his whole sense of self, ripped apart in one minute. And Francesca, in an attempt to protect her own, had wreaked havoc on a family. Enzo

Pittaluga's quote—echoed by his brother—came back to her, "An over-flow of good converts to bad." Shakespeare's words had special meaning here.

She'd gone far to protect her son, to protect her family, from evil. And in doing so, had created the very thing she'd hoped to avoid.

Francesca gasped.

Dom was descending into the root cellar. Allison centered herself, knife in hand, ready to spring.

THIRTY-NINE

Pushing off the wall, Allison flung her body against Alex, catching him off guard and knocking the gun from his hand.

She took advantage of the split second of confusion and grabbed the gun. Her knife fell. She kicked it toward Francesca, who bent to pick it up.

Now that Dom was coming, her client looked scared. Alex may have been the kidnapper, but it was Dom calling the shots.

"Alex!" Dom was halfway down the rope ladder now, and it swayed under his weight. He bent to see what was happening. When he spied Allison, his face contorted in rage. "One fucking task, Alex. One fucking task."

Alex stood feet from the ladder, still in shock.

And Dom couldn't let go of the ladder, or he would fall. Rain poured through the open cellar door, impeding his vision. Allison eyed the gun in her hands with wary distaste.

Heart slamming against her ribcage, head pounding, she steadied her hand and aimed the gun at Dom, then Alex. The sirens were louder now. She fought to stay calm.

Alex moved.

"Stop!" She pointed the gun in his direction. "We're in a really close space. And I have a wicked migraine. Don't tempt me."

The sirens stopped.

"Let Alex go," Francesca said.

Allison glanced quickly at her. "Are you serious? They kidnapped you, Francesca."

Francesca lifted the knife. She pointed the tip at Allison. "He didn't know. Let him go."

"Francesca, this is serious." Allison kept her eyes locked on Alex, then on Dom, keeping the gun level and her expression hard. "I can't let him go."

"Please. Let. Him. Go." Francesca raised her arm, poised to throw the knife at Allison.

Allison, white-knuckled and furious, took a step toward Alex. "Do it, Francesca, and I pull the damn trigger. I mean it." And in that moment, she did mean it.

"Put it down, Aunt Francesca." Alex's voice was thick—with sadness? Regret? Fear? Allison wasn't sure and didn't care. None of it mattered now.

Francesca let out a howl like a trapped and injured animal, low and guttural and agonized. But she dropped the knife and fell to her knees.

"Stay put, both of you," Allison said, keeping the weapon trained on the two men. The police would be down here any minute. Patience, Al, she told herself. Breathe.

FORTY

In the shadows of the late afternoon, Linden Street was quiet. Allison pulled up to the Edwards' house with a rock in the pit of her stomach and a headache laying siege to her skull. But she forced herself out of the car and returned the wan smile of the two girls sitting on the porch—Kellie with an "ie" and, next to her, arms wrapped around long, skinny legs, Tammy Edwards.

"Hello, Allison," Tammy said. She looked across the porch, into the sun, squinted, and cupped a hand across her forehead for shade. "Do you want my mother?"

"Is she home?"

Tammy nodded. "I don't think she'll want to talk to you, though."

"Are you okay?"

Tammy glanced at her friend, as though for confirmation. Kellie smiled gently. Tammy shrugged. "My father's in prison."

"I heard. I'm so sorry, Tammy."

The girl started to shrug again, seemed to think better of it, and said instead, "He said it was unavoidable."

Allison climbed the steps and sat next to the two girls on the dusty porch flooring. "I want to tell your mother that I'm sorry."

"She's not much for apologies."

"I did what I thought I needed to do at the time. We—I—thought you were in danger."

Tammy took a long time to answer. She stared at her toenails, newly painted a coat of pearlescent pink, girlie and fresh. "When I overheard Denise talking about a kidnapping, I knew. I knew she was using me, and I ran. She didn't see me as a star. She saw me as a way to get to someone else." Tammy looked at Allison. "I also knew my father was involved. That she had been using him, too. That he had set her up with me as a favor to the Gretchkos."

"And that's why your mother kept your whereabouts a secret, isn't it? To protect you. And to protect your dad from the police."

Tammy nodded. "Mom's known for a while Dad does odd jobs for the Gretchkos. But she didn't know about this. She was angry. At him, at me."

"But more than that, she was scared." Allison guessed. "Scared that if the police started digging around, she'd lose you and your father."

"Maybe."

Tammy glanced at Kellie, who reached out and touched her friend's hand. Thinking about Kellie's alcoholic mother, Allison figured Kellie knew, as did Allison, about family heartache. About the lengths one would go to hide a loved one from pain—and accountability.

But sometimes, there was no hiding from the truth.

In this case, we came along and shone a big, fat light on everything, Allison thought. Now Tony Edwards was implicated, and Tammy was a witness. Allison thought about Mia's story, about Thomas Svengetti and the others. She knew it was Tony Edwards who had chosen to play with fire, not her, but she wondered at the fate of this family. She prayed they'd make it through whatever was in store.

Allison rose to leave.

"Don't you want to talk to my mom?" Tammy asked.

Allison shook her head. It was time to leave this family alone. She touched Tammy briefly, gently on the shoulder and smiled at Kellie. Her heart ached. No matter how one tried to do good, it seemed, there were always unintended consequences. The path to hell, Enzo Pittaluga had said. How right he was.

Mia pulled the shawl around her shoulders and snuggled down into the couch, against Vaughn. Allison watched them, happy to be here, surrounded once again by people she loved.

Jason was in the kitchen, making coffee, and Brutus was on the floor, next to Allison, his head on her lap. His severe underbite made breathing difficult, but that didn't stop him from lying on his back, legs in the air, showing Allison just how thrilled he was to have her home by taking a nap.

It had been a few days since the last day in Ithaca, and Allison finally felt ready to talk about the ordeal. She knew in the days ahead, there would be police inquiries and reporters, and even that promised discussion with Jason, but for now she welcomed peace.

Mia said, "So why did Francesca write 'Gina' on that wall? In the hopes someone would find her?"

Allison hadn't stopped wondering the same thing. "I don't think so. I think Francesca was more than willing to give up her own life by that point. She blames herself for Gina's death. She saw the kidnapping as some sort of penance, and she was offering it up for Gina. I bet that second word was 'sorry.' In the misery of captivity, in the midst of being taken by the man she'd tried to protect, Francesca saw her life for what it was. A tragedy."

Vaughn nodded. "And Gina's ghost? Just a crazy Maria story?"

"Gina is a ghost, at least in the sense that her memory lingers, a reminder of guilt and regret."

Jason came in and handed Allison and Mia coffee. He sank down onto the floor next to Allison and rubbed Brutus behind the ears. "Why did she stay in that house all those years? Did she say?"

Allison shook her head. "I think in the beginning, she was trying to stay out of sight. She was paranoid that her former husband and his family would find out the truth and lay claim to her son. But when Alex was older? I don't know. Habit? Fear? Another form of penance?"

"Thinking that if she gave up her life, Alex could keep his?" Mia said.

Allison remembered the way Francesca had threatened her with the knife. A mother's desperation. After forty plus years of sacrifice, her actions made a certain sense.

Mia took Vaughn's hand and smiled. "I'm just thankful things worked out."

Vaughn smiled back, but Allison caught the hint of worry in his eyes. He and Mia were so good together, but would it last? Vaughn's world was still fragile. The cleansing light of honesty had strengthened his will and his life with Jamie, but Allison knew that Vaughn still felt vulnerable, and the Benini plight showed him just how vulnerable he really was. Even with Tammy back home with her mother and Frances-ca's kidnappers in jail, Vaughn looked on edge. It would take a while to get normalcy back. Maybe he would never know normal.

She didn't think she would, either.

Vaughn looked down at his hand, the one clasping Mia's. "Enough about all of this. It will be nice to get back to work. Routine is sounding pretty damn good."

Allison nodded. "Maybe we can stay out of trouble for at least a few weeks." Jason shot her a sharp look. She winked. "Just kidding."

Mia stood, gently disengaging from Vaughn. She re-wrapped the silk shawl around her and stepped into silver ballet flats. "If you folks will excuse me. Vaughn, you need to pick Jamie up from the police de-partment in an hour. And I have a date to keep."

"With Svengetti?" Allison asked.

It was Vaughn who responded. "She promised him the scoop."

"So the Feds have what they need on the Gretchkos?"

"For now," Jason said. "Francesca's documentation helped. And Maria's murder is being pinned on Andrei Gretchko. We'll see if it sticks."

"I guess Tammy will need a new manager," Vaughn said. "Hard to manage musicians from jail."

"Actually, I'm afraid Tammy doesn't need a manager right now. After all this, she still wants to go to Juilliard. I just don't know that any music career is in the cards. She says her mother is against it, is fighting the contract. If Tammy wants to pursue opera, she'll need to find her own voice, to fight for what she wants. And as we all know, that's not so easy."

Gently, Allison pushed Brutus aside. She stood and gave Mia a hug, then walked her to the door. "Thank you," she whispered. "For everything." Allison looked behind her, at Jason, who was petting Bru-tus and chatting with Vaughn about baseball. "I know you talked to him."

Mia nodded, gave Allison a poignant smile. With a glance back at Vaughn, Mia said, "Don't hurt him, Allison. My son loves you." She opened the door and stepped out into the summer heat.

Allison, face tilted up toward the baking sun, watched her go.

WENDY TYSON

Wendy Tyson's background in law and psychology has provided inspiration for her mysteries and thrillers. Originally from the Philadelphia area, Wendy has returned to her roots and lives there again with her husband, three kids and two muses, dogs Molly and Driggs. Wendy's short fiction has appeared in literary journals, including *KARAMU, Eclipse, A Literary Journal* and *Concho River Review*. *Deadly Assets* is the second novel in the Allison Campbell series.

In Case You Missed the 1st Book in the Series

KILLER IMAGE

Wendy Tyson

An Allison Campbell Mystery (#1)

As Philadelphia's premier image consultant, Allison Campbell helps others reinvent themselves, but her most successful transformation was her own after a scandal nearly ruined her. Now she moves in a world of powerful executives, wealthy, eccentric ex-wives and twisted ethics.

When Allison's latest Main Line client, the fifteen-year-old Goth daughter of a White House hopeful, is accused of the ritualistic murder of a local divorce attorney, Allison fights to prove her client's innocence when no one else will. But unraveling the truth brings specters from her own past. And in a place where image is everything, the ability to distinguish what's real from the facade may be the only thing that keeps Allison alive.

Available at booksellers nationwide and online

Visit www.henerypress.com for details

Henery Press Mystery Books

And finally, before you go...
Here are a few other mysteries
you might enjoy:

MALICIOUS MASQUERADE

Alan Cupp

A Carter Mays PI Novel (#1)

Chicago PI Carter Mays is thrust into a perilous masquerade when local rich girl Cindy Bedford hires him. Turns out her fiancé failed to show up on their wedding day, the same day millions of dollars are stolen from her father's company. While Carter takes the case, Cindy's father tries to find him his own way. With nasty secrets, hidden finances, and a trail of revenge, it's soon apparent no one is who they say they are.

Carter searches for the truth, but the situation grows more volatile as panic collides with vulnerability. Broken relationships and blurred loyalties turn deadly, fueled by past offenses and present vendettas in a quest to reveal the truth behind the masks before no one, including Carter, gets out alive.

Available at booksellers nationwide and online

Visit www.henerypress.com for details

THE AMBITIOUS CARD

John Gaspard

An Eli Marks Mystery (#1)

The life of a magician isn't all kiddie shows and card tricks. Sometimes it's murder. Especially when magician Eli Marks very publicly debunks a famed psychic, and said psychic ends up dead. The evidence, including a bloody King of Diamonds playing card (one from Eli's own Ambitious Card routine), directs the police right to Eli.

As more psychics are slain, and more King cards rise to the top, Eli can't escape suspicion. Things get really complicated when romance blooms with a beautiful psychic, and Eli discovers she's the next target for murder, and he's scheduled to die with her. Now Eli must use every trick he knows to keep them both alive and reveal the true killer.

Available at booksellers nationwide and online

Visit www.henerypress.com for details

CIRCLE OF INFLUENCE

Annette Dashofy

A Zoe Chambers Mystery (#1)

Zoe Chambers, paramedic and deputy coroner in rural Pennsylvania's tight-knit Vance Township, has been privy to a number of local secrets over the years, some of them her own. But secrets become explosive when a dead body is found in the Township Board President's abandoned car.

As a January blizzard rages, Zoe and Police Chief Pete Adams launch a desperate search for the killer, even if it means uncovering secrets that could not only destroy Zoe and Pete, but also those closest to them.

Available at booksellers nationwide and online

Visit www.henerypress.com for details

DEATH BY BLUE WATER

Kait Carson

A Hayden Kent Mystery (#1)

Paralegal Hayden Kent knows first-hand that life in the Florida Keys can change from perfect to perilous in a heartbeat. When she discovers a man's body at 120' beneath the sea, she thinks she is witness to a tragic accident. She becomes the prime suspect when the victim is revealed to be the brother of the man who recently jilted her, and she has no alibi. A migraine stole Hayden's memory of the night of the death.

As the evidence mounts, she joins forces with an Officer Janice Kirby. Together the two women follow the clues that uncover criminal activities at the highest levels and put Hayden's life in jeopardy while she fights to stay free.

Available November 2014

Visit www.henerypress.com for details

FATAL BRUSHSTROKE

Sybil Johnson

An Aurora Anderson Mystery (#1)

A dead body in her garden and a homicide detective on her doorstep...

Computer programmer and tole-painting enthusiast Aurora (Rory) Anderson doesn't envision finding either when she steps outside to investigate the frenzied yipping coming from her own back yard. After all, she lives in Vista Beach, a quiet California beach community where violent crime is rare and murder even rarer.

Suspicion falls on Rory when the body buried in her flowerbed turns out to be someone she knows—her tole painting teacher, Hester Bouquet. Just two weekends before, Rory attended one of Hester's weekend painting seminars, an unpleasant experience she vowed never to repeat. As evidence piles up against Rory, she embarks on a quest to identify the killer and clear her name. Can Rory unearth the truth before she encounters her own brush with death?

Available November 2014

Visit www.henerypress.com for details

SHADOW OF DOUBT

Nancy Cole Silverman

A Carol Childs Mystery (#1)

When a top Hollywood Agent is found poisoned in the bathtub of her home suspicion quickly turns to one of her two nieces. But Carol Childs, a reporter for a local talk radio station doesn't believe it. The suspect is her neighbor and friend, and also her primary source for insider industry news. When a media frenzy pits one niece against the other—and the body count starts to rise—Carol knows she must save her friend from being tried in courts of public opinion.

But even the most seasoned reporter can be surprised, and when a Hollywood psychic shows up in Carol's studio one night and warns her there will be more deaths, things take an unexpected turn. Suddenly nobody is above suspicion. Carol must challenge both her friendship and the facts, and the only thing she knows for certain is the killer is still out there and the closer she gets to the truth, the more danger she's in.

Available December 2014

Visit www.henerypress.com for details

THE RED QUEEN'S RUN
Bourne Morris

A Meredith Solaris Mystery (#1)

A famous journalism dean is found dead at the bottom of a stairwell. Accident or murder? The police suspect members of the faculty who had engaged in fierce quarrels with the dean—distinguished scholars who were known to attack the dean like brutal schoolyard bullies. When Meredith "Red" Solaris is appointed interim dean, the faculty suspects are furious.

Will the beautiful red-haired professor be next? The case detective tries to protect her as he heads the investigation, but incoming threats lead him to believe Red's the next target for death.

Available December 2014

Visit www.henerypress.com for details

34267574R00172

Made in the USA
Lexington, KY
30 July 2014